At Van Eyckmann's Request

ROBERT J. STAVA

www.wyvernfalls.com

*to John Dickson Carr
and to the art of fair play...sort of.*

CONTENTS

	Acknowledgments	i
1	The Mohican Club	9
2	Mr. Easton, isn't it?	17
3	Van Eyckmann's Request	29
4	Taron Hall	37
5	Mind Your Step, Mr. Matthews...	47
6	Snakes in the Garden	61
7	Old Acquaintances	69
8	May All Appearances Be Forgotten	75
9	Lunchtime Favorites	85
10	Missed Connections	97
11	Missing Persons and Voices in the Dark	116
12	The Voyage of the Black Dragon	129
13	The fate of Akma, and a Curse	157
14	One Potato, Two Potato	167
15	Dinner is Served	171
16	Kimmi's Tale	179
17	Trick or Treat	199
18	Delgado's Desserts	209
19	End Game	219
20	Aftermath	237
	Notes for the Curious	248

ACKNOWLEDGMENTS

ACKNOWLEDGMENTS

I owe a debt of gratitude to John Dickson Carr and Ian Fleming who were the first 'adult' authors to inspire me as a young reader, and, of course, the wry influence of Washington Irving whose presence is still very much alive here in the lower Hudson Valley, especially around Halloween. I've visited his house often for inspiration. Special thanks to my family, my wife Tomiko for her candid feedback and unwavering support, Carlos Cabrales for handy legal pointers, Anna Cabrera for her merciless editing and invaluable assistance, Tam Hernandez for properly whipping this 2nd edition into shape, Tom Laemlein for his unrelenting humor and friendship, and Mark Wyszynski for being such an excellent friend through times thick and thin.

...and of course whatever mysterious forces are at work here along the Hudson River Valley that continue to fire my imagination....

ROBERT J. STAVA

1. THE MOHICAN CLUB

The eight men sat around the long, polished oak table that had seen its first coat of varnish around the time President Cleveland had first taken office. Outside, a stiff October breeze snapped and buffeted impatiently at the lead-paned, Moorish-looking windows, three stories up. A few random leaves skittered along the gallery outside, the dry rustle of summer's dead dreams riding on the threat of coming winter. The gallery, with its spiraled brownstone columns, bas reliefs of scowling Indian faces, and crumbling rails, was more ornamental than useful for longer than anyone alive could remember - like many things at this building in Brooklyn known as the Mohican Club.

Built in the 1870s, in its heyday it was a premier gentleman's club for wealthy businessmen seeking some relief from the pressures, overcrowding, and incessant pollution of Manhattan. A large square edifice, it was a hodgepodge of building styles: an eclectic combination of ceramic roof tiles, brick and brownstone facades. It featured Arabesque arches, stained glass, triple-fluted chimneys and, for those who troubled themselves to look up these days, a running two-foot-high bas relief sculpture that decorated all four facades between the second and third stories. Beginning at the front of the building on Prospect Park West, it appeared at a glance to depict the history of New York and the founding fathers of the club in a series of chronological scenes involving Dutch traders, Indians and canoes, English warships, corn, marshes, deer and bear, a man at a desk with a map depicting trade routes behind it and a scribe taking dictation; the usual Colonial imagery suspects.

The north face of the building revealed an even more interesting story. In fairness, that facade was usually in shadow and was partially obscured by the two English oak trees that stood between the building and the old fashioned tennis courts (which hadn't been used since, say, another President named Dwight took his last look around the Oval Office). Only the window washers that came twice a year got a truly good look at those frescoes while making their rounds and without fully understanding why – this particular cleaning company employed south-of-the-border immigrants who generally weren't experts on Dutch colonial history – they would lower their scaffolding as they passed them, cleaning the windows as efficiently and quickly as possible.

Many would cross themselves while doing so.

This north facade sequence depicted an odd and vaguely disturbing series of events that predated the other sides. These involved Dutch traders as well, but landing in the Banda Island chain in the Strait of Molucca in the East Indies in somewhat less-than-friendly circumstances. These events were dated in and around 1620, though you would have to be close enough to read the roman numerals embossed on it to grasp this. The Dutch Governor was shown striking a traitorous deal (nutmeg and mace were the key spices involved) with what appeared to be the shaman or darwashi of the local village, kidnapping one of the wealthy merchant's daughters, then letting his Japanese mercenaries loose to gather up all the men and slaughter them in front of their wives and children after his demands weren't met. The men were shown drawn and quartered, then decapitated, before their horrified families. One scene depicted the Governor meeting with the darwashi, a scowling, muscular man who towered over the Dutchman. Either time or an errant vandal had disfigured the face of the taller man until it was no longer recognizable. Then the fleet was shown traveling with their spice-laden vessels back to the Hague and to the Lord's Seventeen where their cargo converted to chests of gold crowns and bullion, shipped off to New Netherlands and presumably to the new beginnings depicted on the next fresco.

None of which was much concern to the eight men gathered around the table on a cold night in late October. The twenty-eighth day of the month. Three days before Halloween. Three hundred and ninety years after the events depicted up on the wall outside.

Of the eight men gathered, six were prominent Brooklyn businessmen. The seventh was an attorney.

The eighth was an imposter.

It was the attorney who was in charge of the gathering. He sat at the head of the table, an elderly man in his mid-seventies with the silver hair and hooded eyes of an aging barrister, dressed in a discreet but very expensively tailored dark gray suit with Barclay cufflinks and a gold Zephyr watch with Swiss workings on his left wrist.

His name was William H. Lowe and he was a senior partner at Makepeace Lowe, one of the more discreet and long standing New York firms which many considered to be dinosaurs in the 21st century. The type of law firm whose attorneys enjoyed flush expense accounts, a Friday dinner at Del Monico's and their mixed drinks served in decent crystal and in separate decanters.

The room was long and spacious, paneled in quarter-sawn oak that had gone nearly black from the years when pipes and cigars (and large social events at old men's clubs) were the norm for Brooklyn's upper crust. Fourteen feet above the parquet floor, the ceiling featured heavy beams between yellowed plaster. The side tables near the windows had Louis C. Tiffany lamps hand-crafted in the original factory in Corona, Queens from the early 1900s. On the opposite wall was a heavy oak sideboard with an assortment of VSOP brandy decanters and Waterford crystal glasses, a large cut-crystal pitcher with ice water and slices of lemon floating in it, along with a polished silver platter with an assortment of after-dinner sweets, none of which had been touched. Behind the attorney was a substantial fireplace with an elaborate carved oak mantel that ran floor to ceiling, its hearth faced with pale green ceramic tiles depicting a rural forest motif with deer, hunting dogs, oak tree leaves, and acorns. A fire laid earlier in the evening crackled in the grate, occasionally popping as a knot in one of the logs exploded.

None of the men gathered at the table with one of the senior partners of Makepeace Lowe were here to swap spook stories around the fire, however, and the brandy and sweets were laid out simply as a courtesy. The express purpose for their attendance was to hear out the terms of the last will and testament of their late business colleague, Lars Van Eyckmann.

The seven men were each from very different professions. Moving counter-clockwise from Lowe's right they were seated in this order:

Geoffrey Washington, senior partner in Washington Harris, an exclusive real estate company that catered to an elite clientele in the Manhattan market. An imposing black man at six foot four, he offset any doubts with infectious charm and impeccable manners that gave him the air of a conservative father bent on making your (albeit very expensive) choice in urban living quarters a wise and fruitful course of action. His three children all went to private schools, his second wife Nadine ran an employment agency in Manhattan and was a trustee on several important charities (Mrs. Washington #1 was still wallowing in middle-class obscurity in Flushing, Queens, along with Geoffrey Junior who enjoyed the enriching experience of public inner city schools) and he owned a pre-war building on Prospect Park West near Carroll Street with an elegant balcony overlooking the park that no one ever used.

"Big Joe" Lefferts, Wall Street analyst originally from Edison, New Jersey, owned several pre-war buildings in Kensington but lived out in Bensonhurst with his wife Barbara and two children and a golden retriever named Elmo. At five foot six (with lifts in his shoes) Joe, born Josef Lavianni, made up for his lack of vertical stature with a dynamic force of personality that immediately reduced by several inches anyone in his proximity. He'd made his nest egg in the financial "Hang 'em High" Reagan boon years but was now mostly out of the game except as a consultant and frequent Wall Street commentator on MSN and Fox News. Prematurely bald since his early 20s and now in his late 40s, he had the flint-eyed features of a born gunslinger and a meticulously groomed goatee of red hair with a sprinkling of gray. With it was the requisite pit-bull stubbornness and nose for fresh blood that had made him a small fortune in his heyday. Even in the middle of winter, he favored striped short-sleeved shirts and bold ties that, oddly enough, usually featured some absurd motif like flying elephants or Hawaiian girls in grass skirts. They had the calculated effect of putting his clients at ease – being one of the few fathers to proudly wear his Father's Day gifts – and throwing his enemies off their stride. The wackier, the better.

Juan Delgado, owner of several restaurants and part of the original spearhead of gay entrepreneurs who in the late '90s transformed Fifth Avenue in Brooklyn from a dingy crime-riddled wasteland of tired bodegas, dollar stores and run-down restaurants with chipped Formica counters, to a shi-shi destination of the cool-and-hip, seekers of overpriced tapas eateries and shabby chic tables made of beat-up wood instead of beat-up Formica. This much to the excitement of local realtors, who wasted no time in elastically rezoning Park Slope to include any dilapidated slum building from Flatbush to Twenty-third Street, anywhere east of Third Avenue, or Second Avenue for the less scrupulous. Juan currently owned quite a few of those buildings and lived in a penthouse condo on Union Street that had been featured in Architectural Record. Twice. He was also currently in a long-term relationship (in Delgado-ese, that was defined as "longer than two weeks") with a twenty-two year old personal trainer/boy toy named Chi who also taught yoga. Although pushing 45, Juan was blessed with preternaturally smooth skin which, combined with a subdued flair for fashion and a thick head of hair, often allowed him to pass for fifteen years younger.

Derek Anderson was tall, gangly, and handsome. He had the easy going lopsided smile and slightly weathered look of a guy you'd expect to run into at the yacht club bar having a vodka martini, musing about how he'd put the spinnaker up a few seconds too late on that last leg of the regatta. He appeared to have genetically engineered hair with just the right mix of gray at the temples. Anderson was an executive at Time Warner and was married to Suzanne, a perky blonde who could have stepped right out of a Cosmopolitan magazine ad for (genetically engineered) forty-year old housewives. They owned a spacious limestone on Third Street near the park and were closet Republicans posing as conservative Democrats – even to the degree of being members of the local co-op – yet despite the almost eerie perfectness of their lives they still remained childless, although recently Suzanne had been secretly scoping adoption websites for Caucasian infants at least vaguely similar in appearance to either her or her husband. None of this "Save the Africans" shit for Mrs. Anderson, not that she had any specific issues with any of those people. She just wasn't keen on one being part of her household. For the moment, Derek was in the dark regarding all of this, in part because Suzanne was fostering some resentment towards her husband: she was convinced he was sterile (he wasn't) but hadn't been able to bring herself to say as much.

Jeffrey Wang was founder and owner of what had started out as a boutique fashion store, Brooklyn Britches, which had grown into a globally distributed brand with deep penetration into the Asian market, particularly Japan and Korea, as well as Europe and Russia. It didn't hurt that part of the Brooklyn Britches marketing pitch involved eco-friendly manufacturing with sustainable facilities, local workers paid above minimum wage, and sponsored community recycling days for old computers, phones, televisions, electronics, etc. (and turned a healthy profit at reselling salvageable items to charities while the rest wound up in a toxic dump in the middle of China where the villagers would be lucky to see 30). Their sole ad strategy revolved around posing bitchy looking models with pouty lips in and around decrepit warehouses while managing to look simultaneously bored and sexually interested. Given the lucrative Brooklyn real estate market these days, the buildings they were shot in were probably in Newark. At 45 and unmarried, there were many who suspected Mr. Wang was gay, or at least playing for both teams, though in truth this was not the case. With his athletic build, immaculate appearance, and striking looks he certainly looked like he could be gay. But in fact Mr. Wang had an insatiable appetite for young models 16-18 years of age (and maybe one or two who slipped under the bar with a fake I.D.), sometimes two or three at a time. There had even been two paternity suits that had been discreetly settled. Since he was riding the crest of success, looks, and eco-popularity that, for the foreseeable/sustainable future at least, promised an inexhaustible supply of women, marriage was about the last thing on the planet he was interested in.

David Hilderman, Executive Director at Steerman Roche, an international engineering and design company based out of London. With his intense, dark haired looks and pencil thin mustache, Hilderman looked like he would be right at home with a crisp set of khakis and puffy-sided cavalry pants. Throw in a riding crop under his arm, an Aussie field hat cocked on his head and one could easily see him directing troops against Rommel alongside that old gasbag Montgomery. A monocle wouldn't have looked entirely out of place either. Unlike Anderson, Hilderman could be found on occasion at the yacht club bar – the New York Yacht Club bar actually – where he was a member and kept his seventy-seven foot ketch, "Solomon's Seal", berthed much of the year. At 53, he was the oldest of the group and recently a grandfather. His wife, Helen, was a sweet woman, pretty-yet-frumpy in a 'British school marm' sort of way, with her pile of salt and pepper hair and pince-nez glasses. The Hildermans lived in a spacious neat-as-a-pin brownstone on the promenade at Brooklyn Heights next to where the late actor George C. Scott had lived. And they had been on speaking terms with him no less. Secretly David enjoyed the company of actors and actresses and could, when called upon, demonstrate a distinct flair for theatrics. Hilderman was good with the peckish-but-good-natured British charm but was also a shrewd businessman who quietly ensured that he would always come out on top, a quality often underestimated by his friends and enemies. He'd also made some lucrative investments through several business acquaintances in the Caribbean which had paid off handsomely over the years.

The seventh man was not who he was pretending to be.

He was supposed to be Grant Matthews, another Englishman who was a senior manager in Voight Bannerman, a long-established U.S. construction company with a smattering of international clients. Matthews' specialty was in landing building projects with high-profile clients like Donald Trump, King Zayed (and quite a few sheiks from UAE as well), the MTA, and two terminals at JFK. He was something of a rock star in the usually anonymous ranks of construction management. Also he was single, having recently broken off a three-year relationship with a model/fashion designer/bartender who went by the single name Kara. His pride was a 2009 Aston Martin kept in his private garage on Montgomery Place where he also had his rooftop penthouse condo. At 39, he was the youngest and, with ten on and off years of triathlons under his belt, arguably the most physically fit of the group.

He was also, as of 5:36 the previous morning, dead.

The real name of the man presenting himself as Mr. Matthews was John Easton, and he bore more than a passing resemblance to the man he was posing as. He was also 39, athletically built, with straight sandy brown hair, gray eyes, and the rugged good looks one associates with Steve McQueen or Daniel Craig. After that, any similarity between the late Mr. Matthews and Mr. Easton parted ways. Jonathan Aaron Easton knew about as much about capital construction as he did about space shuttle reentry window calculations. But death he knew a thing or two about. He was a Detective Superintendent with the Royal Turks and Caicos Islands Police Force, Criminal Investigation Department, and just three days earlier had narrowly missed being laid out on the permanent horizontal plane himself.

Now, against his better judgment, he was sitting in the top floor room of a once prosperous men's club at least half a century past its prime, pretending to be one of seven men named as beneficiaries to the estate of the recently deceased Lars Van Eyckmann, about to be read the terms of that man's somewhat bizarre last will and codicil. How he came to be occupying the chair he was currently sitting in was in some ways no less bizarre....

2. MR. EASTON, ISN'T IT?

Three days previous John Easton had been on American Airlines Flight 170 from Miami to JFK. He was under strict orders from his commanding officer to take two months paid leave after wrapping up a major investigation involving an American investment banker by the name of Robert Princeton in a Ponzi Scheme to the tune of two billion dollars, give or take. Princeton, originally a poor-local-kid-makes-good story from Bridgeport, Connecticut, had apparently first hatched his scheme while in college at UCLA and had been on a roll conning everyone he came in contact with ever since. It had been going on so long that he probably woke up and lied to himself in the mirror every morning and every evening before he went to bed. And yet by age 45 he owned three islands in the Royal Turks, a sizable chunk of real estate in Barbados, a private jet, two 80 foot yachts, six Arabian horses and the majority share of the local cricket team. Or rather, he convinced people that he owned all this through an elaborate network of bank accounts, advertisements, testimonials, etc. He also was the head of four corporations bearing his name, Princeton Financial being the largest (with over six hundred employees, not including a few dozen carefully chosen international bank officials unofficially on his payroll); he was involved in eight lawsuits and one palimony suit, not to mention being the focus of several investigations. The CIA, the SEC, and of course the Royal Turks and Caicos Police Department were very interested in Mr. Princeton's more questionable activities, particularly his offering ridiculouosly high rates of return on CDs along with an alarming level of control in TCI Bank Ltd.

Detective Easton had been working undercover for a year and a half to crack the case, posing as an unscrupulous and merciless up-and-comer in the investment world and had worked his way very carefully and subtly into

Mr. Princeton's inner circle until he was counted as one of his most trusted deputies. What he found both appalled and shocked him. When it came to money (particularly when it was accompanied with the number of zeroes that became associated with any digits next to Princeton's name), an uncanny level of greed and bad behavior set in. Aside from the predictable ranks of climbers, gold diggers and opportunists, a good many sober-sided individuals and prudent personalities began to shed their common sense and jump on the money wagon. When the bank numbers began to reach the stratosphere, a new level of lunacy began to set in along with suspicion, paranoia, inflated egos, and a sense of entitlement to even more and more of the green stuff, which snowballed until one's value system became completely warped out of any recognizable relation to the vast majority of the rest of the planet's population: I deserve to have first class accommodations and be seated at the best table in the house; I deserve to have only the finest tailor-made clothes and travel only business class; I deserve to drive a gas-guzzling Cadillac SUV and have the international airport suspend its flights while I take off in my private jet.

And Easton's personal favorite, the classic rationale used by gold digging divorcees and widowers the world over: I'm entitled to the lifestyle I've grown accustomed to.

It was difficult to maintain one's perspective and not get caught up in the lunacy, let alone keep one's hands from strangling these people. And on more than one occasion Easton began to recognize the corrosive effect it was all having on his soul. Like the day he didn't get his usual table at Barclay's and ended up reaming the maître d' a new one ("Do you know who I am!? Now get me that goddamn table now or you'll be bussing tables here tomorrow night!") and for a moment believed his obnoxious behavior was actually justified.

In spite of this, he managed to keep his eye on the ball and amass a mounting pile of evidence that would guarantee Princeton a long and fruitful visit behind bars.

Or so he thought.

Instead, the investigation took a wild turn into near catastrophe just as it was being wrapped up. The Americans beat the RT&C officers to the punch when the SEC announced in the U.S. media that a warrant had gone out for Princeton's arrest. Without any heads-up to the Royal Turks and Caicos police force. Easton was forced to move into high gear and fast which is when, as is always the case when superiors start hammering for quick results, mistakes start getting made. There had been a near riot at TCI Bank Ltd. When, in a panic, citizens in the area showed up demanding their money, terrified that the Americans (or anybody) were going to freeze the bank assets and leave them high and dry. No small concern when you're one of the many living hand-to-mouth in the lower end of the Caribbean income strata.

But the real excitement started when representatives for the Mexican and Haitian drug cartels Princeton had been secretly laundering money for showed up at the Princeton Financial offices, weapons drawn, looking for their money. Someone – correctly as it turned out – had informed them that Princeton kept a substantial amount of valuables in the safe located in the private meeting room adjacent to his office. It was cleverly concealed by a secret panel in the wainscoting. To make matters even livelier, the two groups from rival factions arrived almost simultaneously. Easton, who had returned armed with a stack of warrants and a dozen constables to help carry them out, arrived just in time to get caught in the crossfire.

The ensuing gunfight was a fiasco. The two drug gangs involved were, like most, known to be exceptionally short on discretion and good manners. Nine Princeton Financial employees were killed, fifteen more wounded. One policeman was dead, three more also wounded, including Easton who was creased by a bullet near the femoral artery in the thigh – another half inch and this would most likely have been his final case – and sixteen Mexican and Haitian gunmen lay on the floor, their search-and-destroy days behind them permanently. Miraculously, Princeton, who had been caught in situ removing a leather carryall containing cash, passports and three small gold bars when the first gang showed up, was unhurt aside from being pistol-whipped across the side of his head and being unburdened of his stash.

The media fall-out was also a disaster. The press was all over the event like a bunch of half-starved crows, pecking at every shiny detail and juicy tidbit. The TCI News was bad enough, but when the TCI Post got its inflammatory teeth into it the frenzy really began. Soon even the BBC and CNN were endlessly replaying surveillance videos, devouring hours of TV time with interviews with the survivors and eye-witnesses and, when those began to shed their glimmer, interviewed families of the deceased, then their neighbors and cousins, then the neighbors of the cousins, and their neighbors and so on until every possible shred of news that could conceivably be milked out of the story had been drained dry.

Easton was already out of the Islands by then. His superior, Police Commissioner David W. Hutchison, under whom Easton had loyally served for eight years, had deflected as much of the blame as possible. But the politicians and press were clamoring for scapegoats and, as always, there were those who were willing to provide them. There was nothing off about Easton's investigation or even how he had handled the conflagration at Princeton Financial. In fact, he had handled it right by the numbers and it was doubtful any of his peers on the force could have done any better given the circumstances. But Easton, despite an impeccable if unorthodox record, was not one to suffer fools gladly. It didn't help that he had made an enemy of the Chief Minister, whom he suspected was involved with Princeton and might be one of the primary reasons TCI's star billionaire had avoided serious inquiry for so long.

The Chief Minister was already listing badly under a barrage of unrelated corruption charges but he still had his connections in the police department. One of those was a young investigator by the name of P. J. Sharpton who was weaseling his way up the promotion ladder and currently had much to gain by seeing senior officers like Easton out of the way. It didn't help that during one heated exchange of words, Easton had called him "Assistant Super Pee Jam Shithead" to his face and that the name had unofficially stuck in the locker-room.

He had a sneaking suspicion that Sharpton might have tipped off the cartel in order to deliberately skew Easton's case. There was no concrete evidence yet, of course, but he was working on it. If it did exist, Easton was going to make it his personal mission to see that Sharpton went down and went down hard because the constable that died, Drex Pearson, was a close and personal friend of his.

While the Police Commissioner did his best publicly, two days after the shoot-out he quietly called Easton into his office for a private talk. Rumors and insinuations had begun circulating that maybe Easton's investigation wasn't a hundred percent kosher…a fair amount of cash was unaccounted for… Easton was a renegade officer who had mishandled the situation and gotten a lot of innocent people killed…

His picture (how was it they always managed to find the most unflattering, criminal-looking shot?) was plastered all over the local news. The TCI Post was clamoring for justice claiming crime was out of control followed by the old standby; 'England was stepping in and taking direct control of the country explicitly because of events like this.'

Hutchison was buying none of it of course. But he was also a practical man. He asked if Easton's passport was current (it was) and recommended that one of his favorite officers make use of the substantial amount of vacation time he had accumulated, supplemented by some medical leave, of course. The message was clear: Get lost for a couple of months until the storm blows over and business gets back to normal.

Easton wasn't happy about it. He'd devoted a substantial amount of his life the past two years to bringing Princeton down and wanted to claim his due. Pearson, one of the few constables Easton felt he could genuinely trust, was dead. And, although he was dedicated to the oath he had sworn years ago, in his heart he wanted to see someone pay dearly for that. Pearson had a wife and three kids. But he was a realist as well and he suspected that living in the muck and mire of corrupt finances and politics for so long was beginning to leave a whiff of rotten odor around him. Setting professional feelings aside, his internal barometer indicated it was time for a change of atmosphere. So the next morning he booked a flight to Miami, with a connecting flight in New York to London.

The plan was vague. Mill around London a few days. Head over to Southampton to see a few friends and visit his sister and her family. Then off to Nice for a few weeks where an old friend maintained an apartment. Chase topless French women around the beaches, scuba dive in the Mediterranean and enjoy a decent bottle of Cotes-du Provence Rosé with a fresh loaf of baker's bread and rosemary olive oil (with plenty of raw garlic) while watching the sun set.

The overnight flight to JFK was looking to be uneventful. Half the plane was empty. The cabin lights had been dimmed, minimalist blankets issued, the whispering whine of the jet engines soothing. The pain in his thigh was tolerable after a couple of Vicodin HP chased by two tiny bottles of the "Select" Robert Mondavi Cabernet American overcharged for on their flights these days and he had just settled into his economy class seat to doze off – he was able to book the one by the emergency exit so he could stretch his leg out – when someone sitting in the gloom across the aisle flicked on the overhead light and leaning over politely tapped him on the forearm.

"Mr. Easton, isn't it?"

Finally, perhaps for the first time in years, he was truly letting everything go and about to fall into the fuzzy arms of a deep sleep and then this. A clipped British accent that sounded vaguely familiar.

Easton had to force his eyes open several times before he was able to get enough of his wits about him to risk looking over to his right. An impeccably dressed English businessman was sitting there, legs crossed, looking ridiculously out of place in the Economy section. He wore a tropical tan Savile Row suit with a pink shirt and a striped tie. The requisite silk kerchief jutted out of the breast pocket.

He raised an apologetic eyebrow at Easton's obvious disorientation.

"Quite sorry. It's been a few years, hasn't it?" He reached a well-manicured hand out. "Hilderman. David Hilderman."

Despite the Vicodin HP and wine, Easton managed to snap to his senses fairly quickly, a trick he had conditioned himself to do over years as a policeman. He also had an uncanny recall ability for faces and facts, a talent that had served him well as an investigator. He'd crossed paths with Hilderman nearly four years previously in Jamaica when Hilderman's daughter Angela got caught up with the wrong crowd and picked up on drug possession charges. The Hilderman's had been vacationing at a posh Marriott in Port Royal for a few weeks and Easton happened to be at the police station in Kingston investigating the dealers who sold her the stash (a few ounces of high octane weed), as they were also connected with a series of crimes in Providencialle on Grand Turk. Hilderman zeroed in on Easton, probably because he was the only white officer in the precinct at the time, and asked him to look into it. When push came to shove, even in the 21st century, political correctness apparently went straight out the window. At first he wasn't interested – Easton wasn't much on soft-pedaling privileged kids. But he also didn't care for the way a couple of the constables were joking around with the dealers. Like it was all a big game. And the way they enjoyed making a spoiled British girl slumming with the bad boys sweat. Or the other ladies, a pretty tough bunch, who were in the holding cell with Angela, looking at her like they were interested in having her for a midnight snack. Without bending the rules too much, he managed to get her off on a stiff fine and a warning, probably pocket change to the Hilderman's, then promptly forgot the whole thing.

Until now.

He managed to muster up a ghost of a smile and sit up a little straighter. Force of habit when around his own countrymen. After shaking Hilderman's hand, he gave a thoughtful nod and said, "Certainly, I remember. How is Angela?"

Hilderman cracked a side smile, which came off a little stiff. But he looked pleased. "Fine, fine. Met a decent fellow finally and got married two years ago. Just had their first child last month. Which makes me a grand-dad for God-sakes." Easton was worried that Hilderman would then follow up with the tortuous photos-of-my-grandchild ritual but was spared. He did feel a slight pang however, at the reminder that, while Hilderman was now a grandfather in his early fifties, at thirty-nine he had never married, let alone had any children. At least that he was aware of. He didn't have a clear-cut answer for that: none of the usual "haven't met the right woman yet", "not really the family type", or "devoted to my career" though the last was probably the closest fit. It would be more accurate to say he never put a whole lot of thought into it. Maybe I'd better at some point, he thought. Tomorrow. Or in ten days when I'm curling my toes in the white sands of the Mediterranean.

"How about yourself then? Any interesting cases? I read all about the Princeton fiasco of course. Sorry to hear it." Hilderman paused, then added quietly; "That prick really had it coming to him if I don't mind saying. I sincerely hope you're taking some time off. The press have been bloody vultures..."

Easton merely grunted in reply. He wasn't much in the mood for small chit-chat. He laced his fingers over his stomach and fell into a contemplative look at the bulkhead wall in front of him. The miniature television monitor there showed a satellite map of the East Coast of the United States, with a yellow line indicating their flight path and a large white plane icon indicating how far they had come along it. Which wasn't much.

Probably a good two hours to go.

He realized Hilderman had not spoken in a few minutes. A quick glance confirmed what he already sensed: the other man was struggling with how to properly phrase what was obviously going to be another request. Probably an awkward one. The giveaway was in the left forefinger tapping the armrest methodically. A diamond cufflink glinted in the dim light.

The David Hildermans of the world didn't fly economy even at gunpoint or threat of extended Chinese torture. Ergo, Mr. Hilderman had somehow acquired knowledge that Easton was on the plane and had sought him out. Easton did what all good cops did: played the patience game.

After another two minutes ticked by, Hilderman finally arrived at a decision. The finger paused in mid tap. Then he abruptly stood up and looked around, crossed the aisle and slid into the cramped window seat next to Easton. There didn't appear to be any other passengers within earshot.

Like their first encounter years ago in Kingston, he went right in for the direct approach.

"I have a business proposition for you, Mr. Easton." He leaned in a bit on his elbow, fingers half covering his mouth and speaking quietly but clearly in Easton's ear. "That is, if I can talk you into a short layover in New York. I assure you I would make it financially worth your while." Easton stiffened. He wasn't sure he wanted to hear what was coming next.

"Three million dollars?" He wasn't sure his ears were functioning correctly. Perhaps there had been collateral damage from the recent gunfight he had been in. Easton tried to recall how extensive the follow-up physical had been. Had the doctor checked his ears? He couldn't remember. For over half an hour Hilderman had outlined what had turned out to be an increasingly bizarre and most likely highly illegal business proposal.

In a nutshell, it involved this: Lars Van Eyckmann, a reclusive and eccentric billionaire (as if there were any other type) had recently passed away from natural causes. No one knew his exact age, but his associates estimated him to be somewhere in his late eighties. And in the previous few months, his health had appeared to be failing. He had lost weight, his already gaunt features appearing even more sallow and skeletal, his responses odd and distracted.

Van Eyckmann was the senior member of the Mohican Club's Executive Council, which consisted of seven members, all selectively culled prominent Brooklyn businessmen. In other words, not necessarily the wealthiest, but the real movers and shakers in the borough's high society. The club itself was something of an anachronism, despite loosening its membership requirements to accommodate women in the 1960s and minority groups in the '80s in a too-little-too-late attempt to embrace the changing times. In the previous ten years, many of its social functions had diminished despite some strategic marketing moves such as the sponsoring and hosting of the Mystery Writers Club's monthly meetings and making the spacious banquet rooms on the lower floors available for local weddings, christenings, bar mitzvahs (and baht mitzvahs once they came in vogue) and a variety of other private functions which would have been considered heresy in its heyday. In truth, these days it was only Van Eyckmann's deep pockets that were keeping the whole club solvent and one step ahead of being sold off piecemeal and parceled into condominiums or anything else for a quick buck. The good old days (good for those who happened to be white and wealthy at least) of grand old gentlemen's clubs had faded out along with three-martini lunches and two-pack-a-day smokers and so-called "proper" American values. Its death knoll had sounded well before that actually, but it had continued to limp along on life support through the adamant if vain efforts of old money like Van Eyckmann's.

Even so, for the past ten years the seven members of the Executive Council had met regularly and almost religiously. For those "newer" up-and-comers like Delgado and Wang, it was close to a secret fetish having been first approached then invited by Van Eyckmann's representatives to become part of the exclusive club-within-a-club inside of the Mohican's hallowed if musty walls. Though not a name that had been seen with any substance in the media since the 1950s, Van Eyckmann was still well known behind closed doors in the inner circles of business and the arts in Brooklyn.

Lars Van Eyckmann was a commanding and intimidating presence. With his long, angular countenance, fierce eyes, jutting brow and prominent nose suggesting the prow of an oncoming man-o'-war, he had a reputation as a merciless businessman with seemingly unlimited funds at his disposal. The word was that he was descended from a long line of Dutch merchants that had originally made their money in the East Indies spice trade in the early 1600s. Though only five feet five, like Josef Lefferts he more than compensated for his lack of height by sheer force of will and personality. He was also not above pulling little tricks to reinforce this, such as having the legs of all the visitor's chairs in his office sawed down a couple inches (and his special desk chair custom made an inch higher than standard) so that anyone sitting in his office would be forced to look up at him – a tip an old business acquaintance named Benito employed successfully as well. But mostly he was content to use his iron will to mold others to his bidding, usually in the form of shadowy back room dealings and favors given or called in, but not above an occasional one-on-one brow-beating. Few knew what really went on in the seemingly black heart of the man, but they did know this: if Van Eyckmann took a liking to you, doors would suddenly open and opportunities would present themselves. If he didn't, the devil himself would make a better partner.

Of his family, little was known. He had no direct descendants aside from a bastard son and a wife who had died under mysterious circumstances years back. There were rumors she was mentally unstable and possibly had taken her own life. There were also rumors of other family members including other children—some stillborn, others deformed in some manner—who didn't survive long. Also a sprinkling of aunts, uncles, and cousins who had faded in and out of the family tree. There were some distant members of the Van Eyckmann bloodline living in Westchester and Putnam counties as well, but Lars was a man who valued his privacy and he was extremely effective at enforcing it. He still maintained his estate in Wyvern Falls, a scenic village situated on the Hudson River north of Tarrytown. No one really lived there during the week other than a skeleton staff (if you were one of the kids spinning stories over lunch in Wyvern Falls Elementary, a staff of skeletons) that included a very well-trained and expensive security detail. It was located near the bluffs overlooking the river just north of town, though few were privileged to see it other than in a few old black and white images hanging in the Historical Society or a glimpse from out on the river of its dark stone towers, goblin-topped gables and chimneys looking like some sort of fairy tale nightmare.

The seven members of the Executive Council had all received identical phone calls two days before informing them that the senior benefactor of their organization was deceased and that they were required to attend a reading of his will by the estate attorney on the 28th of October. Of the group, Hilderman had known Van Eyckmann the longest and he was able to shed a little additional light on what was coming. One thing Hilderman was an expert at was getting the low-down on "what was coming." Even from Van Eyckmann. What Hilderman knew was this: aside from the usual charities, stipends to remaining Van Eyckmann relatives and a bastard son, and a perpetuity to maintain the estate, etc., a substantial chunk of the estate was being willed to the seven members of the Executive Council to the tune of twenty million dollars each.

But there was an unusual catch: the members had to maintain the club for the next five years, and all seven original members had to stay overnight at the Van Eyckmann mansion, Taron Hall, on Halloween as part of an old family tradition. It was part practical joke and part test, Hilderman explained. Van Eyckmann was not the sort to just hand out money without exacting some price in return. In this case, Hilderman was told, part of the plan was a few surprise arrangements designed to scare the wits out of the club members (and provide some excellent entertainment). Otherwise, the money would be in forfeit and they would have to return it in full.

"Van Eyckmann was a bastard all right," Hilderman added, "but he wasn't the hundred and twenty percent bastard everyone assumed he was." Over the years, Hilderman had struck up an odd sort of acquaintance with him, and had even had the rare privilege of dining at Taron Hall on several occasions, the only member of the club to do so. One night, after two glasses of rare brandy from his private stock, Van Eyckmann had confided some of this. The rest Hilderman had very carefully and cleverly extracted from Bill Lowe over the years and at various social functions.

Van Eyckmann may have been a bit of an anachronism, but he was quite serious and committed to the Mohican Club and he took special interest in those he deemed serious and seasoned businessmen – hence the age requirement of the Executive Council – worthy of investing in and developing. Especially in this age of instant millionaires and infatuation with excess, which he found especially gauche. So he took care and pride in developing protégés in the next generation who he considered worthy businessmen and quietly mentoring their careers. Of course, he wasn't above a practical joke or two as well, as a test to measure their mettle. And to amuse himself. Even cantankerous old (rich) Dutchmen had their own, albeit peculiar, sense of humor.

Which brought matters to the latest catch: the unexpected death of Grant Matthews. Hilderman had received a call from a contact in the police department within minutes of the body being discovered - he was in the middle of a meeting for the Miami Port Tunnel at the time - and immediately the damage control machine sprang into action. The initial investigation didn't suggest any foul play but it wouldn't be until after the full autopsy results came that it could be ruled out. Easton was well aware that, unlike television crime dramas where every investigation gets magically resolved for better or for worse in one hour less commercials, these things usually took weeks and weren't always conclusive. He'd also seen his share of forensic labs and was yet to see one with the incredible hi-tech equipment and sleek interior design one otherwise only sees in architectural magazines.

Stocked with exceptionally hip and well-dressed people, of course.

So far, the real New York City investigators had determined this: Matthews had been out to a few bars the night before with friends around SoHo and had finally wound up before midnight at Pravda on Lafayette Street. At the cozy upstairs bar there, he'd crossed paths with his ex-girlfriend – she was with another date – and wound up in an intense but quiet argument. An hour and three "Russian Marys" later, they had left together and wound up back at Matthew's condo in Brooklyn where, after sex and a few lines of cocaine, they both passed out. Which was all she wrote until the girlfriend – her real name was Linda Fisher – woke up a few hours later to find her man bereft of any signs of life.

The medical examiner's initial report suggested that "a congenital heart defect combined with illegal use of controlled substances had resulted in the suspect's death." Translation: While high on Bolivian Marching Powder, New York's rock star celebrity engineer had blown his engine after fucking his brains out.

Hilderman was too well-mannered to use that description of course, but that's what Easton's ears heard. However one opted to phrase it, the result was the same for the future of seven prominent businessmen in Brooklyn. Each of them was about to be out twenty million dollars unless they could come up with a solution. Fast. Hilderman was the first to know this of course. After weighing the matter carefully, he decided to contact the other club members and fill them in on the essential details. The first order of business was to lock the clamps down on any of this getting out to the press, at least for another five days or so. Money changed hands. Arrangements were made. The ex-girlfriend suddenly had relatives to visit in California. The corpse of Grant Matthews became "John Doe" for a bit. The whole matter went quiet. Very quickly.

The following week Grant Matthews would die again, publicly, exactly as he had the first time.

In the meantime, a suitable replacement had to be found for the reading of the will. Hilderman was en-route back to New York when, as fortune would have it, he glanced at the passenger list and caught Easton's name. He was always insistent about knowing who was on any plane he was on, something of an obsession since 9-11. Even if it meant scanning a hundred names.

A quick word with the flight attendant confirmed it: Detective Superintendent John Easton was in Seat 28B. And Hilderman, whose recall was as excellent as the detective's, remembered he bore more than a passing resemblance to his late Executive Council colleague. Not just that, Hilderman had already been considering the idea that Easton would be a good candidate for what he had in mind, and wondering how he would reach out to him on such short notice.

Fate worked in strange ways.

"Three million dollars," Easton repeated. "And all I have to do is pretend to be this engineer guy for a few days. Isn't impersonating another person for financial gain slightly illegal, Mr. Hilderman? And uh, have you forgotten I am a Detective Superintendent with CID of the Metropolitan Police?"

Hilderman let out a quick snort. "Yes, I am aware of your profession, Mr. Easton. First, please call me David. May I call you John?"

Easton smiled, but it was not one of his friendly smiles. He chose one from the I'm keeping this polite for the moment box instead. "Let's keep it to Detective Easton and Mr. Hilderman for now."

"As you please...Detective." Hilderman seemed amused. And

confident. "But I only ask you to hear out my proposition before making a decision to entertain it....or arrest me."

Easton cut in. "Before you continue, Mr. Hilderman, I do have to remind you (again) that I am a police officer and that anything you say could that could incriminate yourself would probably not be advisable."

"Of course. I understand."

Easton cut in. "But just out of curiosity, if each of you and your colleagues in the "Executive Council" are due to collect twenty million dollars each, and you're proposing to pay only three million to the man putting his neck on the line to impersonate one of you. What exactly were you looking to do with the rest of the money, if you don't mind my asking?"

Hilderman chuckled. "Not at all, Detective. I was getting to that. In your case, half the balance of that money would be going to the family of Constable Pearson who was killed in the line of duty with you three days ago. To be paid out as an annuity. The rest would be distributed to the Royal Turks and Caicos Policemen's Charity. All of it anonymously of course."

If Easton was momentarily caught off guard, he hid it well. Although the smile left his face.

"I have to be honest, Mr. Hilderman. If this is some sort of joke, I don't find it at all amusing."

Hilderman let that sit a minute. Then: "I assure you, Detective, this is no joke. If you agree to undertake this...impersonation...I will not only agree to pay you three million dollars, I will double it. Six million dollars guaranteed. I can have the papers drawn up within hours of getting to New York. Nothing specific to anything not legal of course. The wording will have to be cleverly chosen and I would not wish to do anything to compromise your career or integrity. Say an inheritance from a rich, forgotten uncle in the Midlands or something. But six million (before all the usual taxes), at the end of...let's say seven days. Wired into a bank account of your choice."

Easton sat up. He was seeing red flags everywhere. "Now why on earth would you wish to do that?"

"Because, Detective, I not only wish to engage you to impersonate Grant Matthews, I want you to find out who murdered him."

3. VAN EYCKMANN'S REQUEST

Easton still wasn't really clear why he accepted. It wasn't the money. Certainly he could make use of it, but he'd passed on several opportunities in the past for a simple reason: Easton refused to be owned by anybody, and he'd seen too many people in his life sell themselves out and knew the price that ultimately came with it. Especially given his latest case with Princeton. He'd been appalled not only by how those like Princeton manipulated people around them with money, but how seemingly rational and decent people could turn into greedy, back-stabbing monsters – like Gollum in those Lord of the Rings movies – willing to do anything to get it. Like junkies and crack. And it wasn't just the big ticket screw-overs, it was the little insidious behaviors that came with the smell of green, the posturing and 'brownie-point' behavior of people around those with money, drawing favorable attention to themselves while belittling their colleagues. The tit-for-tats, the insecurities, the sarcastic quips, the rolling eyes, the melodrama and frail egos, in short, the all-around juvenile behavior more suited to grade school than so-called adults.

So Easton had kept his nose clean. And perhaps that had cost him in other ways, but at the end of the day that was a price he was willing to pay. Years ago when he was heading off to the Metropolitan Police Academy after a four year stint as a Paratrooper, his father, in a rare moment of dispensing personal advice, surprised him as they sat in the parking lot of the Falmouth rail station. He turned off the engine, looked him straight in the eye, and told him, "Son, there are a lot of things you can do in life to make money, and lots of it. But it always comes with a price. Don't ever forget it. Stay true. Oh yes; and always wear um, a glove you know. No rush to have any little Easton's running about the place just yet if you catch my drift."

That was it. The sum total of fatherly advice he had ever been given. Direct at least.

And he hadn't forgotten.

Mainly though it had been the offer regarding Constable Pearson. That arrow had hit home. Pearson had been a close and reliable friend for many years. One of those dutiful and unassuming civil servants that are the real backbone of whichever particular branch they are in, always showing up on time, never complaining, almost always getting overlooked when promotions and pay raises were handed out. Pearson practically had to be forced at gun point to take vacation time. And policemen in Grand Turk weren't exactly rolling in the money. Crime was on the rise as the economy continued to slide like a listing ship in the wake of the recession. Pearson had three children and a wife. His meager pension and life insurance settlement would only stretch so far. Easton would be more than willing to help, but this whole offer Hilderman was laying before him wasn't adding up completely to a hundred percent. And then there was the last hook: a private murder investigation. Of course, Easton had no jurisdiction to act in any official capacity in the States, other than Hilderman mentioning that he could arrange for him to be issued a private detective's license within twenty-four hours. Easton couldn't remember the last time he had been involved in an actual homicide investigation though. He had recently been part of a group that had received SWAT training and there was the occasional security training for private clients that he did on the side, but none of that involved good old murder investigation, the meat-and-potatoes type of work he had originally cut his teeth on. Which made him even more suspicious: Hilderman was offering him a tailor-made opportunity and was willing to pay him handsomely to do it. The timing was dead-on and the package was wrapped up all neat and perfect.

Maybe a little too neat and perfect.

But he had decided to play along. For now. Carefully.

Easton had canceled his connecting flight after they arrived at JFK. After some hassle with his luggage, he joined Hilderman at the departures ramp at Terminal 8 where Hilderman had a Lincoln Town Car and driver already waiting. Hilderman was on his BlackBerry with his attorney most of the time. From what Easton could tell, Hilderman was doing most of the talking and the attorney doing most of the listening. He had a steely delivery once he was rolling and Easton decided Hilderman wasn't a man one would choose to cross lightly.

He also decided then that he would never fully trust him.

The driver left them off at an incongruous building not far from the Brooklyn Bridge in lower Manhattan where Hilderman's company maintained a suite of apartments for business purposes. They were quite nice in a modern, chic, and completely non-descript sort of way. What

Easton thought of architecturally as "High-End Anonymous." A harassed-looking attorney showed up with a stack of papers for Easton to sign (which he insisted on keeping duplicates of) and handed him a P.I. license. He had a half-hour briefing by Hilderman on "Being Grant Matthews" during which a suitcase of the aforementioned's clothes arrived in a Louis Vuitton suitcase, freshly dry-cleaned and pressed. Easton balked at this and after some back and forth compromised with swapping out his personal effects and underwear.

He wasn't overly concerned about playing his part. The only person he needed to convince over the next few days would be Van Eyckmann's attorney Lowe, who, according to Hilderman, had only met Matthews in person once a few years back and then only briefly to sign some papers. The other businessmen were in on the whole set-up and there were no papers to sign for the next few days.

Another gust of wind hammered at the windows again and the lights flickered momentarily. A mild nor'easter. Nothing serious unless you happened to be a fisherman out in the middle of the dark ocean or in a small airplane struggling through the crosswinds. Easton sat leaning forward with his fingers interlaced. He was wearing a dead man's suit – a sharp fitting gray Armani with a black turtleneck – with an envelope inside the left breast pocket containing a short note printed in elegant copperplate script on expensive cream colored linen paper:

You are hereby asked to appear
at the Mohican Club
3rd floor Meeting Chamber
October 28th, 2010
7:00 PM

At Van Eyckmann's Request.

Very to the point. Van Eyckmann apparently was a man accustomed to giving orders and having them obeyed. An hour earlier, Easton had met the other members of the Executive Council in the first floor bar where there had been awkward introductions. Hilderman had given Easton a reasonably thorough (as thorough as one could be in a couple of hours) breakdown of Matthews: what he was like, his mannerisms, friends, known quirks, and, more importantly, how to conduct himself with the other members of the Executive Council. Fortunately, Matthews had no close personal or professional ties with the other members. Except for Hilderman. Their companies had worked on several high-profile projects together in the past. Hilderman didn't seem to have a high opinion of

Matthews. In fact, he sounded disapproving. Aside from Matthews having eaten at Delgado's restaurant once, Hilderman wasn't aware of any interactions with the other members outside of their monthly meetings at the club. Still, clearly no one was comfortable with the idea of pulling off any sort of deception with one of New York's leading law firms. But Hilderman had been calm and very assertive on this. Words were whispered as hands were shaken and, after a round of drinks, the mood smoothed out considerably.

Lowe looked around at each of the men in turn. Before him on the table was Van Eyckmann's last will and testament in a neat, perfect stack. It didn't appear to be very thick.

"Gentlemen, thank you for coming this evening. As you are well aware, Mr. Van Eyckmann passed away on the 22nd. In accordance with his last wishes, he will be buried in the family plot this next Monday, November 1st, at his estate in Wyvern Falls. The service is scheduled for 9 AM. You are all expected to attend of course, to fulfill your part of the arrangements."

Juan Delgado made a slight rolling gesture with his forefinger. "And what, um, exactly are the 'arrangements'?"

Lowe, fingers steepled, shot Delgado the look of an indulgent schoolmaster. "I was about to get to that." One could almost hear the unspoken 'young man' hanging in the air at the end of the sentence. "Gentlemen, as you know, Mr. Van Eyckmann, God rest his soul, was something of an unusual man and the terms of the will that he dictated to my firm are no less so. I am not here to judge nor comment on it as such, merely to convey his wishes. So please bear with me and I will do my best to answer any questions afterward." With that, he produced a pair of reading glasses from his jacket pocket with the practiced ease of a conjurer, went through the ritual of putting them on with his right hand while his left picked up the first sheet of paper, and began:

"I, Lars Van Eyckmann, resident of the Borough of Brooklyn and of the Village of Wyvern Falls, being of sound mind and body and well over the age of eighteen years, and not being actuated by any duress, fraud, mistakes, deceit, witchery, astral manipulation, the acts by deceitful ifritis or undue influence by sinister forces, do hereby make, publish, and declare the following to be my Last Will and Testament, revoking all previous wills and codicils made by me.

"I declare that I was married to Isadora Van Eyckmann who was not of sound mind, was, in fact, nutty as a holiday fruitcake and is deceased, may God rest her soul (here Lowe paused to clear his throat uncomfortably), being a worthless bitch who bore me no children.

"I acknowledge that I have sired one bastard child, Edgar, born out of wedlock to one Francis Walters, but deny him any right or claim over my properties other than what is to be specified herein. Should any others come forward seeking to make claim upon my estate, they shall be seen for the gold-digging imposters they are, probably being Jewish in descent, and should they persist will be met with the full extent of legal repercussions that may be levied upon them by my counsel.

"I do appoint William Lowe, my attorney of record, as Executor of my Last Will and Testament. If he is unable or unwilling to serve, I then appoint Harold Makepeace as alternate Executor. My Executor shall be authorized to carry out all provisions of this Will and pay my just debts, obligations and funeral expenses, except mortgage notes secured by real estate, as soon as practical.

"I also name the following beneficiaries of my will, all fellow members of the Mohican Executive Council:

Geoffrey Washington, Josef Lefferts, Juan Delgado, Derek Anderson, Jeffrey Wang, David Hilderman, and Grant Matthews, all of Brooklyn, New York. Each of these gentlemen, as per prior arrangement with my Executor, will be granted the sum or equivalent of twenty (20) Million Dollars to be transferred to their persons within twenty-four hours of the following conditions being met:

1.) Each of these men shall be required to spend twenty-four hours at my estate, Taron Hall, located in the town of Wyvern Falls commencing at eight AM of the morning on the thirtieth day of the month of October following my death. This is required as part of a long-standing Van Eyckmann family tradition.

2.) They must also subsequently agree, in written form, to maintain the Mohican Club, remain faithful to its charter and attend monthly meetings, etc. for the next ten years.

"For the first condition to be met, ALL existing members of the Executive Council must be in attendance and remain within the Estate Grounds for the entire Twenty-four hours and not a minute less, or the Twenty Million Dollars for ALL the members will be completely forfeit. As for the second condition, if any of the existing members should become deceased, incapacitated, decapitated, or unable to fulfill their obligations to the club in any way, the remaining members are permitted to select a suitable successor. If they unable to arrive at a successful decision, a successor will be appointed by the Executor.

"Regarding the balance of my estate, the rest of all outstanding monies shall be set up in an annuity fund to maintain Taron Hall in perpetuity, less operating and accounting expenses to be paid out at the discretion of the Executor. The entire contents of the estate, including ALL my personal belongings, shall remain exactly in their current state. The existing staff shall be retained at their current salaries, plus a one-time award of ten thousand dollars each. My illegitimate son shall receive a yearly stipend of one hundred thousand dollars to keep his mouth shut plus a one-time award of one million dollars.

"His mother shall receive $1.

"My relatives, Victor and Sybilla Vandereems of Dutchess County, shall receive a onetime award of fifty thousand dollars, as they have made feeble attempts at civility over the years and sent me their insufferable family photo Christmas cards every holiday without fail.

"It is also my desire that a trust be set up in my name for.... "

Lowe ran through the final gritty details to the end, which had no bearing on the seven men present, finally wrapping up with:

"I remain ever faithfully yours and wish you continued success in your endeavors, Lars Van Eyckmann.

Lowe's last worlds trailed off into the air, followed by an uncomfortable silence. Some of the more ridiculous words he'd just had to read seemed to hang in the air around them like awkward little ghosts not sure where they should go. Another knot popped in the fireplace. The wind continued its forlorn howling outside. He laid the sheets of paper back down on the table, carefully cornering them with his index and forefingers. He looked around at each of the men in turn.

"Any questions?"

Easton was curious which of the men would speak up first. He had a whole list of questions, but doubted the attorney could or would be interested in answering them. Plus, he knew it wouldn't be wise to draw unnecessary attention to himself. Observing everyone's body language, he figured it was Delgado who would speak up first. He had been drumming his fingers lightly on the table for the past few minutes. What bothered him was the look on everyone's face at the mention of twenty million dollars. Even Hilderman's. These were wealthy men, and, while not exactly pocket change, it didn't explain the intense look everyone had. He was also curious why no one flinched at some of the eccentric wording which appeared to suggest an old curmudgeon skating along the edge of lunacy.

Then everyone gave a start as Lefferts' hands came down on the table with a resounding slap and he burst out laughing. "Hahahahaha...Holy Christ! That's insane! The old clod was crazier than a bag of rabid weasels and anti-Semitic to boot! Astral manipulation? Deceitful ifritis? What in the fuck is that!? I have no idea!" This prompted another round that had tears streaming from his eyes. This trailed off into a series of fitful snickers as he realized no one was laughing with him.

Seven sets of eyes looked at him flatly.

After an awkward pause, Delgado jumped in, affecting a slight lisp. "So...William, let me get this straight. All seven of us have to drop everything and in two days be up at Van Eyckmann's gothic train wreck of a house for twenty four hours? Wyvern Falls??? Is this place near any known civilization? Do they have hot water? Do they fight Indians on the weekends???"

Lowe managed a slight chuckle. "It's not quite as terrible as all that. But, considering the sums involved, it might be worth it for you to take on an Indian or two."

It took the members a collective moment to realize that Van Eyckmann's stalwart lawyer had actually made a joke.

A few of the members suppressed a laugh under their breaths.

Lowe placed his hands flat on the table. "Gentlemen, I won't mince words. My client, Mr. Van Eyckmann, was, shall I say, somewhat eccentric in his ways and not exactly the most tactful when it came to his choice of language. While I personally find some of the wording of his will objectionable, my personal feelings have no bearing on its content or on my role in executing it. Asking, no, requiring the seven of you to spend an evening at his estate in order to receive your respective inheritances is certainly odd in my estimate, but certainly no harm will come of it. Of course, you do so of your own free will.

Easton decided to throw his hand in. "Excuse me, Mr. Lowe, but what can you tell us of this "family tradition" Mr. Van Eyckmann referred to? Are there any specifics? Anything we are required to do while up at Taron Hall?"

Joe Lefferts cut in, "Heh, what, do we have to dance around the family mulberry bush or toss rose petals from the highest window?"

"Or," Jeff Wang said quietly, "Perhaps we'll be 'required' to conduct a séance to contact Mr. Van Eyckmann and receive investment advice from the other side...?"

"Actually....now that you mention it, I believe there is something." Lowe went through the papers again until he found what he was looking for. "But it appears you will have to wait to find out. According to this, Mr. Van Eyckmann has left an additional set of instructions for each of you up at the Hall. Unfortunately, however, they are sealed. I'm afraid you'll just have to wait until all of you get there...."

4. TARON HALL

Easton caught the 6:41 express train out of Grand Central Station. Hilderman had offered a ride up in his limousine but Easton preferred to travel alone and collect his thoughts. Plus, it was his first opportunity in life to play commuter and take a train out of a station he'd only seen in the movies up until then. It really was a magnificent station that still evoked the aura of a bygone New York with its cathedral-like ceiling with discreet pale green constellation frescoes, the stars twinkling pinpricks of light, its enormous iron-mullioned windows and broad stone staircases, and the iconic clock at the information station in its center. These days, it was kept clean and well-policed. Like all well-designed train stations, its atmosphere and architecture managed to inspire calmness and hustle and bustle at the same time, the type of space that made you want to hurry up and enjoy it. One half expected to turn the corner and run into a hurrying 1940s businessman in top coat and fedora or a lady in a square-shouldered suit, perhaps with bright red lipstick, swept hair pinned back up on one side under a raked hat, a cigarette perched in one gloved hand.

The lines were short at that hour, so Easton indulged himself by purchasing a round trip ticket from an actual human being at the old-fashioned ticket booths on the south side of the main floor (he wasn't big on ticket machines except in a pinch) and managed to secure a coffee and turkey sausage/eggs/spinach on an "English muffin", or an American facsimile of one, down on the lower mezzanine where the food courts were. He noted that while the subways in New York were much nastier and aromatic than the tube in London (what was with the band of Mexican musicians with their embroidered black leather boots and Elvis pompadours?), Grand Central was all spit- polished brass and stonework, while its London counterparts like Waterloo and Victoria looked like a couple frumpy aunts with their dust-caked frameworks, florescent lighting, and patchwork modifications.

Except for the bathrooms.

In England these days, even the public restrooms were all modernized and reasonably clean. In Grand Central, as Easton had discovered, the men's bathrooms were apparently located in a different dimension from the rest of the station, a dark and evil Bosch-like dimension that reeked with the sour and putrid aromas of unwashed bodies and unwashed clothes, of continuous hacking and phlegmy coughs, and strange activities, rustlings, goings-on in the stall next to you, the explanation for which were better left unknown.

A place Easton probably wouldn't have wished on his own worst enemies.

Other than that Grand Central was fabulous.

He settled into the third car, choosing a window seat that would afford him an unobstructed view of the Hudson. It was one of the newer M7 Metro North cars, with its sharp blue trim, high-backed seats, and stainless steel siding. He never tasted anything quite like the so-called English muffin, but all in all the egg sandwich was surprisingly good. The coffee was strong and mellow.

As the train rolled out slowly through the maze of tunnels under Midtown towards Harlem, Easton mused over his impressions of the past two days and what he saw as his immediate future. In general, he felt pretty good and rested, if out of sorts staying in Manhattan. After so much time in the open expanses of the Caribbean, the grit, noise, bustling crowds, and hemmed-in canyons of skyscrapers was overwhelming, a physical assault on the senses. There didn't seem to be anywhere one could get more than a cursory glance at a patch of sky. And the people. Apparently, United States Immigration had insisted on bringing in millions of people from every corner of the earth and jamming them into a few square miles to see what would happen. The result was the semi-organized chaos that is called New York City. He had to admit though, the energy was infectious. Everybody was in a rush to get somewhere else. Usually with some zip in their step. Food was ordered and served double time and cab drivers were in a perpetual competition to find the fastest shortcut to anywhere – from one neighborhood to another, one streetlight to another, even one side of the street to the other. It was enough to make your head spin.

But Easton found himself enjoying it.

Physically he had never felt better, aside from the fact that his leg was still stiff and he had to change the bandages twice a day. Even so, he had done a lot of walking the past couple of days and did his basic workout of sit-ups and push-ups (three hundred of the former and one hundred of the latter) and stretches in the mornings. He had come to the conclusion that the mental and cultural shock of New York had been good for him. An unexpected reset to purge the bad taste of the past few days, weeks, hell…the past few years out of his system.

He still had no clear idea what exactly was going on with the whole Van Eyckmann business. Very little of it added up or made any sense at this point. The arrangements and will were bizarre at the least, compounded by the retainer he was being paid (although, after years of living in the surreal financial universe of Mr. Princeton, not that unreal) and, underneath it all, the nagging idea that he was being carefully manipulated through this latest turn of events.

Hilderman was the first one who came to mind. But Easton sensed there was more to the picture. Some other workings that perhaps even Hilderman wasn't aware of. Call it a policeman's instinct. Or paranoia. There just wasn't enough information yet.

So instead Easton ran over what he did know.

A very wealthy and eccentric millionaire, or perhaps billionaire. An exclusive club of hand-picked, highly successful businessmen, all from Brooklyn. All within a ten-year age group, give or take. One suddenly dead on the eve of inheriting twenty million dollars. A bizarre requirement for that inheritance that read like something out of a "B" horror movie script. Something Hammer Films would have cranked out in the '60s, probably starring Barbara Steel and Christopher Lee, with Peter Cushing as the mad Dutchman.

There was the coincidence (?) of running into Hilderman on the plane, the everything-happening-so-fast-no-time-to-explain pace of events that effectively kept everyone off balance, the thousand or so things that could go wrong at any given moment and send the whole damn thing south. At least in addition to a bunch of Grant Matthews I.D.s, he still had his own passport and detective's badge, and, thankfully, his nine-millimeter Beretta 92F in a shoulder holster under his left armpit. Not the sturdiest of side arms but deadly accurate.

As for what was coming down the pike, he would wait and see. One thing he was fairly certain of: it was going to be an interesting twenty-four hours.

7:15 AM.

Easton nursed his coffee and took in the magnificent scenery of the Hudson Valley as the train worked its way north along the river. The sun was breaking over the hills to the east and igniting a storm of color in the cliffs on the opposite side. Autumn had come late this year and the trees were still a riot of scarlet, warm yellows, bright oranges, and sienna's, set against old cliffs of reddish-brown rock that ran in their ranks along the west bank, some hundreds of feet high. The intermittent piles of cumulus clouds under thrusting tendrils of cirrus looked like something Albrecht Dürer would have dreamed up for one of his 15th century woodcuts. Easton was quickly grasping why a whole school of art had erupted in the region. It had a spooky exuberance that had you pining for drawing or painting materials whether you were an artist or not.

There was something about trains that Easton found romantic and exhilarating, that reminded him of his childhood in England. But this Hudson River business was something altogether different from Falmouth where he grew up. Apples to oranges, perhaps, but everything seemed larger and more aggressive in scale: the grass was thicker, the trees taller, the sky broader. There was a brashness that was echoed throughout the atmosphere. It was, even hundreds of years after the term was coined, a new world.

A thought crossed his mind: what an amazing country. And these damn Americans have no clue what they've got.

The stops whirled by: Yonkers, Dobbs Ferry, Hastings-on-Hudson, Irvington, Tarrytown, Ossining.... Finally the conductor called his stop: "Wyvern Falls. Please check your belongings. Mind the gap as you exit the train..." Easton stepped off onto the long concrete platform and had a look around. A handful of commuters trudged towards the antique-looking metal stairwell that had been recently renovated and painted a forest green. Overhead, the clouds scudded in a cerulean sky. Upstairs on the overpass where a 120-year-old station spanned the four tracks, a Lincoln Town Car was waiting.

Easton didn't get to see too much of the town proper. The driver, a grim-looking South American type with acne scars who looked like he hadn't smiled in decades, wasn't exactly forthcoming with helpful tourist hints. The road veered up a steep incline and became Main Street, a curving tree-lined affair with a series of restored mid-Victorian row buildings that featured cafes, bakeries, a few clothing stores, and a True Value hardware store. There was an old-fashioned theater (The Alhambra) that looked pretty active with performing arts, the requisite "Coffee House," a Greek restaurant, an abandoned barber shop featuring cobwebbed windows, three antique shops, and two bars. They came to a wide intersection labeled Route 9B and went left. Heading north, they crossed a short bridge that spanned scenic waterfalls (the Lower Falls of town terminology) where a picturesque-looking old stone mill, complete with waterwheel, was sited along the cascading water. The street led past a few more desultory businesses, including a run-down auto parts store, a furniture store that looked as though it had given up stocking new inventory twenty years ago, and a deli. Then some Victorian houses, some restored, some looking like they were wishing to be restored, one or two looking like they were on life support, and then the car was winding up out of town heading north.

After a brief stretch of empty road, Easton began to notice discreet entrances set in the woods on either side that hinted at large estates hidden from the road. A few miles out of town, the driver pulled into a large wrought-iron gate with eight-foot stone pillars on either side supporting a stone arch. The effect was positively feudal. Two fierce-looking iron dragons in asymmetrical poses watched from the top of either pillar, looking ready to leap down and tear to pieces any trespassers. They looked surprisingly realistic. And very old.

"Taron Hall" was carved in relief letters on a marble plaque set on each pillar. A graphic designer might have noted that the letter font looked distinctly Art Nouveau, like Benguiat perhaps. The pillar on the left had a modern intercom box mounted on it but a hidden security camera must have identified them – the driver simply rolled down his tinted window and after a moment the gates released and swung open with a heavy click.

Beyond, the leaf-strewn drive went diagonally up through a sparsely wooded slope and over a steep rise, suggesting a road that led to nowhere in particular. The effect was mysterious, secretive. For a fanciful moment Easton wondered if there was even a house up there at all, or if maybe they would top the hill only to find a decaying ruin of a madman's dream. The crumbling remains of a stone wall that ran along the slope like a remnant from a lost civilization only enhanced the idea.

The car continued up at its discreet pace, the tires muffled by the carpet of leaves that stretched in all directions.

They passed a squat-looking caretaker's house to the left that was half hidden in the trees as the gravel drive curved right, then left. The grounds were heavily wooded and much of the natural details were left in place to provide privacy from the main road. As they emerged from the last bend to the estate proper, Easton also understood it was intended to heighten the drama of the estate, particularly for those seeing it for the first time. The dark wooded trail crossed a short stone bridge that spanned a brook and then the trees fell away revealing a huge spired mansion built of dark granite.

Taron Hall.

As the driver eased up towards the stone arched porte-cochere, Easton got a quick look at the place. It certainly rivaled anything he had seen similarly in Europe. Christ, it did look like it was right out a Hammer Film. He wouldn't have been surprised at all to find Christopher Lee and Peter Cushing waiting to greet him at the front door. The hall was three stories of Gothic-looking gables, chimneys, arches, eaves, and peaked windows. The front of the house was dominated by a square turret while on the back side he could just make out a taller circular tower with a tall spire that would no doubt offer a magnificent view of the Hudson. The architecture was not quite like anything he had seen before. Hidden galleries, small balconies amongst angled brow windows, soaring peaks, and an abundance of leering faces and gargoyles (and a few fantastic creatures not immediately recognizable) suggested an architect who had read a few too many Brothers Grimm stories.

The ones with unhappy endings.

The whole mansion gave off an air of brooding menace, suggesting a decaying lineage of not-quite-sane generations falling into eccentricity, or worse. What better way to spend your first Halloween in America?

The car fell under the shadow of the porte-cochere, a square affair of pointed stone arches and a glass roof, where Easton noted a few other cars parked, including a dark gray Maserati. Next to it, Jeffrey Wang was having an animated discussion with the valet, who kept glancing at the car with a wild eye that said "give me the keys and fifteen minutes". Easton's driver had enough courtesy to step out and open his door for him before popping the trunk and unceremoniously dropping Easton's small suitcase off to the side with a decisive thump and then wordlessly driving off. It was ten minutes to eight. Christopher Lee and Peter Cushing were nowhere in sight.

Wang had finally turned over the keys and walked up to Easton, fists on hips in what was apparently one of his stock poses. A general subconsciously sizing everything up. His other favorite was 'arms crossed with fore finger tapping.'

"Welcome to Castle Frankenstein," he said with a nod over his shoulder. "You're almost in time for the festivities to commence. That kid is going to be off for a joy ride as soon as I'm out of sight. Didn't tell him I have a GPS tracker hidden in the car that comes up on my BlackBerry? I'll know it even if he's just tooling up and down the driveway. Should make for an interesting conversation when I leave tomorrow. So...enjoy the ride up?"

"Brilliant."

Wang nodded. "It is magnificent. Few New Yorkers have any clue what an amazing natural world is sitting right outside their doorstep. And people in Brooklyn tend to think anything north of the George Washington Bridge is a foreign country."

Easton smiled. "Well, it's my observation that people who stay in any place too long tend to think of anywhere else as a foreign country. Whether they're from Brooklyn, Beijing, or a back-ass alley in Brisbane." Wang laughed. He had an easy going charisma that was more apparent when he was apart from the other club members. Easton could easily see how he'd have all sorts of women chasing him down. A dash of boyish innocence, a smile that was quick and lit up his whole face, sharp looking and rich. He was the type a girl would kill to bring home to her parents.

"Well, we'd better get inside before Lowe, the starched attorney, sports a wrinkle in his suit and drops dead of shame. I think he's eager to read us the rules and regulations so we can get this party rolling and wake up tomorrow richer men."

"After you."

Massive oak double doors that looked like they could stop a battering ram (or at least give it a run for its money) opened on oiled hinges into the cavernous gloom of an atrium lined with medieval-looking wood paneling that lead into the main hall with plenty more oak paneling, a gallery of oversized oil paintings in the manner of old Dutch Masters of seascapes, hunting scenes and a bunch of presumably dead relatives that Easton conservatively guessed would cost him a few years' salary, and cleverly inlaid marble floor of intricate patterns that suggested the Far East. At the opposite end of the entrance, a broad staircase swept up to a landing that split and curved symmetrically up either side to a second-floor gallery. The newel posts at the bottom were of intricately carved wood that transitioned into iron dragons clutching yellow glass globes on their heads. Above the staircase landing, the ceiling cut away into a large skylight three floors up, filtering sunlight down in rays that danced with dust motes. Anyone standing there would have looked like they had been personally sanctioned by God. Easton wondered how often Van Eyckmann had taken advantage of it.

To the left, a door opened into a broad parlor that spoke of an immensely wealthy merchant who occasionally indulged in sportsman-like activities. Or liked to convey to others the idea that he did. A broad circular table of polished teak was in the center. Beyond this was a huge floor-to-ceiling stone fireplace that a small family could probably move into, in front of which lay a bona fide tiger-skin rug, complete with stuffed head, glass eyes, snarling teeth, and all. A pair of elephant tusks intricately carved with Indian motifs soared up on either side of the broad mantel, framing a life-size portrait of a long-faced young man – a relative of Van Eyckmann presumably – dressed in 17th century costume, right hand resting triumphantly on the pommel of an ornate sword resting point-down on the ground, left foot resting on a vanquished native-looking man who didn't look overly happy at being dead. It was one of those portraits with the creepy life-like eyes that followed you around the room, letting the spirit world know whatever you were doing in the room. It probably added up to no good.

To the left, three floor-to-ceiling windows with heavy curtains looked out over the front lawn and an ancient looking old English oak with twisted limbs that looked like it was succumbing to dementia. Set along the windows were several damask-covered couches and chairs which, with their ornate detailing, Easton thought of as 'Gaudy Victorian'. To the right was a broad desk, some ornate bookcases filled with sets of old books that looked like they had never been read, and an arched entrance into a larger room beyond that hosted a grand piano and a harp. The rest of the room was a curio collection of memorabilia of less fortunate peoples from distant lands. Interspersed with display cases of eastern artifacts were stuffed birds and small animals, a gilded bird cage, and old Victrola with an oversized hand-painted speaker or "Morning Glory." There were a few high-back leather chairs near the hearth that looked as though you should be required to smoke a pipe, or at least a cigar, to sit in them. In one corner was a life-size statue of a traditional Samurai warrior with its curious array of armor slats, an iron-masked helmet with a large metal "V" at its front, intricate shin guards, and metal boots chased with black bear fur.

The center table was set with an assortment of coffee, tea, orange juice, and pastries. The silver service glowed in the morning light slanting through the front windows. The other members of the Executive Council were all there, along with the imperturbable Mr. Lowe, who stood by the fireplace like an expensive prop, hands clasped behind his back, waiting patiently for the members to sort themselves out. A heavy mantle clock that looked like a refugee from a Bavarian castle indicated it was almost 8:00.

Lowe came to life with an inclination of his head towards Easton. "Mr. Matthews, pleased you could join us. Would you like any coffee...tea, perhaps?" A pointed glance at his wristwatch indicated Easton would have to step to it if so interested.

Easton, leaving his suitcase by the entrance to the room, sauntered in and acknowledged the other members with a short smile. "No, thanks. Enjoyed my breakfast on the train ride up." He dropped his overcoat on one of the chairs. Most of the group had dressed conservatively: Hilderman and Washington were probably born in suit and ties, Joe Lefferts was in chinos and a bright yellow sweater, Derek Anderson was in Yacht-Club-Bar casual with crew-neck sweater, blue blazer, and Docksiders. Jeffrey Wang looked like he had raided Ralph Lauren's closet for his autumn wools: all muted browns, beiges, greens, and plaids (had he the requisite chiseled rectangular features, he could have stepped right out of one of Lauren's ads – the ones where all the models, both male and female, look eerily like Ralph himself). Apparently not shy on making a statement, Delgado had apparently taken his cue from a gay French boatman's catalog with his broad horizontal-striped shirt, knotted red scarf at his neck, and pants that looked like he had airbrushed them on. Easton had a hunch this last bit of fashion bravado wouldn't have flown if Van Eyckmann was still alive, but apparently Lowe had no regulations in his Executor manual regarding this.

After a quick round of handshakes, the men organized themselves into a rough semi-circle around the attorney. Coffee cups and saucers were set down. Everyone stood at attention.

"Gentlemen, on behalf of your late colleague, Mr. Van Eyckmann, I would like to welcome you to Taron Hall." He picked up a small stack of envelopes from a side table and handed them individually to each member. Like the invitations from the other night, each had their names embossed on them. For a dead guy, Van Eyckmann was turning out to be quite the event planner, Easton thought. Not quite right. Lowe's firm must be carrying out preplanned instructions. But to such lengths?

"In each envelope you will find an itinerary for the next twenty-four hours. Also you will find a list of rules and guidelines for your stay. I'm obligated to add that these are to be adhered to, to the letter, or you will be in violation of Mr. Van Eyckmann's wishes and thus forfeit your respective inheritances. I do hope that is explicitly clear...yes?" A round of nods traveled the room. "Also, I'm afraid I'll have to ask you to surrender your cell phones and or PDAs. They will of course be returned to you tomorrow morning."

Eyebrows went up. Delgado actually looked stricken. Uneasy looks went back and forth. No cell phones? BlackBerrys? It was Geoffrey Washington who spoke up first this time. He had a deep rich baritone that made you want to sit down, relax, and agree with anything he was about to say.

"Mr. Lowe, surely this isn't completely necessary? All of us are businessmen. With important matters to stay on top of," said the Voice of Reason. "Should there be any sort of emergency....?"

The lawyer made a "hey, not my idea" gesture with both his hands. "I'm terribly sorry, Mr. Washington. Mr. Van Eyckmann has always had a very strict policy about cell phones and personal digital assistants here at Taron Hall. Not for any particular reason that I know of. He just hated the damn things. For what it's worth, I do think they are a nuisance. I would have thought that it would be enough to simply ask guests to turn them off, but I don't make the rules or terms. I'm simply here to ensure my client's wishes are carried out."

Hilderman stepped in. "It's true. I've only had the privilege of dining here twice. Lars was adamant. He wasn't convinced I carried only one phone. I thought he was going to have the butler strip search me."

"Speaking of which...." Lowe gestured towards the hallway entrance.

As if summoned up like a conjuror's trick, a tall dark-skinned man in the full livery of a house servant – looking like he had stepped straight out of central casting for the colonial Victorian era – materialized in the entrance from the main hall. To make things even more exotic, he wore a turban with a feather in the forefront and a pair of very old-fashioned silk slippers with curled toes, which explained why no one had heard his approach. He was tall, well over six feet, with a bushy blue-black beard that curled forward at the chin, and glittering, angry-looking eyes. He looked like some sort of half deranged djinn that if crossed, would have smoke puffing out his ears and nose in short order. Easton made a mental note of both the man's demeanor and the size of his biceps. He decided he was looking at a very dangerous man.

"Gentlemen, I would like to introduce you to Kimmi, chief caretaker of Taron Hall. He will be your first order of contact should you require anything or have any questions while you are here."

Kimmi gave a bow and threw everyone a grin that stopped well short of his eyes. Held at chest height in his gloved hands was a broad silver platter, apparently for the collection of the offending electronic devices. Easton couldn't recall the last time he had seen gloved hands. Some official event for the Governor back in the Bahamas maybe. Or maybe watching the Queen on BBC 1? He also noted that something was wrong with several of the fingers. Deformed? Or perhaps broken at some point and reset badly.

The caretaker glided into the room and waited patiently as hands went through the well-oiled rituals of pulling out cell phones and BlackBerrys, depressing the off buttons and putting them back into their cases before handing them over. Easton wasn't much bothered. It was the first thing he was in agreement with Lowe on: he thought the damn things were a nuisance. But he also didn't like the idea of not having a personal direct line to the outside world. Then again, who was he going to call if he needed help? His Captain in Grand Turk? Easton decided that whatever was going to happen in the next twenty-four hours, he was going to have to rely strictly on his own wits, which was just fine with him.

He also suspected this was going to be an interesting night. Probably not the good kind of interesting either.

5. MIND YOUR STEP, MR. MATTHEWS...

Easton stood on the stone-flagged terrace at the back of the mansion, admiring the view of the Hudson River spread out below. Two sets of broad steps on either side curved down through landscaped gardens to a lower terrace with a large fountain in its center. The effect stirred a deep chord somewhere within Easton, like a vague childhood recollection just out of reach. For some reason, it made him think of a temple of sorts. A place he had visited? Seen a photo of? The answer eluded him.

The estate was certainly sited well, the rear lawn atop a bluff that overlooked a winding inlet that became Murderer's Creek a hundred feet below. With the exception of two tall Norwegian maples, the trees had been kept thinned on the west side to offer an unobstructed view of the river. To the north, it snaked up past the rolling slopes and reddish brown cliffs of Rockland County and eventually to Albany. It had turned out to be a pristine autumn day on which the skies were a bright China blue and the sun promised to stay up there forever. A heavy barge plowed its way up the river in front of a blue and yellow tugboat. Behind him loomed Taron Hall like some sort of lurking relic from another era casting its oppressive shadow into the future.

It had been quite an adventurous day so far.

Easton subconsciously patted through his jacket pockets and wished for the tenth time that day that he had a pack of cigarettes, even though he had quit years ago. It was uncanny how such a ridiculous habit could still have its ghost of a grip after so many years. Drinking, drinking made sense. You put a liquid in a container, you transfer the liquid into your mouth, almost immediately (for most people) your nerves calm down, you relax, the world starts to look a little better. No big deal until it starts to get the better of you. Easton recalled a certain rant by the American comedian

George Carlin: "Hey, people need to take the edge off. Earth is a stressful place." Cigarettes, on the other hand, are a complete kick in the mouth to common sense. You take a bunch of dried leaves, roll it in paper, set it on fire, and suck it into your lungs. Over and over and over again. Then you're wired up and stressed, your lungs are blackened and you reek of something dried and burnt. A process that, once repeated enough times, somehow enables users to convince themselves that they are enjoying the moment. Easton personally thought the whole physical addiction business was utter bullshit. A loophole that smokers clung to to rationalize their dance with insanity. Anybody can stop for the three or four days it takes to flush out your system. Quitting was easy. Staying quit was a whole different story. The real crux of the problem, he had decided from personal experience, was throwing that on/off switch in the brain that enabled/disabled the whole lunacy of the habit. And being able to step away from that switch whenever those trembling fingers crept towards it, which they would inevitably do time and time again. Rough day. Good day. Bad news. Good news. Boss chewed my ass off today. Boss gave me a raise. That driver really pissed me off. What a fun ride! And the classics like: just had sex. Gotta have one with my morning coffee. The list of rationales was as long as the history of mankind. Name any experience in the panorama of human drama and you could find a reason to smoke for it.

And yet, in spite of knowing all that, he still longed to whip out a pack, stick that damn coffin nail in his mouth, light it right up, and blow a big cloud of smoke in the Devil's eye.

Scratch that. He remembered a scene from an old Warner Brothers cartoon where Sylvester the Cat, wracked with guilt from finally murdering (so he thinks) Tweety Bird, stays up all night drinking and tormenting himself with guilt, finally just takes an entire pack of cigarettes, rips off the end and pops the whole thing in his mouth, lighting up all twenty at once.

That was looking like an excellent idea at the moment.

Fortunately the point was moot. In bogus Latin-speak: no cigarettum, ergo, no smokus.

That was how you quit.

Despite the sun, there was an autumn chill in the air. Easton had on a double-knit turtleneck and a wool blazer with dark gray slacks that felt fairly warm and comfortable. As he stood near the stone rail, he let his eyes wander around the grounds again. After the kick-off meeting in the study that morning, the group had broken up and been shown to their respective rooms to settle in and unpack. Easton's was off the second floor hall to the back of the house and offered a small covered porch with views of the Hudson. It was large enough to accommodate two wicker chairs and a table with a heavy glass ashtray on it. If the sunset was as good as the weather promised, he was going to have a postcard seat to enjoy it.

His room was impressive in a heavy-handed Victorian sort of way. The heavy ornate furniture, heavy brocaded curtains, and heavy mahogany paneling that ran floor to ceiling seemed to press the very oxygen out of the air and with it any inclination to do things one might normally do in a bedroom, such as have sex or even just sleep. It appeared that the last time an interior decorator passed through, the light bulb had just been invented. After years of living in the openness of the Caribbean, the air of the bedroom was positively.

The upper wall panels were intricately hand carved with a leaf and acorn motif that adorned the cove panels around the room. Atop the shelf formed by those were an odd collection of beer steins and Dutch wooden shoes. One wall sported the mounted head of a twelve-point buck above a couple of ancient-looking flintlock rifles and above the bed itself was a panoramic oil of Henry Hudson's Half Moon somewhere up near Storm King on the river that would eventually bear his name.

The bed was a large, ornately carved affair that looked like it might be better suited to having a Tudor knight sleep in it. At least the mattress was reasonably comfortable and the linen was fresh and top quality. Across from it was a predictably heavy fireplace with tiles depicting what might be a Hudson Valley hunting scene, similar to the one in the Mohican Club. This one, however, included some Indians in the woods in the background. They were either running after game or running for their lives, Easton couldn't quite tell which. The room included a seating area, a short table near a huge armoire that Easton could have slept in, and an adjoining bathroom done in old marble, white plaster, brass, and dark oak wainscoting. The sink had rust and greenish stains streaked in it, presumably from the taps. The tub was an old claw-foot affair with a jury-rigged curtain and shower head and spigot apparatus of such complexity it looked like something out of a cappuccino-maker's laboratory. The tub was deep enough to compete with its European counterparts. (Easton had never understood why American baths were so shallow, hardly deep enough to cover one's toes.) But this was definitely a tub with the serious bather in mind. All the fixtures seemed imbued with extra weight and patina. Even the faucets, with their rounded prong spigots and white porcelain caps, seemed more there. More solid.

Easton spread out his shaving kit and toiletries, then, heading back into the main room and picking up the envelope with his name on it, sat down near the windows and read. Enclosed were three sheets of foolscap, two with typewritten instructions. The first was a welcome note from Lowe detailing the rules of the house – most of which the attorney had already covered in person – followed by an itinerary that read as follows:

Schedule for 31/10/2010:

8:00AM: Check-in and announcement by William Lowe, Executor. Light fare included.
8:30AM – 12:30PM: Free Time for Executive Council Members*.
12:30 – 1:30 PM: Lunch for guests.
1:30 PM – 6:00PM: Free Time for guests
6:00 PM – 8:00 PM: Dinner. A full course meal will be served.
  8:30 – 10:30 PM: Halloween reading of the Van Eyckmann history in the library (Brown Room). To be followed by a séance in the library
  10:30 PM: ?

Schedule for 01/11/2010:

  8:00AM: Meeting in the Blue Room, concluding remarks by Mr. Lowe. Full breakfast will be provided.
  9:00AM: Services at the Funeral Plot by the Reverend George Franklin Callahan.

*Strict adherence of house rules are to be observed at ALL times

The second was a detailed breakdown of the general rules of the house as well as Van Eyckmann's specific requirements for their stay. The third page was a basic plan of Taron Hall's first and second floors identifying key rooms as well as a map of the estate grounds. Easton was very interested in the rules but first went back to the itinerary.

Séance? Good God! What kind of lunacy was he now involved with?

Easton shook his head and let out a chuckle. This was going to be even more interesting than he originally thought. He looked through the specific requirements. Aside from what Lowe had already brought to their attention, there were a few others worth noting: guests were allowed to travel anywhere on the estate grounds but were strictly forbidden to go past the perimeter fence that surrounded the estate. RSG, the security company maintaining the grounds, had hidden cameras all around the perimeter and would know immediately if anyone tried to leave the estate. There was a list of staff and their respective roles at the estate including Mr. Kimmi, which was minimal: a cook, four maids, a valet, a groundskeeper, a driver and the security team which consisted of three men. Plus a local catering company from Briarcliff Manor, Francine's, that had been brought in to handle meals for this event. They had four staff listed. Easton decided he would have a chat with the security team first just to get a sense of why Van Eyckmann would go to such extravagant lengths to protect his privacy. He would have to be careful though. Often these security personnel were moonlighting policemen or retired policemen themselves and had an uncanny way of smelling out one of their own.

Then there was the last item that Easton found particularly weird: "Full costume attire will be required for dinner and after-dinner activities. Your costume has been tailor-made and can be found in the wardrobe in each of your respective rooms."

Then: "The name of the character you will be attending tonight's events as is Lieutenant Rogier Osterman."   .

Easton had reread the last line three times, not quite believing his eyes. What the blue fuck!?

He couldn't wait to see the costume.

Afterwards, he had decided on a stroll around the estate grounds, partly out of habit – anywhere he went, he always staked out the surroundings to better understand the geography, potential problem areas, and potential escape routes – but also out of plain curiosity. He had only a vague understanding of the geography and history of the Hudson Valley except for what scraps he might have picked up as a young student in history classes covering what his countrymen called "The War of Independence." Or ridiculous Hollywood melodramas like The Last of the Mohicans where Daniel Day Lewis ran around with his hair strategically windblown, looking like his deerskin suit had just been dry-cleaned. He was also intrigued by what he had seen of the village on the way up and, in the back of his mind, was considering staying over an extra day after he'd fulfilled his obligations for Van Eyckmann and his club of loony millionaires and do a little exploring.

After a quick wash, he headed out the front entrance and down the main drive. The morning was cool and inviting for a stroll. Here and there came a rustle from the underbrush as large gray squirrels (and the occasional black one – apparently Taron Hall was an integrated neighborhood) poked around for acorns or walnuts or whatever it is squirrels poke around for in the fall. Occasionally a dispute would break out and a couple of them would chase each other up a tree in a staccato of angry chitters. The drive was skirted by what looked like very old growth trees; Norwegian maples, plane trees, English and red oaks that soared up sixty to eighty feet. Filling in here and there were groups of river birch, spruce, hickory. Though just past their peak, the trees were still a riot of scarlet, orange yellows and browns. The grounds had a subtly disorganized pastoral feel that looked wilder the further from the house one ventured. Once over the bridge, the road was the only indication of man's intervention. On one of the many rock outcroppings on either side, Easton could easily have imagined a bronze-skinned native perched there with a Mohawk and a couple of eagle feathers poking up out his headband, bow slung over his shoulder, and hatchet in hand. With doeskin leggings not quite fresh out of the prop trailer.

The caretaker's house was near the top of the drive, looking squat and blocky. It was two stories of grey stone, heavily-framed windows, and deep pitched roofs of slate. It also sported its share of gargoyles and other mythic creatures. It had a small driveway and parking area tucked around the west side, where four cars were parked including the Town Car Easton had arrived in. One of the cars was a Lexus, the other two were Acura's. Apparently, working security for Van Eyckmann was a lucrative gig.

Easton walked around the house twice before the front door opened and a heavy-set-looking man with a shaved head stepped out onto the front porch. He looked like the actor Russell Crowe, plus ten years plus forty pounds and minus the hair. He also looked, despite a wrestler's physique sliding into middle-aged paunch, like he was quite willing and capable of removing your head or any or all of your arms and legs on a moment's notice. He stood with his hands clasped behind his back, steel gray eyes measuring up Easton. He wore black slacks, polished black boots and one of those dark wool sweaters favored by Special Ops with the padded shoulders and elbows. A shield-shaped patch on his left arm said "Rowe Security Group". A shortwave walkie-talkie was holstered at one hip, a nine-millimeter Glock holstered at the other. He gave Easton a smile that was neither friendly nor unfriendly.

"Morning," he finally said.

Australian accent.

Easton paused near the front of the porch. "Morning," he said back. Then he looked up at the canopy overhead. The autumn sky peeked through here and there. A minute or two passed in silence. Just a couple of men contemplating the weather. A flock of geese honked in the distance. From closer by came the piercing cry of a predator bird. Once. Then twice. It was followed by a chorus of agitated squawks Easton immediately recognized as crows. He cocked his head.

"Hawk?"

"Bald eagle."

"Really?"

"Really."

"Interesting. Can't say I've ever heard one before. Directly at least. Are they as impressive as they sound?" Mentally, he kicked himself. Would Matthews have seen one up close? In New York City? Hard to say. Probably not. Easton just didn't know enough about the New England area. Or much of anything about America when it came down to it, aside from a few trips to Miami and connecting flights at JFK or Newark. Even so, he'd have to watch himself more carefully.

"Definitely." Another minute ticked by. Then: "More so actually. You see one up close, you'll understand quick-like why the Yanks decided on them as a national symbol and stamp them on just about anything. Bloody fierce-looking things. And big. Would be a might careful about letting the little ones play about when there's a Baldy in the neighborhood. Crows can't stand them. Only bird stupid enough to antagonize an eagle."

Easton chuckled. "Duly noted. I'm Grant Matthews, by the way."

The man nodded. "I know. We're always fully briefed on any visitors staying here at the Hall. Paul Knightbridge. I'm chief of security here at Taron Hall. For the immediate future anyhow."

Easton looked over at the gate with its cameras and call box. "Security really that much of a problem around here? Looks like a serious operation you have here."

"It's always a problem when you're talking money like Van Eyckmann's. You might be surprised how many attempted break-ins we've had this past year. Then again, you're a card carrying member of his elite club, so you must."

Easton winced inwardly. "Well...Lars wasn't exactly open about discussing his own private affairs, let alone what fun and games were going on at his private shack up here in the...– " (He searched for an appropriate word – "booties" was all he could come up with.) "He was a secretive man. And to the best of my knowledge, in a whole other financial circle from our little club."

"Yeah, well he's in a whole other circle now, financial or otherwise." Knightbridge turned to go back in the house but paused and looked back over his shoulder: "A pleasure chatting with you, Mr. Matthews. If you should need anything I'm easy enough to find. Or pick up any phone in the house and dial zero. Direct line to our switchboard here."

"Much obliged. I was thinking of taking a stroll around the grounds. Might be my only opportunity."

"Mind your step, then. The poison ivy around here is vicious." He paused again, this time with his hand on the door and, as if speaking to himself, "And, seriously, mind your step. This area can be a...an unhealthy place."

"Oh...and Mr. Matthews?"

"Yes?"

"Let me know if you see our gardener. Can't seem to find him and the lawn's a wreck."

"Sorry?"

Knightbridge chuckled. "Oh, bit of a running joke with the staff around here. The gardener has been missing for decades. Good day, then."

Easton continued on, keeping to the south end of the property. There appeared to be an old iron fence, a good seven-feet high, marking the property line, but it was mostly lost in a thick tangle of vines, creepers, and no doubt copious amounts of poison ivy. A branch off the main drive led up to a large Gothic-looking barn which was where Easton guessed the cars would be kept. With its four sets of wide double doors, it had clearly originally been designed as a horse stable. One of the bays was open and Easton could make out Wang's Maserati parked inside, its engine quietly ticking over in the autumn air. The valet was polishing the hood with a chamois cloth.

Easton poked his head in the doorway.

"Morning."

The valet jerked his head up. "Hey, how's it hanging?"

"I believe I'm 'hanging' just fine." The valet looked like he'd just graduated from high school. Easton nodded at the car. "Been out for a spin?"

"Just around the drive." His eyes narrowed. "You're not going to rat me out to Mr. Wang now, are you?"

Easton shook his head. "No, mum's the word. But I wouldn't recommend going for a joy ride around town with your friends. I think Mr. Wang is a pretty sharp-eyed customer. Especially when it comes to his car. Just a word to the wise."

The valet had a look on his face that said that was exactly what he was thinking of doing. Easton glanced around the shadowy interior of the barn. It appeared to be jammed with an assortment of vehicles, many antique-looking. Further back were piles of junk – old furniture and stuff. Easton thought he could make out what looked like an old horse-drawn carriage towards the back. Christ, the place was a pack rat museum.

"Interesting place you have here. Mind if I have a look around?"

"Knock yourself out. It's just a bunch of old junk anyhow. The old man, he never threw out anything. And I mean anything." He cocked his head sideways, as if he'd just solved a complex mathematical equation. "Say, your English, aren't you?"

"Bingo."

"I can tell. I'm good at accents. My sister Amy, she can't tell a Scotsman from an Aussie. But I watch a lot of British shows...Doctor Who, Pinky and the Brain and all that." Without missing a beat, he jumped into what he must have thought was his best Pinky imitation "Oy say Brain, if we give peas a chance, won't the Lima beans get jealous!? Wot!"

Easton winced. "Um, well done. But I think that's an American cartoon you're referring to."

"Really? Ahh, who cares. Want to hear my James Bond?"

"Actually, no."

The valet looked up, surprised. Easton caught his eye. He wasn't much for chit-chat today, particularly with an eighteen-year-old who considered himself an expert on the English language from watching too much bad television. "You have a name?"

"Tommy."

"Tommy." He echoed. When he wanted, Easton could instantly switch into what some would call "too-long-a-day-police-interrogation tone," which usually was good at getting him answers, quickly.

"Tommy Robbins." The kid was tall and gangly with longish brown hair cut in a swept Beatles haircut. Not a bad-looking kid, but he had a slightly submissive demeanor. Easton had a hunch he probably got bullied a lot in school.

When Easton didn't respond right away – just kept staring – the kid offered: "From town. I'm... from town." He began shifting on his feet from side to side. "You up here for the week? Sometimes the old man has people up here for a week. But they don't look so hot when they leave. Sometimes a little messed up. One time...ah, never mind. I said too much already...."

"Messed up how, Tommy?"

"I really shouldn't say. Mr. Kimmi....Mr. Kimmi....nope. Not saying another thing." He shuddered and went back to polishing the car like it had become the most fascinating task in the world.

Easton nodded, hands in his pockets. Another old trick. He walked into the barn and had a look around. To the left of the entrance was a small office area with a square-paned window looking into the main area. Inside, Easton could make out an old oak desk, a new water cooler, an old coat rack being used by an even older pea coat, a Vargas calendar on the wall that stopped tracking dates in 1944, a tacked-up ad from the same year that showed a bunch of Sherman tanks charging through the clouds over a sprawling factory complex with the banner "Come Visit Tank Town U.S.A.!", inferring that at one time God (or Heaven at least) officially endorsed Chrysler Tanks Made In America. On the desk were a bunch of automotive trade magazines – the kind with high-end sports cars, not the suburban muscle car mags with oiled models stretched suggestively over the hoods – which suggested that the kid, or somebody around here at least, was really into serious cars. And wonder of wonders, on the desk was an old-fashioned black rotary dial telephone. Looking at it, Easton felt a pang of nostalgia. Such a simple thing once taken for granted: a common household technology icon from his youth now looking obsolete and vaguely absurd. Easton wondered if he was looking obsolete and vaguely absurd these days. He also wondered if the damn thing still worked.

"It still works," came the kid's voice from behind him.

Easton looked back at him. Tommy was still polishing the Maserati. If he kept at it, pretty soon he'd be polishing the paint off it. Tommy managed to shrug while his hands kept going.

"Everybody asks. Mr. Van Eyckmann wasn't a big believer in

55

technology. Never even had a cell phone. Can you believe it? The phone is still hooked into the house system. Someone needs their car all they need to do is dial "3" from any phone inside the house."

"What if one needed to dial outside the house?"

"Have to dial '9', then the number. Just like a hotel."

"Just like a hotel," Easton echoed. This last tidbit he knew already from his helpful little information list but again, old policeman's habit, never let on what you know or don't. He continued past the office taking it all in. The second story above was partially floored in, the central part was open up to the second floor and a peaked four-sided turret. Shafts of late morning sunlight cut through the air in beams that danced with dust motes. A heavy chain and pulley system hung up in the rafters, probably for moving heavy objects, maybe bales of hay back in the days before automobiles.

"I'm Grant Matthews, by the way," he offered without turning around. The place was fascinating. And enormous for a garage/barn. Six stretch limousines could fit in here comfortably with plenty of room left to chase your prom date around. At the moment, the only other modern vehicles were a Cadillac Escalade, a plain old regulation-length limo, and Wang's Maserati. Further back was an old Buick – a '57 Roadmaster if Easton's guess was right – with flat tires and more wonders, an old Rolls Royce Silver Ghost from the 1910s that looked dusty but otherwise in excellent condition. Despite being a ninety or so year-old car it still had a majestic power to it with its sloping running boards, three rows of seats, long silver hood with the double RR ornament above the radiator grill. Next to it in the shadows was what looked like a circa 1950s hearse with a cracked windshield and then an early 1960s Jaguar. Then a set of horse-drawn coaches including a two-seater hansom, a baroque-looking carriage with peeling gold leaf, and a late 19th century hearse. The coaches looked neglected, a collector's curiosities now forgotten. Even the spider webs looked dusty and abandoned. Beyond the vehicles were piles of crates, trunks, and furniture.

"Quite a museum you're in charge of here."

"Well, not exactly in charge. I just take care of the guest's vehicles. And sometimes odd jobs around the place. Place is kind of spooky. Sure. But the pay is decent and, if you caught him on a good day, Mr. Van Eyckmann was always good for a tip."

Easton saw a flash of silver, then a coin flying in his direction. He caught it out of the air in front of him. It was an antique silver crown. Dutch. He looked at the date: 1620. The kid wasn't joking. Not a bad tip at all. He also had to admire the kid's reflexes. He'd stopped polishing with his one hand, reached in his pocket and flipped Easton the coin with the speed of an accomplished magician. Either that or Easton's eyes were getting old.

He tossed the coin back at Tommy, who caught it with a snap of the wrist, then with a bit of bravado started walking the coin back and forth across his knuckles. He seemed pleased at the opportunity to show someone he could do more than just park and polish cars.

Easton strolled deeper into the barn. He wasn't an expert on historical carriages but he had no reason to believe these weren't original. The question was why? What the hell was a 300-year-old carriage doing with a Rolls Royce and a 19th century hearse? Just another rich man's eccentric collection of toys? Possibly. But, just as someone once told him you could learn a lot about someone by the books on their shelves, Easton thought you could also gain insight on someone's personality from the things they collected. Even the way they collected them. What he saw here was equal parts disturbing and bizarre.

And that was just the surface.

Deeper in the gloom he began to make out even stranger things. A medical table with leather straps. Old wheelchairs. A child's tricycle with the tires rotted off. What looked like an old Victorian dollhouse. Old metal and wooden signs, wicker chairs that were disintegrating, a porcelain dentist's chair with rotting leather cushions, a pile of lady's parasols from another century. Further back even stranger things; what looked like the bow of an old sailing ship, complete with figurehead and bowsprit, one of those creepy automaton fortune teller boxes (The Amazing Rhandi! Sees All! Tells All! Only 5 cents! the faded gold type announced) one finds at carnivals or old arcades, some sort of cages from a traveling zoo perhaps, all sorts of statues and trunks and what looked like an old carousel.

He found himself particularly drawn to the old hearse. Chalk it up to morbid curiosity. It had huge old brass lanterns on top of elaborately-carved columns at each corner and oval windows with peeling gilt trim. Inside, moldering black curtains in remarkably intact condition still hung, trimmed with tiny black tassels. A crumbly spectre of death from another century. Easton did a double take. It was difficult to tell, given the angle and poor lighting, but for a moment it appeared there was something in there – what looked like a bier with a corpse stretched out on top. That was absurd, of course. The only thing that would be in there –should be in there at least – would be a coffin. But Easton couldn't resist. He stepped over to the rear of the carriage where the two curtained access doors were. He grasped the tarnished brass handles with both hands and taking a deep breath, turned them downwards. The latches let out a short squeak of protest but gave in readily enough.

The doors creaked open.

There was something in there.

Easton couldn't discern exactly what at first, but the space was certainly occupied by more than just the shadows that seemed to have amassed there. There was a shallow platform of sorts with two fixed handles, apparently a sort of system on rollers for trundling the coffin in and out of the narrow space within. As if on its own accord, Easton watched his hand reach down and tug one of the handles.

As if recently oiled, the platform accelerated out of the back – too fast – and the bier, it was a bier, slid out and in one fluid motion see-sawed on hidden hinges and slammed down at an angle. Reflexively, Easton reached down to grab it and was instantly frozen in horror.

There was indeed a corpse on the bier. Clad in the formal policeman's dress uniform he had been buried in was Constable Pearson.

The past few days hadn't been kind to him. His dark skin was gray and ravaged by tropical rot. Cheeks sunken. Viscous fluids had pooled around him and stained the bottom end of his clothes. The smell was horrendous. Old meat rotting in the tropical sun. Easton, trained as he was to react in extreme situations, found himself unable to do anything for the space of what seemed an eternity. Over Pearson's left chest was his set of ribbons and commendations. A worn and rubbed St Christopher's medal hung around his neck.

Then Constable Pearson's eyes flew open.

They were the colors of congealed egg whites, the pupils milky and indistinct. Even so they locked Easton's gaze. The jaw was moving. The fetid air of the grave wafted out. Sounding like it was coming through rusty slats, his ex-colleague managed to croak:

"J-o-o-hhhhny...." Easton was trying to scream but his lips remained clamped in place, "Red S-s-sky mo-morning Johhnnyyyy....B-bad bad. Careful o—fff the C-captain...'e's c-ccoming ffor you..." Then, still full of tricks apparently, Constable Pearson reached up with claw-like fingers and grasped Easton's head in a steely grip. They felt like metal icicles. Easton's face was forced in close.

"Ah-ah-ahm sorry about...the money...J-J-Johhnny...."

A sharp laugh came from behind Easton.

Without thinking he snapped his head around. Tommy was standing a few feet away, working the polishing cloth between his hands. "Should have warned you about that. I swear that old hearse is rigged to scare the shit out of people. Either that, or it's haunted."

Easton looked down in shock. The platform was still there, at an angle where it had levered after popping out the back of the hearse, but it was empty and coated with a film of dust. Of course it was. Constable Pearson was buried in the policeman's cemetery back in Grand Turk fifteen hundred miles away. Unless he'd followed up on a flight after Easton's.

Unlikely.

Airlines tended to frown on selling airfares to dead people, policemen or not. And Immigration? Forget it. Especially since 9/11.

Easton straightened up, unconsciously brushing off his sleeves. His nerves were still jangling and he felt a desperate need for fresh air. What in the hell?

He glanced at Tommy. "Haunted. Right."

Out front of the barn he took a couple of deep breaths, hands hooked in his belt. Another Easton trick: he let his eyes look off into space at nothing in particular and forced his mind to clear for a second.

Nothing. Think of nothing.

Disengage.

Then:

What in the fucking blue blazes was that? The whole episode now replayed in high-definition, crystal-clear colors. Was he hallucinating? Does Vicodin HP bring back the dead? He tried to recall the fine print on the warning label: Do not take with alcohol. Do not take with other prescriptions without first consulting your doctor. Do not operate heavy machinery while taking.

May result in advice from dead and decomposed constables.

Nope. Didn't recall the last one.

But he did recall what Pearson had said.

Red Sky Morning Bad-Bad.

One of many dumb sounding code phrases between Easton and his constables that had developed over the years, though no one could say where or when they'd originated. This particular one was a play off the old fisherman's saying: "Red sky at night, sailor's delight. Red sky at morning, sailor take warning". Translation: "Shit was about to hit the fan, big time – brace yourself."

But what was that about 'the Captain'? What Captain? Captain Hutchison?

Bullshit. This was all bullshit. Easton began walking west towards the river, Talon Hall towering off towards his right.

Then he realized something heavy was shifting around in the right lower pocket of his jacket and he stopped in his tracks. He reached down and pulled out a medal on a chain. A St. Christopher's medal on a chain. From somewhere nearby he heard a whippoorwill call out, a forlorn sound.

"No way," he said to himself. "No. Fucking. Way."

Yes way apparently. There no doubt it was the same St. Christopher's medal he had last seen around Pearson's neck at the funeral as he lay in his casket. It had a nick in the lower corner where one of the 9mm bullets that had killed Pearson had creased it. And he had seen that casket closed. As one of the pallbearers, he had carried it out to the cemetery and seen it lowered into the ground with his own eyes. From church to the grave. Uninterrupted.

Not possible.

Possible.
Not possible.
He looked down. It was still in his hand.
Possible then. Like it or not.

6. SNAKES IN THE GARDEN

Easton continued across the grounds which opened up as he passed the hall. Towards his left he saw what appeared to be a sprawling late-Victorian-era greenhouse. From the looks of it, very Art Nouveau influenced with its swirling ironwork, organic-shaped panes and overall organic style. The framework was painted a dark green instead of the usual white, or had been. Large swatches of it had given over to rust and some of the panes were broken, the framing bent, probably from the heavy snows of winters past. The whole thing was odd but not in a way one could specifically put one's finger on. Partly it seemed too heavy and big for a traditional greenhouse with its large central atrium framed by flying iron dragons, wings spread, that spiraled up into an intricate glass tower latticed with iron bird outlines. The suggestion was that the dragons were pursuing the flock of birds up in to the sky. The effect was a strange and whimsical work of fantasy.

Easton simply took what had just transpired in the barn, boxed it up in his mind, and set it aside for later consideration while he focused — deliberately — on this new subject.

To either side the greenhouse branched out east and west. The east branch appeared to have suffered the worst damage. Nearly a third of its roof had collapsed. The west section appeared completely intact. Easton walked up to the main doors. Weeds and tufted grass had grown on either side. The doors themselves had a pair of glass nymphs as a motif. The transom of the door featured a full-sized relief of a woman's face, stern and unforgiving, sculpted so that she appeared to be judging whoever stood before her seeking entry.

"Mind if I come in?" Easton ventured, looking up.

Nothing.

At a closer angle, he realized the face had cruelty and disdain in its lines, the lips suggesting a sneer. A Medusa's face minus the snakes.

Easton grasped one of the curved metal handles and yanked. The metal wouldn't give at first, then finally released with a screech of protest. The hinges sounded like they hadn't worked in years. The temperature was a good ten degrees warmer inside and smelled of both dried and dead plants and vegetation run amok, dirt and things old and baked. Easton wasn't much of a gardener, but he made a guess that the greenhouse hadn't been used in a good ten years, maybe even twenty.

Actually, it had been thirty-five years since the estate gardener had last entered the front doors.

Since then, the plants had run riot. Wisteria and English ivy had grown up and around the framework both inside and out. The center atrium had a series of wrought iron benches along its circular perimeter, arranged around a white marble fountain choked with stagnant water, coated with green algae, and with some sort of black slime on its surface.

Must be a damn mosquito factory in the summer, Easton thought. He was surprised it hadn't been drained.

Rising out of the center pedestal in the fountain was a full-sized bronze statue of a nude woman surrounded (and being grasped) by nymphs. Her demeanor – from her up-reaching arms, heavy lidded and open lipped expression and up-thrust hips – all suggested someone in the throes of sexual ecstasy. Something in the whole tableau, however, struck Easton as slightly off, subtly revolting. For starters, there were the surrounding nymphs, whose poses and gleeful expressions suggested they were in part responsible for the woman's state. Then there was the woman herself: middle Eastern possibly, with almost Asian features, broad mouthed, large breasts with abnormally large aureoles and nipples, the pubic area with an apparently exaggerated thatch of hair. It wasn't anything specific, but the sum of all the details that suggested something alien and monstrous. Easton couldn't fathom who could have been used as a model and concluded that the artist must have had a very strange and distorted imagination.

From the main circular atrium, glass doors (left open) gave access to the east and west wings which were filled with heavy long table racks for plants in various states of collapse. Many of the plants were dead in their containers. A few holdouts, however, had defied the odds and even thrived. The place looked like a post-apocalyptic ruin: Site #4095 – Remains of greenhouse, circa 1910.

With assorted vines and creepers climbing up into the ceiling structure and a complex system of sprinkler pipes and window controls, the lighting was distorted and murky in certain areas. To the back of the atrium was a brick and stone wall with a solid iron door in its middle. A large storage area for the gardening equipment presumably.

Easton skirted the fountain, brushing aside some of the hanging creepers that drooped from the atrium dome above. From the east wing of the greenhouse came a faint rustling. Field mice perhaps. The door looked as though it would stop a tank, despite the large patches where the dark green paint had rusted off. It had a sort of Romanesque look with its heavy rivets and thick trim. To either side were niches with marble urns filled with a scrabble of dead branches. The door had an oversized metal handle which Easton grasped in both hands and wrenched down.

No go.

He put his right foot against the frame for better leverage and yanked again.

Nothing. Then…an inch.

He pulled again, the chords on his neck standing out. Metal screamed in protest. Rust flaked off the hinges. Easton prayed he wouldn't throw his back out. An inch became two, then three, then a foot. He peered in and saw that the storage area was in fact a sort of gallery with a long and narrow swimming pool. The walls – bricks that had been plastered over but which were revealing themselves as chunks crumbled off over time – ran about fifteen feet from floor to ceiling. The roof was an arched glass arcade from which hung the remnants of a complex canvas awning system that must have been designed to diffuse the sunlight, depending on the time of day. Now the rotting canvas hung in tattered strips along with dangling ropes and pulleys, the effect not unlike the rigging and sails of an old abandoned sailing ship. The pool itself was choked with debris including, oddly, an old-fashioned wheel chair. Amidst random dead leaves and branches, Easton could also make out odd bits of furniture, netting, old seat cushions, and such. Apparently at some point someone decided the pool was better suited as a large garbage bin.

Past the end of the pool was a dais with a sculpture of a man sitting on it, and, beyond that in the gloom, Easton could make out a couple of doors that would presumably lead to the changing rooms.

Old-fashioned swimming pools always creeped Easton out for reasons bordering on the irrational. Something about the narrow walkways, the old-fashioned iron ladders, the tiny tiles that didn't fit in with his modern image of what a swimming pool should be: broad blue tiles, chrome ladders, and wide walkways that suggested cleanliness and health and chlorine and exercise. Old swimming pools somehow made him think of words like old, moldering, cramped…and drowning.

This pool was no exception. Although admittedly a lot of Easton's feelings were tied in directly to the time when he was a young student and became lost while exploring his grade school's off-limits areas – in a building that dated to the turn of the century – and became trapped in the old swimming pool room.

splashing, something (dead) had been splashing in the water
for three hours.

He worked his way along the side of the pool until he came to the
statue at the far end. He realized that his original impression was off the
mark. As he cleared the far edge of the pool, he could see that what he had
thought was a throne on a dais was actually an old Gothic chair set atop a
shallow wooden platform on which a figure was seated. The figure was clad
in heavy denim overalls and a work shirt and had gloved hands that rested
on the arms of the chair. The head, which was now a desiccated skull with
its jaw hanging open in a frozen scream, had the remnants of a wide-
brimmed straw hat on it. As Easton bent forward, a large black beetle
meandered out of one vacant eye socket, its antennae probing in the air.
The clothing was slashed and torn as if the man had been mauled by a
mountain lion.

Easton had found the missing gardener.

"Christ," Easton muttered under his breath. The condition of the
corpse suggested that it had been there for quite a while. What was left of
the skin appeared mummified, dried to a chestnut brown. It was hard to tell
at a glance but Easton wouldn't have been surprised if the corpse had been
here for quite a long time – even ten or twenty years. He would have
expected all the soft tissues to have been consumed by bacteria and smaller
insects but apparently not. Perhaps the room had acted as a sort of slow-
cooking oven.

He took a short walk around the body, taking mental notes, tallying up
dozens of questions. How had he died? Was this the act of an animal or a
human? And who had placed the body here? Covering his face in the crook
of his elbow, he pulled out a handkerchief and, wrapping his right hand in
it, reached behind the corpse and gingerly probed around until he felt the
bulge of a wallet, which he extracted.

Stepping away, he flipped it open. The leather had hardened from
years of exposure to the elements (and body fluids no doubt, if the stains
were any indication) and looked to be one of those plain and inexpensive
things one finds at a flea market. Inside were some bills – 47 dollars in all,
hardly a fortune – an old-style New York State driver's license and Social
Security card indicating that the owner was Iraklese Krodos, aged 48 at the
time it was issued, which was June 18, 1975. It was valid until 1979. Unless
Mr. Krodos was running around with an expired license, it was looking like
he had been enjoying the view here from around the time disco mania was
convincing people polyester print shirts were a great thing to wear. It gave
an address of 18 Churchill Street in Ossining. There were a few business

cards as well, local businesses mostly, an attorney in White Plains, and a dog-eared wallet photo of a dark-haired young woman and a baby. It looked like the typical mediocre studio portrait taken by photographers delusional enough to call themselves "professionals." Daughter? Wife? There was no name on the back. She looked pretty and most likely Mediterranean, with her dark eyes, dark curly hair, and since the picture was found in the wallet of a man by the name of Krodos. Their clothes and hair said "1970s" loud and clear.

Easton dropped the wallet in his coat pocket. He was in a dilemma. He had been hired, ostensibly, to investigate one man's supposed murder. Now he had discovered another possible crime. His instincts were telling him – blaring at him through a bull horn actually – to drop the whole game and go straight to the local police before the shit got any deeper. But, for one of the few times in his life, Easton wasn't fully trusting his instincts. This crime scene, if that was what it was, was years, decades old actually. Twenty-four hours wasn't likely to swing matters one way or another. Bringing in the authorities would throw his game in the toilet, deep six any possibility of Pearson's widow and family getting any of the money Hilderman had promised. And he already was going to have a few difficult questions to answer for.

Or he could keep quiet on all this until he could figure out just what in the hell was really going on. For starters: how does a body sit in a greenhouse on a billionaire's property undiscovered for three decades? Was the body here the entire time? Too many questions. Better yet, run over and dump it in Knightbridge's lap and let him deal with it. He took one step back towards the pool and paused.

Something crashed in the atrium outside.

The sharp tinkle of glass breaking.

Followed by a rustling sound.

Easton drew his Beretta and ran lightly towards the iron door on the other side of the pool, keeping on the balls of his feet to minimize the sound he was making. Creeping up to the door, right hand holding the gun up and the other cupping the grip, he glanced around the iron frame.

And froze.

Impossible.

The statue had changed.

The figure of the woman was turned around and facing him, lips drawn back in a snarl, hands now curved into claws as if to throw a spell or hex at him. The nymphs had changed as well. The expressions of ecstasy had become livid snarls. They were all staring at him.

Then he saw the snakes.

At least a dozen copperheads were writhing on the floor around the fountain. Heading toward him. They were big, too, three or four feet long, and looked like they meant business. Tongues flickering. Undulating bodies as thick as his arm. He had no idea how poisonous the snakes were but decided he wasn't up for sticking around to find out.

Easton dodged back inside the pool room. In one motion he re-holstered his pistol and grabbed the edge of the door to pull it shut.

No deal.

A wedge-shaped head bigger than his fist came around the corner. Easton jumped backwards, the hair standing up on his neck and forearms, heart racing. Ever since he had been a kid, he'd been terrified of snakes. Lizards, alligators, and other reptiles: no big deal. But something about snakes – their undulating bodies, the dry rustle of their scales, the thought of those vicious needle-like teeth – struck a deep chord of loathing and dread in him, to the point that he felt physically ill.

His Beretta held 15 hollow-point rounds, staggered, in its clip. But then, firing his pistol might raise all sorts of problems.

Then again, so would getting killed.

Before he could decide, he heard a hiss and the snake struck, snapping the air where his foot had been a moment before.

Easton was backpedaling down the pool room. He saw shadows moving along the tiles and looked up. More snakes were up on the roof.

What the hell!?

The first fingers of panic brushed his heart.

He felt something long and sinewy along the back of his neck and nearly screamed. Twisting around, his hand grabbed blindly. Dust and debris came down on top of him, along with a whole section of canvas awning. He did a half spin, losing his balance. Then he realized his right foot was dropping down into nothing and with that a flash of understanding – too late! – he was toppling into the pool.

There was enough time for split second thought – Shit!! – as he was falling. His hand snapped out reflexively. His fingers grasped and then almost immediately slid right off the rim of the pool, but the effort was enough to check his fall into the debris pile and, more importantly, enabled him to fall in feet first. Had he gone in body first, he would have most certainly been impaled on one of the narrow upturned table legs. As it was, his feet landed on the angled underside of the table and went out from under him. He landed square on his ass, then his back hit the rim. A bolt of pain shot laterally across his back.

Easton let out a heavy grunt as the wind was momentarily knocked out of him.

He lay for a moment staring up at the glass roof and the swaying remnants of the awning system.

And then at the undulating bodies of the snakes above.

Trying to get in.

His chest hitched as his lungs kick-started themselves again.

Shaking his head and flinging broken chords and large shreds of canvas away from him, he saw that he had landed (fortunately) in the shallower end of the pool. The pool itself was only 15 feet wide or so, and about 40 in length. But, with all the loose junk, it was a treacherous pit and he quickly realized that he would have to be very careful about how he worked his way out.

Then the first snake made the rim of the front end, paused, its tongue flicking the air to pick up his scent. Then it plunged into the pool.

It was quickly followed by two more.

Christ!

Easton started scrabbling backwards, managing to move a few feet before the table he was on tipped, settling to one side, and he slid deeper into the pool. Something sharp snagged his ankle. Rustling. Small objects creaking. Slithering. The damn things were coming fast.

Not possible.

He saw a thick shadow moving under his left foot.

Then panic did race through his nervous system, like a lit match on dry gunpowder, obliterating any other thought in its path. The four-alarm message blaring at every muscle fiber was "Get out! Snakes!!! GET OUT NOW!"

He scrabbled even faster, gaining the top of some old cracked leather cushions. He felt a sharp pain in his leg as his shin banged the edge of an old wooden cabinet. Then he lost his balance and slid off — to his left this time — onto a bunch of old banana crates which collapsed under his weight. He plunged a good two feet deeper into the mess. Something moving at the top of his peripheral vision. He snapped his head up.

Inches away was a broad flat-shaped head, looking impossibly huge this close. /the jaws opened. Inner mouth: glistening pale flesh. Two wicked looking fangs, translucent. He could actually see the tiny drop of venom at the tip of one.

Poisonous.

Purely on instinct and reflexes, his right hand moved on its own orders and snatched the neck of the copperhead just as it struck. Right behind the head, as luck would have it. The scales were somehow simultaneously dry and slimy. His instant shudder of revulsion was forgotten as the thing immediately coiled its body around his forearm in three powerful loops. Hissing and writhing, it attempted another strike and nearly succeeded when it slipped a couple inches forward out of his grip. His other hand shot out and grabbed the neck ahead of his right and squeezing with all his might twisted and wrenched.

The snake's neck bones snapped.

A final wisp of fetid breath reached his nostrils, then the thing went limp.

Easton flung it away from him. Another one was rustling through the debris, coming at him from below, while a third was looping its way along the top of a tangle of chairs. Easton pulled his feet up underneath him in a squat, then leapt for the rim of the pool.

He almost made it.

The crates slid apart under his feet, bleeding off most of his forward momentum. His fingertips actually touched the edging tiles before he slid face down into a pile of old burlap sacks laid over something harder below. He sensed rather than saw the next copperhead coming at him and rolled to his side just as it struck, grabbing two of the sacks as he did so. The next strike was at his face and he brought up the two sacks and caught the front end of the snake, using them like an oversized catcher's mitt. In a choking puff of dust, he snapped the mouth shut and flung the creature away after its dead brother just as the third one came up from below. Easton was running short on options. As the third copperhead struck, he defended himself with his feet put together, kicking both out at the same time and praying for the best.

A dull thud as the snake's fangs struck the inside edge of his left heel, drilling into the spot where it met the sole. If Easton ever had any doubts about spending the extra money to get genuine leather-soled shoes in his life, he wasn't having them then. The copperhead's fangs impacted so hard they stuck.

Easton jackknifed his feet in and winced as he heard a gruesome double snap.

Then the coppery body with its diamond patterns arched and coiled up in agony, the enraged hissing sounding more like a scream. Easton shuddered. There was a wet smack as its bloody mouth struck his shoe once, then twice, then he forced himself to reach down and grab it, and, before it could coil around his arm, chucked it deeper into the junk pile.

He managed to finally vault himself up and out of the pool.

Then there was a crack of glass breaking and another copperhead dropped in from the roof. It dropped down on to the opposite side, writhing. Then Easton saw four more come in through the front door. More tinkling glass and, as he looked up, a flailing copperhead landed right on him. It instantly coiled around his neck. Even as he reached up and grabbed its glistening body, the edges of his vision went a soft gray, then darkened. Again the sensation of rippling muscles under cool scales against his skin made his gorge rise in revulsion.

The last thing Easton saw just before he passed out was the oversized wedge-shaped head whipping around, jaws open. His right arm was coming up to block it, but it was moving much too slowly. Then the world went black.

7. OLD ACQUAINTANCES

David Hilderman sat in the study at the back of the house tamping cherry-scented tobacco with his thumb into one of the two Eagle Claw meerschaum pipes he owned. He was reclining in Van Eyckmann's high backed red leather chair at a broad polished teak desk, partially swiveled so he could gaze out the tall windows that looked out over the rear gardens and the Hudson River beyond and below. One leg was crossed over the other, English fashion. Hilderman was reflecting on the magnificent view while his hands went about their orderly ritual of preparing his pipe as if on their own accord.

Perpendicular to the desk was a large studded-leather couch on which Geoffrey Washington was relaxing with one of Van Eyckmann's imported Havana cigars poised in his right hand. A thick whorl of smoke was curling up into the air.

Unlike the public rooms up front, which were really stage dressing for Taron Hall's infrequent visitors, this room had been Van Eyckmann's private study and domain. Broad and spacious, it had all the trappings of a wealthy man's command center. Situated in the southwest corner of the mansion, the décor vaguely evoked the Van Eyckmann history of successful Dutch merchants and was one of the original rooms of the house when it was first built in the 1600s. Unlike the low and Spartan rooms typical of the time, this one was palatial in design, paneled in oak, with 15-foot ceilings with heavy beams. In the center of the ceiling was a framed rectangular panel with a painted mural depicting what looked like fantastical scenes from The Arabian Nights. The upper third of the walls was covered in stamped dark leather, the lower third with heavy paneling. Heavy Persian rugs covered the wide planked flooring.

To the right as you entered was a broad medieval-looking fireplace that seemed large enough to sit and eat lunch in (if you didn't mind sharing it with a few hundred years accumulation of smoke and soot). Above the heavy mantle, the flue was hidden under a massive wedge that tapered up into the ceiling. On it was the Van Eyckmann coat of arms, which consisted of red and yellow fields with blue and yellow trim, a sword in one corner and the profile of a dragon in the other. The fireplace had a large iron grate with ornate dragon andirons and a fire tool set with pokers, shovels, and bellows made of oak and red leather that looked powerful enough to fill a passenger balloon. An ancient blunderbuss rested on the mantle. To one side was a firewood locker and an old water bucket that hadn't been used in decades. Before it was a fleece throw rug and a heavy Dutch couch and chairs from the early 18th century.

To the left of the entry was a sideboard possibly ten feet long, above which hung a mural-sized map of the Near and Far East which had been commissioned around the time the house was built, with ancient trade routes indicated on it, some which would have surprised more than a few expert historians. The far left wall had broad French doors leading out to the terrace that wrapped around the back of the house. Behind the desk, the wall at the rear of the room had a few display cases including a few elaborately detailed ship models of galleons, caravels and East Indiamen ranging from the 17th to mid-18th centuries. A large tapestry depicting a battle on a forgotten Spice Island was flanked by crossed swords and halberds on either side. On either side of the fireplace was a door, one of which let onto a short hallway that led to the main dining hall, the other to a small private room that included a toilet. To either side of the doors were tall glass-fronted bookcases that were filled with books someone had read, including ledgers and journals dating back hundreds of years, atlases, books on regional history, and, discreetly to one side, an assortment of books and grimoires on arcane subjects such as necromancy, demonic possession, spell casting, voodoo, and on more mysterious practices out of deep Africa and ancient Egypt, including more than a few rare first editions including William Frazier's *Golden Bough*, Abdul Al Azrad's *Necronomicon*, Charubel's *Grimoire Sympathia*, Von Wilderstein's *Forgotten Cults*, Aleister Crowley's *Summoning on Erapus*, a folio of stories translated by Sir Richard Burton and, of course, S.L. MacGregor Mather's *Key of Solomon the King*.

Certainly interesting reading for a reclusive billionaire.

A few other objects were scattered throughout the room: a large wooden globe dating from the 17th century, some scattered statues including an authentic seven-foot tall 10th Dynasty Anubis, a life-sized Turkish eunuch, a stuffed white tiger in a stalking pose, ears flattened, and, in one corner, a 3,000-year-old sarcophagus containing a 2nd Dynasty king no one had ever heard of. (The priests of that era thought they had eradicated all remaining traces of his name.) To round it out was a set of real shrunken heads atop one bookcase, a wood carving of a one-foot-high Bantu demon sporting an impressive array of razor-sharp teeth, a display of a winged reptile (genus unidentified) with a six-foot span, assorted sailing ship bits including lanterns and carvings, and weird odds and ends collected over quite a few generations of travels.

Washington took a pull on the Cuban, taking guilty pleasure in a habit that was completely verboten in his own home. (On occasion he would sneak across the street to Prospect Park to enjoy one of his slim imports on one of the benches there, at the expense of the inevitable flat-eyed no-nooky-for-you-tonight look from his wife upon returning). Letting out a series of perfect smoke rings, he turned the cigar around to study it. These weren't exactly the general imports the guys down on Wall Street strutted around with. These were specially grown, cured and rolled on Van Eyckmann's private plantation, and sent up via diplomatic courier. During the later 1800s, the Van Eyckmann's had moved their Manhattan facilities to a more lucrative (and much cheaper) location in Brooklyn where they were still packaged to this day.

Washington was probably smoking up around a 100 dollars in his fingers.

"I have to say, David, these are most thoroughly delightful and delectable." He drew out the words as if cigar smoking was the most pleasurable pastime anyone could possibly conceive of.

Hilderman's fingers reached the end of their ritual, putting a match to the pipe bowl just as the study door opened and Juan Delgado, Jeffrey Wang, and Derek Anderson stepped in. Juan waltzed into the room, making a face and waving his hands melodramatically just as Hilderman drew on his pipe and let out a few experimental puffs. The rich smell of cherry tobacco immediately diffused throughout the room, at odds with the harsher aroma of the Cuban cigar.

"Ugh, Barbarians. It's 2010, boys, haven't you heard anything about second-hand smoke? This place stinks worse than an Italian poker game. Never mind what you're doing to the artwork in here. If I didn't know better, I'd say you're trying to kill the rest of us off and collect our shares."

Hilderman swiveled around and leaned forward on his elbows, left eyebrow raised either in amusement or annoyance. "Oh, these walls have survived a couple hundred years…and more than a couple of pipes and cigars," he said around the pipe clamped in his teeth. "Besides, you've taken in far worse things through that mouth of yours."

Delgado pulled up short, hands on hips, with a look that indicated he was about to let Hilderman have it – which would have made for an amusing scene given his flamboyant attire – but the Englishman beat him to the punch and said icily, "Now sit down. All of you. We have a few things to discuss."

Without further words, the three men quickly found chairs near the desk. Without fully registering it, they found themselves looking slightly up at Hilderman.

"Gentlemen, I expect I have no need to emphasize how important it is for us to keep our wits about us and get through the next 24 hours." He glanced at his watch and corrected himself. "22." He glanced over at Derek Anderson. "Has Mr. Lowe departed yet?"

Anderson smiled his lopsided grin. "Ayuh. Left 20 minutes ago. Said he had more paperwork to sort out and was taking the next train back to Manhattan. Should be the last of him until tomorrow morning."

"Excellent." He looked at each man in turn. "Derek. Jeff. Juan. Geoffrey. None of us can afford to make a mistake at this point. 20 Million Dollars. Last year, any of us would have chuckled at that number. This year everything has changed. Seriously changed. For all of us."

Delgado sat with his arms crossed, still fuming. Wang was leaning back in his chair, legs out and ankles crossed, fingers interlocked and thumbs touching. "What about Lefferts? Where's he with all this?"

"Good question. I'm not completely sure. He's taken some hits the past year like the rest of us. But he hasn't been up front with me about what his real situation is. And he's been over in Europe for the past several months. I'm hoping I'll have a chance for a little chat later today or tonight."

"And what about East...I mean Matthews. Our old buddy, Grant?" Wang looked around sideways, his fingers beginning to fidget.

Hilderman took another draw on his pipe. "Mr. Matthews is on board with the program. Although I understand he may be taking a vacation to Europe after tonight's festivities. A long vacation."

Wang pulled his feet up and leaned forward, shaking his head. "David, I don't know....Christ, I don't like this. Any of this. There's too many things that could go..."

He was cut off by Hilderman who suddenly put a vertical forefinger to his lips. Hilderman shot a quick nod to Derek, who, with surprising agility, bounded to the main door and threw it open.

Kimmi was standing right there. Holding a tray with a silver tea service. He gave a short bow. "Kimmi thought you might enjoy a little tea before lunch."

Hilderman had a narrow look on his face. "Been standing there long, Mr. Kimmi?"

The butler gave up one of his little smiles. His teeth looked like antique ivory. "But of course not. Mr. H. Kimmi just thought our guests would enjoy tea. I bring."

"Very thoughtful of you. You may set it down on the sideboard." Hilderman's look said he didn't find it thoughtful at all. The butler glided over to the sideboard and began meticulously preparing the tea at a speed that make it ready by dinner. Hilderman's impatience began to get the better of him. "Mr. Kimmi, if you please. We appreciate your hospitality, but we have business to discuss and would appreciate some privacy. Yes?"

Kimmi snapped a look back at the Englishman and, for a split second, there was murder in his eyes. Every man in the room caught it – Washington even recoiled in his seat, almost dropping his Cuban – then the veneer of self-control reasserted itself on his features and he gave Hilderman a slow and controlled nod.

"To hear is to obey," he said ambiguously.

He glided back out of the room and Anderson, eyebrows raised, gave the heavy oak door a shove. It swung shut with an oiled click.

An uncomfortable silence hung in the air. Then Hilderman spoke again: "I would say there's more to Mr. Kimmi than meets the eye, wouldn't you all agree?" He sat back and drew on his pipe. A cloud of rich-smelling tobacco wafted up to the ceiling. "And Jeff – all of you actually – be very careful what you say around here. Despite appearances, I think it's fair to say Taron Hall has very thin walls."

8. MAY ALL APPEARANCES BE FORGOT

Easton sat up abruptly, disoriented. He was at the rear of the pool room, sitting on the floor. He reached up with his left hand, reflexively pulling off the coil of rope and a pulley that was draped around his neck and threw it away, shuddering.

There was no sign of the snakes anywhere. Nothing on the roof. There was some broken glass and pieces of rotted ropes and canvas littered the tile floor, but that was all.

From the outer room, someone was calling his name, "Grant? You in there? Grant?"

He stood up, brushing himself off, which was when he realized the chain of Pearson's Saint Christopher's medallion was wrapped around his right hand. He didn't recall grabbing it out of his pocket, but there it was. He held it up and let the medal dangle in the rays of light coming through the glass panels.

There were two fresh scratches on the face piece.

He looked back. The mummified gardener was still sitting in the chair. That much was definitely real at least.

"In here."

There was a grating rasp as the door was wrenched open and Joe Lefferts stepped tentatively into the room. "Jesus, Mary, and Joseph. What the hell is this place?" He looked up at the ceiling and at the debris hanging from it as if it could all come crashing down at any moment. Which in fairness it could.

"Pool room. Or was." Easton brushed dust off his jacket sleeves, discreetly palming the medallion into his pocket. "You didn't happen to run into any large snakes out there by any chance?"

Lefferts gave a start. "Snakes? Heck no. They have snakes around here? LARGE snakes?"

Easton let out a smile as he stepped past him. "Don't worry. I think your tie scared them off." He glanced into the foyer. The statues were back in their original positions. Of course.

No snakes.

Easton glanced back, "Oh, I think I found Van Eyckmann's gardener. Ex-gardener. He may need watering." As he stepped out of the front doors, he heard Lefferts swearing again. That was when he noticed something awkward about his left shoe. A quick inspection revealed the sole was torn up with two jagged holes; some sort of viscous fluid that looked like it was mixed with blood was smeared around it. No sign of the fangs though.

He wiped his sole on the floor several times in disgust. Outside the greenhouse, he took a few steps, then stopped. He glanced back up at the sculpted faced glaring down at him from over the transom. With a start he realized it was a Medusa's head. Now he could clearly see there was a rat's nest of snakes writhing around it.

He flicked his fingers off his chin at her in a universal gesture. "Up yours."

The kitchen was big enough to cook for a small army but somehow managed to retain an air of coziness and country charm. Somebody, probably a woman, had at some point made a concerted effort at domesticating the space: the whole atmosphere bore no relation to anything else in the house. With its oversized sinks, heavy wooden beams, and Dutch cupboards, it looked like a set piece for a movie set in the 1700s. The center island was hewn out of heavy oak boards bearing centuries of nicks and scars and had a suspended overhead rack clustered with iron skillets and copper pans. The only "modern" touches were the farmer's-style pendant lights and the bank of three huge Vulcan ranges with overhead iron vents along the inside wall. Only one looked like it had been used in the past 20 years. Next to them was a large stone hearth with two iron doors inset on one side for baking bread – the original oven. It probably hadn't been used since the house had been rigged for gas a hundred years earlier. Along the outer wall were the sinks and two large sets of diamond-paned windows with bronze latches that over-looked the back lawn. To the left as you faced the back wall was a heavy door with heavy steel hardware that led into the cooler. To the right past the sinks was a small country table, a closet, then a side door that led out onto a covered porch.

Between the entrance and the stove was a broad counter where the caterers were setting up under the cook's baleful eye, well out of earshot of the three men. The caterers looked like college students, three women and a man who looked like an uptight gay theater type in between gigs. The head caterer was a short, middle aged man who reminded Easton of the late actor Marty Feldman. He even had eyes that looked in different directions. He had the fussy-but-discreet mannerisms one usually finds in maitre'd's at expensive restaurants. One of the girls, Easton noted, was a striking brunette with a thin figure who he caught looking at him more than once.

Easton was sitting at the table with Hilderman, a mug of hot apple cider in front of him and a bowl of peanuts which the cook, a stern looking Portuguese woman in her 50s, had mustered up for them. Leaning against the island was Knightbridge, a bottle of Palmer's Pumpkin Ale in one hand, a lit Marlboro in the other. Easton was strongly tempted to ask him for one, but managed to resist. Christ, did everyone smoke in this house?

Hilderman looked cross. Knightbridge looked concerned. He pulled on his cigarette and blew smoke up at the ceiling. "Mr. Hilderman, I need one – no better make it two or three – extremely convincing reasons I shouldn't be on the phone to the local police department right now."

Hilderman glanced back to make sure the caterers were focused on catering then reached into the breast pocket of his jacket and produced a silver money clip. Four crisp one hundred dollar bills were extracted and laid out on the table.

"How does four reasons suit you?"

Knightbridge stubbed out his cigarette in a small serving bowl and set down the beer but made no move towards the table. He crossed his arms. "It doesn't. While I appreciate your generosity, Mr. Hilderman, this is really a police matter."

"Of course it is, Mr. Knightbridge. I'm not suggesting otherwise. What I am suggesting is that you simply hold off notifying the authorities until tomorrow. Then take whatever steps you feel necessary. I'm quite sure Mr. Lowe would agree. I know the mayor and police chief personally and am quite confident they will be cooperative and understanding. Besides, I'm sure I needn't remind you, Van Eyckmann retained your services to handle things around here. So handle them." He stood up and walked to the inside door but before leaving paused. "Besides, you may need a good recommendation if your contract here is up, which I understand it is as of February."

With that he left, quietly closing the door behind him.

Knightbridge picked up the four bills from the table, walked over to the massive refrigerator next to the sink (a stainless steel restaurant-sized piece), pinned them under a magnet and, pulling a notepad from his pocket, wrote "Happy Halloween" along with a smiley face and put it in with them. Then he turned to Easton and gestured with an open hand towards the outside door.

"How about a little walk?" It didn't sound like a question.

They took a stroll out to the gardens at the back of the house. Behind Taron Hall was a broad, stone-flagged terrace bordered by a low stone wall. A short flight of steps led down into a second garden terrace that was focused around an oval marble fountain with a large bronze sculpture of Neptune and his maidens emerging from a ship wreck. Neptune appeared to be erupting from the water with his trident in one massive fist and a barnacle-encrusted conch shell pressed to his lips like a horn in the other. The fountain was filled with old water, black and oily. Looking at it now, Easton tried to recall why he'd had a sense of deja vu about it earlier but came up empty. To either side were heavy-looking arbors of dark wood snarled with wisteria and English ivy. Two ancient oak trees rose up on either side. To the north, a winding path led to a gated area with a decrepit chapel and a hulking mausoleum, along with a scattering of gravestones. Presumably this was the family cemetery where Van Eyckmann would be laid to rest in the morning.

Which led to another question in Easton's mind: where was the body now? There had been no mention of a wake or anything outside of the funeral services tomorrow morning.

From beyond the fountain, another stone wall dropped down about 15 feet. From there, the grounds pitched down into ragged stone cliffs with around a 150-foot drop into a creek – Murderer's Creek according to local maps. To the southwest, Raadsel Point, with its own low bluffs and remains of a Revolutionary War fort, jutted out into the Hudson. Further to the north, the river snaked up toward West Point and Rhinecliff.

Knightbridge stepped up to the stone wall and leaned on it with both hands. A stiff breeze off the river plucked at his jacket sleeves. With it was the spicy scent of dry leaves with a touch of maple and woodsmoke, mingled with a tinge of river water. Easton stepped up alongside, hands in pockets.

Again, he waited patiently and let Knightbridge speak.

"Nice view, yeah?"

"Impressive. I'm begging to grasp why the Yanks fought so bloody hard here."

"Scenic real estate all right. Got nothing quite like this back in Melbourne. I'll cut straight to the chase, Mr. Matthews. Or should I say, Mr. Easton?"

Easton didn't respond right away. He studied a distant point on the opposite side of the river. The game was up then. Somehow, he wasn't surprised. A small smile played across his face.

"When did you know?"

"It's my business to know. Lowe was suspicious from the start. Asked me to look into it. If I had any doubts, I didn't when we met earlier today. When I stepped out on the porch, I didn't smell engineer, but I definitely smelled cop." Knightbridge tapped the side of his nose with his forefinger, looking amused. "Good nose. Can smell a 'roo fart a mile away."

"That was it?"

"Pretty much. That and Matthews was from the East End, though I understand he covered it well. Your accent – definitely not. In spite of your name."

"Got me there. So what's your plan now? Call Lowe and deep six this whole charade?"

Knightbridge didn't respond right away. Then he gave a brief shake of his head. "No. Can't say my own record is squeaky clean. And I can't say my late employer was exactly a saint. More like Satan actually. But I am a professional and I take my job seriously. And I am paid to take care of things, as Mr. Hilderman pointed out. Mr. Lowe already suspects as I said, but men like him are good at knowing, then unknowing. As long as the money is flowing in their direction."

He tapped his nose again. "I just wanted you to know because I got a bad smell about all of this and what's going to happen in the next 24 hours. From what I dug up on you, I'm convinced you're a reliable sort. Do we understand each other?"

"Five-by-five."

"Good. What are you carrying?"

Easton told him.

"Good again. Not as sturdy as a Glock but very accurate. I don't trust Hilderman any farther than I can throw him. And Kimmi seems to be running on his own agenda. He shows up seven months ago out of nowhere after the previous caretaker vanished and suddenly takes charge of the house. No word from Van Eyckmann who this guy is, why he's here, no orders to look into what happened to his predecessor. Or him for that matter. Extremely unusual. Acts like he owns the place. This whole thing is feeling hinky. And Van Eyckmann slinking around this guy like, like, what would the Yanks say? Like he's got the goods on him. And I can tell you, I've never seen or heard of anyone getting the goods on Van Eyckmann. Wasn't aware it was even possible. Van Eyckmann wasn't just wary of this guy, I can tell you, he was terrified of him. And hated him at the same time. Fear and loathing. I asked if there was anything I needed to look into regarding our new housekeeper and Van Eyckmann shot me a look that would freeze fresh lava. "Mr. Kimmi is none of your concern Mr. Knightbridge, and I mean none. Do we understand each other?" Van Eyckmann's health began going last year. But in the past month he began acting really screwy. Like a half-wonked wombat with a nest of fire ants up its arse. Jonathan – might I call you Jonathan?"

"John."

"John it is then. Well, John, the atmosphere around here has gone from paranoid to worse. And Kimmi has gone from being his usual belligerent-manservant-self to being pretty much openly hostile. I was beginning to have serious questions about what the exact nature of their relationship is. Was. And where Hilderman fits in. I don't know what sort of deal he cut with you to play along with this whole scheme, but I can assure you of this: every one of those so-called successful businessmen are in serious fucking financial trouble."

Easton did a double take. "Really? You don't say?"

"I most certainly do say. Geoffrey Washington – Washington Harris? Teetering on bankruptcy. Between the implosion of the high-end real estate market in New York and being blackmailed by a massage parlor out of Chinatown – one that supposedly favors young ladies, very young ladies if you catch my drift – good ole Geoffrey is on the ropes. There was an incident. A little role-playing that got out of hand, a girl died. Now they're squeezing him good. Tack on two kids in private school and a wife who likes to get the home palace redecorated every year and you get the picture."

"Juan Delgado? His restaurants are running on fumes. One – the trendy Thai soup kitchen – hasn't paid its employees in weeks and just racked up a dozen health code violations. When the Brooklyn real estate market was flying wild and high, he floated one loan on another to double his holdings but now he can't dump 'em fast enough. Actually, he can't dump them at all and a brutal murder/suicide in his biggest building on Fourth Avenue a month ago cost him quite a few tenants. Not like the Wild West days before Giuliani, when tenants felt cheated if they didn't have a brutal murder/suicide in their building.

"Derek Anderson? According to Human Resources at Time Warner, he isn't even employed there any longer – he was laid off in the last round of cuts in September. Not sure his Barbie-doll wife knows. Otherwise, she might be concerned that he's been tapping into their retirement accounts and going through cases of single malt scotch like soda pop. And there were rumors about a fling with one of the interns at TWC. A couple of flings, actually.

"Jeff Wang. His sales projections are way off the charts – the wrong end of them. The new Brooklyn Britches clothing line was a complete flop in the Asian markets, the U.S. retail markets are flat, and he is about to be served papers by some humanitarian groups for illegal waste disposal and profiteering. And the IRS is auditing him. From what my sources say he owes a cool five million in undeclared taxes.

"'Big' Joe Lefferts? Probably the most stable of the bunch, but even his fences are buckling. Turns out he's been doing a little insider trading to pad out his nest egg and his kids' college fund – I heard his oldest daughter has her eye on Harvard or Princeton Law School. Apparently, the SEC received a tip and smoked out one of his moles and it's only a matter of time before the noose closes.

"And Grant Matthews – the real Grant Matthews – is – was – about to be the focus of a sting operation by the ATF for illegal gun smuggling and dealing coke. No kidding. "Loose cannon" doesn't begin to cover it. He was also named in a lawsuit arising from a crane collapse in Midtown in which several people were killed or grievously injured. He might have been pushing the construction schedule a bit hard and may have cut some corners. Sloppy. You might want to think long and hard before passing yourself off as him going forward.

Easton's jaw was tightened. He was getting the distinct sensation he had been played for a sucker. But then he knew that. The whole shtick about Pearson was very shrewd. "What about Hilderman? What's his story?"

"Hilderman? Oh, he's a piece of work that one. Steerman Roche is also in serious trouble after losing funding on the Hudson Tunnel and two major projects they had cooking in Abu Dhabi and Dubai – the jobs were shut down with only a week's notice. He was also on the SeaLand development project in Monaco that also folded, although the Prince quite graciously paid everyone's fees out of his own pocket. Real gentleman, that one, bit of a rarity in this day and age.

"So it hasn't been a banner year for Mr. Hilderman. Plus, he has a serious gambling habit. I heard he went down 20k at the baccarat tables on his last visit to the Monte Carlo Casino. He's also a man you want to keep a very close eye on, John. The Hildermans of this world will take whatever measures necessary to ensure that they come out on top and smelling like roses, and this one has a very long and lucid record of stepping on backs to get where he is, yeh?"

"Lastly, we have the esteemed William Howard Lowe. Probably the squarest of the bunch, considering. Even so, Makepeace Lowe is a law firm still living – and spending – in a different era. No real dirt on him other than being a closet homosexual – the discreet type – which would bring his wife and family to ruin if it ever got out at this point. Old money from Boston, you understand. The company has been on life support for years. As their main client, Van Eyckmann was the chief reason Lowe isn't down at the pawn shop hawking that exclusive watch right now."

"Right. You seem to have an awful lot of information at your fingertips for the local security man."

Knightbridge chuckled. "Got that right, mate. Lars Van Eyckmann had a lot more than just this rock pile up here that needed protecting. And he would go to great lengths to protect his interests. Very great lengths. I happen to be a man with a wide range of specialties, if you catch my drift."

"I believe I do. I also believe I'm not completely convinced as to why you're sharing all this with me."

Knightbridge was drumming his stubby fingers on the stone rail. They stopped. The watch on his left wrist was consulted.

"Because the situation is changing. None of these men got to where they are today being jolly chaps. These men are jackals, which is one of the reasons Van Eyckmann singled them out for his club. The problem is that they are now desperate jackals, and they will stop at nothing to save their skins. I know you're a capable mate, but watch your back, John. Also, there's more you should know about Hilderman. He's got his own agenda going. But it will have to wait. I believe they are about to serve lunch." The fingers were drumming again. "Why don't we plan on meeting this afternoon, say by the family plot over there 3 PM. Another nice open spot."

"Fine. Paul, I have another question for you. Do you ever have a problem with snakes around here? Large ones with coppery scales?"

Knightbridge gave him an odd look. "Copperheads? Not this time of year. Way too cold. Even then, only out in the woods up in the hills. Pretty rare these days around here. Why? You saw a copperhead around here?"

Easton shook his head. "Thought I did. May have been my imagination"

Still something else, some sort of subtle question mark kept prodding his instincts. More than that he wasn't sure. So he prodded back. "Aside from Hilderman what else?"

"What?" Knightbridge seemed to be distracted.

"There's something else not right here."

"Oh, there's a whole fucking truckload of not right going on here. But for starters: the gardener's body."

"What about it?"

"Just that it wasn't there two days ago. When I was inspecting the grounds. Between Friday and today, somebody put him there. And I'd really like to know who."

From the back study, one of the curtains fell back into place as a hand disappeared. Geoffrey Washington's congenial face – the fatherly and calm face that made laying out a few cool million as a down payment on a midtown condo the most solicitous and wise act one could undertake in life – had been replaced by another face – a cold granite face with predator's eyes. Dead eyes. Eyes on a hidden face that perhaps a dozen young prostitutes in special Chinatown massage parlors witnessed in the last few moments of their lives. Had his wife Nadine seen that face, she would have run screaming down the stairs and down the street and would probably still be screaming when she showed up at the local precinct for police protection.

Washington turned towards Hilderman. "They're talking. A lot." His head tilted as he took a pull on another of Van Eyckmann's cigars and blew smoke at the ceiling.

"So it seems. Mr. Easton may be turning himself into a liability."

"What about the money?"

"If Easton starts talking, there may be problems."

"Problems?" Washington echoed.

"Complications. But there may be a backup plan. Mr. Van Eyckmann didn't put all his money in investments. Hardly."

"You mean to tell me he kept it around here? At Taron Hall?"

"In a manner of speaking. Come, let's join the others for lunch."

"David, would you like me to take care of Mr. Easton?" A slight gleam was in his eyes.

"In due course. Patience, Geoffrey, patience."

9. LUNCHTIME FAVORITES

A buffet had been laid out in the main dining room in the north wing of the house. The room itself was entirely paneled, floor to ceiling, in oak and the east wall had the requisite tall windows looking over the front lawn. On the north wall was a set of double doors that led into a ballroom that had been sealed off since the 1930s. On the west wall was an elaborate oak-mantled fireplace with an alabaster hearth. To either side were medieval-looking sideboards, one with crystal decanters and glasses for an assortment of juices, hot apple cider, and tea; the other laid out with plates and silverware that would have probably cost Easton a year's salary and a variety of dishes including lobster salad, cold meats, Maryland-style crab cakes, spiced red potato salad, two soup tureens – one of New England clam chowder and the other a pumpkin/apple bisque – along with a tray of cookies and sweets.

The polished table was a heavy, narrow affair of oak, aged nearly black with years that looked long enough to land a jet airplane on. Five high-backed chairs were set on each side, with an additional one at either end. It had an embroidered runner and four candelabras that someone may have swiped off the set of The Munsters, along with bowls of apples and grapes and pine cones. Three massive chandeliers that hadn't been used in decades hung from the paneled ceiling which framed an elaborate series of four paintings. Each depicted a different season with mythical looking creatures.

Wall sconces were staggered around the room, along with paintings depicting various Hudson Valley scenes, including a beautiful rendering in oil of Washington Irving's home, Sunnyside. The heavy drapes had been drawn open and weak sunlight ventured in. The room had a heavy, oppressive feel that seemed more suited for formal black tie dinner parties than a casual lunch, although some attempt had been made to cheer it up with seasonal decorations, carved pumpkins, flying witches and goblins, and miniature skeletons and banshees with shreds of cheesecloth garments – most likely brought in by the catering company.

Easton pulled up a seat at the table with a plate piled with salad and crab cakes and a large bowl of the pumpkin/apple bisque (which he chose out of simple curiosity), along with a mug of the spiced hot apple cider. Two things had become immediately clear to him after entering the dining hall after his conversation with Knightbridge: the first was that the atmosphere had completely changed. Nothing he could directly put his finger on – he had only known these men a short while and was here under forced circumstances to begin with. It was more a subtle sense of avoidance, eyes averted, conversations vaguely uncomfortable. It was the feeling an undercover officer had when his cover was blown and he was about to get cut out or slated to be killed. The second was that, no matter what was going to happen between now and the next morning, he was going to need as much energy as he could get.

The group sorted themselves out with Hilderman, Washington, and Anderson clustering at one end of the table. Two seats further on, Wang and Delgado were engaged in a heated debate over which restaurant served the best sushi in Park Slope. Wang was adamant that it was a traditional but very "local Park Slope" restaurant on Flatbush called Geido. Delgado was fixed on Blue Ribbon Sushi on Fifth Avenue. Easton caught a bit of their exchange:

Wang: "Blue Ribbon is a joke. They crank up the house music like a night-club and no one there is even freaking Japanese for chrissakes. How the hell are you supposed to digest your food with all that music blasting? And the service is terrible! Last time we had dinner, I couldn't find the waitress with a Geiger counter. She acted like we should be oh so honored to be served by her."

Delgado: "You are so yesterday! You mean to tell me that sitting around with a bunch of granola-eating co-op flunkies with limp hair and hairy armpits is your idea of proper dining? Ughh! And the walls – all that drawing and graffiti?" Delgado was rolling his eyes. "Spare me. It looks like some hippy teenager's bedroom."

"What!? Do you even have a clue what real Japanese food is?"

"Puhl-eese, Jeffrey. I may look Hispanic, but when it comes to order and sensibility I was born Japanese. Besides, what would you know? You're Korean."

"What!?" Wang hissed in disbelief. For a moment, Easton thought he was going to launch himself at Delgado and throttle him with his bare hands. To his surprise, Delgado reached over and pinched Wang's cheek.

"Darling, lighten up! It's only a restaurant. You're so uptight! Come by my gym on Union Street next week and I'll have one of my boys loosen you up."

Wang's cheeks shot crimson. Delgado was still shaking one of them like a reprimanding aunt. A grin flashed across Wang's face and he pulled up his napkin, wiped his chin, and chuckled. "Thanks but no thanks, amigo. Homey don't play that game. You need to start hiring some hot little senoritas over there. Then I'll apply for a platinum membership...."

Easton's attention was sidetracked as Joe Lefferts slid in next to him. Lefferts had piled enough on his plate for an army.

"Mind?" He pulled up his chair without waiting for a response. Easton suspected Lefferts seldom, if ever, waited for responses.

"Not at all. Planning on running a marathon?"

Lefferts smiled. "Good idea. Have to look into it next spring. Actually, nah. I was born with the metabolism of a humming bird. Have to eat twice my body weight every day just to stay alive."

Easton could believe it. Lefferts looked like the kind of guy who could burn up calories just sitting there. He was constantly buzzing and brimming with frenetic energy. He wolfed three bites out of a massive sandwich in a matter of seconds. From what Easton could tell, he'd piled one of everything on it.

"Have to tell you Easton, er, Matthews," Lefferts said. "This whole shtick up here is one of the wackier things I've ever been privileged to be involved in. And I've had the privilege to be involved with some pretty whacked out things, believe you me."

Easton was trying to figure out how Lefferts managed to eat and hold a conversation simultaneously. He decided it must be some sort of ventriloquist's trick native New Yorkers were taught at birth.

" 'Whacky' doesn't begin to cover a fraction of it. So, how much do you really know about Van Eyckmann?"

"Lars? Not a lot, come to think of it. Met him at a New York businessmen's dinner one night at the Waldorf 15 years ago. He looked exactly the same back then. Cadaverous old man with sly eyes. Cripes, I think Van Eyckmann was born old. Came out of his mother's belly at age 65. No kidding. Anyways, we got to talking and it came out he has a club – a businessmen's club – over in Brooklyn, and he's on the lookout for, I think his exact words were "men of a certain caliber," who were not only successful but interested in shaping the future of the 'Borough of Brooklyn' which he felt was the finest of the five and deserving of guided attention. His words, not mine. Something about the Van Eyckmann's having been a prominent local family since the 1600s and having a vested interest in keeping it on the right track. Especially since the wonder years of the '60s and '70s when the Great White Flight had New Yorkers fleeing to the suburbs in droves and leaving whole neighborhoods to the drug dealers, gangs, prostitutes, and squatters. Shit, even I remember those good times. I had an aunt on Sixth Avenue in Park Slope and the life expectancy of your car on the street there was about fifteen minutes. Good times my friend, good times. Even so, I'm not sure how much I was buying what he was selling. It didn't all sound a hundred percent. So I did some checking."

"And?"

"Some things just didn't quite add up. About his family history. On the other hand, his finances did add up. Much more than you could imagine. Mostly under the radar. You won't see Van Eyckmann's name on any Forbes list, but he certainly belongs there. In fact, no one knows exactly how much he's actually worth. His family bank accounts go back hundreds of years though. And those are in the hundreds of millions. That much is legit. One thing was also true."

Easton noticed that from down at the other end of the table, Hilderman was looking at him intently. He looked straight back without blinking. "What was that?"

"Whores. You can make their eyes water but you can't make 'em blink."

Easton did a double take. "Come again!?"

Lefferts laughed. "Bad joke. I've got plenty of them. No, what I meant to say was doors. Once you mentioned Van Eyckmann's name, all sorts of doors would open for you. Opportunities would happen. In my case, people start showing up with serious amounts of money to invest. Suddenly, a house you're looking to buy is available at an incredible price. One day you get a call from your local car dealer that the Lexus you weren't sure you could afford has a special one-day discount. That sort of thing. The guy is better connected that all the Mafia families put together. The kind of money Van Eyckmann has gets things done. It gets people a little crazy as well."

Hilderman finally looked away and said something to Washington, who didn't look pleased.

"It can also get people killed," Easton said.

Lefferts chomped down the last of his sandwich. "Yep. That too."

After lunch, Easton decided to explore the mansion and get a better idea of the layout. Pulling out the building plan from his jacket pocket, he unfolded it and quickly concluded that the only two rooms on the first floor he hadn't yet seen were the library, which was immediately to the right upon entering through the front doors, and the conservatory, which was in the wing to the left at the back of the house at the end of a short hallway between the parlor and study. After considering a minute, he snapped the paper with his forefinger and headed off to the library.

Like all the first floor room entrances in Taron Hall, the library was accessed through two massive oak doors that looked like they'd been nicked from a medieval castle. Opposite the main hall from the parlor where they'd first met that morning, the library was a mirror image of the other room in dimensions, but had a bay window with cushions and pillows. However, much of the room was occupied by floor-to-ceiling bookcases, leather wing-backed chairs, and an octagonal reading table in the center. Over the table was an Art Nouveau iron chandelier with yellowed globes that suggested lotus flowers. Like the parlor, the library also had a massive fireplace opposite the door. And, like every room it seemed, the floor was oak planked with antique-looking area rugs faded with age. The room smelled of old books and old furniture.

Sitting at the octagonal reading table was Kimmi, who closed an ancient leather-bound tome with a snap as Easton walked in. He looked at Easton with what looked like an alarmed expression and hissed, "It's you!" Then quick as a snake, he managed to look somewhat irritated, despite the smile he drew up instantly on his face. The effect was odd. For a moment, it appeared to Easton that he could see another, disturbing face hidden underneath the man's skin.

Eyes glittering, Kimmi inclined his head. "I mean...good afternoon, Mr. Matthews....and welcome."

There was a momentarily awkward moment as Easton was nonplussed at finding the so-called caretaker sitting at a table in the middle of the day. For a brief moment, he pondered whether or not he could take him in a fight. He decided he probably didn't want to find out.

"Catching up on some homework?"

A deep-throated chuckle, the kind you associate with an evil henchman just before he pulls the trapdoor lever that lands you in a pit of spikes.

"In a manner of speaking, my friend." The old book with its metal clasps was laid carefully on the table with both gloved hands. "Merely passing the time before this evening's entertainment begins. I trust your accommodations are all in order and to your liking, yes?"

"In order, yes. To my liking? The jury is still out on that. I'm more of modern room kind of guy." He strolled over to the bay window overlooking the front lawn. Next to it was a large bronze sculpture of a cowboy on a bucking stallion. Easton wasn't an expert on art but he was pretty sure it was a Frederick Remington and that it was an original. His hands were stuffed in his front pants pockets as he gazed out at the front lawn. A pair of black squirrels were capering across the lawn. They did a couple of loops in their undulating gate, then shot up the trunk of the nearest oak.

He opted for the direct approach. "Where are you from, Mr. Kimmi?"

"From, my friend?"

"Yes, from. I'm trying to place your accent and choice in fashion but I have to confess, I'm at a bit of a loss." Watch it, he chided himself, you're asking questions like a cop.

Kimmi must have picked up on this as well. There was a moment of silence. Easton felt the man's eyes studying him carefully. He half turned, throwing a casual smile. "You're not from India, are you?"

A measured wait before responding. "No, my friend, I am not."

Although not the most prudent of actions, Easton couldn't resist baiting him a little bit. "Sumatra?"

Another measured wait. "No, my friend. Your interest strikes me as odd."

"Just natural curiosity. I'm always interested in where the hired help comes from."

"I am not the...'hired help' as you call it, my friend." The voice was growing oily with threat. Easton could almost smell the man's temper beginning to simmer.

"No, I suppose you are not."

Still smiling, he looked at the man with raised brows, waiting him out.

Kimmi's expression appeared frozen on his face. It was a look Easton had seen on hardened criminals just before they decide to leap and try to run that shiv into your guts in and out like a sewing machine. Instead, Kimmi inclined his head again.

"T'yandu."

"Sorry?"

"A very small island in Malaysia. That is where...I am from."

"Ah. Wouldn't have pegged you for a Malay. Thought they tended to lean towards the short side with broader features, no slight intended." Kimmi's perpetual use of "my friend" was starting to get on Easton's nerves. And there was one thing he was completely certain of: Kimmi was lying to him.

"None taken, my friend. But I said I was from an island in Malaysia. I did not say I was Malaysian."

"Fair enough. I thought, however, that Mr. Lowe introduced you as the chief caretaker here at Taron Hall, no?"

"Of sorts, of sorts. Mr. Van Eyckmann and I have been acquaintances for a long time, a very long time. We met many years ago on one of his adventures, during which we crossed paths and arrived at an...arrangement." Kimmi spread his hands in a deprecatory manner. "And the rest is, as they say....history."

Easton began to stroll around the room, taking in the bookshelves with their dusty volumes and folios. The room had a discarded feel to it, like an old stage set fallen into disuse. He paused at a framed photograph propped on one shelf that looked like it had been taken sometime around the First World War. It showed a bunch of men standing in front of an old pusher biplane – a DH2, if Easton wasn't mistaken. The location might have been somewhere in the Middle East, or even India. Two of the men were dressed as airmen – presumably the pilot and gunner – while the rest were apparently civilian businessmen. One was dressed in tall boots with flared trousers, a leather collarless jacket, and a cap. With his narrow face, sharp nose and steely eyes, he looked like the portrait of Van Eyckmann or perhaps one of his close relatives. The ages wouldn't have matched up – the man in this photo looked middle-aged or older. The other man was a dead ringer for Kimmi, right down to the clothes. It was difficult to tell, given the graininess of the photo, though.

"Relative of yours?" Easton queried. When he received no response, he half turned around.

Kimmi was gone.

Easton shrugged and walked over to the octagonal reading table where the book had been left. He tilted his head so he could read the barely legible embossed title on the cover:

Night of the Thousand Deaths.

Lovely, Easton thought. Must have just missed the top ten bestsellers' list in the Times.

His next stop was the conservatory. This room, as it turned out, was somewhat misleadingly named, as it wasn't exactly a true conservatory. It was more like an exotic den with a lot of extra plants. And trees. True, it had a series of large skylights that could be swung open on milder days, but apparently the glass atrium at the back had been walled in at some point and replaced with a semicircular couch and a large stained glass oval window. The room had a lofty, spacious feel to it, enhanced by a series of slender fluted columns that ran up to the ceiling two stories above. Their capitals were carved stylized lotus leaves. Between them ran slender, multi-paned windows and, to the west side, a circular wrought iron stair went up to a gallery festooned with hanging planters. It looked like something right out of a Victorian novel; the room was filled with cane furniture gone nearly black with age with overstuffed tan cushions and pillows. In addition to several exotic-looking plants, the room had six full-sized date palm trees. It looked like a wonderful room to enjoy the morning paper with a scone and a hot cup of coffee and Easton wondered if he would have an opportunity to do just that on the morrow.

He had a hunch he wouldn't.

Reclining with his feet crossed on one of the larger couches – the word davenport came to Easton's mind (he wasn't clear what that really was, only that his grandmother had always used the term when referring to her couch) – was Geoffrey Washington. His arms were spread out on the back of the sofa. He looked like a guy enjoying a football game in his family room on a lazy Sunday afternoon.

"Mr. Matthews!" he said, rolling out the syllables in his deep baritone, as if Easton was an old college buddy dropping by for a beer and an afternoon ball game on the telly. "Please, please, have a seat!"

"Thanks, but I prefer to stand." Easton stepped into the room, taking in the unusual details, his hands in their customary front pants pocket position. He noticed a pair of thick glass doors leading out to the back terrace. They had scrolling iron frames that together formed a stylized dragon. Easton was beginning to wonder what Van Eyckmann's obsession with the damned things was.

"Fine, fine. So....what do you think of Taron Hall so far? Quite the 'River Cottage'...wouldn't you say?"

Easton glanced back from the doors. "Eh? Oh. No, I wouldn't exactly call it a 'River Cottage.' Some sort of hideous set made for an old Hammer Film perhaps, but definitely not cottage."

Washington frowned at him, struggling to decide if he was being insulted or not. "You seemed to be making good friends with our security guards around here." The jocularity was leaking out of his voice. Easton continued to stroll around the room, taking apparent interest in a pair of rare orchids set on a wrought iron table.

"Knightbridge? I wouldn't say 'making friends' either, Mr. Washington. Though when a dead body pops up in someone's garden shed, it is worth discussing with security, is it not? Or perhaps dead bodies don't shock you all that much?"

It would be fair to say Washington already had it in for Easton for a few reasons, the one blinking at the top of his list being that, British or not, Easton was a cop. And Washington had had enough of cops sniffing around his business over the past few months, particularly in regard to his extracurricular activities in Chinatown. Actually, there was more to the story than even Knightbridge had uncovered. The girl who had died was named Chi Lin, she was 15, and, in his own sociopathic way, Washington had grown to care for her over the past year that he had been a client at Wu Tan's off the Bowery near Canal. If the way one grows attached to a particular person could be categorized by the term "care." It was just that one night in late May, right after a quadruple header of having four major condo sales fall through in one day (in addition to a royal bitching-out session by Mrs. Washington over an upcoming dinner party invitation list — did she honestly think he had nothing better to do at work than to listen to such trite rubbish?), he had been, well, a little tense. Perhaps a lot tense. And, in those few moments, he had forgotten himself, again, his hands seemed to work of their own volition. Suddenly, in the spasms of his ecstasy, he became aware just how tight his hands were gripping Chi Lin's delicate throat and that her usually tender-but-distant gaze had gone into the realm of distant – and unfocused – and then it was far too late, though that hadn't stopped him from climaxing. In fact, it had actually made him even more aroused. Somewhere deep in the recesses of his heart, there had been a momentary pang, but more that of a child who realizes he's just broken a favorite toy than any sort of empathetic human emotion. From there, it had gotten somewhat matter of fact: cleaning up and dressing himself (in reverse order of his carefully folded clothes, as his mother had always taught him) as was his usual routine, then carefully re-dressing Chi Lin in her school girl uniform and folding her hands over the mounds of her tiny breasts to suggest that she had simply dozed off on a short nap after a hard day at school. His mother had taught him always to be good to little girls and to clean up thoroughly when he was finished with his "business." She was such a nice little girl, ran the warped logic of his thoughts, except when she was bad. Why did she have to be so bad and do those dirty things to him? Things that made him feel ashamed and unclean? He didn't want to do these things, she made him. Invited him. Seduced him. Proper little girls should know better than that. Wasn't that why they were in school? He had urges, ones he was powerless to control. But he would try. That's what good boys did. He made a promise to himself right then and there that this would stop, this would end. No more. But…he was the victim here, didn't anybody understand that? Mother did. I miss you, miss you, dear Mother!

And then the little pang in his heart winked out like a snuffed candle (and a very tiny one at that) and Washington's thoughts switched gears as he considered his late afternoon appointments, automatically "A and B" listed the names on the invitation list his wife had run past him that morning, and briefly considered whether he should renew the lease on his Lexus or look for something more sporty. After double checking the full Windsor knot in his tie, he quietly closed the door (after softly whispering "Zài jiàn, Chi Lin….jìng cháng lian xi á – let's keep in touch) and notified the elderly Madame at the front desk that he was slightly disappointed with his appointment and then simply walked out the door into the frantic hustle of Chinatown. Just another appointment on just another day. Then, a week later, the phone calls had started from Wu Tan. Asking for money. Not enough to break him – Wu Tan was either a very shrewd guesser or had the drop on Washington's income – but just enough to make the big man sweat. Which he paid. And sweated. And planned. He knew that at some point Wu Tan would have to be taken care of – not by him certainly, perhaps someone like Knightbridge could be brought in, discreetly, under the pretext of a cleverly crafted story. Washington was an expert at cleverly crafted stories. But then the NYPD detectives began showing up. Which made Washington agitated. Not because of this latest incident – he had information on Wu Tan's that would have the NYC district attorney's office down on them like a hammer. No, it was the three other small bodies that had subsequently found themselves out in a Staten Island landfill (and another in a culvert off the Belt Parkway near JFK) that had him nervous and edgy. And Geoffrey Washington was not a man who took well to being nervous.

It made him upset. Angry.

It made him do, well, *things*.

So it would be fair to say there was quite a lot that Knightbridge, Hilderman, and any of his colleagues (or even wives, although Mrs. Washington #1 had more than a few suspicions over the years, #2 was too caught up on her own narcissistic fast track to notice) really knew about the whole Geoffrey Washington subcontinent that existed behind the familiar and friendly Geoffrey Washington coastline most visitors were familiar with.

So when Easton made this last comment it was like, well, putting a hammer to a bullet primer.

Washington surprised him by leaping to his feet and covering the distance between them in three strides, pulling up close – too close – to Easton. Like a schoolyard bully looking to escalate a fight. He looked down at the detective with dead, cold eyes. The only suggestion of anger was his flared nostrils. Easton looked up at him with a calm he didn't quite feel. Christ, the man was fast! he thought.

"You seem to like to disagree a lot." His pores were oozing menace.

Easton considered a smart-ass response then didn't. "Do you have a point, Mr. Washington?"

Washington looked like he would enjoy nothing more on earth than making that point with his bare hands. On Easton's neck. For a few seconds, there was only the sound of Washington's breath going in and out of his nose like a pump. Then Washington grinned. The effect was ghastly.

"The point, Mr. Matthews, is that Mr. Hilderman wished you to remember that we have an agreement. A very important agreement. One none of us would like to see jeopardized. Yes? Otherwise there would be problems....and, Mr. Matthews, I am very good at fixing problems...I enjoy fixing problems...Do we have a problem here? Problem?" Washington sounded like a parrot stuck on repeat. The metallic aroma of insanity was wafting from him. Easton was beginning to suspect that he was on his way to becoming unhinged. Cancel that. Was past there already.

"Are you threatening me, Mr. Washington?"

"I'm reminding you, Mr. Matthews...not to be a bad boy,"

Easton tilted his head to the side and said evenly, "Consider me reminded, then." He didn't care much for where this was going. *Bad boy? What was this, school kids on the playground?*

As he moved to step past Washington, the realtor grabbed his bicep in a vise-like grip and tried to pull him in close. Easton's reaction was pure instinct. Executing a textbook judo take down, he spun his arm clockwise, breaking the grip, then grabbed Washington's forearm, jerking it up as he stepped behind. At the same time, his right foot swept the other man's. The result was instantaneous. One minute Washington was pulling Easton in, the next he was flat on his face with the detective's knee in his back, his right arm being yanked up behind him. In the process, Washington's shoulder had caught a wicker side table by the corner and smashed it, toppling a priceless orchid to the floor, its ceramic pot shattering. Part of the pot banged off his skull and rolled away.

The realtor's attempt to struggle was met with another harsh jerk of his arm. The pain was excruciating. Easton bent over and whispered in his ear. "Steady now, Mr. Washington. I can break your arm quite easily. Now listen up: you'll want to be on your best behavior from here on out. You may be a tough guy with the little ladies in massage parlors but that won't wash with me. Got it? Nod twice if you understand." To make his point, he gave a sharp yank on Washington's arm. His eyes had flared a little wider at Easton's reference to his little secret, now beads of sweat popped out on the man's forehead.

One nod. Then two.

"Good boy. Now do I have your word you'll behave if I let you up?"

Another nod.

"Excellent. Otherwise, Hilderman will have to find a doctor that makes house calls." Easton released the realtor's arm and stepped back carefully, his guard up. Washington must have been in considerable pain, but was doing a respectable job of hiding it. The only tip-off was the clenched jaw muscles. He very slowly got up, arm dangling, portrait of an injured middle-aged man. Then in another instant, he was flying at Easton, hands spread like giant claws .

The interesting thing about judo is how it redirects an opponent's energy into working against him. It also has a bit of "weee!" factor in the way the throws are executed. One minute, 250 pounds of six foot three realtor were barreling at Easton with the intent of inflicting serious bodily injury; the next, he was sailing through the air upside down, describing an arc that landed him on the top of a wicker couch that toppled over with a resounding crash. For a brief comic moment, Washington's legs were standing straight up in the air, then they dropped out of sight.

Easton circled around the couch warily. Washington was sprawled on his back, motionless. There was a small gash on the side of his head where it had struck the base of a small iron table. Easton stepped over carefully. It was difficult to tell if the realtor was breathing or not. His chest wasn't moving. Easton knelt down at his side and put two fingers to the side of his neck.

There was a pulse.

Which was confirmed a split second later, when Washington's eyes flew open and his arms grabbed Easton by the neck. The man's hands were huge but Easton grabbed the backs with both of his and drove his thumbs in on the pressure points and pried them off. Then he drove his fist up into Washington's jaw.

The realtor's eyes rolled back and there was no second guessing the results this time. He was down for the count.

Easton stood up, shaking out his fist, hoping he hadn't fractured any knuckles. He flexed his hand a couple of times. It would be sore for a few days but nothing some aspirin couldn't fix. Christ, the man had the constitution of an ox. Easton's hand felt like he'd hit a butcher's block.

As he turned to go, he saw he had an audience. Kimmi was standing in the doorway, arms folded, a sly look in his eyes. Next to him one of the house servants – a short middle-aged woman in an old-fashioned uniform – stood with her jaw hanging open.

Easton brushed off his arms and stepped around the damaged furniture. "My apologies for making a bit of a mess. Mr. Washington and I were having a go at a little arm wrestling. Afraid it got a little carried away. He may need to sleep it off though."

"You should be more careful when you play."

Easton tried to think of a quick comeback, but was fresh out. He needed to get out and get some air.

"Will do."

With that, he brushed past them and out the door.

10. MISSED CONNECTIONS

Outside, the breeze was kicking up. Dead leaves leapt up into the air like whirling dervishes. The sun was slanting into its late afternoon golden spectrum and the first touches of salmon and orange brushed the clouds scudding overhead. Easton turned his collar up and crossed the lawn with long strides.

The chapel and family crypt was a forlorn looking place on the verge of falling into ruin. On the northwest corner of the property, it was sited, presumably, so that those resting in eternity would have a decent view of the river. Easton never quite understood that part of funeral planning: he wasn't clear how one being dead could see anything and, if you did buy into the afterlife/spirit world shtick, it didn't make sense to him what difference it made where you were buried if you became an incorporeal being. His own firsthand experiences had made him highly pragmatic over the years — he'd seen plenty of people die (including three men he had dispatched personally) and had yet to see any of them come back, or ring him up, or show up around his flat as a skulking ghost

Pearson was wearing the medal.

...to haunt him for his sins. To be sure, he had seen some odd things now...

When he was buried. Snakes. October.

...and then, living in the Caribbean, it was unavoidable. But nothing that couldn't be explained under the cold hard light of reason. Which granted, doesn't make for exciting stories of prematurely dead boyfriends speaking to their loved ones through psychics to help them get on with life.

The same medal sitting in your pocket.

...or television series about worried looking housewives with false eyelashes and handsome-yet-non-descript sensitive and supportive husbands. ("I'm the Ghost Therapist, the actress always seemed to be saying. I'm from California. I can help. Help the endless stream of troubled spirits find resolution and eternal peace." Within an hour. Every week.)

The snakes. The snakes, John.

As Easton came up to the Iron Gate surrounding the cemetery, he actually smacked himself upside the head, as if that would drive that voice out of his head. He didn't like that voice. At all. It was the voice of the irrational. The voice that reads horoscopes every day in anticipation and dread. The voice that is convinced that the U.S. government is actually sitting on a stockpile of alien hardware (and a real alien or two, supposedly) over in Area 57. The voice that says 1-800 Psychic is a completely sane call to make at 3 o'clock in the morning, that Santa Claus and the Easter Bunny are as real as rain. In other words, the voice of...

Aunt Bethany.

...someone who puts stock in such ridiculousness.

Easton suddenly felt a wave of (fear/heat/awareness?) creeping up his spine and threatening to engulf his consciousness. With it, blind panic. A memory...

The phone call. It started with the phone call from Aunt Bethany.

...from...All at once, it erupted full blown in his mind. Like a door being thrown open or a gas bubble long buried in the muck of a swamp, the memory wobbled up and burst on the surface of his mind. The whole scene resolved into crystal clearness. A memory he had no idea he had forgotten.

Hi Auntie B.

As simple as that. The phone hadn't even rung. A 13-year-old version of John Easton running out the door to meet up with friends at the park for an afternoon football match. He'd just finished tying his shoes and was going out the front door, past the phone in the front hall, the old black Bakelight one with the rotary dial. That sat under a lithograph titled "The Winning Hand," which depicted three roguish-looking gentlemen that Easton thought of as the Musketeers and a vexed looking friar playing cards in a shadowy tavern by the ocean, if the press of ship's masts in the background were any indication. It might have even been Falmouth Harbor. The winner had just laid his cards down, a triumphant smirk on his face (which perhaps bore more than a passing resemblance to one of his relatives, pointed goatee and all) while his fellow players looked confounded, vexed at what was clearly an unexpected turn of events.

He hadn't even thought about it.

Just picked up the phone which hadn't rung and said automatically...

Hi, Auntie B.

...like he would have greeted the postman or bus driver. There was a brief silence on the other end, then that rich musical laugh he knew so well. Her deep, sexy voice: "Hello, Johnnie." And Easton going red to the roots of his hairline. Aunt Bethany, his mother's younger sister, with the emerald eyes, arched eyebrows, and auburn hair. And crystals and healing herbs and tarot cards and arcana and so on.

"So, my knight errant has the gift too....Have you been opening doors, Johnnie...?" Easton standing there confused/aroused/ashamed/curious – conflicting emotions his aunt never failed to trigger in him as he entered his teenage years – now aware something else had just happened between him and his aunt – something unexpected and somehow intimate. And chasing on the tails of those feelings – fear and disgust. At experiencing something, well, girlie. Easton even at 13 not being much for the touchy-feelie school of emo-boys.

The doors, John. The day you picked up the phone. Then you went out to play and when you came home, you were in trouble. Because when your mom came home from work, all the doors in the house were open, even the closets and cupboards. She nearly blew a gasket....

Aunt Bethany, wild card black sheep of the family. Never settling down. Always running on some hair-brained scheme or another. Going on at family gatherings about her past lives (inevitably something exciting and exotic like caravan slave, Egyptian sorceress, high priestess of Atlantis). Disappearing for months on end. One year, it was the month-long sojourn re-enacting Gaelic rituals with a bunch of so-called Druids on some remote island off Ireland. A two-week retreat on astral travel in northern California. A week-long gathering attempting to contact aliens from a volcano on a south Pacific island. At one point claiming she was a seraphim angel of the third order and the next month an initiate in the Order of the Golden Dawn that an accountant in Sussex had made a half-baked attempt to revive, most likely as a calculated attempt to spice up his pathetic sex life. Easton's father calling her the Christmas Fruitcake, nutty as a drunk squirrel, clinically insane. Easton's mother, the responsible older sister of her family, exasperated, secretly loaning her money from the Easton cookie jar. Whispered conversations with words mentioned like "medication," "shock treatment," bi-polar disorder," The somewhat racy flirtations between Easton and his aunt. The time during his older sister's wedding when he barged in to his own bedroom unaware that his aunt was using it as a changing room, the brief glimpse of her pale, pointed breasts before beating a hasty retreat (and his subsequent Dear Penthouse teenage fantasies where his clothes fell off as well, with predictable results). Later dancing with her at the reception, a wine-laced whisper in his ear. "Be careful when you open doors, Johnnie, you never know what you'll find..." which fueled a whole additional set of Dear Penthouse fantasies.

Nothing ever technically went beyond just that – a bit of harmless flirtation. One of them, maybe both, engaging in a little daydream fantasy. The problem was this: for a brief time after that out-of-the-blue phone incident, strange things began to happen to Easton. It was as if some invisible imp had nonchalantly walked by the switchboard in his head and thrown a switch he never suspected existed.

The one marked *psychic ability*.

For the most part, it was harmless, benign stuff. Picking up people's thoughts when in close proximity, as if on a short wave radio. Sometimes they came in as words. Other times, images. A girl a year ahead of him at school that he knew only vaguely (her name had been Karin...no...Corinne, Corinne Delancy) walking down the hallway, barely looking at him but "Cute ass!" shot through her brain into his as he strolled by. Two little kids at the corner store in the aisle thinking "Candy! Candy" almost simultaneously. Another kid – maybe 16 with greasy hair who was walking awkwardly from a beating his father had dished out the night before – eyeing the bottles of Schnapps behind the counter, cooking up a questionable scheme to steal them. An elderly woman named Mrs. Tyler concerned about the lump she'd found near her breast that morning and why her daughter seemed to hate her so much and how she was terrified, not of dying but of being forgotten...and so on. Sometimes banal. Sometimes nasty. Sometimes bizarre. Sometimes hilariously normal. People and their thoughts ran the entire gamut, it appeared, sometimes exactly as expected and sometimes not. Or, as one writer once pointed out: sometimes good, sometimes bad, most of the time just balancing out.

Personally, however, Easton struggled day in and day out. His emotions were tangled: guilt, voyeuristic curiosity, shame, outrage, hearing things he knew his friends wouldn't believe in a hundred years. Mostly though, he found his new-found talent unnerving. It flew in the face of everything he'd been brought up with...

My knight errant has the gift, too.

...in what was a very practical and proper British household where one did one's chores, handed homework in on time (neatly written), minded one's manners, and used the fork and knife properly at the table while sitting up straight...well, to some extent. Some nonsense was tolerated but, by and large, the Easton's were a pragmatic bunch and not prone to flights of fancy. His father worked for British Rail and his mother dabbled in real estate and worked part-time at the local library. Easton had a younger brother who was a gifted and semi-successful musician who would go on to tour as a bassist with Peter Gabriel, Kate Bush, and Pink Floyd, and an older sister who married a barrister and lived in Kent. All ran pretty much on an even keel.

So discovering he had some whacky talent that threw him in the same corner as his (Hi, Johnnie!) wickedly attractive aunt was both exciting and highly disturbing. There were several more incidents of Easton picking up the phone before it rang and finding his aunt on the other end. Until he made a conscious decision to stop picking up the phone. There were a few run-ins over holidays and such, when his aunt would tease him about coming to visit (she was living the next town over at the time). She could show him how to use his gift, develop it, master his destiny, etc. but Easton consciously or subconsciously avoided all of these invitations and clung like a lifeline to his sports, studies, and anything else that had some semblance of normalcy.

All that stumbled along for a year and a half until the incident with Gerald.

Correction: Gerry. As in Gerry Holdsender.

For a split second, standing in the present at the gate of Van Eyckmann's chapel, Easton was struck with amazement at how completely and thoroughly he had taken the memory of Gerry Holdsender and what happened that July day and un-remembered it.

It was a hot day. One of those hot July days in a string that went on forever. It was impossible to sleep at night. Even the seagulls looked tired and worn out by the heat, sulking in clumps on the docks and wharves. The games Easton was playing with his friends, especially Norm MacDonald, were getting flat and uninteresting. Gerry had been a friend of his who was being phased out of favor, the way friends will be in the formative years of adolescence. Gerry was two years older, dark haired and wild-eyed, and possessed of one of those personalities that is practically required by universal law to continually test the boundaries of sane and rational behavior. This was stimulating on one level (and made for excellent story material over lunch break) but continually grated on your nerves on another. Gerry had a big, mischievous grin and flashing eyes that got girls nervous and his friends more so when he got hot on cooking up some scheme. Since the previous year, Easton had struck up a friendship with Norm. They seemed to have more in common – fantasy art (Frazetta, Valejo) and horror/sci-fi books, movie stars (Charlotte Rampling was the best, Julie Christie a close second, though Easton had a secret crush on Diana Rigg). Gerry's ongoing antics and sometimes gutter mind – he was dead set on being the first of their neighborhood bunch to get laid, being the first to have achieved near-mythical first and second base status – did not fit in with all this. In retrospect, maybe it was just his sense of one-upmanship, jealousy, general dementedness, or all of the above but out of the blue – it had been months since they'd talked, Gerry suddenly knocked on the Easton's back door one Saturday morning in July and said he had been....

"...working on plan, Johnnie-boy, you have got to see this!!!"

Easton was slightly annoyed – he and Norm had been hanging out in the Easton's living room watching American cartoons on BBC2 and kicking around various plans for that night (one farfetched one which involved asking out the McMurray sisters, who were twins a year older than them on a double date to the cinema in town.). But here was Gerry all fired up about some new scheme involving, if Easton wasn't mistaken, the medium-sized bundle wrapped in a towel in both his hands. Norm came to the door finally to see what was up.

"Hey, Ger! What's the rumpus?" he said over Easton's shoulder.

Carefully, as if he had just nicked the crown jewels out of the Tower of London and was showing off a peek to his mates, Holdsender pulled back a little bit of the towel to reveal the business end of a scale model brass cannon perhaps fifteen or sixteen inches in length. "This is the rumpus, lads! Got it from me old man's study. Always wanted to try out this puppy and see if she really worked...."

Easton blinked twice. True, they were at that age since the previous summer when they'd taken mischievous delight in experimenting with fireworks, torching their model airplanes with various types of flammable liquids (including one spectacular event where they took a 40-inch balsa wood Avro Lancaster model Norm had built years back and launched it off one of the nearby cliffs into the ocean while pretending to be German anti-aircraft gunners, having first soaked it in lighter fluid and sending it off engulfed in flames, thus earning a week of "Holy-Shit-did-you-see-that!?" conversations).

But this was a whole new category on their radar.

And in a flash, Easton had a premonition. He looked at the grin on Holdsender's face. The brass cannon cradled in the towel, the bright sun filtering through the chestnut tree in the Easton's back yard, and the slight breeze with its summer scents pushing through the screen door and felt his gut drop like an elevator. For a split second, he saw red, splattered everywhere, and holes through Holdsender's face, then the image vanished as Norm clapped him on the back and pushed him through the screen door out into the back yard. "Mad, Ger, completely mad!"

There was a field back behind their houses owned by the Aryons, just past a dense grove of chestnut and oak trees (which doubled as their Sherwood Forest, as necessary), the field where everything from the Battle of Waterloo to Arnhem to the Falkland Islands was fought in previous years. Today, however, it was to be the site of Gerry Holdsender's latest experiment. As they walked diagonally across the field to another copse of trees on the side opposite from where the Aryon's farmhouse lurked, Easton's stomach continued to have butterflies. He had picked up more images too from Holdsender: Gerry spotting him and Norm on some of their more recent antics, his thoughts darkened by jealousy and competitiveness with a few pin needles of anger at being overlooked by his peers. If there was one thing the Gerry Holdsender's of the world could not abide, it was being overlooked.

The spot.

Near the trees facing towards the small brook there. Holdsender carefully laying out his bundle which included the cannon, its wooden carriage, a small garden shovel and, to Easton's alarm, a nail set and a hammer.

A nail set. And a hammer.

Easton heard his voice from far away. "Gerry, is this really a good idea? I...I...what exactly are you planning to do?"

Holdsender shot him an annoyed look that said "never, ever, question Gerald Holdsender, laddie."

"What you think, you little wanker? I'm sticking this cannon in the ground, which has been carefully filled with a measure of gunpowder and shot, which I will then proceed to fire across yon stream, yeah?"

MacDonald now chimed in. "Uh, Ger, are you sure about this?"

"Sure I'm sure. Spent the last three days figuring it all out." (Another lie, Easton intuited – Holdsender had cooked up this little beauty just this morning.) "Now clam up a second, ladies, while I tend to the arrangements." With that, he busied himself with the hand shovel, digging out a small trough which enabled him to bury the cannon at a muzzle-up angle. He then cleared a small hole around the back of the cannon where the touch hole normally would be. .

"Shotgun primer," he explained, in response to John and Norm's curious expressions. Easton remembered thinking "fuse, why isn't he using a fucking fuse???" But things were on a roll. Holdsender made like he was an artillery commander sighting his piece across the little stream, while he motioned Easton and MacDonald to stand back with fanfare. He even made a show of wetting his thumb and sticking it out to check the wind direction. With that, he knelt over his set-up, placed the nail set on the shotgun primer jammed into the touch hole, and shouted in a mock German voice "Eins. Zwei. DREI!"

And brought the hammer down.

Easton remembered hearing a dull "crump!" Then his ears ringing. Then glancing down and seeing bright red sprayed over his tee shirt. Then realizing Holdsender was staggering, then dancing around like he had bees in his pants. It was almost comical. Except for the screams. Holdsender was screaming a high-pitched, shrill scream. Easton and MacDonald were frozen in place, two statues cast in lead. Holdsender reeled around. Where the cannon had been was a scorched hole in the ground. Easton was trying to process why his shirt was so red and what those little pieces of raw meat (?) were doing on it. His prized Sex Pistols "Never Mind The Bollocks" shirt with the sleeves torn off (a band he would never listen to again after this day). MacDonald's jaw hung open in shock. Then he saw Holdsender's face.

It was horrible.

Like something out of a movie.

It was punched through with holes. Easton didn't know such a thing was possible, though he would grow to understand it completely in later years as a homicide cop. The right eye was gone – just a mashed hole with a chunk of shiny brass protruding from it. Part of the cheek was gone, a gaping wound revealing the inner mouth where several teeth had been smashed by the flying shrapnel. The upper shirt was torn and blackened, the skin peppered with small and big holes. Of the left hand, there were only mangled ribbons of flesh and bone. The right still had the hammer in it, of all things. Holdsender, eyes glassy with shock, staggered up to Easton and fell to his knees.

"Help.....me......!!!" Holdsender's voice turned into a strangled gurgle. And Easton saw bright arterial blood leaking out of the side of his neck.

Next to Easton, MacDonald finally kick-started himself and started yelling "FuckfuckohfuckI-I-I-ohfuck!!!!!!" and jumping up and down like a rabbit on a hot plate.

That was all it took.

Easton bolted and ran. Panic bright and sharp as the pieces of brass jutting out of Holdsender's face shot through his veins and obliterated all thought. He went at a dead sprint back towards his house.

The screaming was still going on in his brain. Holdsender. It trickled into a mewling plea: "Don't leave-oh-oh-oh-help-memememe... backcomeback...." which turned into a whimpering cry, which, coming from a guy with Holdsender's reputation, was utterly unnerving. Easton ran like the wind. Bolted through the trees, branches whipping his face, leaping over fallen branches like the very devil was hot on his heels. He had a brief thought of Robin and his Merry Men looking on from between the yew trees (had he thought himself a noble warrior? Look at me now!! I'm one hundred percent pure chickenshit!!), shaking their heads at such cowardly behavior, but that vanished in a wisp as well. He had no idea if he was injured as well or what had happened to MacDonald or anything at all but only that he...

Run!

...was scared shitless and somehow this perfectly good Saturday morning had taken an abrupt left turn into nightmare city.

He made it all the way to his back yard before collapsing to his hands and knees, his breath coming in great whoops. A second later, MacDonald, who, as it turned out had been right behind him the whole time, caught up and began pacing circles like a wounded animal, hands holding his sides, which were cramped from sprinting. He continued on his rant "Fuckfuckholyfuckwhathappened???" to no one in particular.

Easton glanced down. Seeing there were bits of gore still clinging to his tee-shirt, he tore it off. For another panicked moment, he thought he was seriously wounded and ran his hands all over his torso before doubling over and vomiting his breakfast of bangers and mash all over the lawn. Miraculously, neither he nor MacDonald had a scratch (aside from what they'd sustained blitzing full tilt through the woods), considering Holdsender had set off what amounted to a large hand grenade. Part of it was pure luck – Easton wasn't even aware that a two-inch chunk of razor-sharp brass had whizzed inches by his left ear. –The other part was that partially burying the cannon, coupled with Holdsender's position hunched over it, had inadvertently spared them the worst.

After Easton's breakfast had diminished to an acidic trickle, he wiped his mouth, sat back on his haunches, and looked up at the sky, tears running down his cheeks.

Holdsender's voice had faded to a whisper...

"hepmehelpmeohnoohno...."–gluck– "idonwantodiealonecomeback..."

...and Easton smacked the side of his head with his palms repeatedly, begging it to stop please make it fucking stop and then abruptly it did.

Holdsender was dead.

It felt like the scene had played in his head for hours, though only a space of a few minutes had elapsed. Easton felt a momentary vertigo as he returned to the present, his hand on the cold iron post of the gate outside Van Eyckmann's chapel. A sob escaped him and his eyes brimmed with tears as the power of the memory convulsed through his body.

26 years and it hadn't diminished an ounce.

There had been all sorts of fall-out of course, including a police investigation. Easton and MacDonald were quickly cleared of any wrongdoing, (Although for years afterward, Holdsender's mother would spread vicious stories to anyone who would listen of how Easton and MacDonald had set the whole thing up, that they'd had it in for her poor little boy, and she'd even heard them outside the window one night talking her son into the whole mess.) As an adult and a police officer who had seen his share of violence and death, Easton knew in retrospect that it was what it was: a stupid stunt by a bunch of stupid kids gone terribly wrong. Or at least one monumentally stupid kid and two idiots who stood by and let him do it. It was hardly the first time in history and was unlikely to be the last.

But that hardly made it any easier.

There had been long talks with his mom and dad who, by and large, were supportive if ineffectual. Apparently, that particular chapter had been omitted from their parenting guide, the one on "What to do if your son's friend blows himself up and dies." But one night, his grandfather, who had dropped by with an old sideboard he'd restored for his dad, had come in and sat on the edge of his bed – this after two weeks of Easton walking around like a automaton, completely withdrawn into himself, refusing to talk to anybody. (Norm's parents had whisked him off to an aunt in Northumberland and Easton wouldn't see him again for two years.) He looked at him long and hard. Easton stared out the window, wishing he was somewhere, someone else, anyone else but John Easton, coward, chicken-shit, runner-away-from-mortally-wounded-friends. He was stricken with red hot shame and his grandfather was the last person on earth he wanted to face. He knew his granddad had fought in the Eighth Army and faced Rommel at Tobruk, fought his way through Sicily and the boot of Italy, before being seriously wounded at Sword Beach on D-Day.

Granddad Easton favored unfiltered Lucky Strikes – something to do with a Yank doctor who had saved one of his legs (and, more importantly, his life) and had what they used to call a "tobacco and whiskey" voice:

"Listen up lad," he'd said, "That was a fair terrible thing you had to witness. And, yes, you did the wrong thing. You should have stuck by your mate. And you probably want to find a deep dark hole to crawl into and stay there for the rest of your life, yes?" No response. "But you're thirteen, goddammit. And you don't know shit about anything, lad. Well...maybe now you do. You've been given a hard lesson." Easton blinked. This wasn't one of his grandfather's bull and bluster stories about knocking the stuffing out of the Jerries, usually told after a few pints. He had no idea where this was going.

"Look, I saw, no, I lived everything you went through, for years. I saw and did a lot of terrible things. Not just that, I saw men, even hardened veterans, go off half-cocked and charge a Jerry machine gun nest like they had balls of iron one day, and the next be cowering in their foxhole, crying like little babies for their mums the next. Courage is situational. And the bravest soldiers usually just get themselves dead. Shite load of monkey chuff your medals do you then. The point is, the point is there's no point at all in punishing yourself forever over this. You panicked, lad. It happens. But you can make good on it." He reached over and put a gnarled hand on Easton's shoulder and patted it. Which was about the closest thing Granddad Easton had in his repertoire approaching affection. Then his free hand traced a symbol that was carved in the center of the headboard of the bed which was a vertical sword in a circle against a background of rocks – a castle? – with some worn-out letters that looked like C-V-J. Easton had no idea what it meant but his father told him the bed was handed down through generations in his family. It was a heavy and crude affair bearing centuries of nicks, bangs, scratches, and scars from little boys' pocket knives, but Easton had loved it all the same. It was a good bed. A safe bed. Now, like everything else in his life, it just felt like an empty collection of wood posts and dowels and blankets.

His grandfather didn't say anything for a moment, then: "'The true heart finds justice.' Something like that. That's what my granddad told me at least — I used to sleep in this same bed myself when I was your age..." Then his grandfather stood up and made to leave but paused at the bedroom door. "You will make good on it, lad, because you're an Easton and have steel in you. Like it or not. Someday you'll understand."

Easton had held his sobs in check until the door had quietly closed. Internally, his emotions were in a maelstrom. It wasn't any one thing, it was all of them. It was the noble image...

My knight errant

...of himself that he had built up over the years that had evaporated in a wisp the moment it was tested. It was the shame of running away from...

Helpmememe

...a mate in need and letting him — *ohgod* — die alone. But the cut ran much deeper than that, which was something his granddad couldn't possibly understand. And that was that Easton had known. He could have prevented the whole thing and he didn't. He could have said, "Holdsender, it'll never work. You're going to blow yourself to kingdom come." Instead, he had stood by like a helpless schoolgirl and watched his friend do something mind-bogglingly stupid that would cost him his life. And with that came a spear of guilt. Part of him, perversely, might have even wanted it to happen. The sinister little voice in his head that said, "Yeah, you're such a smart cookie, Holdsender, we'll see..." But the worst, by far the worst, was the screaming he had heard in his head long after he was out of earshot of Holdsender. The parlor game "gift" he had uncovered was also a curse, a sword that cut both ways.

After that, Easton did change. He shut down any association with anything resembling "psychic" after that. Just dropped it into a crate, slammed the lid shut, threw a massive iron padlock on it, and tossed it overboard into the deepest ocean of his mind. His survival response was to slam the door shut on the whole convoluted aunt-psychic-sexual-tension-parlor-trick thing for good by sheer force of will. In his mind, it had proven to exact a terrible price. A price he swore he would never pay again.

But his grandfather had been right on one thing, Easton would make good on it. That day, Granddad Easton had thrown him a lifeline out of the whole mess and, though it would take years to consciously realize it, Easton had taken it.

He made a career out of making good on it.

Of acting on it. Of saving people's lives.

Of living and acting and reacting in the real-world.

His aunt had been confused, hurt. But she sensed – how could she not – the depth of his torment and respectfully withdrew out of the lives of her sister's family. Easton hadn't seen or talked to her in 26 years. In time, Easton had come to a sort of resolution of what had happened. Much of that came gradually, over time, seeing how the world worked. And how people, especially the Gerry Holdsenders of the world, worked. That there was an inevitability to so many things in life. More than likely there was nothing he could have said or done to convince Holdsender to abandon his fateful project. And had he done something to physically stop him that day, it would have happened the next. Or the week after. Or a month after. Or it would have been some other crack-brained stunt. Jumping from a cliff into the ocean backwards. Playing chicken on one of the snaking roads along the coast. One truth Easton would swear on a stack of Bibles: one cannot save another person from himself.

Easton shook his head like a dog with a flea in its ear. Then he heard a voice, his Aunt Bethany's voice, close – as if she had spoken directly into his ear.

"My knight errant..."

Easton looked around wildly, the hair rising on the nape of his neck. No one was there, of course. Aural hallucination. Glancing at his watch, he saw that it was 3:10.

The chapel was small and gloomy inside. The air smelled of damp, mold, of old air hanging out in old corners. Dust and debris and old leaves were scattered everywhere. The space was roughly 15 by 30 feet, with a low stage opposite the entrance featuring a lectern and a bier. A row of pews was set up on either side, covered in dust. Behind the bier loomed a life-sized statue of Christ suspended on a life-sized cross, both carved of white marble. From what Easton could tell, a suspiciously Aryan-looking Christ, with a long straight nose, thin eyebrows, and a distinctly European face. He had no doubt that, had the artist been using colors, the hair would have been blond and the eyes blue.

Some wit had left a note taped to the Savior's groin.

As Easton stepped forward, his foot bumped into something. Bending down, he saw that it appeared to be one of those little hymn books with a thick black leather cover. This one looked old and the binding was water damaged. Without thinking, he bent down and picked it up, blowing the dust off the cover. He was about to drop it on the nearest pew, then changed his mind. Still walking up to the altar, he turned the book over in his hand a couple times before cracking it open.

It wasn't quite your typical hymn book, as it turned out.

Glancing at the front piece, the type was set in the crude and somewhat uneven rows of an antique press from some few hundred years ago:

> Being a short account of the Black Dragon
> on her maiden voyage to the East Indies,
> 1619-1622
> Lieutenant Piers Maynard

It appeared to be a journal of sorts, printed in tiny print with occasional crude woodcut illustrations. Easton fanned through it, then dropped it in his coat pocket. The shadows were growing long in the chapel and there was no sign of Knightbridge.

Or perhaps there was.

Easton stepped up on the small pulpit to have a better look at the note someone had taped to the loincloth of Christ. Written in sloping block letters he read:

Easton: sorry for missing you, mate. Found something really bizarro you'll probably never believe. Look for me down in the basement over at the hall.

-PK

Easton pulled the note off and, folding it, put it in his pocket. Then the door to the chapel slammed shut with a resounding clang, followed by the weighted click of a padlock being thrown.

After his second conversation with Easton, Knightbridge set off for a short walk around the grounds to clear his thoughts. There was a gathering tension in the air he didn't like. The kind of feeling he'd felt on one of his SAS missions in the Falklands just before the bullets started flying and people started getting killed. The business with the gardener was just one more thing that wasn't adding up. Along with about a few dozen other things Knightbridge had been quietly tallying over the past few weeks.

For example, there was the business with the cats. Wyvern Falls had always had a minor problem with a feral cat population. Over the past month, however, they'd been zeroing in on Taron Hall like it had been painted in catnip, yowling and hissing around the grounds at all hours.

And in the past week at least three had turned up dead near the house, necks broken.

Knightbridge walked over to the chapel, just to scope it out. It was one place on the grounds he'd never spent much time investigating, aside from a casual poke inside to make sure no vagrants or itinerant teenagers were taking up residence or utilizing it for a hideaway to score some cigarettes, pot, or whatever crap kids got into these days. He had yet to find any sign of either.

Today, however, proved to be different.

For starters, someone had recently oiled the old massive padlock that hung from an equally old massive chain strung through the double iron doors. Second, the usual autumn debris of old leaves and twigs had been recently shoved aside, presumably by someone entering the chapel. As he did for every lock on the estate, he had a key, including an archaic iron one for the chapel, though he had never actually used it. Although, he mused as he inserted it and fumbled around with the tumblers, even the most amateur lock picker would make short work of this one. It looked to be a couple hundred years old.

With a heavy click, the lock fell open and Knightbridge entered, noting the footprints around the entrance. They appeared to be from a man's dress shoe, maybe a size 9 at a guess. That would match at least two of the guests. He did a quick turn around the inside of the gloomy little building, pausing to look at the lectern and crucified Savior looming up behind it. Like most things about Van Eyckmann and his estate, the whole damn thing gave him the creeps. He wasn't much concerned about the threats Hilderman had implied earlier – he'd already decided to get the hell out after his contract was up, money be damned. He had enough socked away to keep him off the streets for a while, hell, a couple of years if he played it right, and, aside from that, he'd been getting way too bored with this latest gig. It simply wasn't his style to be puttering around the grounds of an old mansion, digging up intel and dirt on enemies and business colleagues (and even arranging for a few of them to get into dire straits, depending on his employer's whims). Knightbridge was happier as an action man and dealing with clear-cut objectives, dealing them out to those who really deserved them. He had no immediate family to worry about, aside from an older brother in Melbourne. His only son had been killed seven years before in the hills of Afghanistan and he hadn't spoken to his ex-wife in years. He still had a few contacts in the DC area. Maybe it was time to start poking around for government contracts again.

He hadn't said as much to his two subordinates, Gerry Wallace and "Spanks" McGoohan. Both were ex-navy Seals and competent when it came to muscle but not necessarily the brightest bulbs in the box. He'd picked them up through his network of contacts when he'd first gotten wind of his current contract almost two years ago. In a way, they were subordinate security types right out of central casting: they didn't talk much and played cards or watched TV in their down time (usually sports or porno, though Wallace was strangely addicted to watching Sponge Bob Squarepants and apparently thought it the pinnacle of hilarity, and Knightbridge had caught McGoohan sneaking in Oprah and Dr. Phil episodes when he thought no one was paying attention). Right down to both men's irritating habit of calling Knightbridge "Boss" when he walked into the room like he was the head of some mob syndicate instead of some lunatic billionaire's two-man security detail.

Still, it had been a good gig. The pay was ridiculous, the medical outstanding, and bonuses were awarded for "special" assignments. Like the local con artist who wrangled getting onto the estate as a delivery truck driver, then "fell" on the ice and filed a bogus injury claim and lawsuit to the tune of a million and a half dollars. His so-called slipped disks and debilitating spinal injuries hadn't prevented him from taking construction jobs on the sly afterward. Until one night he'd taken too many painkillers, drank a fifth of Kentucky bourbon and broke his neck when he toppled over the Lower Falls at four in the morning.

With a little assistance.

Then there was the Chinatown pimp who had tried to blackmail Washington the previous year. Something to do with a little girl who turned up dead during a little weekly role-playing visit (he had deliberately omitted that bit of intel while talking to Easton). That noble entrepreneur was currently enjoying the view from inside a Staten Island landfill (not far from two other bodies that Knightbridge didn't know about). There was generally a certain level of crude justice to these dirty jobs which didn't rattle Knightbridge's moral compass too much – Van Eyckmann never called upon him to deliver the goods to someone who hadn't had it coming in spades.

A smirk crossed his face as another thought occurred to him: he probably wouldn't have the luxury of such distinctions if he went to work in Washington.

Maybe it was time to get the hell out of the business altogether.

Which brought him to Easton.

He liked him.

And didn't like him.

The first because he had a good handle on the man's metal. Partly instinct, partly the intel he had dug up, partly years of having to go into situations with a man you just met and having to gauge whether you trust him. It wasn't a stretch to fill in the blanks between the lines. Wouldn't be squeaky clean. Hardly. But the kind of bloke you could depend on to do the right thing when the chips were down.

The latter for the same reason. Being around Easton really bothered him. Because it forced him to consider just how far off his moral compass he may have strayed over the years. He had a hunch he didn't want to look at those measurements too closely.

While these thoughts were drifting through his mind, Knightbridge had pulled up short before the crypts located on the south wall of the chapel. His eyes had been idly wandering across the inscriptions when subconsciously something began to nag at his mind.

Something odd.

A finger mentally tapping on his brain.

What?

Names? Dates? Striations in the marble? Variations in the time/space continuum?

He backed up a couple of steps, hands clasped behind his back. A deep furrow creased his brow.

Think! What in the blue fuck is it!?

Names.

Dates.

He looked at the inscription right in front of him almost at eye level.

Lon Van Eyckmann
Died 1880
"I shall be satisfied when I awaken."

Then to the left:

Ludwig Van Eyckmann
Died 1750
"May the Lord grant eternal mercy."

And the newly chiseled inscription to the right:

Lars Van Eyckmann
Died 2010
"May he rest from mortal suffering."

The lower row contained the remains of Lars' wife who had passed away in 1971, along with two other Van Eyckmann's with female names – presumably wives or daughters of the Van Eyckmann ancestors. The upper row had blank slabs, reserved for future generations of Van Eyckmann's.

Knightbridge looked up and down and crosswise again.

Dates. For starters, there were the dates. Three generations of Van

Eyckmann's dying exactly 130 years apart. With no birth dates indicated. Where were the generations in between? Was he to believe the Van Eyckmann's had such robust genes that they lived, what, 130 years or more? Highly unlikely. Not completely impossible, but running around just outside the limits of credulity. There had to be a more rational explanation. The crypts below listed both birth and death dates.

Eloise Van Eyckmann. 1940-1971. Aged thirty-one years. May God rest her eternal soul.

That added up. Sensible and standard, Five-by-five as Easton had said.

So what, then? Every other Van Eyckmann buried elsewhere? Not worthy of the family crypt? That wouldn't quite tally either – the years were too far apart. It would have to be two generations of Van Eyckmann's if they had children at say, their early 30s. All of them. Which didn't quite ring Kosher either. So what the blue fuck, then? What made these three so special that they were entombed side by side, having died exactly 130 years apart, no birth dates thank-you-very-much?

This was going to require some digging. Intel. Knightbridge decided he wanted to have a look at Lars Van Eyckmann's body, which was cooling its heels in the basement meat locker back at the hall. But first, he decided he would have a look at the small cemetery outside to see if that would yield any clues. Easton would be by in an hour or so. Breaking out a sticky note pad, he began to write.

Outside, the wind had picked up a notch. Knightbridge zipped up his jacket to the top of the collar. The temperature was dropping and he'd thrown the light jacket over his sweater earlier. It was a lightweight but warm windbreaker he'd picked up at Eastern Mountain Sports, their in-house brand. Some sort of GoreTek material supposedly.

Going to be a bitchy one for the Trick-or-Treaters and Jack-o-Lanterns tonight, he thought. The wind threatened to snatch the Knightbridge Security Group high-peaked bill cap off his head. Fucking Dunderberg Imp, came his next thought. Going to snatch my damn hat and fly off to Sugarloaf Mountain or wherever the hell those little Dutch shits tot off to these days.

He wasn't even quite sure what a Dunderberg Imp was. Something someone had mentioned over drinks in a local pub one night. Had to do with sailing ships and goblins and some other nonsense.

Hands in pockets, he stepped over to the south side of the chapel where, amidst overgrown weeds and crabgrass, were a bunch of old tombstones. Twenty-one to be exact. In three rows of seven. The rearmost row looked to be the oldest, so Knightbridge started there.

These tombstones were tilted at odd angles and carved out of some sort of soft limestone. The inscriptions were barely legible in some areas, completely worn off in others. The stones were stained with old moss and countless winters. Knightbridge had to squat down on his haunches and peer in closely to make out what scant information was left.

None of the graves were family - that much was immediately apparent. They all appeared to be officers, with Dutch names, and they all passed away in a period between the late 1630s and the early 1650s. Nothing too odd about that, aside from the fact that someone had elected to bury a bunch of officers in a private family graveyard. One thing Knightbridge did know was that Van Eyckmann's relatives had first staked their claim on this particular piece of real estate in 1634. He also recalled that the first Van Eyckmann to land his feet in the New World was a sea captain. Which still didn't explain why the officers were buried here. Unless they were still serving their captain or were here at Taron Hall for some other reason. But why chose to be buried here? Why not sent back to wherever their respective families were?

Questions.

Knightbridge quickly set them aside, as it was all idle speculation until he could get more facts. Intel. He crab-walked over to the next row of tombstones. These were all cut from the same reddish-brown stone that was popular amongst the colonists in the 1700s. The folk art adornments and distinct scrolling letters were another tip-off.

This group proved an odder mystery.

Again, no Van Eyckmann's pushing up the daisies here. Seven men with seven different names and seven different birth dates with one common denominator: they all died in 1750. On the same date. October 31st.

The ones in the third row were in the best condition, having been carved of polished gray granite. Again, the same pattern as the second row except this group all slipped their mortal coils in the year 1880. Which, put together with the dates inside the chapel, added up to some seriously fishy business. What kind of fishy business, Knightbridge couldn't even guess. Ritual suicide? Every 130 years? He'd never heard of such a thing. He went back to the first graves and began to write all the names and dates down on his notepad. After five minutes, he stood up, knees popping. A cold feeling was beginning to settle at the bottom of his stomach.

That sinking feeling that time was running out.

It was October the 31st. 130 years to the day after the last group wound up in this graveyard. And there were seven guests staying tonight at Taron Hall. It didn't take a rocket scientist to figure out that if something wasn't done – and quick – there would be seven fresh graves in the family plot tomorrow.

The question was *what?*
Knightbridge put his notepad away and headed back to Taron Hall.
This time, he was running.

11. MISSING PERSONS AND VOICES IN THE DARK

The cellar of Taron Hall had two means of access. The first was via a circular stone staircase located under the stairs of the main hall. The second was through a small entryway under the front stairs that was cleverly concealed by a pair of mulberry bushes. Using the latter might appear odd to anyone observing him, so Knightbridge opted for the straightforward approach. He went in through the front door and headed straight for the cellar door.

As he passed the parlor to the left, he ran almost dead on into Hilderman who was coming down the main staircase.

"Mr. Knightbridge! We've been looking for you. A moment of your time, if you please!"

Knightbridge pulled up short and shot Hilderman a clearly annoyed look. "Now's not necessarily a good time, Mr. Hilderman."

"Now is certainly the time, Mr. Knightbridge. Mr. Matthews has gone off his rocker and assaulted Mr. Washington! I insist you find and detain him immediately!"

This at least got his attention. "Matthews? Explain."

"In the conservatory a few minutes ago, Mr. Washington was knocked unconscious. The man is violent and clearly unstable, I insist..."

"Noted." Knightbridge cut him off. "I have some pressing business at the moment but will be glad to look into it shortly. I'll contact my security and have them locate Mr. Easton directly."

Hilderman was glaring at him. His voice took on a steely tone: "The man is a menace! I..."

"NOTED, Mr. Hilderman." A muscle on the right of Knightbridge's jaw began to twitch. Hilderman hadn't even noticed the switch in names. He pressed it once more. "I'll take care of it. Besides, Mr. Hilderman, I believe you were the one responsible for bringing him into this mess. Easton, that is."

"I'm afraid I don't know who..."

"Save it, Mr. Hilderman. I assure you I will take care of it promptly."

Without waiting for a reply, he turned on his heels and ducked through the arch under the stairs, leaving Hilderman with his finger pointed in the air and a mixed expression of anger and surprise on his face.

With their rough-cut stone and old oak beams, the cellar stairs suggested that they might lead down into a medieval dungeon or a mad doctor's laboratory. The wall sconces had been converted to electricity at some point during the 20th century, when bulbs were small and dim and cast only a feeble glow. The smell of must and damp and old things left in the dark too long hung in the stairwell like a frail old relative with no place left to go. Knightbridge had grabbed a Maglite from the low shelf by the door (being the sort that stored flashlights and other necessities at key areas around his base of operations) but kept it off for the moment. He knew from previous experience that the basement at Taron Hall was a rabbit warren of rooms and hallways added piecemeal over the centuries and the unwary could get lost down there for hours, days, maybe even eternity.

Mostly it was storage rooms filled with junk, but it also included a furnace room, a laundry area, a well-stocked wine cellar, and a large workshop with enough benches, lathes, saws, clamps and equipment to turn out some serious furniture if anyone had a mind to do so. Although from the few times Knightbridge had popped his head in there, it looked like no one had used the shop in decades.

There was also a utility room, a back-up wood locker, and a large meat locker. The last, located at the end of a short hallway that turned at right angles to the back of the house just under the kitchen, was where Van Eyckmann's body had been placed as per his specific instructions until he could be entombed in the chapel. There was to be no embalming or preparing of the body other than to dress him in his best suit.

At the bottom of the main stairs was a fairly large Great Room with a heavy beamed ceiling and diamond-paned half windows on the north and south walls. The windows were latched and made of yellow glass that had buckled in places from a losing struggle with hot and cold over the years. Knightbridge had been pushing Van Eyckmann to either rip them out and replace them with more secure, modern windows or at least to have them framed in from the outside as they were a major security risk. His requests had repeatedly fallen on deaf ears and nothing had been done about them. The room also contained a huge stone fireplace with years of dust accumulated on its mantel, an old staghorn chandelier suspended in the center of the room that looked like it had been lifted from a Bavarian hunting lodge, and a bunch of heavy tables and chairs stacked up against one wall. The hearth was framed by old-fashioned Dutch-style blue and white tiles depicting river scenes. To one side of it was a wood locker, the other a set of built-in shelves. The room appeared to have been a sort of auxiliary banquet hall at some point in its past.

A door to the east led into a short hallway with a series of storage rooms and a hidden exit under the front entrance. On either side of the door were old floor-to-ceiling built-in cabinets with glass-fronted doors, now filled with broken crockery, assorted junk, and assorted spiders, the latter mostly of the large, bloated, and leathery kind one always seems to find in forgotten corners of old houses.

Knightbridge went through the archway to the west and followed the hall to the meat locker. Before it was another door set discreetly in an old stone archway. This led to the real Mad Doctor's Laboratory where Van Eyckmann conducted his private experiments and indulged in his private activities. It was also the one door Knightbridge didn't have a key to and, being a man who knew when to stay ignorant, he left well enough alone. The meat locker, however, was lit by a series of caged bulbs that had been strung from the ceiling. At the end of the hallway was the massive door with its oversized steel-hinge latches right next to a dumb-waiter that went to the kitchen above. The locker had enough square footage to stash away an army's supply of food for six months. It also had, in addition to sinks and a preparation area, a large stainless steel table in its center where packages were often piled when first brought in. It was the same table Knightbridge had laid a plastic sheet on before he laid out Van Eyckmann's body after the frantic call had come in from the head housekeeper three days before. *I found him in his bedroom this morning. He isn't moving or breathing and he's as cold as ice – please come right away.*

The locker had no outside windows and was lined floor to ceiling with tile. It was airtight, of course. It had been constructed in the 1920s by a German engineering contractor brought over especially for the job with what was then state-of-the-art technology. Which still worked fine nearly 90 years later.

Knightbridge pulled out his keys again, fanned through them, and, after two tries, found the correct one for the locker. Intimidating as the door was, it swung open quite easily on well-oiled hinges once the latch was pulled. It had been designed so that even a diminutive house servant could open it readily enough.

Knightbridge stepped in and flipped the bank of switches on the inside right wall as he entered. Rows of overhead fixtures came on and brought the room into overly bright, sharp relief.

He stopped in mid stride, eyes registering alarm, a single word coming out under his breath, barely audible.

"Fuck."

The table was empty.

The chapel was nearly pitch black.

Easton came up to the main doors and gave the handle a shake. The door gave a little bit, but wouldn't budge more than that.

Some joker had locked him in.

For the second time that day, Easton gave himself a swift mental kick for quitting smoking. If he hadn't, he would have at least had his trusty Zippo lighter in his pocket.

Goddammit!

He patted his pockets anyhow, just out of reflex. Nada.

Then he turned and banged with both fists on the doors.

"Hello!!? Anybody out there? Hey, open up!" he yelled. "Anybody!?"

Nothing. He thought he could hear the faint crunch of footsteps on gravel walking away. Some bastard had just locked him in here. But why? Wasn't he required to be at the formal dinner in a few hours, dressed in some ridiculous costume?

Or had the rules changed? And the next question – who? One of the Mohican Club members? Or someone else...Kimmi, perhaps?

He banged the door one last time in frustration, then turned around to face the twilight gloom of the chapel. There was a dirt-smudged rosette of stained glass over the door that let in some of the waning light from outside, but not much. Like the rest of the chapel, it had apparently been put on the Ten Most Neglected list, and near the top at that. Easton paced up to the small pulpit, turned around, paced back to the doors again.

Now what?

He didn't have a clue.

Knightbridge was back at the Hall. Easton realized that the most likely scenario was that someone from the house had locked him in here, and, unless one of the other two men working security chanced by, he could scream at the top of his lungs until he was blue in the face.

He climbed up onto the small stage area and began to check the walls on either side of the crucifix for any signs of a second door.

Nothing.

Christ, didn't these people believe in fire codes or anything? Right. Does the Pope shit in the woods?

Easton wasn't one to give up easily. He was on his third pass of the back walls, perhaps thinking he could wish a door into existence, when he paused. Something had caught his eye from the periphery of his vision.

The hairs began to rise on the back of his neck.

Turning slowly, he realized he wasn't alone in the chapel. Someone was sitting in the pews.

It was a woman.

Even in the murky light, Easton could make that out quickly enough. She was seated near the back, perfectly still with hands folded in her lap, her demeanor suggesting someone who had been waiting patiently for hours. He couldn't make out much more, other than that she was on the small side, had long straight hair, and had a very straight, almost regal posture.

Easton was completely stumped.

She wasn't there when he came in. Of that, he was positive. He definitely hadn't heard the front doors open or close. He'd be willing to swear frontwards and backwards on a Bible on that score. All evidence suggested she had materialized out of thin air. Which was, of course, impossible.

Ergo, there must be another explanation. A secret entrance perhaps? Not impossible at all, given the age of the estate. Which begged the next two questions: who was she and what on earth was she doing here?

Silence stretched on for seconds. Then minutes.

Easton took a step forward, hands clasped in front.

"Hello?"

His voice sounded abnormally loud in the musty air.

More silence. He let another minute tick by. The whole thing was now striking him as odd. Not scary. Just odd. There was no sense of threat or danger, just the sense that this woman was simply sitting there, patiently. Watching him. Waiting?

Now Easton was curious.

He stepped off the stage and walked down the aisle toward her casually, as if he was out for a stroll on a sunny afternoon in the park instead of locked in a neglected mortuary chapel with a mysterious apparition on, well, Halloween.

The woman continued to look straight forward, even as Easton drew near the pew she was seated in. He sensed her eyes following him. One row away he stepped in and leaned against the back of a pew.

"Hi," he said. "Any idea how one might get out of here?"

The face turned quietly towards him, fading sunlight from the rosette window catching one cheek.

Easton's eyes widened.

She was extraordinarily beautiful, he could see that at a glance. And exotic. Asian? Southeast Asian? Very possibly. He couldn't quite put his finger on it but there was an unusual slant to her features that defied ready classification. And as someone who had looked carefully at a lot of faces in his career, that was a rarity. After a while, one starts to see repeating patterns in specific features, one person reminds you of another you crossed paths with, or interviewed. Or arrested.

Not this woman. She appeared to occupy her own exclusive category.

She had large almond eyes, roundish, and pronounced cheekbones. A fine upper lip with a full lower one – an aristocrat's mouth – but one that appeared to be on the verge of a smile. With her deep bronze complexion, she might have been some imaginative sculptor's dream of the Far East.

That was all Easton could tell. She appeared to be wearing a simple, non-descript dress. She was either freezing or had the constitution of an Eskimo. She also didn't appear to be in any hurry to supply him with any answers.

Easton decided it was up to him to get the ball rolling. He'd also decided he'd had enough of this damned Grant Matthews charade. Money be damned.

"I'm Easton. John Easton. Who are you?"

She turned and looked at him with a concerned expression. "Who do you think I am?" Her voice had a musical, almost sing-song quality. He couldn't place it.

"I don't know. Who are you?"

Pause. "You don't know?"

This was getting cryptic. "No, I'm quite certain we've never met before. I never forget a face." Even as he said it, however, Easton realized he wasn't completely sure. Sitting in this chapel with a mystery woman who might have dropped in from another planet, he realized he wasn't sure of anything.

And yet she did seem familiar.

Easton chuckled. Where else would one meet a woman like this? Locked in a mortuary chapel, naturally. On Halloween. Happens all the time. Of course. Why not?

Well, he could think of a whole list of why nots.

For the moment though, he decided he would play along.

"Actually, no. I don't know. Now let's try this again. I'm John Easton. And you are...?"

She looked directly into his eyes then. Easton got his second surprise in as many minutes. They were deep and hypnotic brown eyes, old and as mysterious as the Orient. And yet...something else...he had an uncanny feeling he could stop everything right there and stare into those eyes for an eternity. Longer, if necessary.

Again, a long silence that would have been awkward under any other circumstance.

Then: "Aun-mai."

She spoke it with her odd accent, as if the syllables accelerated out of her mouth.

He cocked his head. "Sorry?"

"Aun-mai."

For a rare moment, Easton was unable to think of anything to say. What came out sounded like "Shhmmmph." More of a snort than a word. Followed by: "Well. That's...that's...well, that's quite a beautiful name actually." He immediately felt like a horse's ass. What an incredibly idiotic comment! Easton mentally kicked himself. Get it together, old man. A little long in the tooth to start acting like a blushing school-boy. Next thing I'll be shuffling my feet and wringing my hands. Good Christ! Mercifully she didn't respond.

Easton cleared his throat. "Well, Aun-mai, a pleasure making your acquaintance. Now, just out of curiosity, how did you get in here?"

She stared at him, looked briefly over her shoulder at the front doors, then back at him again. Easton raised his eyebrows. Then looked over at the doors. They looked as locked as ever. He looked back at her.

"You came in through those doors behind you?"

This time a little smile snuck across her lips.

Easton had a hunch he was being teased. He also had a hunch he wasn't much in the mood for it. "Look, Aun-mai, I don't know why you're here, or how you really got in here, but I..." To his surprise, she jumped to her feet and swiftly stepped right up to him and without any hesitation put her finger to his lips. She shook her head slowly side-to-side. He could smell her – a hint of oranges and cinnamon mingled with a deeper, muskier scent. How unusual, he thought. He realized her face was only inches from his own. Drawing him in with those damn eyes. For a crazy moment he thought she was going to kiss him. Instead she spoke.

"They are just doors..." cryptically, then: "But I have something for you."

"Really."

"Yes." With that she reached over and picked up a large bundle wrapped in a musty, heavy cloth. Easton hadn't noticed it earlier. The cloth was an indigo blue and smelled like it had sat in an attic (or tomb) somewhere for a very long time. He was fairly sure there had been nothing on the pews earlier but couldn't swear to it.

"What is it?"

She stepped back and held the bundle up for him. "For you. Tonight."

He carefully took the bundle from her – it felt somewhat heavy – and removed the cloth. It was a sword in its scabbard. Quite an antique from the looks of it. Certainly one meant for business, though Easton could hardly be called an expert on such things. It had a solid leather-bound grip and a utilitarian hilt of braided metal chased in silver. The scabbard appeared to be made of some lacquered leather also chased with silver trim. He pulled the sword partway out. The blade looked pitted and weathered but still gleamed with an edge on it. Someone had recently oiled and sharpened it. He could just make out an engraved Latin inscription:

"Verus Cor Justitia"

Easton was a little rusty – a lot rusty, actually – on his secondary school Latin, but if he wasn't mistaken the second two words meant "Core of Justice". Vera. Verae. Verus. True. Cor. Core. Heart. The True Heart of Justice then. That gave him pause. A memory tickled around the edges of his thoughts. Then he shook his head.

Coincidence. Had to be.

He closed the weapon with a solid clack.

"Aun-mai, what is this? I mean, where did you get this?"

"For you. Tonight," she repeated.

The penny dropped. He had completely forgotten. "Ah. For the dinner. The costume." It all began to make sense. She must be one of the two maids he hadn't met. But then...Easton seized automatically at the rational solution. Maid. Costume. Sword. Maybe a bit of a joke, one of Hilderman's boys having a little fun with him. Or even Knightbridge. Halloween prank. That made more sense. Knightbridge was the only one who knew he'd be headed to the chapel. Of course.

Still holding the sword in both hands, Easton smiled and gave a short bow.

"Thank you."

She smiled back at him, a genuine smile that lit up her face and made his heart leap just a tick, and said something that sounded to his ears like "Sintakammu." He had no idea what she had said, but the sound of the words was almost sensual. Not quite. More like a promise.

Easton cocked an eyebrow. "Sorry?"

Aun-mai shook her head as if to clear it. "Semiga Beruntung," she said, equally as cryptic. Seeing his nonplussed expression she added, "Good luck." Then, in a reflexive gesture, she brushed his cheek with her fingers. Her touch was cool and soothing.

"I'll need it." Easton struggled for a moment with the urge to grab her palm and kiss it. And with it came a sense he wanted to linger here with her a little longer. Instead, he tucked the bundled sword under his arm and headed to the doors. He gave the handle a shove. It swung open with a creak of protest. Unlocked. Of course.

They are just doors.

"I hope to see you..." Easton trailed off as he looked back, "...later."

There was no one there.

Of course.

Knightbridge was tapping his fist on the door jamb.

"Fuck a duck," he said. Then he hit the jamb as hard as he could. He'd been in similar situations before. Usually military operations where, for any one or more of a number of reasons, a mission just went FUBAR. Fucked

Up Beyond All Recognition. Incompetent leadership. Incompetent planning. Bad intel. Sudden change in the weather. All of the above.

Generally he had a pretty good instinct when a situation was starting to go south.

He was definitely getting that feeling right now.

The cats. Grant Matthews kicking the bucket. Easton getting roped in and decking Washington. Things were starting to fray around the edges. Including his nerves.

But not much. Knightbridge was in his element when things starting rocking and rolling. It was prolonged inactivity where he began to get sloppy. Even so, this was definitely a major problem. His major problem. If someone had come in and snatched the body of the great Lars Van Eyckmann himself, right under Knightbridge's nose, then there was going to be hell to pay. In spades. Frowning, he did a cursory search of the locker, then proceeded to check through each room in the entire basement.

The ancient octopus of a furnace. The wine cellar that cost a small fortune (in particular, the four bottles of 1907 Hiedsieck champagne and one bottle of 1945 Chateau Mouton Rothschild that together would have topped a cool million – Knightbridge waltzed straight past those without blinking an eye). He did a quick once-over of the various storage rooms but the undisturbed layers of dust told him what he needed to know.

No body. No sign one was there.

Knightbridge stepped over to the window where the reception would be better and took out his handset.

"Wallace. McGoohan. Come in." He pressed the send button. The speaker gave out a cough of static.

Nothing.

"I said, come in."

Send. Another cough of static.

He looked up at the ceiling. "Over. Anybody there?"

Nothing. Empty airwaves.

Bloody Hell.

Probably had their sets off and were sitting around playing video games or wanking off to porno movies. Dammit. He checked his watch. 3:05 PM. He needed to get the house searched immediately from top to bottom and he was going to need help to do it. First things first, however. Upstairs to find out what in the hell had happened to Washington.

He found them on the second floor in Washington's bedroom, which was located at the southeast corner of the house. The room was enormous, with a bay window overlooking the front lawn and a fireplace situated directly over the one in the downstairs sitting room. A stack of birch logs was burning brightly in the grate, lending a suggestion of warmth to the drafty room. He passed Juanita DeVera, the older of the two maids, leaving with her hands crossed and perpetually downcast expression – whenever Knightbridge ran into her she always had the doomed look of someone awaiting an imminent tragedy – as she exited the bedroom.

The room was furnished much in the same fashion of all the guest rooms. Best as Knightbridge could figure, one of the Van Eyckmann's had hired an interior decorator to overhaul them sometime in the mid-1800s and left it at that. Aside from the upstairs being wired for electricity sometime in the late 1930s, the rooms looked like a movie set for a period film about a dying aristocracy.

Washington was on the four-poster bed, propped up against the headboard with a bunch of pillows, with one of those blue sports ice packs pressed against his jaw and a glowering look in his eye. Lefferts was seated next to him, lips pursed, idly toying with a tall glass of ice water with his fingertips. Hilderman was standing by the bay window, apparently studying something of interest out in the yard. Wang and Delgado were seated on an ornate Victorian couch near the fireplace, Delgado flipping through an International Décor magazine he had dredged up someplace, while Wang was riffling through a copy of Wired until he found the article on the latest iPad he'd been looking for. He didn't appear too happy about whatever updates the hip technology magazine was feeding him. If it weren't for the furrowed brow, he could have been a poster boy for Apple. Derek Anderson was nowhere to be seen.

All eyes zeroed in on Knightbridge as he stepped into the room. He tended to have that effect on groups. Hilderman half turned, one eyebrow cocked in irritation.

"Nice of you to join us, Mr. Knightbridge."

Ignoring the sarcasm, he replied, "My pleasure. Now what's this about a scuffle in the conservatory?"

Delgado was the first to pipe up. "Scuffle? Scuffle!!? The man is a brute! He broke Geoffrey's jaw, for heaven's sake. You need to arrest him! He's a…"

"Thank-you, Mr. Delgado." Knightbridge said, cutting him off before his hysterics could get under sail. He strode over to the bed and took a quick look over Washington.

"Let's have a look now." He pulled the ice pack away from the larger man's jaw and turned his face this way and that. There was a decent-sized lump and the skin was beginning to bruise but Knightbridge figured he'd live. Though hardly a qualified doctor, Knightbridge knew enough about trauma in the field to assess the difference between serious, not-quite-serious, and for chrissakes stop being a sissy. This case was somewhere between the second and third.

"I expect you'll recover, Mr. Washington, with a couple of aspirin and ample use of that ice-pack. Now, would you care to tell me what happened?"

Washington continued to glare like a sulking bully and didn't answer.

"Fine, I'll be happy to track down Mr. Easton and have a word with him. Now if there's nothing else, I have a few other pressing things to look into."

Delgado slapped down his magazine and looked at Knightbridge in alarm. "Nothing else! Look at the poor man, he's ..."

This time it was Hilderman who cut him off. "Put a sock in it, Juan. Mr. Knightbridge, I'd like to have a word with you if you don't mind. Now."

"As you wish. Will this be a family discussion or shall we speak somewhere else in private?"

"In private."

They ended up in a small oak-paneled room down the hall that had been converted to a telephone room sometime in the last century. It had a bench, a chair, two framed water colors of duck hunting on the Hudson, and an oak writing desk next to which was mounted an ancient telephone, the wooden box type with the fluted ear piece connected by a cloth cord, double chrome-plated bells, and a hand crank on the side. Though clean, the room looked like no one had had occasion to use it in the last hundred years.

Hilderman closed the glass-paned door for privacy.

"All right then, Mr. Knightbridge, let's lay some cards on the table. Obviously, you've uncovered the truth behind Mr. Matthew's identity. Does Lowe know?

"He suspects."

"Does he plan to act on his suspicions?"

"Well, Mr. Hilderman, I can't speak for what he will or won't do, but no, I seriously doubt he'll act on what he knows. Van Eyckmann is dead. There's no immediately family barking around here for handouts. Everybody plays along, everybody gets their pay day."

"Very good. Then we all understand each other. I am concerned however, about Mr. Easton. Can I rely on you to keep him in line until tomorrow morning?"

"I'll have a word with him. I'm not sure what happened this afternoon between him and Mr. Washington, but Easton doesn't strike me as an impulsive sort or quick to anger. But there's a much more pressing problem. We seem to have a problem around here with old corpses popping up and new ones disappearing."

"Come again?"

"It's Mr. Van Eyckmann. His body's gone."

126

"What!!?"

"Gone. Vamoose. Flew the coop. Mr. Hilderman, I don't know what in the blue hell is going on here, but someone is fucking with us. My job is to maintain a safe and secure situation around here and I take my job very seriously. So if you have any information that might shed some light on these events, I think you'd better tell me. Now."

Hilderman's response was to bow his head and rub the bridge of his nose with his thumb and forefinger. "Christ almighty. Gone?"

"Gone." Knightbridge considered his next words carefully. "Look, Mr. Hilderman, I'm well aware of why you and your colleagues are here. But I'm going to go out on a limb here to be square with you: I may not like you personally, or your associates, but I have to tell you I have reasons – strong reasons – to believe staying here at Taron Hall tonight is an extremely bad idea. For all of us. I know about the money and I know about Van Eyckmann's peculiar will. I also know that none of that is worth a kangaroo turd if you're not alive to spend it. I don't say that lightly. I think the smartest course of action would be to load everybody up and go book a suite of rooms at Mad Anthony's Inn in town and come sort this out in the morning."

Hilderman looked at him sideways. Knightbridge could clearly see the suspicious gleam in his eye. "That's a pretty strong statement, Mr. Knightbridge. Do you have some specific information that our lives are in danger?"

"Not…anything I care to share just yet. Listen, Mr. Hilderman, I'm a combat vet-"

Hilderman put his hand up. "Yes, yes, of course, Mr. Knightbridge. I know all about your glorious history in the Falklands and Middle East…" Knightbridge could see the almost smug look on his face – the look of a civilian who had no concept of what a front-line veteran went through outside of what he learned from too many bad movies and story books – and knew he was about to be dismissed. "…but I'm afraid we have a bargain to fulfill with the late Lars Van Eyckmann and we are men of our word. Your concerns are noted, but we are staying as per our original plan. I expect you to do your job and stay vigilant. And I expect to hear back from you once Mr., er, Easton, has been located."

Knightbridge fought down the strong urge to backhand Hilderman. He'd lost count of the times he'd seen the same idiotic self-confidence on the battlefield. Usually preceding a lot of people getting killed. But he also knew he had no concrete evidence to call the whole thing off. He was wasting his time here. He had to get over to the gatekeeper's house, get his team to put their asses in gear, then find Easton. Then locate Van Eyckmann's missing corpse.

"Very well, Mr. Hilderman. We'll talk again shortly." He opened the door and stepped out onto the rich carpet of the hallway. Hilderman was leaning against the desk, arms folded and staring off into space.

The next time the two men would meet, one of them would be dying.

12. THE VOYAGE OF THE BLACK DRAGON

Easton entered through the kitchen just as Knightbridge was trotting out the front door. Such are the quirky paths of fate: had both men chosen the same entrance, subsequent events might have turned out differently. Might being the operative word.

Then again, as Easton had observed, there was a certain inevitability to so many things in life.

He ran into Juanita stacking dishes from lunch on a sideboard next to the sink.

"Pardon, ah, buenos dias, Senorita."

Juanita immediately stopped what she was doing and faced Easton, drying her hands on her apron. She managed to fish up a feeble smile, though she looked at him worriedly as if he were certain to tell her something terrible. "Bueno."

Easton thought for a second, flipping through his smattering of Spanish and finding only meager scraps. "Sorry, but the other, ahm, maid?" He wasn't sure how much was getting through. Juanita's eyebrows went up slightly.

"Maid? Ahhhh, yes, yes! Maid!"

Easton attempted a gesture with his hands. "Other maid. Is she young? Uh, uh, jovenes? Si?"

Juanita processed this for a second. "Ah, yes, jovenes, bueno!"

"And pretty? What what, bonito? Um, muy bonito? Yes? I mean si?

Juanita's lips grew into a full smile. She nodded vigorously. "Ah, muy bonito! Bueno! Bueno!"

Easton felt he was getting somewhere. "And ah, her name is Aun-mai? Si?" A pause while the penny dropped. He could almost see the gears turning in her head.

"Yes, yes. Si!"

The words hung in the air for a moment. Easton wasn't quite sure what else to ask. He also wasn't quite sure he'd gotten the answer he was looking for. Finally he shrugged. "Well, thanks for clearing that up." With that, he turned and headed out towards the main hallway.

Juanita seemed pleased he was satisfied but found his English accent very confusing and difficult. The same with the man Hilderman. But she felt she had grasped the main point this nice Englishman was trying to make. Her husband, Tom Mackenany, a local roofing contractor in Wyvern Falls, was very close with his Aunt May who lived in New York City. Apparently this Englishman knew her and was paying her compliments by saying she was young and beautiful. She couldn't wait to get home and tell him later.

Upstairs in the telephone room, Hilderman stood in the same position Knightbridge had left him, one arm across his chest, the other bent, finger tapping his chin, thinking. Things were definitely, most definitely, not going to plan. He had been working towards this night for years, a query here, a prod there, an innocent question casually dropped into a conversation then quickly masked by dropping the subject. Hilderman could run a conversation like a master magician's act when he wanted to. Verbal sleights of hand, clever redirects.

He'd found out about Van Eyckmann's bizarre will a year and half ago by pure chance during a lunch with Bill Lowe at Smith and Wollensky's on Third Avenue, somewhere around the second half of Lowe's third martini. He immediately began making mental notes, Hilderman style: 20 mil. Twenty-four hours, Taron Hall. Who could he count on? Who was expendable? Drawing sides, connecting numbers, dates.

The trick about came about a month ago when Lowe rang him up for some advice on an engineering lawsuit he was handling. Another lunch, this time at Delmonico's. Bill was still on his first martini when he started babbling on about Van Eyckmann's erratic behavior, the arrival of Kimmi, the premonition that he would die on or near Halloween, just the same as every other male Van Eyckmann had done time and time again. They were a cursed family. Preparations had to be made. Hilderman listened, his mind pouncing on possibilities like a cat at its prey.

Hilderman didn't believe in curses. But he was a firm believer in the power of green.

Matthews was already becoming a serious liability and would have to go soon or he was going to blow it for all of them. In fact, Hilderman didn't like the pattern he was seeing: all the executive members of the Mohican Club falling into various financial straits almost simultaneously. Hilderman didn't believe in coincidences either.

As the saying went, the first time is happenstance, the second time is coincidence, the third time is enemy action.

So he began laying his own plans.

The day after Van Eyckmann's death he took the train up to Taron Hall, ostensibly to assist with the arrangements (as one of Van Eyckmann's personal friends) and ensure all was running smoothly. In reality to find out if there was any additional angle he could find to stack things in his favor. What Knightbridge would have called intel.

What he found was Kimmi.

They had a long and interesting talk in Van Eyckmann's study, while Hilderman sat in Van Eyckmann's chair and smoked Van Eyckmann's tobacco and pondered what it would be like to control Van Eyckmann's vast finances and be lord of his manor. As Kimmi talked, it began to look like more and more of a real possibility. A mansion like Taron Hall would be, well, befitting a man of Hilderman's ambition and stature. He wondered what his wife would think and what their first dinner party would be like.

Every man has his Achilles' heel, it is said.

Even before money, Hilderman's was Pride. He briefly wondered what the faces of his associates would look like when he brought them to Taron Hall.

But, standing in the telephone room, he was beginning to have his first creeping doubts, which was so un-Hilderman-like that it took him a few moments to grasp that was what they were. It dawned on him that maybe Kimmi was much more than he had originally guessed and that maybe, just maybe, he wasn't a lead player here but a pawn in someone else's game.

It took a few minutes for Easton to locate the staircase to the basement. He poked around for a good ten minutes, calling out Knightbridge's name, before giving up without finding any sign of him. Before heading upstairs to his bedroom, Easton stopped off in the dining room, where he'd seen some decent bottles of single-malt scotch on the sideboard. Oblivious to the caterers bustling about the room with -ike efficiency, after some consideration he poured himself a hearty glass of the Bunnahabhain, a twelve-year-old Isle of Islay Scotch with a rich caramel color. He took a tentative sip and decided it was a keeper. It had a full-bodied flavor and a smoky aftertaste that seemed perfect on a cool autumn afternoon. In a habit most would consider a sacrilege, he tossed in a couple of ice cubes for good measure and headed up the main staircase.

He could hear a heated discussion coming from Washington's room in the front and bee-lined for his bedroom in the back. Someone had laid a fire in the hearth while he'd been out. Outside, the trees were swaying and the cold fingers of the autumn wind snatched and rattled the windows. He set the bundled sword down on the dresser and walked over to the porch windows.

He had to admit that he was intrigued by this latest encounter. Who was this Aun-mai, really? Was she even real? The sword on the dresser made a pretty compelling case for her reality but then how had she gotten in and out of the chapel without him seeing or hearing anything? Which, being nearly impossible without some sort of trick, suggested another question: was this some sort of setup? If so, by who and to what end? Too many questions trailing off into too many directions. Easton at least had enough sense to know when he was chasing his own tail and let it go. Kicking his shoes off, he set the glass on the end table and dropped onto the bed with a bounce. He bunched up some pillows and propped himself up against the headboard, then took a long pull off his Scotch and let its warm tendrils flow through his veins. He decided then and there that there was nothing better he could think of than enjoying a cool glass of excellent Scotch on a biting fall day.

After a few minutes ticked by, he remembered the small booklet he'd found earlier and fished it out of his jacket pocket. Cracking it open he looked at the title again:

Being a short account of the Black Dragon
on her maiden voyage to the East Indies,
1619-1622
Lieutenant Piers Maynard

Certainly nothing he had ever heard of before. Which wasn't surprising as it appeared to be an obscure account of an obscure voyage. Why on earth it was left sitting in a neglected mortuary chapel he had no idea. Obviously someone had dropped it there, by accident or by design. He checked his watch. He had nearly two hours before dinner, plenty of time to catch up on a little history.

First, Easton reviewed what he knew about the Spice Trade, cobbled together from years of reading historic accounts, one of his private hobbies. (He was particularly a buff on the history of buccaneers and the Spanish Main but he gobbled up pretty much anything nautical from the 1600s onward.) He recalled that it was a tumultuous time. The East Indies, specifically the Moluccas, were originally monopolized by Arabic traders, the Portuguese, with the Spanish muscling in during the 1500s. South of the main island of Ambon were the Banda Islands, the only place in the world at that time where nutmeg was grown. By the 1600s, aggressive Dutch campaigning had resulting in their monopolizing the spice trade, particularly in nutmeg and mace (with pepper trailing close behind), commodities that were worth as much as gold in a European market still clawing its way out of the Dark Ages and craving anything that would add some level of improvement to their bleak food palate. Or at least mask the poor quality of it. Once entrenched, the Dutch East India Company (VOC or "Vereenigde Oostindische Compagnie") shrewdly manipulated the market to ensure maximum profits in Europe (and even more so in India, which outstripped the Europeans in spice consumption by a wide margin) and enforced their control with a brutality only marginally matched by the Portuguese and Spanish. But in the early 1600s, the situation was far from stable or monopolized. The Dutch spice factories were continually vexed by duplicitous native merchants who appeared to change their agreements as often as they changed their clothes. There were the English, just gaining their international confidence and sea legs with the defeat of the Spanish Armada and then Queen Elizabeth's chartering the British East India Company, which began securing bases in India and then probing for trade opportunities in the area. In fact, they had set up a small outpost on Rhun Island, located just west of the main island Palau Banda 20 years earlier, openly flaunting their trading under the noses of the Dutch and treating the whole situation like it was one great big joke. But behind the scenes (and English nose-tweaking) were the political and economic chess games that would define the rest of the 17th century.

The account, as it turned out, was one of the early gambits to Rhun Island, an expedition in the spring of 1619 led by a Captain Horatio Cecil Forester, a name which vaguely resonated somewhere deep in Easton's memory. A name he'd come across in one of his many historical readings, perhaps? He paused and looked off at a distant point on the ceiling for a minute but couldn't find the connection. With a brief shake of his head he fell back to his reading.

It took him a bit to get into the archaic rhythm of the language and syntax, which was a mixture of old and modern English. The elongated double "s" that looked like a pair of "f's" continued to throw him off as did the "eth" endings. The actual language went in clunky passages like "And as sich, we setteth sail on the eve after the Sabbath on the nineteenth day of May, in the year of our Lord Sixteen Hundred and Nineteen years, set forth upon the dark sea, God's wounds...." But after a bit the narrative began to take hold and his 21st century mind began to automatically translate.

This particular book was a report by Forester's second lieutenant of that ill-fated expedition to challenge the Dutch, possibly an effort to gain some notoriety (or, more practically, additional income) through publication of the events. Or perhaps Lieutenant Maynard had some ulterior motive in mind. Difficult to say, though Easton had yet to come across anything like it. Certainly it was a time when life for a seaman outside an active commission was precarious, even for officers, and one could hardly be blamed for looking to pad one's purse by any means possible, as it were. There was a brief introduction that made mention of "varius eyewitnesses and testimony" that contributed to the telling of the account which referenced a list of names appended at the back.

The expedition had left London in early May of 1619, commissions in hand from the directors of the British East India Company, off to the Orient (Easton had to reread these passages several times to finally grasp this). The voyage was fairly routine by modern standards and got off to a good start. Winds were favorable, the three ships, one galleon and two caravels, were well stocked and morale was generally high. Forester's flagship was the five-hundred ton Black Dragon, the other two ships the Katrina and Providence, both 300-ton vessels. Lieutenant Maynard was second-in-command aboard the Black Dragon. The first chapters covered details of the ship's daily activities from Maynard's diary, told in his buttoned-down style:

Friday 26 May 1619

This day, just past seven bells, the wind grew high and though the fleet made good progress -we've come in sight of the coast and I've had my first look at Spain. Mr. Abbott, first mate, asked to borrow my glass to have a better look himself. Many of us have never been past the Coast of France or Netherlands.

Breakfast of radishes in the Morning room, ran the crew through gunnery drills on the main deck. Nicked a minute off their time, but still far too slow for my comfort.

Ordered a reef in the mainsail in the early evening as we had a very fresh gale, which brooked better than I thought I should be able to do. May God favor our endeavor!

The next few entries covered sightings of whales, waterspouts, dolphins, and flying fish (several of which were caught) as the fleet worked its way down the coast of Africa. Then the unnerving experience of St Elmo's Fire dancing around the rigging as they cleared the Cape of Good Hope through pelting rain, sleet, hail, and towering seas. Maynard reported the fleet took moderate damage, including the Katrina losing a foretopmast, yards of torn rigging, and a total of three sailors lost overboard. As small price to pay in those days. (Easton could only marvel at the tenacity and courage it took to navigate the oceans back then. It was a time when the majority of sailors didn't even know how to swim and life vests were a non-existent fantasy of the future. If a man went overboard in anything other than optimum sailing weather, there was no chance of turning about to rescue him.)

There was the usual reports of dysentery, dengue fever, scurvy, rickets. Maynard made regular visits to the ship's sick bay, run by a surgeon by the name of Dickering, to make notes on the status of the crew and check on their general well-being. Dickering, described as a lean man with a large, thin nose, thinning black hair, and "acerbic demeanor" was nonetheless a personal friend of Maynard's and the two men would often "engage in discourse over fine literature and arts over a few pints of Margate Ale into the late hours." They shared an interest in the Greek classics and Dutch Masters. From the reports, Maynard came off as a dutiful and attentive officer and surprisingly well-read for a man of poor means.

Little was mentioned directly in the account about Maynard himself, other than that he was from an under-privileged background, grew up in Surrey, and was in his early 20s at the time of the voyage. He got on well with his fellow officers except for the First Lieutenant, Miles Tattersill, who was described as "a puffed uppe Peacock better suited to preening himself than any effective duty." Tattersill was clearly one of those officers from a politically connected family that Forester was forced to take on, minimizing the effect of his incompetence by giving him as few responsibilities as possible. As to the captain, he was described as charismatic, gruff, and clearly well-liked by the crew. Maynard appeared to be in awe of him.

Friday 19 June 1619

This morning the commanders in the fleet came on board and dined here. I was joined by many officers of the Katrina including my counterpart on the Providence, Mr. Sheply, whom I am well-disposed toward, in the coach (a room outside the captain's main cabin, Easton recalled) where we supped and were very merry. On this day, however, Mr. Sheply appeared in some distress. Though it took a few quaffs of grog to draw out the source of his vexation.

The previous day the fleet had put in at the port at Benin and succeeded in the getting of provision. Fresh fruit and a number of black skinned men were acquired to fill out the crews and some of the officers (no sich luck for myself) were engaged to do some sight-seeing in the port. Mr. Sheply, as it turned out, had been to see a fortune teller of sorts – a woman of African descent, her skin the black of a moonless light and eyes dark as the deepest jungles (his words, not mine) – and the fortune she saw in his hands bode ill. She claimed to have seen visions of death, screaming skulls and burning bodies in our future. And a terrible event in store for the noble Captain and our fleet. Being a superstitious lot, the crew fell into a melancholy fit and returned in an ill temper to their ship.

I myself hold little stock in the caterwaulings of such types and take pains to avoid them at all costs. Sich women live to make trouble and vex others so that they may join in their misery....

Captain Forester and his little fleet made it intact to the Indian Ocean and over to Calicut within eight months for more provisions and a little side trading. The English had already established several ports and a thriving trade conduit with China. Then it was off for a game of dodge-and-weave with the Dutch through Malaysia and the Molucca Islands, picking up a little more trade on the way at Bantam. Finally, after a year at sea, they sailed boldly into port at Fort Nassau on the island of Palau Banda, calling on the flummoxed Dutch harbor officials and offering to trade. (Their offer was politely refused – Maynard noted that he was amazed the fort didn't send them off with a broadside up their arse). After cheekily announcing themselves at Banda, Forester sailed for Palau Rhun to the west to support the beleaguered garrison the English had there already.

Five years earlier, the Bandanese locals had signed a contract accepting the King of England as their sovereign but the British foothold in the Banda chain was tenuous at best. And since the spring, things had taken a distinct turn for the worse – the Dutch had sent a new Governor VOC -to clean things up and set the situation to rights: A captain by the name of Lucas Van Eyckmann.

Still, Captain Forester had a few aces up his sleeve, the foremost being the goods he had to trade with – steel, copper, medicines, and even some Chinese porcelain he had acquired in the short layovers in Bantam and Calicut. And weapons. Cannon, powder, and shot. The Dutch, in the meantime, were still trying to pawn off heavy wool, damasks, and basically junk goods, which the Bandanese merchants were far too savvy to be interested in.

So for nearly a year, Forester and his men were set up at Palau Rhun and trading for spices right under the noses of the Dutch, treating the whole thing like it was one big joke. It was a good set up. Every few weeks, Forester would send one of his ships back to India, laden with nutmeg and mace and anything else they could barter for. Half the product would be shipped back to England while the other half, at a much higher profit, would be sold locally to the Indians, who were far outstripping the European market in their insatiable desire for spices.

For Forester and his crew, the island was a tropical paradise. Brilliant skies, white beaches, turquoise waters, unlimited sweet meats and fresh fruits, and a near-celebrity status amongst the Bandanese women. Women who believed in a seriously reduced amount of fabric coverage compared to their European counterparts. For most of the crews growing up in northern Europe at the tail end of the Dark Ages, they had died and awoken in heaven.

Sunday 6 June 1620
(The Lord's Day). Very calm and hot. Rose and drank a good morning draught with Mr. Pickering on the quarterdeck, the sunrise brilliant and clouds piled up as if painted there by a Dutch Master. Accompanied the Captain last night to a feast of sorts held ashore. The Captain has done well with the native merchants here. I myself came acquainted with a young local – Sera – an exceedingly pretty lass. I'm fairly smitten I believe! But too much wine last night and now my head akes so…Mr. Newberry, our ship's chaplain, is shortly to commence his sermon for the men and I fear the Captain is still dead asleep….

Forester and his officers quickly fell in with the orang kayas – the caste of wealthy Bandanese merchants who controlled the purse strings of all the local trade, in particular nutmeg and mace. Maynard recounted several of the elaborate feasts and one in particular, hosted by one of the more cunning merchants, a fellow by the name of Khali-mior, or Datuk Khali-mior. Over the course of months, Forester had become close friends with him, both apparently sharing a roguish streak and knack for bluff and daring and a love of good liquor, though Maynard clearly didn't trust the merchant and cited his "elusive manners concerning matters of importe" suggesting he was quite the slippery customer. Khali-mior was also possessed of five beautiful daughters, all of whom he adored (as well as possessing a harem of seven ladies who the sailors all adored.) He was also, despite his congenial manner towards his guests, vehemently against his daughters getting involved with any foreigners, English, Dutch, or otherwise. Nor would he allow any of them to marry below what he saw as their proper station, which narrowed their options considerably.

Which may have been the idea.

The youngest daughter, as is so often the case, was the most free-spirited and head-strong. She was also the most striking of the five girls and there was something about her, something in her aura, energy, smell – words outside Maynard's limited vocabulary but hinted at in his clumsy descriptors – that made the sagest of men lose their minds. A real head-turner apparently. Her name was Akma and apparently it was her primary mission in life to push her father's patience well beyond its recognizable boundaries and nudge him right up to the edge of a nervous breakdown. Certainly Maynard, whose austere writing style tottered on the verge of stodgy, was completely smitten as well.

Khali-mior was apparently one of the more important ruling merchants in Banda and as such had a bevy of advisors and henchmen. One of these was a tall and somewhat mysterious man, a Darwashi or wizard, who went by the name of Karim Maghra. No one seemed clear exactly from whence he came or how he insinuated himself into Khali's inner circle. He was simply there one day and in short order set himself up as Khali's most devoted sidekick/bodyguard/personal assistant (Easton's 21st century interpretation). It was clear Maynard didn't like this man from the get-go, from his dark complexion, his crafty eyes, arrogant demeanor and, apparently above all, the glittering looks he gave Akma when he thought no one was paying attention. Or as Maynard intoned, his sinister designs on Akma noted, being a man of questionable character and in clear congress with the Black Arts. (Easton let out a chuckle reading this comment,) It was also apparent that Akma was tweaking the nose of the devil – Karim – while her sights were clearly set on Captain Forester. Who, it seemed, was utterly oblivious to her affections and the volatile atmosphere that was building. Part of this may have been due to the fact that he was married and devoted to his wife and clearly had no designs on Akma or any of her sisters. Which no doubt upped the ante and inspired Akma to zero her sights on him all the more.

This didn't appear to go beyond a little harmless flirtation (either Maynard was too circumspect to say or simply didn't know) with Akma doting on the captain and secretly leaving him little gifts in his chambers on the occasions when he stayed over at Khali's manor, but nothing overt, despite some wagging of tongues and whisperings into ears in certain quarters. If Dukat Khali was aware of any of this, he kept it to himself. But clearly Karim Maghra was aware. The gleam of jealousy in his eye became increasingly apparent and in short order, plots and schemes were formulated.

Wednesday 15 August 1620

This morning, which rose infernally hot and humid, saw Mr. Pickering and I finishing the last of my supply of pickled oysters which my boy brought up from the hold. Discipline among the men remains good — mainly through sheer force of the Captain's will. He is that caliber of man that cause the crew to mind themselves and be loyal, and that very caliber that as of late has occasioned my thinking.

I grow concerned at the plots and machinations that I catch word of — clearly the daughter of Khali-mior is quite taken with our Captain, clearly his heart remains true to his wife Sophia (even so, I would not fault the man for taking his pleasure as it suits) and clearly it is this magician, this Karim Maghra, who is the source of these designs against our commander. Could he be so blind as not to see this, when even such a country sod as myself can? Perhaps fortune has intervened this week with the latest news; a Dutch fleet under the command of Captain Van Eyckmann having arrived at Fort Nassau this week past.

There are rumours that he has been sent upon orders of the Dutch East India Company to set to rights the devious means by which the Bandanese make deals with both the Dutch and ourselves and make insult of the "Eternal Compact" charter signed many years earlier. This Dutch Captain is of stern repute having survived a most treacherous massacre of his own commander some years back by the Bandanese and mayhap be on a mission of revenge. I had hoped this recent turn of events would turn the Captain to a more sober mind, and yet still he treats the matter as all a big game and methinks this is a little much....

It wasn't a game to Van Eyckmann.

His orders from the Lords Seventeen back in the Hague were circumspect and, as far as he was concerned, far too vague. Clearly written by a bunch of soft politicians who were probably being bribed off by

English royalty. Van Eyckmann was a man with a reputation as a strict taskmaster to those under him and a merciless enemy to those who opposed him. He was also convinced he served the right arm of God. Through the summer, he had been developing a plan to take care of the English and deal with the Bandanese merchants in one swoop. One day in October he decided it was time to pay a visit to the Island of Rhun.

That apparently was when all the real fun started.

(At this point Easton reached for his glass of Scotch, gave it a swirl, and took a healthy swallow. He made a mental note to go back downstairs and write down the name of the bottle when he got a chance. A glance at his watch: A quarter past four – still plenty of time. Then, legs crossed, he got back to reading.)

After Van Eyckmann and his fleet pulled into the harbor at Rhun Island, things began to happen fast. Forester received word almost as soon as the Dutch galleons tacked around the point. He put his crew on alert and all shore leaves were ended. Guns were oiled and readied, swords checked and sharpened, cannons cleaned and primed. Lieutenant Maynard made mention that some of the crew had "gone a bit soft with idleness and inaction," despite keeping up the routine of gunnery and sailing drills. There were several disciplinary actions noted requiring the ship's quartermaster to administer a few floggings and there were six cases of desertion. But by and large, the English fleet got their act together and double quick.

Khali-mior's district was on the far side of Banda from where Van Eyckmann's fleet was anchored. He lived in a palatial Batak-style house, complete with servants and gardens. A short boat ride away was the village of Neira with its leeward harbor where Forester's fleet was holed up, their flags with Saint George's Crosses fluttering lightly in the limpid breeze. Although tempted to sneak out and ambush the Dutch fleet despite being far outgunned, Forester decided after much deliberation that it was his duty to get back to England with his spice-laden ships and let the East India Company directors decide on the next course of action. The captain was no coward but he was also no fool and his orders were specific: go to Banda, acquire as much spice as could be crammed into the three ships, and high-tail it back. And in no way provoke the Dutch with anything resembling an act of war. Period.

Easton took another sip of Scotch and stretched his legs. Now that he was becoming truly absorbed into the story, it felt like the walls of his room had melted away as the scene from hundreds of years ago began to take full shape and color in his mind, it seemed to him that...

...Forester and his four ships were just about to weigh anchor when a Bandanese outrigger was spotted oaring furiously towards them. He was in the main cabin aboard the Black Dragon reviewing his charts (Easton could almost hear the creak of rigging and the stomp of feet on the deck overhead, the persistent lapping of water alongside the ship's hull) when Lieutenant Maynard's fist began hammering on his door...

"Yes?"

"Captain, Captain!"

"Come in."

Lieutenant Maynard practically crashed through the door – Kingsley, the captain's steward, just narrowly escaped being smashed flat against the bulkhead as he reached to open it. Forester looked up from his charts, one eyebrow cocked.

"Steady now, Mr. Maynard, is something amiss?"

Maynard knuckled his forehead in a quick salute. "Aye, Sir, indeed!" He pulled his hat off and bowed, long ringlets of copper-colored hair falling down around his face. The air in the cabin was stifling in the tropical heat, despite the thick lead-paned windows at the stern being open. Forester's great coat was draped over the sea chest behind him and he was in his linen shirt and leather doublet. "You have a visitor, something terrible has occurred. I would beseech you to..."

He was interrupted by raucous yelling and footsteps stomping down the gangway. The visitor in question tumbled into the room. Kingsley stood to the side, looking horrified. This level of rudeness was unprecedented.

The visitor was Khali-mior and his appearance was terrible. His usually immaculate clothing was in tatters and blood-stained. Tears were running freely down his cheeks. He looked as though he had aged ten years since Forester had seen him the day before. Without any warning, Khali rushed to the desk and fell to his knees, pawing at Forester's thigh-high jack boots in a weirdly supplicating pose. Forester was both appalled and alarmed to see his friend in this state.

"Captain, oh, Captain, you must help me...please help me!!!" Khali sobbed. Without waiting for a response, he gushed on. "They've taken my Akma, my poor Akma!!! Oh, it is terrible, you must help. They've taken all my daughters from me but Akma... I know she has had eyes on you. My poor Akma! You must help! Oh please..." At which point, Forester grabbed the man by the shoulders and, standing up, shook him like a dog.

"Datuk! Stop it! Pull your wits about you!" and, when that didn't work, he slapped him hard across the face.

Which did work.

Khali-mior looked at him, stunned. Forester forced him into a chair and had Kingsley fortify him with a healthy glass of French brandy to get some color back in his cheeks. Then he began to talk. There had been an incident the night before. A work detail of Javanese slave laborers on the other side of the island at Lonthar was building a factory, guarded by a detachment of Dutch soldiers from the garrison at Fort Nassau. The previous night, someone had thrown a bottle of alcohol with a flaming wick through the open window of the barracks. In short order, the Dutch had rounded up some of the villagers and discovered through one of them that it had been a signal for the natives to attack.

Tensions had been running high since the new Governor VOC had arrived. Many of the natives were refusing to work under the new Dutch rules and in the groves on Banda, much of the nutmeg fruit hung rotting on the trees. Van Eyckmann had been a young officer under the previous governor when that notable was ambushed and killed by the Bandanese fifteen years before and he still had an axe to grind. Granted, Governor Verhoeven had been a fool and his naiveté had cost him, but to Van Eyckmann it had become a personal matter. He had escaped the ambush but his reputation had been smeared. Some wagging tongues suggested he had been a coward and fled. Others that he had fought a gallant delaying action until overwhelming numbers forced him to retreat to the safety of the ships. Either way, Van Eyckmann had slunk back to Holland under a cloud of failure that rankled his not-inconsiderable ego. This time around he was looking for payback.

What followed was an orgy of destruction and violence. Homes were looted, then torched. The Ronin – Japanese mercenaries Van Eyckmann had specifically recruited en route to the East Indies – were put to work on the natives. Blood ran in the streets. The night – October the 29th – would hence be known in the island history as "The Night of a Thousand Deaths."

In the midst of all this, word had gotten back to the Dutch commander that the real culprit was a merchant by the name of Khali-mior on the other side of the island. The soldiers had come into the village and gone directly to Khali-mior's house. Khali himself was over at another village on the south coast, where he had been attending a feast honoring the marriage of another orang kaya's son. At the time the soldiers were putting the torch to his own district, Khali was out cold with three empty wine gourds on the pillows around him. The soldiers had stormed through the front door at his house and seized all five of Khali's daughters, along with a good amount of his belongings (and the harem, of course), then demanded that the terrified servants tell them where Khali-mior was. They left one alive to tell Khali that it would be in his best interest to go straight to Lonthar and surrender himself by noon the next day. After that, they would send back the heads of each of his daughters, one by one, for every hour he delayed.

Khali-mior was beside himself. Was not Forester sent by his mighty king to protect the orang kaya of Rhun Island? What to do?

Forester stood motionless while he listened to all of this, hands crossed, head bowed. Only a twitching muscle in his jaw betrayed any tension. Khali-mior finished his story and for minutes there wasn't a sound except for the lapping of waves against the hull and the occasional creak of a sailor moving on the deck overhead. Then he quietly ordered Maynard to fetch his launch.

"Captain?"

"You heard correctly, Mr. Maynard. You will fetch my launch. Khali-mior will remain here as our 'prisoner' and I shall return to the mainland with Lieutenant Tattersill and a dozen men. You will wait here until the tide goes out tonight. If we do not return by then, you will take over command of all the ships and sail directly back to England as quickly and safely as you can manage. I will have Kingsley draw up a set of orders to make it official."

"Captain, I must protest. I cannot allow you to go confront the Dutch in this manner. 'Tis madness!"

Forester stepped up and looked Maynard straight in the eye. Titles aside, Maynard was the closest thing he had to a friend. "Mr. Maynard, Piers, I beseech you, as your captain and as your friend, this is how it must be done. It must appear to be handled as an act by a single person, not the act of a nation. Do you understand? I will confront this Van Eyckmann directly and he will answer to me, none other. The first lieutenant will accompany me as far as the port but I will arrange to go to his ship alone. Anything else would risk the interests of our country, our king."

"But Captain…"

"There is no but, Lieutenant. I, and I alone, am directly responsible for this turn of misfortune. Khali-mior has taken an oath to our king and has proven loyal to us and has now paid a terrible price. If there is any hope of undoing any of this, I must act quickly and decisively, aye?"

Lieutenant Piers Maynard looked him straight back, his own eyes reddening. "Aye, Captain, your orders will be carried out to the letter. I give you my word." Lieutenant Piers Maynard had served loyally under Forester for the past five years and throughout that service had never once disobeyed an order or broken his word. Within the next fifteen minutes, he would do both.

Forester and his landing party arrived at the village to find it completely destroyed and abandoned. Most of the buildings had been torched, dead bodies strewn everywhere. On the outskirts, the severed heads of many of the villagers were mounted on bamboo poles. Some wit had stuck a clay pipe in the teeth of one of them. Lieutenant Tattersill looked pale and his lips trembled but, to his credit, he kept his breakfast down. Forester had serious doubts that he would be any use if it came to a fight but he wanted him out of the way if a useful commander was to be left in charge of the fleet. Besides, the dozen seamen he'd recruited for this mission looked plenty able to handle themselves.

Forester headed straight for Khali's house in long strides, appalled at what his eyes were seeing. The Bandanese might be duplicitous, crafty, and double-dealing, but he could not in any way find that as a justification for the sheer level of brutality that had been inflicted here. His calloused hand was clenched tightly on the hilt of the sword at his hip and the look in his eye was cold and murderous.

Someone would pay dearly for this, on his oath.

He almost didn't recognize the house of his former host. It was half burned down and the rest looked like a pack of Mongols had been having a go at it. A spacious steep-roofed building elevated on stilts and patterned after the sweeping style of the Batak boathouses of Indonesia, its ornate woodwork was scarred and burnt and it looked like the heavy plank front doors had been kicked in. A quick search revealed that the place had been thoroughly looted. He found one of the servants sobbing in a fetal position by the pool in the back garden.

Dropping to one knee he grasped the man – he couldn't recall his name but thought he might be the cook – and pulled him up. One of his ears had been sliced off, leaving a raw, bloody hole. Forester had no time for civilities.

"The women. Where did they take them?"

The man, an elderly native with a shaved head and a broad face, simply shook his head and whimpered.

Forester shook him again. "Khali-mior's daughters – tell me where they took them. Now."

From behind Forester, an oily, venomous voice said, "To the ship, of course. Where else?"

Forester snapped his head around, standing up and unsheathing his sword in one fluid motion. Standing there as if he'd been summoned out of the tendrils of smoke floating through the morning air, was Karim Maghra. Arms folded, eyes glittering, looking for the world like a djinn conjured out of the Arabian Nights.

Except this djinn appeared to have had a rough night of it. His turban was singed and torn and his clothes were spattered with blood. His pantaloons were sliced in several places. It appeared several of his fingers had been broken.

"Where's the Dutch ship?"

Maghra nodded to his right. "Ships. Four. At Lonthar." About three miles to the east.

"You managed to survive."

"A wise man avoids a fight he cannot possibly win."

"Aye, as do all other sorts of men."

Karim didn't respond immediately. He simply tilted his head. Then his nostrils flared. "Perhaps so, my friend, but you must make haste! I believe Akma and her sisters are in imminent danger! You must save her, you must!"

The Dutch ships rode quietly at anchor in the harbor at Lonthar, the brilliant tropical skies overhead giving no hint of the atrocities that had just transpired since the previous night. The largest ship, a 600-ton galleon christened the Voetboog was Van Eyckmann's flagship and a source of extreme personal pride. He'd invested no small amount of his private funds in having the stern and bow emblazoned with ornate and decorative gilt work in a rare public display of opulence. And, in keeping with the VOC tradition, the ship was christened based on the county seat where the Van Eyckmann family resided.

Captain Forester had found the flagship's launch waiting for him in the smoldering ruins of the harbor. Some of the buildings were still burning brightly in the morning light. The coxswain, who was in charge of the boat, had strict orders to take only Forester to the ship. "The governor's been expecting you," he said cheerfully, his broad flat face with its too-small eyes tilted up at Forester. "Where's the Orang Kaya?" He had a big clenched smile with a jaw that jutted out proudly despite the atrocious condition of his teeth and he had a sly look like that of a cat.

"I presume you mean Khali-mior? He has the luxury of being held prisoner aboard my own ship until we can get to the bottom of this matter."

The coxswain shrugged as if this was of no consequence.

"Suit yourself. My orders are clear though, only you and the merchant allowed on board." He stepped aside and indicated with his hand that Forester should climb in. To make his point, he kept his other hand resting on the pommel of the heavy-looking sword slung from his hip.

Tattersill and the rest of the Black Dragon's seamen were left to wait on the remains of the main wharf. Forester sat in the stern sheets, a grim look fixed on his face as the boat rowed out to the Voetboog. The still water of the bay was filled with flotsam and debris, but the four Dutch ships swinging idly at their anchors like some sort of tranquil seascape painting gave no indication that they were in any way connected to the massacre the night before. Forester tried not to look as one of the oars rolled over a pale corpse as they passed. The knuckles were white on the hilt as he clenched his sword even tighter.

Van Eyckmann's flagship was a masterpiece of Dutch nautical engineering. With her broad hull, curved decks, and heavy armament, she combined speed, stability, plenty of space for cargo, and plenty of guns to protect it. She had a high-swept stern with gilded dragons adorning the top and a long prow that jutted well out over the water. As the launch drew in closer, Forester could see sailors and soldiers alike quietly watch them from the decks and aloft in the rigging. And lined up amidships like grim sentinels were the Ronin, a strange and exotic mix of ragtag mercenaries, ex-Samurai who had been stripped of their status for reasons ranging from the loss of their feudal lord to the vagaries of the changing political landscape in Japan at the time. Some were naked but for a heavy black cloth wrapped about the groin and waist; some were dressed in various bits of lacquered armor that glinted brightly in the morning sun. A handful of the wealthier ones had complete sets from their fur-trimmed armored boots to their iron helmets.

The launch pulled up alongside and, without waiting, Forester clambered up the ship's ladder and stepped through the bulwark entrance-way. For a moment, it looked as though the Japanese mercenaries, with their fierce expressions that seemed carved in light brown marble, were going to maintain an impassable armored wall. Forester paused, left hand resting on the sword hilt slung at his left hip, but he made no threatening move. He simply stared back at the opaque sets of black eyes staring back at him. Then silently the ranks melted away right and left and he saw a trim and almost foppish elderly-looking man stepping down from the quarterdeck, followed by a half-dozen men who seemed to be officers. He had a narrow face, hooked nose, and an almost feminine-looking mouth and was dressed in a studded doublet with a fall of Flemish lace at the neck. He also wore damask pantaloons of gold and maroon. The steely-eyed glare (and the way the surrounding crew suddenly found important things to look at on the decking) suggested to Forester he was about to meet the notorious Governor Lucas Van Eyckmann.

"Captain Forester, so nice of you to finally join us!" he said in clipped, cultured tones.

Forester returned with a curt nod. "Governor Van Eyckmann VOC, I presume?"

Van Eyckmann stepped up close but to Forester's relief made no attempt to shake hands. "You presume correctly. I am surprised to see you alone. Where is Khali-mior? My men have been looking for him. He is wanted on charges of treason and conspiring to incite a revolt. Do you have knowledge of his whereabouts?"

"Aye, indeed I do, Your Governorship. He is at this moment cooling his heels in the brig of my flagship. I thought it prudent to come here in person to sort this matter out."

Van Eyckmann pursed his lips as he contemplated this. Then the hint of a cruel smile. "I see. A most unfortunate decision. But where are my manners? Please, allow me to introduce my officers." Forester received a curt nod from each as they were called out in order of rank (when he named the third one as a Lieutenant Osterman, Easton gave a little start). Did you not receive my invitation?"

"I'm sorry...invitation?"

Van Eyckmann was not a man accustomed to repeating himself. His eyes took on a flat look. "Yes, invitation. To assist us in handling this unpleasant little situation. I sent a messenger to deliver it directly to your ship last night. As our countries are at present allies, I thought it prudent to engage you in this necessary disciplinary action. To make yourself useful."

"Disciplinary action?" Forester was beginning to doubt his ears.

"Yes. Disciplinary action. Punishment for wrong-doing. For conspiring to inflict harm upon the rightful rulers of these islands. And for gross violation of our treaty. That is what this is all about and why you should have brought this Khali-mior with you this morning. Captain, I'm not in the habit of having to repeat myself. Do you have difficulty hearing?"

Forester was beginning to wonder if, in fact, that was the case. He was also well aware of Van Eyckmann's insulting tone.

"No, Your Governorship. I am simply having reservations about what you consider 'handling this unpleasant little situation'."

"Perhaps, then, Captain, you have no stomach for maintaining discipline. These Bandanese are like children. Dangerous children. They must be minded constantly. A plot was afoot to ambush my soldiers. The ringleader has been identified as Khali-mior. Consequences must be meted out to bring those responsible to justice. Law and order must be maintained."

Forester could barely contain his rage. Through clenched teeth, he said, "With due respect, Your Governorship, you've massacred two entire villages of defenseless people, for God's sake. And it is my duty to report as much to the directors of the British East India Company, and the Lords Seventeen, as well. This is not justice, it is a mockery of justice!"

Forester had gotten Van Eyckmann's attention with the mention of the Lords Seventeen, who controlled the Dutch East India Company. Van Eyckmann's officers looked at each other uneasily, unaccustomed to having their leader challenged this openly. The Governor's eyes flared briefly, then he leaned forward conspiratorially and spoke quietly into Forester's ear.

"The Lords Seventeen are a bunch of lily-livered sods who have no understanding of the realities of the situation here, halfway around the world. They enjoy the money that lines their coffers while they lounge about on silk pillows and make decisions on matters they have no concept of, nor any stomach for. Which is why I am here, Captain Forester. My countrymen are God-fearing people, but out here, I am the instrument of God. Judge, jury, and executioner, if need be." He stepped back and this time spoke loudly enough for all to hear. "Now tell me, Captain Forester, do you have the stomach for it?"

"For what, exactly?"

In response, Van Eyckmann raised his hand and made a circular gesture. Sailors, soldiers and Ronin parted on the sweeping curve of the main deck, allowing a disheveled figure in irons to be dragged over to the heavy wooden grate covering the main hatch by two beefy-looking Africans. Forester immediately saw that it was Akma. Her ornately jeweled robes were soiled and torn, her beautiful black hair in disarray and her legs were streaked with blood. Her eyes looked defiant. And terrified.

"To administer justice, my English captain. I believe it is time to carry out the first sentence." He reached into his breast and brought out a folded sheath of linen paper and glanced at it. "And I see that it is – oh dear! – death by dismemberment." He looked over at the nearest Japanese mercenary and held his hand out. "Taro-san, if you would." The mercenary obliged by producing his Katana sword hilt first and with a small bow presented it to Van Eyckmann. The Governor gave an even smaller bow in return. The two Africans let Akma drop to her knees over the grate and stepped aside. They looked like ebony statues, arms crossed, their blue-black skin shining in the late morning sun. Forester looked at Van Eyckmann.

"Unpleasant business. But I am a man of duty, Your Governorship."

"Very good, Captain. This is the Japanese Katana, a sword of exquisite workmanship. They take upwards of two years to manufacture, and are rated by the number of bodies they can slice through consecutively. This one is rated at four, I believe." He handed Forester the sword and stepped backwards. "If you are in a merciful mood, a single strike at the neck should suffice. Otherwise, I suggest the arms first."

Van Eyckmann consulted his papers and began reading out the sentence aloud. He was midway through stating "…for the intent of inflicting grievous harm…" when Forester sprang into action.

It is a very difficult thing to react while someone is speaking, even more so when the speaker is reading a sentence and is in mid-sentence. The attention is naturally upon the speaker, and there is a momentary lag while the brain (or brains in this case) shift gears to the new subject of interest.

Which was exactly what Forester was counting on.

Even so, it was a near thing.

It was the ever-vigilant Ronin who almost prevented what transpired next, although even they were caught by surprise. After all, they were taking their cues from Van Eyckmann's actions, which were genuinely relaxed. Hadn't the man given Forester one of their swords? Plus, as it worked out, Providence was on Forester's side.

Forester leapt toward the hatch grate, swinging the Katana horizontally. It was even better balanced than he had anticipated and, true to Van Eyckmann's claim, went clean through four torsos starting with the large African guard on the right. Almost simultaneously, the nearest Ronin leapt to intervene and lost his hands at the forearms for his efforts with Forester's subsequent reverse cut. The second cut nearly decapitated the Japanese mercenary next in line before getting lodged in his lacquered neck protector. Forester had already released the sword before that was decided and, reversing again, grabbed Akma with his left arm and, knocking aside two sailors, bolted to the gunwale. The third mercenary managed to grab a hold of his left shoulder – Forester spun on his heel and delivered a right hook with his sword hand that sent the smaller man pin-wheeling backwards and stumbling into a knot of other crewmen. Then it was up and over the side of the ship and a good ten-foot drop into the turquoise waters of the harbor.

Down they went. The impact knocked them apart, Forester struggling to hang on to the poor woman before she slipped from his grasp and shot straight down.

The chains!

The story might have ended right then and there. By all rights it should have. But it didn't.

Coming out of shock, Akma reflexively snatched wildly, found the ankle of Forester's boot and locked on with both hands. Forester was thrashing wildly with his arms – unlike most seamen, he actually did know how to swim. But his boots and heavy clothes immediately began to work against him in the water and Akma would have pulled both of them down to a watery grave if a gnarled hand hadn't reached in and grabbed the collar of Forester's leather doublet and hauled the two of them to the surface – much to their surprise – alongside a native outrigger. Forester found himself staring into the fierce countenance of Maghra.

Spewing water, he managed a strangled "What the...?" before he was manhandled on board by another set of brown arms, Akma being unceremoniously dumped alongside him a moment later. They were in a native canoe manned by two other men in addition to Khali-mior's henchman. In all the excitement, he hadn't even seen them (hardly surprising as they were ducked under the stern when Forester jumped). Somewhere above came the loud ka-floom! of a blunderbuss being fired, then a hail of random missiles – belaying pins, blocks, whatever the sailors aboard the ship could quickly lay their hands on – came raining down around them.

Yelling. Shouting. Curses in a dozen foreign tongues. The two Bandanese men laid into their oars as if the devil were on their heels, which wasn't far off the truth. Forester rolled onto his back, not believing this turn of events. In fairness, he had pretty much winged it, starting with rowing out to the Dutch flagship. But in the seconds following their mad leap off the ship, he had pretty much realized that they were jumping to their deaths.

Better than the alternative.

He spat salt water over the gunwale and looked over at his rescuer. Looking at Maghra's ruined hands, he realized that the act of hauling two water-logged people out of the water must have been excruciating. But the man gave no sign. He simply stared at the two of them. Forester had a hunch the only reason he had been rescued was that he had been the only link between Akma and the surface of the bay.

In that he was correct.

He looked over at the young Bandanese woman. She looked barely conscious. She was quite beautiful, he thought, as if really seeing her for the first time. If it wasn't for his Sophia back in Cornwall...

He turned and looked over at Maghra and at the women's heads rolling in the slow surf of the bay. "Her sisters. I couldn't save them."

Maghra stared at him with his strange, glittering eyes. "No, you could not," he said finally. There wasn't any room for discussion.

"I have a landing party on shore. Can you get to the main pier?"

Maghra shook his head. "They are all dead. Van Eyckmann's men cut them down while you were on board his ship."

Something about that didn't ring quite right with Forester, but there was little time to consider it. "Then you need to take me to my ship. Quickly. We haven't much time."

Maghra tossed him an extra oar and grabbed one himself. "No. We must row faster." The oar was a crude wooden affair. Forester dug in and started pulling. The shallow-bottomed outrigger picked up speed. Behind them, there was a flurry of activity on the Dutch ships. Three longboats filled with soldiers were lowered and began hauling towards shore in pursuit. On the galleons, the topmen were clambering up the ratlines like nimble monkeys amidst more shouting and in short order the heavy canvas began to roll out and fill. Anchors were hoisted in and secured. The Dutch fleet began to wear and make for the open water.

Forester had an idea where they might be headed.

Events then began to converge from their separate paths.

One was the dance of the two small fleets which by sheer minutes missed each other. The Dutch fleet tacked its way around the north end of the island, while almost simultaneously Forester's ships worked their way around the southern route. Maynard had fretted as the morning wore on, then decided that, consequences be damned, he would sail to the opposite side of the island and hope to trap the Dutch ships there. At the very least, it would be a show of force that might tip the bargaining chips in Captain Forester's favor. On the other hand, it might spell the end of his career. Maynard was torn between his duty and the bonds of his friendship and loyalty to Forester. The latter finally won out.

Once they made the shore, Forester and Maghra hustled Akma across the island, pausing briefly only to empty out Foresters waterlogged boots and strike the manacles off Akma with a hammer and chisel found at a warehouse near the docks.

They made good time to the opposite harbor located at the southwest coast of the island.

Only to find it empty.

Standing at the top of the low hill near the warehouses overlooking the bay, Forester could only stand there and stare. Maynard and the ships were gone. The Dutch would be coming for them. Maghra actually let out a low chuckle and shook his head. The two Bandanese men – Forester could now see they were little more than teenagers – looked around uncertainly. The sun was reaching its zenith and the temperature was pushing 90. The air was so thick with humidity it felt like something tangible. It wasn't hard to imagine reaching out with an open hand, then squeezing and wringing the water right out of it.

Forester's clothes were beginning to steam themselves dry, his feet were sore and chafed in his boots that had been squelching the entire hike over the island, and his patience was beginning to run short. He wasn't sure why Maynard had disobeyed orders, but, if his measure of the man was correct, he had probably taken the ships to Lonthar to rescue him.

Damn!

He looked up and around.

To the north, the ground sloped up to Api, a small volcanic peak that rose up to around 600 meters. A few plumes of white smoke drifted over the peak. Forester looked at Maghra and shrugged. "Well, then, it appears that my ships are gone, the Dutch soldiers will catch up with us soon, and will no doubt be aiming to give us a warm reception after my abrupt departure. We can either die here or at the top of the volcano. The view is probably better up there. What say you?"

It was Akma who responded, her voice an exhausted whisper. "There's a secret path near here. I can show you. And there is something else...you will see."

"What about them?" Forester nodded towards the two Bandanese men.

"They are dead anyway," said Maghra. "The Dutch have massacred nearly everyone on Rhun. These two hid in barrels near the docks. But this island is small. The Dutch will eventually find and kill everyone." He questioned them in Bandanese dialect. They looked scared, but nodded in agreement. One had a machete-like weapon at his hip, the other a rusted halberd he had picked up along the way. Maghra appeared to be unarmed, Forester still had his sword. But, unless it was oiled and cleaned shortly, it would rust within a matter of a day at most.

Above all, he was a pragmatist. And he guessed at the moment that their options were dwindling to nothing. Best to find a good location and then give a good account of themselves. He pulled out a short dirk that he also kept in his belt and placed it in Akma's slender hands.

"Don't let yourself be captured again. Use this when the time is right."

She nodded, then grasped his hands tightly as he gave her the weapon. She pulled him in closely, locking him with an intense look. Tears brimmed around her eyes. Then she whispered in his ear:

"Cinta Kamu."

He didn't quite understand the phrase, but from the way she said it he could wager a guess. But he was a married man. And a God-fearing, Christian man. So he pulled his hands away, grasped her cheeks in his palms and kissed her lightly on the forehead. His grasp of the Indonesian language was fairly limited, so he said the only thing he could think of at the moment:

"Semiga Beruntung."

Good Luck.

As they gained the summit, the path that wound through the heavy vegetation that clotted the slopes fell away and revealed an amazing sight: a massive, sprawling Buddhist temple built out of intricately-designed brownstone blocks. Perched near the rim of the complex was a series of conical towers with diamond-shaped cutouts built to a scale that defied the imagination, interspersed with flag-stoned courtyards. The ancient towers resembled oversized perforated bells and there were hundreds of them in various sizes ranging from a foot across to ten. Jungle vines and foliage were woven through the complex, giving it a slightly decrepit, abandoned atmosphere. The whole affair was sited around the north side of the volcano's rim, offering a spectacular view of the Bandanese sea below. Behind them, the cone was swathed in a series of mists along with large plumes of steam clouds emerging into the noonday sky.

From somewhere deep below came a low rumble.

The five of them stood spread out on a terrace overlooking the ocean. Akma, her face looking exhausted but still full of beauty, gave Forester a searching look.

"My father?"

"He is safe aboard my ship."

"That is good. Life will be hard. He will lose all his daughters. It is late in his life, but he will have to start all over again." She looked out at the ocean and the azure sky and momentarily closed her eyes, letting the mixed aromas of sea and jungle drift into her lungs, absorbing the moment as if for the last time. "This is a good place to die. I am sorry, Captain Horatio Forester. But...thank you. For giving me a chance." She held up his dirk, the blade glinting in the sunlight. "And for this."

At that moment, there was a muffled cry and something came rolling to a stop at Akma's feet. It was the head of one of the two Bandanese men. Forester lugged out his sword and instinctively pushed Akma behind him. Emerging onto the terrace was Governor Van Eyckmann, a sword drawn in his right hand, with half a dozen Samurai and two dozen of his soldiers. Maghra was nowhere to be seen.

"And so, Captain, we meet again."

If there had been some pretense at civility previously, it was clear that it had all gone by the board. Van Eyckmann's cheeks were flushed from both anger and exertion. The way he kept his body angled with right foot forward and left hand at his hip indicated he was not going to be caught unawares this time. The soldiers fanned out in a rough semi-circle, trapping Forester and Akma. The remaining Bandanese dropped his machete and leaped over the parapet. There was no time for Forester to consider his fate. Instead he stepped forward, the tip of his sword wavering and somewhat low.

"Aye, Dutchman, so we do." A grim smile played across his lips. "Are you man enough to face your business directly, or will you have your lackeys handle your dirty work for you again? I understand your countrymen aren't much for a fight without a little courage from a bottle. Shall I pull up a seat and wait while you fortify yourself?"

"You are sorely misinformed I'm afraid, Englishman. And I will take great pleasure in personally teaching you a lesson – SO!" And with that he bounded forward with a deadly thrust at Forester's neck. Anticipating this, Forester side stepped to the left and met Van Eyckmann's blade with a circular counter which, if completed, would have disarmed his opponent and ended the fight right then and there. Van Eyckmann was too much of an old hand for this trick, however, and fell away to the opposite direction, pulling his blade away and freeing himself. For a moment, the two men stood taking each other's measure, then they were at it again, this time engaging in a fury of expert swordplay that impressed even the Japanese mercenaries.

Sunlight glinted off steel. The swords rang and clanked.

Van Eyckmann was the more traditionally-trained of the two and his style was one of finesse and calculated strategy. But he was also deceptively powerful and quick for his size, and his aggressive personality made him a very dangerous opponent. His sword, a rapier, was well suited to his thrust and riposte style.

Forester was his opposite in many ways. His style was more savage and energetic. In combat, all his repressed emotion and rage came to the fore and he fought like a demon. When he fought, in his own words, a "red haze descends o'er my eyes." His technique had been honed from shipboard fighting, not at the finest fencing schools in Europe, and it had a barbaric ferocity on its surface. But part of that was an act, behind his arm was a crafty and calculating mind. His sword was also suited to his personal style, a narrower blade than the typical seaman's sword or cutlass, but finely balanced and with an intricate guard.

Back and forth went the two men, neither gaining an advantage in the first five minutes. Thrust. Parry. Counter. Feint. Thrust.

Up on this forgotten temple, the battle went on. In the surrounding jungle, the birds had fallen silent. Atop the volcano was a hushed quiet except for the clang of sword play, the grunts and hard breathing, the tamp of booted feet back and forth on the flagstones.

Swordplay, however, is fast and hard work, all the more so when the temperature and humidity are pushing 100 and one is wearing heavy clothes. Eventually, Van Eyckmann's weaker stamina began to tell. His technique began to falter, his moves becoming increasingly defensive. Both men were soaked in sweat. Their breathing grew more labored. Van Eyckmann knew he would have to bring this fight to an end quickly, or his commission as Governor VOC would be over, permanently.

He did a quick left-right feint to get his opponent's guard in so he could execute a quick lower thrust and then things went awry. His foot slipped on the mossy stone and in an instant he felt cold steel enter his abdomen on his right side in a lance of icy agony. Down he went. His rapier clattered on the stonework and rolled away.

The next thing he realized that he was looking up at the bright sky, Forester's boot on his chest, the tip of the Englishman's sword – dripping with his own blood – staining the lace at his throat. The side of his torso was on fire. He realized, almost abstractly, that he was about to die.

He was also puzzled. How did this happen? How did things go so wrong? His was the hand of God. Of righteousness, no? All he could think was: "Why hast thou forsaken me?"

Forester was looking down at him. "Spare the woman and I will spare your life in return."

Van Eyckmann's teeth were clenched. "Swine. You are swine," was all he could think to say.

"Very wel…" Forester's words dropped off mid-sentence as the point of a rapier – Van Eyckmann's rapier no less – emerged from his breast. Then the point withdrew and Forester staggered, falling to his knees, his hand grasping his left breast where a dark maroon stain began to spread under his fingers. He looked genuinely surprised. Behind him stood Maghra, his face fixed in an arrogant sneer.

"No. She is mine!" He stepped up to Van Eyckmann and, for the second time in as many minutes, the Governor had a blade at his neck. This time it was his own. Had he been a man of humor, he might have considered God was getting more comical by the minute.

Forester crawled over to the parapet and slid down on his butt, still looking surprised. Akma immediately ran over and cradled him. Though she did not cry out, tears began running freely down her face as she stroked his cheek. Maghra pressed the tip of the rapier into Van Eyckmann's throat, drawing a pinprick of blood. "Your men will back off, now, my friend. The girl will be mine. As was promised."

Despite his pain, or because of it, Van Eyckmann's head was beginning to clear. "Damn you to hell, you filthy Bandanese dog, I promise you nothing!" Maghra would have run him through the neck right then but for the fist-sized rock that glanced off his turbaned head, sending him sprawling. It had been thrown by one of the soldiers and a split second later, he was tackled and manhandled to the ground. The Governor was pulled away to safety and managed to gain his feet, albeit unsteadily, with the help of two of his men. Maghra was quickly bound and hauled to his feet. Van Eyckmann turned to his soldiers.

"The rest of you take the girl to my ship. And for those two – he nodded at Forester and Maghra – make sure their heads are off, then toss them over the rail!" he said to two of the Ronin. There was a blur of flying hair and a gleaming blade as Akma launched herself at Van Eyckmann, Forester's dirk flashing in the light. A futile effort as it turned out – she only succeeded making in a slashing wound on one of the Samurai's arms. Akma was pulled off and dragged kicking and thrashing down the trail with Van Eyckmann, and the Japanese mercenaries were left to do their dirty work.

(At this point Easton stretched again, took another pull off his Scotch and checked his watch. Still over an hour to go. There were only a dozen pages left and by this time he was so entrenched in this story that had happened – what, 390 years ago? – he wouldn't have stopped if the house were on fire. He checked his watch again. Dinner could wait.)

Van Eyckmann did manage to make it to his ships, which were now anchored in the southwest harbor at Rhun. Maynard had swung in to the harbor at Lonthar only to find it empty of course, then continued on around the north shore and then past the volcano, where his lookout spotted some activity at the ruins near the top.

Forester was fading fast, as he was manhandled into the courtyard along with Maghra, who had been smacked back to consciousness. The two men were bent forcibly to their knees. Then the Ronin, after a few minutes' deliberation (there was an argument over who would behead whom), agreed to let the older of the two begin the honors. He raised his sword and there was a whistling wump! and crack! it was broken in half. Shocked, he frowned and looked at it, then at his comrade-in-arms who was suddenly missing his head. Something heavy ricocheted off one of the temple tops, sending stones flying in all directions and then the other Ronin's head landed, bounced a few times, and rolled to stop. The headless body staggered a few feet, then collapsed on the flagstones, arterial blood streaming out of the severed jugular.

A second and third projectile whistled overhead and the remaining Samurai finally comprehended that these were, in fact, cannon balls – someone was firing on the temple. The first was purely a fluke shot but the continuing salvo suggested that an expedient evacuation of the premises was in order. The surviving mercenary tossed the remains of his sword aside and ran for it.

Tuesday 30 October 1620
A most foul day. And tomorrow is All Hallows Eve.
I have committed a most unforgivable sin, having disobeyed my Captain's order, but I was overcome by the most terrible premonition as I paced the quarterdeck of the Black Dragon. 'Twas almost as if a voice spake directly to my ear. I hesitated but a moment before ordering the ships to weigh anchor and make for the other side of the island where the Dutch fleet was. Perhaps if I could come in at them from upwind I could use the advantage to take them by surprise – the wind was after all picking up.

Alas, as we tacked past the northernmost point of Palau Rhun, the lookout cried from above and drew our attention to a most dramatic scene occurring at the top of the volcano there – a duel between two swordsmen! Through my own glass I could clearly witness that one was none other than the Captain himself! I left third Lieutenant Edwards in charge of the Dragon, taking the precaution to have all the guns run out with orders to fire if anything untoward should occur, and to keep a sharp eye out for the Dutch fleet.

It took nearly two hours to gain the top of the volcano and ere we did we heard a cannon shot but could not fathom the cause. Upon reaching the peak, we chanced upon a most terrible scene; amidst the ruins of an ancient stone temple our great Captain lay seriously wounded and nearby a most peculiar dressed man – clad in oriental armor of sorts – lay stretched upon the flagstones, his head gone (in short order, one of my men did locate the remains of it nearby). There was no sign of the other swordsman nor anyone else, and Captain Forester in his state was not in a position to discourse further on the matter, I can only give thanks that Providence has looked kindly upon us and spared his life…

Forester was barely alive, but the rapier thrust had missed his heart and major arteries, though he suffered a punctured left lung. He had managed to retrieve his sword and was found cradling it to his breast. Maynard and his crew managed to construct a makeshift stretcher (while two of the men paused to marvel at the lucky shot that had taken the head off one of the guards) and manhandle him back to the ship, where he would wallow in his cabin for weeks in semi-delirium under Pickering's ministrations as the fleet made its way back to England. Khali-mior was dropped off at Jakarta, a heartbroken man, yet he would eventually, as his daughter predicted, start a new family and resurrect some of his business standing.

In the postscript Easton would discover that Captain Forester would eventually recover, though his seafaring days would be over – he would settle down in Cornwall with his wife and family and live out his days as a tavern keeper where he had built quite a reputation as a gambler and story-teller. Maynard meanwhile would return to Palau Rhun as captain of his own ship, where he would eventually learn the rest of the story of Van Eyckmann and the fate of Akma. Much of this story he would hear from Khali-mior, whom he met up with in Jakarta, and who would never return to his beloved Palau Banda ever again. This part of the story was told in a hand-written narrative someone had inserted at the back of the book, written apparently by Maynard himself. It took some work to decipher the sloping, faded script but it was at least legible enough. The title at the top of the page said, "The Fate of Akma…and a Curse." Based on largely second-hand sources, the story reeked of the outlandish and fanciful imaginations of the Bandanese and even Maynard dismissed most of it as such, but noted it anyway as there was little else to go on.

13. THE FATE OF AKMA…AND A CURSE

Though seriously wounded himself, Van Eyckmann's wound was clean and his recovery would be relatively swift. For the youngest daughter of Khali-mior, and for that of the Bandanese islanders, fate would not be so kind.

Depending on your point of view, of course.

The following morning, Akma was brought up on deck and lashed to the main mast, in a hideous state. Each of the ship's officers had taken their pleasure with her during the night. Van Eyckmann had decided on a particularly brutal execution for her, even by 17th century standards, on which he had briefed the ten Japanese mercenaries he had carefully decided on earlier at the first watch. His fury at being subdued in front of his own men by an English captain, and subsequently by a Bandanese magician, seeped deep and cruel venom in his heart.

His words were met with eyes alight with sadistic gleam. This particular sentence would require finesse and patience.

They took two hours.

One hundred and thirty cuts. Each designed for maximum pain, none which would be fatal. Thirteen cuts each by the cruelest and most disciplined Ronin who had volunteered for the task. Then the coup de grace, by Van Eyckmann himself. And only after she begged him for it.

There would be no gallant Englishmen coming to her rescue on this morning, nor obsessive village magicians devising plots to free her. This was to be death, slow, cruel and extremely painful.

In the end, however, Van Eyckmann would be denied his final wish. Akma would not beg for her final release into the hereafter. Eyes glassy with pain, she was too far gone for any articulate response. Buckets of seawater were to no avail. She hung limply in her lashing, bleeding profusely (but not fatally) from 130 places. The Samurai had done their work with surgical precision. Finally, after another five minutes of trying to revive her, Van Eyckmann grew bored and with one swift upper cut took her head clean off. The remains were cut down and tossed overboard like so much offal. Tasty morsels for the tiger and hammerhead sharks already feasting in the bay.

Within minutes, Akma was no more.

That night, Van Eyckmann was back in his quarters high in the keep at Fort Nassau, propped up on Persian pillows near an open balcony. The wound in his side was excruciating, but dulled somewhat by the Madeira he had been drinking. The surgeon had fussed over him all afternoon. The day had been a messy business and left bitter dregs in his mouth. From his sleeping quarters, he could look out over the nearest wedge-shaped phalanx of the fort's parapet and over the bay where a brilliant sunset was in its dying embers, fading salmons and reds accenting the cumulus clouds that piled up to dizzying heights into the deeper indigo of night. Above that, the first stars began to make their appearance, southern constellations so different from the ones in his native Amsterdam. The Dutch masters would have a field day with this palette. He was considering how he might bring one of their apprentices down to this part of the world and commission a portrait of himself against one of these impressive sunsets. He had gotten as far as contemplating which set of clothes and how he might hold his sword when a soft thump from the balcony intruded his thoughts.

Van Eyckmann was puzzled. His room was in a tower, a good 40 meters of sheer stone block to the courtyard below. His confusion took a nod towards genuine alarm when the turbaned figure of Maghra glided into his chambers from outside.

"How did...? Guard! GUARD!!"

The shaman held up an open hand and smiled, his eyes glittering in the dim lamplight.

"No bother, they cannot hear. They sleep the sleep of the purple lotus tonight. No, tonight, my friend, there is business only between you and I."

Van Eyckmann pulled himself up, eyes darting around for a weapon of any sort. The nearest was his sword hung on the wall, but he would have to pass by Maghra to get it. Unless he could find a clever way to get him away from it. The thought of an intruder gaining access to this room was never a consideration. Between the balcony and two other windows that only a bird (or perhaps a very patient and determined monkey) could access, the main door, which was bolted shut, was solid teak, six inches thick. How the Bandanese magician had gained access was a curious question indeed, and one that would require serious investigation and probably severe punishment, but for now he had to accept the situation and discover how he was going to get out of it.

Meanwhile, Maghra was standing between him and the only weapon in the room. Arms folded, his usually immaculate clothes were beginning to look the worse for wear, he apparently hadn't dropped in to chit-chat over pleasantries. He fixed Van Eyckmann's eyes with a livid glare, his diabolical face appearing to shift in the flickering candle light.

"We had an agreement. The four daughters were yours. Akma, the youngest, was to be mine. What have you done!?"

If Van Eyckmann had any fear of this man who had already come a breath away from killing him earlier, he hid it well. He might have been addressing a petulant nephew who wasn't getting his way: "Done? I have set an example is what I have done. I've decided the surviving daughters will be sold into slavery after I've tired of them, along with any miscreants throughout these islands who will defy Dutch law. If I agreed to let you have the youngest, it was before she tried to kill me, no? The plan was to let the English captain escape with her, that I might have a legitimate reason to have him killed or at least imprisoned. Now he has run off with the ringleader of this little rebellion in his hold." Van Eyckmann was growing short on patience. "Besides, your little girl attempted to kill the Governor VOC of the Dutch East Indies. That is a capital offense. Take one of the other four. They all look the same. Take one and be gone!"

A mix of rage and homicidal insanity was practically baking off Maghra in waves. Even Van Eyckmann could sense it. One could almost see the smoke wafting out of his ears and nose. One moment he was standing there, arms crossed, seething; the next he leaped like a panther and landed on the Dutch governor, straddling him with his legs and both claw-like hands wrapped around the other man's throat. Not choking, but pulling him up close while painfully extending his neck.

"I will not take one and be gone!" he hissed. "You have taken from me what was mine. Now you will pay!" With that, he did the last thing Van Eyckmann could have expected – he pulled him in close and forced his lips over the governor's. The man's breath was rancid, the taste of something burnt and rotted and somehow alien. Van Eyckmann gave a smothered cry but there was nothing he could do. He tried grabbing the larger man's forearms but they were as immovable as iron. His eyes bulged in their sockets. Then he felt something slug-like enter his mouth and tried to scream, to close his throat, but Maghra abruptly broke their hideous kiss and slammed his jaw closed, forcing him to swallow whatever vile thing had been transferred between them. Something heavy and slimy worked its way down into his stomach. He tried to gag but the gnarled hands held him immobile. The magician's eyes were dancing with sadistic glee.

Still inches away from him, Maghra smiled his terrible smile. "I have infected you with the worm of life, terrible life, and with it, a curse. A curse just for you: You will live for all eternity, all that you love will turn to ash and dust. You will know suffering and loneliness, and your loins will bear only corrupted seed. You beg for it to end, but it will not. And every 133 years, on this night, you will suffer unbridled torment, for every cut my...my... Akma suffered. And I will be there to enjoy it so! Yesss! That is my promise and my gift to you! Unless...unless..."

Van Eyckmann was half out of his mind with disgust and loathing at what had just transpired. He felt violated. And unclean. But he managed to croak, "Unless...what?"

"That is for me to know, and you to spend an eternity finding out." And with that he began to laugh his peculiar, screeching laugh, and kept laughing until Van Eyckmann passed out a few minutes later.

At first, in the bright logic of the morning sun the following day, Van Eyckmann passed the whole thing off as a bad nightmare. That evaporated pretty much immediately as he doubled over and vomited. With it came the revolting taste of the grave in his mouth (and things long dead yet longing to be alive) and the whole episode of the shaman's obscene kiss flooded his conscience with crystal clarity. What didn't come with it was whatever hideous thing he had been forced to swallow. Just ropy loops of black bile.

It would take weeks, and several failed suicide attempts, for the truth to sink in.

There was no sign of Maghra, despite a thorough search throughout the Bandanese Island chain and a generous bounty issued for his head. The magician had simply vanished. Nor was there any answer to the mystery of how he had gained access to the governor's chambers, although the private guards would be found dead asleep the following morning. They would all be executed by the following morning.

Van Eyckmann instead took out his anger (and self-loathing) on the Bandanese natives through the order of mass executions and unprecedented butchery. Many of them were shipped off to Batavia to be sold into slavery and those who remained chose mass suicide over living under this Dutch tyrant's degradations. Within months, not a single original Bandanese native would be left – natives were brought in from other islands, including a large contingent of Javanese convicts – to repopulate the villages and take over working the nutmeg and mace groves. While the reports filtering back to Europe were repulsive and ignominious, despite the public outcry, Van Eyckmann would receive little more than a slap on the wrist by the Lords Seventeen. He was ultimately rewarded handsomely for his "firm" handling of a crisis situation, ensuring a strong and profitable future for the East India Company.

After governing Banda for another nine years, Van Eyckmann

presumably returned to his native Amsterdam and from there disappeared into the mists of history. Maynard concluded his account thus:

The Lord has been good to me and to mine in his manifold mercies, bittersweet though some of those mercies have been. After returning to England and giving a full accounting of my actions to the Directors of our Honorable Company, I was granted command of the Black Dragon, as Captain Forester, due to the extremity of his injuries, was not inclined to continue the sea-faring life. He did, however, take ownership of a quaint sea-side tavern called "Solomon's Bane," where he lives with his wife and family still and where, when the opportunity warrants, I call for a spell. On those nights, the Captain and I will discourse long into the night by the hearth in the great room of his tavern, recounting our adventures with plenty of toasts to the King's Health. I sense, however, a ghost of unsettled business in his countenance regarding the Dutch Governor, though he has never addressed it directly with me and forbids any discourse on it. I have related some of what I had discovered regarding what happened, but never the fantastical accounts of the curse and Van Eyckmann which no sane man could credit. Would that I might find what ultimately happened to that vile and boorish man, but he has all but vanished. All inquiries have led to naught – I only know that he renounced his title some years later and returned to Amsterdam – as a hero no less – but from thence no word has been heard though there are rumours he fled to the colonies under a cloud of scandal....

As for myself, I had the good fortune to settle and marry a fine woman named Alicia, who has born me three good sons and a daughter and now in my later years have gained the esteemed title of Director with the British East India Company. I still think of that day on occasion and would give anything to go back and change the course of events so that my Captain would escape the grievous injury he suffered and that charming young lass Akma avoid her terrible fate...but I cannot. What was, was.

With what felt like superhuman effort, Easton pulled himself back into the present. Maynard's account had thoroughly absorbed him into its distant era and he had that momentary vertigo of moving from one reality into another. What a story! How much of it was true? Much of it smacked of actual events, but most certainly much of the second account was complete fiction with its curses and magicians and whatnot. He also had a disturbing realization – at least some of the story he had just grasped from Maynard's account wasn't actually written. It had details he couldn't possibly have known. It was as if, in the course of reading, he had fallen into a semi-lucid daydream where certain sentences suggested additional details. It hurt his head to think about how such a thing might even be possible, and with that came a prick of fear of...

Hello, Auntie B.

...things (talents) best buried and forgotten trying to claw their way back up to the surface. He tried to focus instead on the truth of history – it seemed ludicrous that barely 400 years ago, men were killing each other, hell, entire nations were going to war over something that was pretty much taken for granted in any kitchen cupboard in the 21st century.

He checked his watch. Still 45 minutes to shower then put on this ridiculous get-up and play out his part in this bizarre schedule of events. A séance for Christ sakes? He was increasingly skeptical that little if any of this was going to turn out as promised or planned, but he was always one to play out the hand he was dealt.

He finished off the watery dregs of the Scotch – most of the ice had melted by this point – and then rifled through the last couple of pages at the back of the small book and noticed some faded notes written in pencil there. Odd. He read the first few lines, eyebrows rising, then stopped abruptly as he realized he wasn't alone his room. Legs still crossed, he placed the book on the nightstand and crossed his arms.

"Been here long?"

Aun-mai was sitting across the room in a high-backed leather chair near the windows, her face inscrutable in the dim light. She appeared to be wearing a headdress of sorts. Her hands were folded in her lap, her legs were pulled up cross-legged, Indian-fashion. From outside, the wind continued to howl and rattle at the windowpanes. Leaves flitted restlessly against the glass. Easton was reasonably positive the room was empty when he entered. But then again, based on how things were unfolding lately, he couldn't be entirely sure. About anything apparently.

"So you know then?" she asked. He was really beginning to like the musical quality of her voice. It made him think of fresh water trickling over the stones of a mountain brook. Or warm waves of velvety sea water caressing a white beach at low tide. Of a distant ocean.

Easton let out a quiet snort. "Hmphf. Well I've been called dense (and a few more colorful adjectives) by certain ladies over the years, but I have been known to figure out a thing or two on occasion." He wiggled the ends of his toes to get the circulation going again. "So...why then? What is it you're here for?"

Her answer was to jump off the chair, made a quick dash across the room, and bound onto the bed, straddling him, her slender hands on his wrists. He saw that she was wearing a confusing array of white gossamer robes with an embroidered vest and a peaked crown of hammered gold. Intricate mother-of-pearl and threaded gold earrings framed her face. Her lips were bright red and her cheeks rouged in a fashion he had seen on Malaysian dancers. Her eyes flashed with a mischievousness that had trouble written all over it and he noticed how long her lashes were.

"You."

"Me?"

"You."

She pulled his arms open and flat against the bedspread and her smile lit up her entire face. Easton had never seen anything like it. Then he realized he was grinning himself. A real honest-to-God ear-to-ear face-splitting grin. A quick thought – have I ever smiled like this in my entire life? He wasn't sure. Probably not. Definitely not in the last year. She searched his eyes intently, drinking him in. He realized he had an instant hard-on. So much for Mexican bullets. There was a tentative tilt of the neck, a teasing brush of lips, once. Twice.

And then they kissed.

Easton wasn't the type of guy to rate kisses, but if he was, this one would have topped the charts. It didn't make sense, really, and this whole thing was like a bomb dropped from Stuka screaming out of a clear blue sky. But there it was. He was aware how full her lips felt against his own, hungry, a little slippery with lipstick, and he could smell her, too – the scent of oranges and spice and a faint sweet and sour smell, an intoxicating blend. She kissed. Bit his lower lip. Kissed again. In one sense, he felt like he had just awoken from a dream. Thoughts flashed through his mind like fireworks:

Not possible. Can't be happening. How? Who? Doesn't...make...sense. Crazy! Completely impossible!

Then:

Here! Now! Great!

I...am...alive!

That was the overwhelming thought. They rolled over atop the bed, first one way, then another. Two people starved of something too long denied. Things went pretty quickly from there. Clothes removed, sent flying to various corners of the room. Suddenly they were under the covers, the soothing deliciousness of two bodies embracing under rough sheets.

Not possible. This doesn't make any sense.

Yet it did. On another level it made complete, one hundred percent sense.

Easton's thoughts were a confusing jumble. Had he ever slept with an Asian woman? No. This was a first. How did she...? Was she even legal age? She seemed so young. Difficult to tell. Even odder, the usual bars that would control his behavior, especially in rolling-out-of-control situation like this, were curiously gone. He felt completely uninhibited, as if he had tossed all reservations aside and was free-falling off a cliff. It was an exciting and terrifying feeling. What about...? But things were happening at a dizzying pace. There was clearly no question in Aun-mai's actions. Her hands and lips moved with instinctive precision. And Easton's level of arousal was quickly eclipsing all rational thought. She guided him in and locked her legs around him and he had a moment to savor that first delicious plunge.

She gasped in his ear.

Warmth. Velvet warmth of her sex. The thrill of being inside her. Panting. Breath coming in gasps. The temperature under the sheets like a furnace. Her pores opening up. Light sheen of sweat across her small breasts. Her smell was intoxicating. It hinted at mysteries. And pleasures. Beyond anything he had ever encountered before.

Easton began to shudder as his climax began to build. He felt like his entire body was going to explode.

And then it did.

She was small, but strong. Easton lay on his back, watching-but-not-watching the shadows play across the ceiling. How quickly our perceptions turn on a dime, he marveled; now the oppressive atmosphere of the room was a thing of intimacy, part of the fabric of a common experience. Aun-mai lay on her side, half wrapped around him in a koala bear hug. His left arm had her in a relaxed embrace. She was playing her fingers along his hair line, studying him. The weird thing was he felt like she belonged there. She fit perfectly. Like she had been born to lie right here in this exact position, right next to him. He felt like the two of them were momentarily in this cocoon outside of space and time, that he could just lie here, this beautiful young woman running her fingers across his head for all eternity and that would be just fine. Fine as wine.

"Aun-mai, how …?"

She put her fingers to his lips.

"Cinta, Kamu," she whispered in his ear. The words raced into his brain and through his heart and through his body. It was a thrilling sensation. A smile touched his face. But his mind was working. The inner policeman wouldn't stay long in his closet. In fact, the door was cracked open and he was waiting there, patiently, peeking out, pencil poised over notebook.

"Aun-mai, I need answers. You need to tell me what's going on here."

Her response was to pinch his nose.

"Do you like me?"

"Do I like you?"

"Yes. Do you like me. A little bit?"

Easton let out a short laugh. "Yes. I like you. Very much. And I don't even know who in God's name you really are. But I'd really like to find out." He felt her finger tips lightly caressing his face, as if seeking to memorize its craggy contours. Or read the history of him as if his face was in Braille. "Christ, it's a cliché. But I do...it's like, Deja vu. All over again.

She smiled dreamily. "You know who I am. You've always known. But now there are other things you must know. About Van Eyckmann. And Kimmi. And tonight." She began to whisper in his ear.

Easton listened very carefully.

After a while, her hand wandered down to his groin and began to speak its own language. Easton listened to that too. The second time she stayed on top.

That was just fine too.

Consciousness seeped into his mind like a rising tide, floating up out of the depths of Morpheus' smooth embrace. He was aware that he felt entirely calm, the way one does after running that mile too far and the body's floodgates open, release a flood of endorphins through the whole system.

Calm euphoria.

He was trying to recall the last time he felt this good. Hell, the last time he had had sex. A month? Two months? The answer was eluding him at the moment. What in the hell had he just done? The lights went on internally and he snapped fully awake, literally sitting up in the bed. He thought he heard a door closing.

Shit!

He looked wildly around. He was sitting alone, clothed, on top of the bed. The covers were all tangled up. No Aun-mai. Of course not. He struggled with his thoughts. And emotions. He must have dozed off while reading. If had been a dream, then it had been the most lucid dream he had ever had in his life. The mother of all lucid dreams. He looked at his watch. According to it, the whole episode had only taken five minutes. It had felt like hours.

A little long in the tooth to be having wet dreams, mate, he thought to himself. He bent over and sniffed the pillows and sheets. He could swear he could smell sex on them. Impossible. Then he noticed two other things. The first was the antique sword Aun-mai had handed him earlier, lying on the bed. It had been in the closet. It had definitely not been on the bed when he first stretched out. The other was the glint of mother of pearl peeking out from under the pillow. He reached and carefully pulled out a small shell earring. With threaded gold hoops.

She had been wearing it.

Impossible.

Still, something jumped in his heart. The dream had been so lucid, it was as real as the thick bed cover under his hands right at that moment. Had it been real? Was someone playing an elaborate hoax on him?

No. Yes. Maybe. He had glanced at the penciled notes at the back of the book. Someone had been doing some additional investigating. Maynard? Akma was just a nick-name.

So of course, Aun-mai wasn't here.

She had been dead nearly 400 years.

14. ONE POTATO, TWO POTATO

Knightbridge jumped into his black Cadillac Escalade that he had left parked under the porte-cochere and gunned it down the drive to the guardhouse. He was definitely not keen on how the whole situation was unfolding. First he would find out what his two screwball sidekicks had been up to, then he would track down Easton and find out what his beef was, then get as many of these lunatics into his SUV as possible and get the hell out of here before something went seriously wrong. Let the town police (or the FBI, for the missing gardener) deal with the whole fucking mess. Knightbridge only needed five minutes back in his office to destroy any incriminating evidence that might be in the fireproof file cabinet (especially the file cabinet – it had a variety of photos and negatives many people, including Hilderman and his associates, would be extremely interested in) or in the laptop next to it, and it was out of Oz we go.

Only as Knightbridge pulled into the drive behind the Continental, he knew immediately it wasn't going to be that simple. For starters, all the lights were out in the caretaker's house and it was pushing four o'clock in the afternoon. On the heels of that, all the vehicles were in the drive. He pulled in behind the Town Car, walked around to the front porch, and spotted red flag number three: the front door was open. Not good. That was when the Glock came out of its holster.

He stepped up carefully to the front door, shoulder up to the jamb, and did a quick peek. In and out. Nothing. It was dark inside. The heavy front door was open about six inches. Since the temperature was in the mid-40s, odds that it was a leisurely mistake were low. There was a double light switch just inside the door to the left, one that controlled the porch light, the other the front hall. Shifting the nine-millimeter to his left hand, he reached around quickly with his right and flicked the lights on.

Still nothing.

Then, a slight rustle from inside. A heavy thump. In one sweeping motion, Knightbridge kicked the door and landed in the front hall, both feet planted firmly on the floor, both hands clutching the Glock in a regulation grip. Sweep left, then right, then …

Something large flying at him. He dropped right and narrowly missed pumping a round into a large raccoon that shot past him and out the door, equally as startled. Then he saw the driver.

The front atrium of the house had a vaulted ceiling, perhaps 15 feet high. The driver had been nailed to it. By what appeared to be a couple hundred nails. Knightbridge wasn't up for a detailed analysis, but at a glance, the source looked to be the assortment kept in the basement workshop, where boxes of old carpenter tools and of old large construction nails were kept. The big iron railroad spike driven through the roof of the man's mouth was a unique touch. He didn't recall seeing that one downstairs. Then again, the place was filled with a ton of junk. Couldn't rule it out.

Impressive. He had no idea who could have done this, let alone managed the logistics of getting the body up there like that, or even why. One thing he did know: the driver, Marco Ruiz, was once a Sandinista bodyguard and was considered by many to be quite a dangerous man. Not exactly an easy target. Especially in the middle of the day. So whatever party was responsible for this was clearly very dangerous.

The floor exhibited a zig-zag of raccoon tracks through the blood. The animal must have smelled it and wandered in. There was no sign of any human prints on the floor.

All bets were off then. He thumbed the safety catch to the Off position and crept through the archway to the left, quiet as a cat. For a man of his bulk, Knightbridge could be surprisingly agile when the occasion called for it. The living room was a gloomy no-man's-land of shapes and shadows. Something was playing on the television, a 50-inch Samsung LED flat screen, though the sound was muted.

Floating across the pixels in glorious high definition were the bland hang-dog features of Doctor Phil, apparently dispensing his usual glib patter of down-home small-town country-doc wisdom to the haggard-eyed, dysfunctional-looking trailer-trash couples. Knightbridge had actually listened to the show once and thought the guy made some degree of sense. Then he saw the trophy wife and saw right through the whole game for what it was.

A fact that was clearly no longer of any concern to "Spanks" McGoohan, who apparently was, as Knightbridge had long suspected, a closet Dr. Phil fan. Spanks' severed head had been left in the middle of the oak-planked living room floor, positioned either by accident or design to face the television. One school of thought suggests that the last image one sees before dying is burned onto the retina. If so, then Spanks went into the eternal night with the good doctor stuck on his eyes. Knightbridge thought that might be a previously unguessed version of hell.

Of the body, there was no sign, though the overturned couch and spray of blood on the walls, floor, television set, and bookcase behind brought a few suggestions to mind. Pistol still gripped in both hands, Knightbridge edged over towards the sofa carefully and did a quick glance. Sure enough, there was a jumble of legs and arms and the Rowe Security Group patch on the shoulder that clinched it.

Knightbridge also noticed several long slices in the upholstery of the couch that looked to have been made by an extremely sharp object.

Like a sword.

A few feet away from McGoohan's body was a Glock pistol. With a hand still gripping it. Someone had come in here and done a brutally efficient job on one of his security men. With a sharp-bladed weapon. Which really didn't make a lot of sense.

That still left Gerry Wallace.

As if in response to that thought, there came a heavy crash from upstairs.

Followed by the roar of Wallace's Ruger Blackhawk .44 Magnum. Knightbridge knew immediately the distinctive sound – he'd fired it himself a few times on the range and thought it a bit of overkill for their particular type of work. But Wallace had a Dirty Harry fetish and got off with toting his cannon-caliber revolver in a shoulder holster.

Three shots, a couple of four-letter expletives, followed by a gargled scream. Knightbridge moved over to the front stairwell as quickly and quietly as he could. Just as he got to the bottom, he saw somebody half bumping, half sliding down the wide staircase. It was Wallace, Magnum in his right hand, white as a ghost and eyes wide with shock. As he slowed to a stop at the base of the staircase, Knightbridge could see that both his legs were gone below the knees. Cut clean off. As he tried to process this, Wallace grabbed his pant-leg with his free hand and looked up into his employer's face.

"Fuckin' eyes, boss, shoot the fuckin' eyes," and with that rolled onto his back and died.

There was a heavy thud and Knightbridge saw something moving in the gathered shadows at the top of the stairs. Creak. Thud. Creak. Thud. Whatever it was, it was coming down and taking its time doing so.

About halfway down, Knightbridge could begin to make out what the hell it was.

A man – presumably – in a suite of armor. The lacquered armor of a 17th century Samurai warrior. Complete with the flared helmet with its strange projections. Almost identical to the one he'd seen in Van Eyckmann's parlor.

Was this some sort of joke?

Apparently not, based on the blood stains and the deadly-looking Katana held in the thing's two gloved fists. It was really the face, however, that got Knightbridge's attention. When showing decomposed corpses, horror movies threw things together out of the prop designer's overactive imaginations.

This was clearly the real thing.

The smell would have gotten his attention, if nothing else. The gagging putrescence of something long dead. A few tattered remnants of flesh, but mostly just a grinning skull. And the suggestion of a greenish light pulsing in the back of the eye sockets.

The sword came up in a glittering arc. Knightbridge was mesmerized. Nothing in his professional experience had prepared him for anything like this.

The sword came down.

The Glock came up.

15. DINNER IS SERVED

Easton stood before the full length mirror, making a few final adjustments to his costume. Although he felt utterly absurd, he had to admit the outfit didn't look half bad. He cut a rakish figure just out of central casting for a part in The Three Musketeers. Boots of soft cordovan leather with wide brims went up to his knees. His pantaloons were of gold damask slitted with deep maroon reveals. Over a loose linen shirt he wore a studded leather doublet that was reinforced at the shoulders, a fall of lace at the neck, and a broad-brimmed hat with a white plume. Slung over his right shoulder was a heavy leather bandolier with a large bronze buckle from which hung the English sword Aun-mai had given him.

Or someone had. He still having difficulty accepting that a woman dead some 400 years was running around dispensing presents (and having sex). Part of him might partially accept it, but that voice was being largely ignored. He was still convinced that somewhere, somehow, there was a human agent behind all of this. How and why he was yet to find out.

After his...daydream...he had jumped into the shower, keeping the temperature close to scalding, then turning it ice cold. That woke him up better than a slap across the face. Partly it was to clear his head of any emotional residue of what had – or had not – transpired. Even fifteen minutes later, the lucidness of the dream still had him in its thrall, It felt more real than most of the real things he had experienced. He could still smell Aun-mai's potent scent in his mind. Which made him wonder how could that be? He had no recollection of ever "smelling" an Oriental woman, and certainly had never been in bed with one, so where did that gem come from? Subconscious. Buried there somehow. Don't think about it!

I'm not crazy!

Famous last words while the straight jacket was put on. Maybe all of this was part of an elaborate nervous breakdown and —here's one – he was really dying on the floor of Princeton's office and his mind had been furiously working overtime constructing the classic Occurrence at Owl Creek Bridge scenario?

No. Sorry. Not buying it.

The really weird thing though was how good he felt. Hell, he felt great. Great in the way one can only feel after a round of really intense and overdue sex. Which was just plain absurd.

Absurd or not, he found himself humming a half-forgotten tune in the shower. He had to fish around in his thoughts a minute before he could come up with the title.

It was Always. By Irving Berlin.

One of the early versions from 1926. Performed by Layton and Johnstone. Easton recalled his grandmother playing an old scratchy 78 when he was a child and it was that more-melodic version, not the jazzed-up Fred Astaire one recorded in the early '30s, that still stuck in his mind so many years later.

The costume had taken him a good ten minutes of trial and error to figure out. An instruction manual might have been helpful. Apparently getting dressed in the 17th century was quite an event and involved innumerable buttons and hooks and bucklings. He had a hunch "getting a quicky" wouldn't have been in the realm of possibility back then.

Feeling vaguely ridiculous, Easton sauntered downstairs to the dining room in his get-up. The one thing that didn't feel out of place or contrived was the sword at his hip. It hung there, heavy, an object of time and purpose. And of violent potential.

The long dining room had been transformed for a Halloween Feast. The centerpieces were a mix of antique decorations – carved sculptures of old goblins and witches and skeletons – with fresh miniature pumpkins and jack-o-lanterns and heavy candles in antique candelabra. Their placement suggested a professional, theatrical eye.

Hilderman and the others were already there, already enjoying cocktails when Easton stepped in. All were dressed in equally flamboyant costumes. Quite a gallery of rogues. An assortment of doublets and jerkins, breeches and boots. Some with lace, Hilderman sporting a traditional Elizabethan collar, Wang with an open-necked shirt with a wide collar. An assortment of rapiers and daggers at their hips. Easton noted that embossed name cards had been placed along the table at their place settings under their "character" titles.

Van Eyckmann's lieutenants.

But why?

It was Hilderman who approached Easton first, holding an oversized snifter of brandy as some sort of apparent peace offering.

"Mr. Matt…" he began, then looking around, "Oh piss on it! Mr. Easton, pleased you could join us." Easton noticed a slight glassiness in his eyes. Apparently Hilderman had gotten a little head start on the festivities. "May we count on you to conduct yourself in a more, shall we say, civil manner this evening?" The last words came out more as a command than a question. Easton glanced over at Washington who was glowering over his drink by the sideboard with Derek Anderson. There appeared to be an assortment of appetizers laid out there on platters of polished silver draped with linen. Washington crammed a large spinach pastry into his mouth and looked back at Easton warily. Anderson was chatting along unhindered, an apple in one hand and a cocktail in the other. It occurred to Easton that it may not have been the wisest organizational planning to have so many men armed to the teeth and drinking, particularly when two of them had been at each other's throats just a few hours earlier. However, he was more than capable of playing the diplomat when the situation required.

"Of course, Mr. Hilderman. More than glad to put any differences between Mr. Washington and me behind us.". I appreciate the drink. However, I only drink Scotch before dinner and brandy afterwards."

"Of course, of course!" (Did Easton see a glint of annoyance in his host's eye?) Hilderman walked with him over to the sideboard set up with drinks. Easton decided to try another option and went with an 18-year-old Aberlour, another single malt he occasionally enjoyed, though his policeman's budget tended to favor the 12-year-old. It had a deep amber color and smooth taste. Hilderman's eyebrows went up as Easton dropped in a couple of ice cubes into his glass.

"Personal quirk," he explained.

Hilderman gave a disbelieving shake of the head   .

"Mr. Easton, listen. I'm not entirely sure how much of this game is up (Easton had serious doubts about that), but I do firmly think it is in everyone's best interest to keep up appearances tonight, follow through with Van Eyckmann's 'requests' until tomorrow morning, when Lowe pops up and the late master of Taron Hall is in the ground. Then we can all claim our respective shares and go our separate ways. Agreed?"

Easton shrugged.

"In which case, since we are all gentlemen here, a truce." With which, he clinked Easton's glass with his own. Easton seriously doubted the veracity of that statement as well, but, being in a diplomatic mood, nodded his head and responded, "A truce, then." It crossed his mind that a lot of issues around the world could probably be avoided if they got all the leaders in a room together and gave each of them a glass of high quality Scotch. Or wine. Or sake. Or shoju. Or whichever drink floated your boat. Just get the best one you can, put it in the other guy's hand, have a healthy belt. Then let's talk.

Then again, he mused, that probably wouldn't help much with this bunch.

Hilderman took up a position at the head of the table and clinked his glass with a spoon to get everyone's attention. "Gentlemen, gentlemen. If you please. Take your seats..." There was a bit of confused shuffling around while name cards were cross checked with printed itineraries, then everyone sorted themselves out. The place settings were organized at the north end of the table, presumably so that conversation could be carried on without resorting to megaphones or shouting. Easton found himself seated in the middle. On his right was Joe Lefferts, then, going clockwise starting from his left, was Jeffrey Wang, Hilderman, Washington, Derek Anderson, and, last, directly across from him was Juan Delgado.

Easton had an uneasy feeling about the whole set-up, the costumes, the assigned names, the whole bizarre will and, even worse, the gnawing sense of the past and present moving on a collision course that would have disastrous results. The rational Easton, the one that had been hammered and honed to perfection over years as a policeman, told him that he was being ridiculous, that he was letting his emotions, the oppressive atmosphere of the Taron Hall and – let's admit it – the fact that it was All Hallows Eve get the better of him. And that made perfect sense.

Almost.

Hilderman was still standing, his glass held up in the air. "Gentlemen, I'd like to propose a toast to our late colleague and – well perhaps not dear – but certainly friend, Lars Van Eyckmann. It goes without saying, of course, that is because of him that we are all gathered here at Taron Hall tonight to fulfill his last will and testament. Some or all of you may find this last 'request' somewhat, shall we say, 'unusual', but in the 15 years I knew Lars that hardly comes as a surprise. Then again, Lars was always full of surprises. (This drew a few quiet laughs.) But all joking aside, he was a dedicated philanthropist and supporter of the business and future of Brooklyn. He was shrewd and, when necessary, merciless in his efforts to cultivate what he felt – and I agree – to be an elite group of the best and brightest of the Borough of Brooklyn. Now some of you may have asked yourself on occasion, why Brooklyn? Why not Queens. Or Staten Island? (This drew a few chuckles.) No great mystery, I'm afraid. When the Van Eyckmann's came to New York, or New Amsterdam as it was back then, there was opportunity here. Particularly after the British took over the town and the church began systematically taking over Manhattan real estate.

Brooklyn was there for the taking, had close access to the trade and shipping of lower Manhattan, which was critical back in the 17th century. Many of you probably have no idea how much real estate the Van Eyckmann family owned. I have only some idea, but it was a lot."

"That's an understatement," murmured Washington.

Hilderman shot him an annoyed glance. "Yes, a lot. And still is. But his one main pride and joy was the Mohican Club. Over the years, the most distinguished members of Brooklyn's business elite have walked its halls and, as you know, you're being chosen by Van Eyckmann himself as its Executive Council should be considered quite an honor. All of you should take some measure of pride in that. So if our required presence here tonight strikes some of you as a little odd, consider that tomorrow all of us will be a little wealthier and able to continue with Van Eyckmann's vision. So to him I say: *Salut!*"

"Hear, hear," someone chimed in amidst a murmur of assent and around the table glasses clinked.

Easton thought he heard Delgado mumble, "Kiss my ass."

The hostile atmosphere at lunch had dissipated somewhat. Either it was the costumes, the liquor, or both. Or maybe none of the above. But at least between Wang and Lefferts, the immediate conversation at least promised to be convivial.

Two younger women dressed in antiquated-looking servant's outfits and wearing black cat masks brought out the first course, which was a light pumpkin bisque, sprinkled with freshly ground nutmeg (how apropos, thought Easton) and a fresh sprig of parsley. Neither of the women, Easton noted, were Aun-mai, one being the striking brunette eyeing Easton earlier in the kitchen. The young theater type, now dressed in a traditional swallow-tail coat and wearing a classic masquerade mask, sailed about offering a choice of wines; a 2008 Pascal Jolivet Pouilly Fume or a 2003 Sterling Vineyard Napa Valley Cabernet Sauvignon. Easton always had a soft spot for a decent Pouilly Fume, so he went with that and was fairly impressed with its airy-yet-snappy taste. He half listened to Wang giving him a lecture on the best French restaurants in Brooklyn. He seemed particularly fixated on one called the AOC Bistro at the corner of Fifth Avenue and Garfield Place – as if Easton had any sort of clue where that might be – while, on his right, Lefferts was going on about celebrities he'd handled investments for over the years. Easton wondered idly about how much the price tag of catering the whole affair was running and decided it was probably more than his salary.

The brunette server's left breast brushed his shoulder as she served his soup, clearly an invitation of sorts (based on the sidelong glance that followed), but whatever interest Easton might have had earlier had dissipated, which struck him as pretty perverse – he was more interested in a dream (or more likely a ghost) of a woman than a full-blooded one right at his side.

He wondered if he needed to get his head examined.

And yet....

He couldn't deny it, something about Aun-mai had really gotten under his skin. His mind kept wandering back to their...what? Encounter? Rendezvous? What in the hell had actually happened?

It was real.

No it wasn't.

The earring.

The sword.

No.

All this bouncing back and forth in his head while, between spoonfuls of the bisque, Easton kept his head going left and right, nodding or making affirmative grunts in the appropriate places. This was fast becoming the most surreal dinner he had ever eaten in his life. Lefferts was repeating his lunchtime trick of stuffing his face vigorously while maintaining an animated conversation, a talent Easton still found amazing. He managed to intercept a passing plate of fresh bread that had a hard, almost-burnt crust but with a chewy, almost sour bread inside. Once dipped in one of the nearby bowls of fresh rosemary and minced garlic olive oil (with a hint of hot pepper), it proved to be heaven in the mouth. Easton had never tasted anything quite like it. He vowed then and there to someday track down the bakery, buy a dozen loaves, and eat nothing but bread and wine for a week.

The soup bowls were deftly cleared away, replaced by clean plates and silverware. Easton picked up on the cold shoulder he was now getting from Miss Brunette and mused on how some things never changed. Salads arrived – hearts of romaine with dried cranberries, glazed walnuts, red onion, and warm goat cheese with a balsamic vinaigrette. After years of eating Caribbean food, the range of flavors was a culture shock wave in Easton's mouth. Wine glasses were refilled and conversation went up a notch.

The main course arrived. This turned out to be a seared pork chop bathed in caramelized slices of Fuji apple and fresh minced ginger cooked in brandy, an assortment of roasted squash and grilled asparagus tips, and a side of basmati rice with almonds. This day was turning out to be one of the strangest Easton could ever recall, but, surreal or not, the dinner was certainly turning out to be one of the best.

He also couldn't help but wonder if they were all being fattened up for the kill.

Juan Delgado quizzed him over the main course on the resorts of the Turks and Caicos Islands and where the best shopping was. (And celebrity hotspots – where does Paul McCartney stay? What about Keith Richards? Easton had no idea.) Lefferts went on about his family vacations in Italy, Monaco, and the Jersey shore. Washington kept avoiding Easton's eye and keeping to quiet conversation over at his corner with Hilderman and Anderson. Hilderman seemed content to keep the whole thing rolling along at a predictable pace, though on occasion he gave Easton a steely-eyed gaze to keep him in check, which Easton simply ignored.

An assortment of desserts arrived – Portuguese almond and custard tortas from a local bakery, along with pumpkin mousse and sweet potato pie, and a choice of port or brandy.

Easton passed on both and opted instead for a hot cup of coffee.

Just before 8:00, Hilderman stood up and signaled the group, again by clinking his glass with his spoon. Easton had to suppress a sudden irrational urge to pull out the pistol hidden in his jerkin and shoot the damn thing out of his hand.

"Gentlemen, gentlemen. It is time now for the next part of the evening's program. If I might impose on all of you to retire now to the library?"

"Ooh, this should be rich," Delgado said under his breath.

"Ah, the Loony 'Toons segment of tonight's entertainment," chimed in Lefferts, addressing Easton. The two men had stood up together and stood with palms resting on sword hilts. The whole thing still felt utterly ridiculous. "Do you believe in ghosts, spirits, spooks, Detective?"

"Wel-l-ll, let's just say I do try to keep an open mind. You see a lot of strange things in my line of work."

"I bet. I bet. Probably a lot of that voodoo crap down in your neck of the planet. Stuff gives me the willies. Did I tell you yet about the time I went down to New Orleans? Totally fucked up story. This college kid, you see, was visiting one of those voodoo museums and accidentally banged into this..."

Easton only half-listened while they walked over to the library at the front of the house where Easton had run into Kimmi earlier. Something terrible had apparently befallen the college student in Lefferts' story but Easton was distracted by Wang going on in his other ear about some haunted house in Brooklyn on Third Avenue where a whole bunch of kids had disappeared the Halloween before.

The lights in the library had been dimmed and a candelabrum with heavy candles had been placed in the center of the octagonal reading table. At the end of the table opposite the entrance was placed a large crystal ball in an elaborately carved bronze stand. Eight chairs had been placed around the table.

The men filed in and sorted themselves out around the table, leaving the seat in front of the crystal ball vacant. A few minutes, later Kimmi appeared in the doorway, gave a short bow, and quietly glided in his peculiar way over to the table, taking the seat before the crystal ball. Somehow Easton wasn't surprised. Outside the stormy Halloween weather ratcheted up a notch and, appropriately enough, there came a blinding white flash followed by a ripping thunderclap that shook the walls of Taron Hall. The library lights winked in response but stayed on.

After allowing everyone a minute to settle in, Kimmi clapped his hands twice and cleared his throat, giving the table a once-over with his strange glittering look. Easton decided that look was getting stranger by the minute. Something about the eyes was not quite right   "My noble friends, I trust the evening meal was to your satisfaction? Each of you has chosen your after-dinner beverage, yes? Then, as it has been ordained in the past, I shall share with you a little story. Fitting for the holiday celebrated this night in the western world, I think. Though perhaps, as it were, not the precise version Mr. Van Eyckmann planned as part of this evening's agenda? Ah, then, so it is, my friends. Sit back and relax. Enjoy your drinks, for I assure you I have a most interesting tale to share..."

16. KIMMI'S TALE

"Perchance, you are aware that hundreds of years past there once existed the Dutch East India Company, known hitherto as the VOC or "Vereenigde Oostindische Compagnie." And, perchance, you are aware that for a time, they exercised complete control over the spice trade of the Far East? No? Much has been written but little truth has been told. But tonight I will give you a full and true account of that which occurred on this very night 390 years ago....

"In the year 1619, there came to the Spice Islands a man, a magician who had given himself up since childhood to the arcane sciences, who had delved into the world of enchantments and their darker secrets, of reading the stars and understanding the spirits, and of spells and creatures and forbidden knowledge that was old when Egypt was young. He was a man who may have been in the bloom of his youth. Twenty? Thirty? None could say but I know. He had seen more than 40 years come and go. But to all he was tall and handsome, and few women – or men – could resist him. (At this, Delgado was rolling his eyes)

"No one knew precisely whence he came – some said he was of the Bedouin nomads of Arabia. Others claim he was from the mountains of Nepal, or Persia, or was of the lost Dravidian sect that still hide in the mountains of China. What was known was that he was well-traveled and fluent in many languages, even languages that were moldering and forgotten by the ears of men in ancient Sumer. Through long and labored exertions and adventures, he traveled throughout the East to the Spice Islands. Therein he chanced upon the island of Palau Banda, where he arrived one day in the court of one of the most powerful orang kaya (a wealthy merchant) there, the man known as Khali-mior. (Easton gave a start here, and his attention perked up.)

"This magician, who went by the name of Maghra, saw opportunity for his purse and pleasure and, as you will soon see, his heart. Thus he presented his services as a darwashi and had been accepted, proving himself by giving wise and fruitful counsel to Khali-mior over the course of the ensuing year.

"Khali-mior was not only powerful, he was also the most respected amongst his fellow orang kaya, as they were called in the East Indies then. He had the largest and richest house, a mansion built in the western style of the Dutch, and a harem of the 12 most beautiful women throughout the islands. Though he had no sons, he did have five beautiful daughters, each of whom he adored. The daughter he loved most, however, was his youngest. She was stubborn-headed and obstinate, but she was possessed of untold beauty and magnificence which every man, young and old, wished to feast his eyes upon forever.

"Her name was Aun-mai."

(At this point, Easton, who had been in the process of taking another sip of his coffee, choked and narrowly avoided spewing it all over his plate.)

Kimmi sat with his gloved hands folded on the table before him, his strange eyes dancing around the table at his guests. It was clear he was taking some sort of – and, as it subsequently came out, perverse – pleasure in relaying this story. The jewels set in the front of his turban glimmered in the dim light. If Easton wasn't mistaken, the largest was a sapphire diamond, one that he suspected would have the undivided attention of a lot of jewelers. Kimmi continued on in his heavy accent:

"Ahhh, this Aun-mai – her father called her 'Akma' or 'my little gem' – was truly a woman to behold, whom Allah hath made none fairer. All the men throughout the islands of Banda knew of her and desired her. Her eyes were round and well-shaped and alive with fire, her nose pretty and properly proportioned. Her lips were as coral with cornelian shine, her figure elegant and majestic, her breast a seduction for all to see (glory be to Him who fashioned it and finished it!). And Maghra was like a man entranced. He wrote her eloquent poems, left rare and beautiful flowers at her window, and used his magick talents to make all manner of gifts to bestow on her – giant moths cast in gold, precious gems and jewelry, silken robes of the finest weave. He most certainly made clear the intentions of his heart and soul. He would make her queen of all Banda, of all the Spice Islands, should she so desire. No wish would go unfulfilled, no desire unsatisfied, he would place the world at her toes and take her heart – and body – to realms of happiness and ecstasy she had never even guessed at in her wildest imaginings. He would have given her, my friends, everything and all a woman could ever want (Easton had serious doubts on that account)…all she had to do was to ask, and he would respond 'to hear is to obey'."

"But was this to be? Would she recognize the greatness and value of the riches that she was being offered? That a thousand princesses would have begged for?" Kimmi snorted. "No! Of course not! She was the spoiled offspring of a rich orang kaya. She had been raised from a mewling infant on the promise that she could already have anything she wanted. And the promises of Maghra, the offerings of his very soul, were toyed with and then cast aside like casual playthings. Ha, ha! Imagine that! A magician of such immeasurable talents, arcane knowledge, and wisdom, a man who had traveled the seven seas and survived countless battles and adventures against creatures, monsters, and savages in lands sane men have never dreamed of, this great man and his riches being…being treated in such a disagreeable fashion by this insolent wench of a princess!"

Kimmi's eyes were wide open, almost glowing it seemed, with the bloodshot whites completely showing around the irises, and bits of spittle sprayed from his mouth as he hissed the last sentence. A few uneasy glances circulated around the table. Delgado, who was seated on Easton's right, leaned in and whispered in his ear "Whoa, someone needs my therapist's number I think!" Hilderman had a flat look on his face that clearly read, "Right, fine, get on with the blasted story and let us have a decent drink and get off to bed." Washington appeared to be entranced with something off in the distance – perhaps daydreaming of one of his illicit visits to Chinatown – while Derek Anderson had settled into a look of polite boredom. Only Lefferts and Easton seemed genuinely interested in the story that was unfolding.

Kimmi's thermostat seemed to settle back a few degrees. His fingers worked of their own accord, moving back and forth like an agitated pair of albino crab legs. "But I must entreat your pardon and return to the thread of my story….

"…presently it turned out there was another. An Englishman who was known by the name of Forester. This other man (of the forest?) was a sea captain sent to command the small settlement of other Englishmen on the island known as Palau Rhun where it was his mission to keep trading under the noses of the Dutch. To these English, the entire matter was that of a big joke, a subject of jest, and a source of insult to the Dutch. And they would pay dearly, very dearly, for their disagreeable behavior…yes, my friends, they would indeed pay.

"And so, as Maghra discovered, it was this Englishman that Aun-mai was in love with, to whom she had secretly betrothed her heart, and it did great violence to the magician's feelings. It would have killed her father to find out so! Her foolishness threatened the honor of her entire family. An Englishman! Pah! Better to fall in love with the swine boar in the jungle.

"Ah, yet there was another issue, in the form of the new Dutch Governor VOC: and his name was Lars Van Eyckmann. Yes, Van Eyckmann. A man of many talents. You've heard of him, no?" Kimmi let out a low laugh, "Yes, of course, my friends. But not the Van Eyckmann of this tale. This Van Eyckmann was cruel – a sadist. And possessed of a single mind. A man, I ascertain, that would share much in common with myself. And it was thus: Van Eyckmann arrived thence to set matters right. Perhaps to settle an old score...You see, he had served under the previous governor, a man of naïve and foolish inclinations who had been lured into an ambush and murdered by the very same Bandanese merchants 12 years earlier. Van Eyckmann had failed in his duty to protect his superior, and thus it was in his mind to exert discipline on these islanders, who were skilled in all manners of craft and double dealing, yes? And these Englishmen, a boorish and tiresome lot, who were they to be trading thus under noses of the Dutch, who had taken their rightful place as masters of the spice trade! These English thieves who would seek to steal the spices and destroy the market these noble Dutchmen had worked so hard and so selflessly to create. Who indeed?

"So one of the governor's spies approached the magician, a man whose noblest intentions had been vexed by Khali-mior's little brat. Was he not justified, I abjure you? That perhaps he might find some recourse if he listened to him, yes? And so, by the light of the crescent moon one October night, a deal was struck. The Englishman and the Bandanese traitors, in exchange for the princess. And so it was agreed.

"But black and treacherous the hearts of men are, are they not? For Van Eyckmann, being an infamous wretch, had no intention to keep his word. None. In his heart, which he had sworn to a fearful God and His Son who had bled out on a cross – a God in whose name countless innocents would be slaughtered – thought it beneath himself to honor his word to a man who appeared no different than the double-dealing Bandanese he served. And it was thus: one night, he ordered the slaughter of all the islanders, or as many as his men could find and put to the sword, then tricked the Englishman into his spider's web by kidnapping all of Khali-mior's daughters. Such was the plan he devised: that he would have everything and the honor of his word be damned!

"Ah, but the Englishman was of an unpredictable and a rogue sort – as so many of them are – and he alighted on the governor's ship and made exertions to rescue Khali-mior's foolish daughter. Many of Van Eyckmann's men, Dutch and Japanese alike, were cut to pieces ere he leaped overboard with Princess Aun-mai in his arms. And Maghra, who chanced to be arriving right then in a native boat, saw his chance to reclaim what was his! Alas, such is God's will, it came about that, to do so, he had to rescue not just Aun-mai, but the Englishman as well, as it was his arms that kept her from certain drowning. How cruel can the gods above be, how cruel! But it was so, and they had to flee as Van Eyckmann was inclined to see all of them dead!

"It came to pass that there was a chase, a pursuit that ended with the English Captain Forester, Aun-mai, and Maghra trapped atop the old Buddhist temple at the rim of the volcano on Rhun. There followed a duel, an incredible battle with swords between Van Eyckmann and the Englishman. Back and forth! Back and forth! Steel flashing in the morning sun. But the little governor, trained as he was in the finest fencing schools of Europe, was no match for the English swine. The fight went on, here, there, until finally the Dutchman, being of a deceitful mind, made a trick. In this he failed and was hitherto run through by this Captain Forester.

"There he would have died, my friends, had not Maghra seen his opportunity to step in and mortally wound the English captain. And what then? More roguery! A rock thrown by one of Van Eyckmann's swine, felling Maghra in his moment of victory. And thus Van Eyckmann survives, the Princess Aun-mai is recaptured. Maghra, however, escapes and, though badly injured, swears that revenge shall be his. It must be! For the next morning Van Eyckmann has the Khali-mior's daughter put to death in a most terrible way. Selecting the ten most skilled swordsmen amongst his Japanese guards, he instructs each one to inflict a cut — just so — not one itself enough to kill, but to inflict much pain. Thirteen cuts each, one hundred thirty in all. The pain must have been exquisite! Such torment! This Dutchman is quite the sadist, no? He wishes her to beg for her death, for her eternal release from this suffering, but in this he will be disappointed. She is but a young woman, after all, and unable to withstand such torments. And it is thus: she is all but dead when he grows tired of his exertions and with one final swing his sword chop! Off goes her head!" He made a cutting motion in the air with his twisted hand to make his point. An oppressive silence hung in the room as Kimmi, with the knack of a natural story teller, let his words sink in. Each man had his own version of the scene just described imprinted on his thoughts, each as equally unpleasant as the other. Outside, the wind continued to howl and rattle at the window panes and somewhere in the vast walls of Taron Hall something creaked and moaned. If there was ever a more appropriate location, night, or weather for such a story, none at the table could imagine it.

Kimmi waited another minute, before picking up the thread of his narrative:

"Maghra knows the instant that the object his heart most desired is dead. He howls like a wretched animal and clutches his breast as if mortally wounded himself. What was to be his, is no more. O what is to be done! For a spell he meditates on this and then the answer comes upon him like a thunder stroke. He makes haste to a secret place on the island, a hidden cave where he has kept the tools and devices he must use and call on at such ill times as this. A square device bearing the seal of Solomon is uncovered and, after making the sand which it is in quite smooth and even, he arranged the points, drew the necessary figures, and began reciting his conjurations. You would not wish to hear those words, my friends. What they summon would turn your skin black and your hair white and freeze the blood in your veins. Such a risk are these words that they must be spoken in a precise manner and order; to not do so correctly is to risk the burning of your very soul in the deepest pits of hell for all eternity. Words not meant for mortal ears. And then he called a name.

"There was a sound. A blasphemous sound. Then... It began. First as a tendril of smoke that writhed in the air like a cobra, dancing this way and that. And it grew and sparkled and swayed and there appeared an ifrit, a powerful variety of the haunting demons of the deserts and wilderness, bound to obey his bidding! A hideous thing of the darkest nightmares, and yet man-like in its fashion. And so Maghra spoke, "Hearken my words, O thing of the netherworld, for I would command thee..." and he described what it was his will to be done. The ifrit responded, "To hear is to obey" and listened. And it was thus that the fate of Van Eyckmann was sealed.

"That very night, the ifrit visited Van Eyckmann's bed chamber in the guise of Maghra to deliver the first part of his curse: eternal life and with it, eternal suffering. And presently the second curse: every 130 years, on the night of his sin, this accursed history shall be re-lived. But with a twist. Van Eyckmann will suffer the same fate he inflicted on the princess, before the eyes of the one who cast his curse. And so it has been...and so it shall be!"

Once again, uneasy looks travelled around the table. Kimmi may have been a consummate storyteller but it was clear from their expressions that more than a few of the men at the table were convinced he was also mad as a hatter. Easton heard a tapping sound and realized it was Hilderman drumming his forefinger on the table, looking at Kimmi with one eyebrow arched in irritation.

"So perhaps now, Mr. Kimmi, you might care to enlighten us. Why are we here?"

On Easton's left, Lefferts leaned back in his chair, both hands flat on the table. "Second that. Oh, and what is the deal with these ridiculous costumes?"

Kimmi looked around the table, eyes sparkling. Easton didn't care for that look. Not one bit. It was a look he'd seen many times on a perp's face just before he or she was planning to do something shit-house crazy like pulling a hidden switchblade to try to gut you. It was the scrambled-neurons dangerous-animal look.

Kimmi was smiling. A big broad smile that managed to look a little too big for his face. One that fell well short of his eyes. "Why, I believe we are here for a séance, my friends. At Van Eyckmann's request."

Geoffrey Washington chimed in this time with his deep baritone, "And the point of us dressing up like a theater troupe of...dandies?"

"Perhaps you prefer to ask yourself? And now I require silence. It is time to summon those who have gone beyond the veil of life and those who cannot leave it..."

Wang looked around. "Don't we need to link hands or something?"

Kimmi shot him a fierce look. "No such nonsense. Now silence. And watch!" With that came another thunderclap that rattled the very walls and threatened to shatter the window panes. Easton felt a blanket of unease envelope him, a hot and tingling sensation that made his skin crawl. Kimmi began to make spinning, almost caressing gestures in the air with his malformed hands and began to murmur in a language none of the men at the table recognized. To Easton, the words, in which a series of phrases were chanted over and over again, made the short hairs on his arms stand up and pricked some deeper primeval nerve deep in his brain. It sounded something like "Ayah...ayah nebakonda...nebakonda... eeza...eezah! Shaitan...Shatain....eeeezah!" before resuming what sounded like complete gibberish.

And then the atmosphere in the room began to change. All of the men sensed it. The temperature dropped a good ten degrees. Breath vapors could be seen in the air. And something else...

Easton caught motion at his peripheral vision. Nothing substantial. A flitting wisp of smoke near the ornate cove molding. Then more. A dancing vapor here and there. Some sort of trick. It had to be. His rational mind insisted this was all some sort of elaborate hoax, staged by someone – maybe even Hilderman – as a Halloween prank. It had to be! Maybe the whole group was in on...

A low keening began, not in any one location. It almost sounded as if it was coming from within the walls. Kimmi was whispering rapidly in his gibberish chant – his eyes had rolled back like marbles and were now only showing the whites. A vaporous howl, an icy breeze. Something batted around the tops of the bookcases like a bird. (A hummingbird trapped in a closed-down shoe store. A random thought came to Easton.) The lights flickered on and off and the entire room began shaking. Books tumbled to the floor.

Then somebody gasped. It might have been Delgado.

Another flash of lightning revealed someone else standing in the room with them, near the windows behind Kimmi. A man of small stature, gaunt, dressed in a black suit, hands hanging at his side. Hilderman craned his neck around to see better.

"Lars!?"

"Oh my God!" someone else said. "Holy shit!" came another.

From somewhere, a curious light brought the man's face into clarity, as if a spectral spotlight had been switched on from above.

"Jesus Christ!" swore someone else. It sounded like Wang.

Standing with them, stiff as a statue, was the late Lars Van Eyckmann himself.

Easton immediately noticed something else, which didn't make sense if this was some sort of apparition summoned from the spirit world.

Van Eyckmann's forehead was ringed with beads of sweat and his eyes were wide with terror.

An idiotic non sequitur went through Easton's head – Dead Men Don't Wear Plaid – and dead men certainly do not sweat.

From his left came Leffert's voice. "Well...this is certainly... interesting."

"Indeed."

Kimmi's chanting had ceased and his eyes rolled back to their normal position – like the creepiest over-sized doll one could imagine. Except something wasn't quite right this time around. The irises had changed. They were now curious vertical red and gold slits, like a reptile's eyes. Easton was fascinated. Kimmi smiled again, this time showing a mouth packed with pointed, discolored teeth, way more than any human should possess. Easton found this fascinating too. If this was some sort of Hollywood staging, it was a first-rate operation.

Kimmi shook his head and kept grinning, like a man who had just woken from the happiest nap one could imagine. "Ah, we have a guest! Our good friend, Lars Van Eyckmann! So good of you to join us, yes?" He began pulling the gloves off his hands finger by finger, like a gentleman at the opera might, revealing the horrible truth of those misshapen appendages: they were scaled and curled with long talon-like nails. A predator's claws. The members of the Mohican Executive Council wore a range of expressions varying from shock to horror to complete disbelief. The air in the library felt charged with electricity. Kimmi began to idly inspect his deformed hands. "Perhaps it is time tell the end of the tale, yes, my good Dutchman?"

Van Eyckmann didn't respond. He simply stood stock still, as if frozen in place, except for a bead of sweat that trickled past his temple and worked its way down his hollowed cheek.

Kimmi continued on, discarding the anachronistic language of his tale. "The ifrit, or Djinn as they are sometimes called in the West, can do...many things. In this case, it was summoned to exact eternal payment. On a 130-year installment plan. So you see, your friend Van Eyckmann has been around for...a while. Including his age at the time, I think we can say 430 years, give or take? Or quoth those here in the West, 'Close enough for government work.' Yes? Poor man Lars. Such punishment, but a very bad man, yes?" He made a slight movement with his one finger and Van Eyckmann's head nodded once, then twice, like a puppet on a string.

"The cycle goes on, one might say. Every time the Dutchman knows the eve of his punishment is nigh, he devises a trick to avert his sentence. It is a game with us, a game I very much enjoy! You see, there is a way to end the curse, to cease the cycle of torment, but he has not found it yet despite his clumsy attempts. Alas, I fear he is to fail this year as well. I believe the plan was for his associates – that would be all of you – to take his place this year. He was told by someone that by substituting his original officers – or at least their proxies – the curse could be dissolved."

Hilderman, to his credit, appeared unimpressed. "And, presuming this whole children's spook story is what you say, who would have told him that?"

Kimmi repressed a laugh. "Why...you, of course."

"Me?"

"Well, I cannot lie. 'Twas myself actually. Having appeared as you one night. After all, I can appear as anyone."

Hilderman actually slapped his hand down on the table. "Oh, for Pete's sake! Are you to have us believe you are some sort of shape-shifting magician?"

Washington added, "Oh, next you will be telling us you are the immortal Maghra?"

At this, Kimmi actually laughed. It was not a pleasant sound. It suggested something dark and deep and unhinged. It was something one might hear in the corridors of a dark cellar of an old asylum in the early hours of the morning.

"Ha ha ha! No, oh, no, my friend! Maghra the magician has been dead 390 years! Such a fool, and an arrogant man. So obsessed with his superiority, in love with his knowledge, so sure of his arcane talents. No, no. He had the formula wrong, the bindings would never work. Whoever taught or sold him such knowledge was as ill-informed as he. More than half the conjurations were mispronounced..."

Then it was as if his voice dropped an octave. "No, you foolish man, I am Kimmi, the ifrit he summoned!" And, with a roar that sounded not unlike an enraged lion, his jaws hinged impossibly wide – revealing rows of diabolically-curved teeth that had grown even more in the last few minutes

– and then he leapt onto Washington and tore his entire throat out in one savage bite.

There was only a moment of stunned silence. Then two things occurred very quickly. The men began their mad scramble to get out of their chairs (with getting the hell out of the room a definite Priority Number Two) but then Kimmi's head snapped around, his homicidal predator's grin dripping blood and gore, eyes with their peculiar slits now glowing like stoked embers, and the men froze. Not froze as in scared, frightened, too terrified to move, though those were certainly somewhere on the list, but froze as in they might have been cast in invisible concrete a dozen feet thick.

Easton was half out of his chair, hands on the armrests, caught right in the middle of leaping out and backwards so he could vault sideways towards the door. It was an instantaneous reaction that required no thought – death was to the left, survival to the right.

Only it didn't happen.

It was like one of those dreams you often have as an adolescent – a type of lucid dreaming – when you awake (or think you do) and can see everything all around you in super-clarified detail, often with an accompanying sense of dread or of an evil presence. Only you are utterly paralyzed and can't move so much as a fingertip. It was like that. Only these dreamers were not dreaming and the presence of indescribable evil was utterly and undeniably real. For the first time in his 39 years, Easton thought he was going to lose his bladder and bowel control and dump right into his pants.

Fortunately, those muscles were frozen too.

Another gargling, maniacal laugh issued from Kimmi's mouth. "No, not so fast, my friends. This party has just begun! First, Mr. Van Eyckmann must suffer his due! And for that, I shall need assistants!" With that, there came a crash as the front door was thrown open, followed by a heavy thump. Easton found he wasn't completely one hundred percent frozen after all – his eyes could move, even if he couldn't blink. And to his right, he saw something move in the shadows of the library doorway. Icy fingers of fear lanced up his spine, panic danced around his thoughts.

The glint of metal. A figure emerging into the dim light of the library.

Easton registered two things instantly: the first was the barrel of Knightbridge's nine millimeter Glock. The second – surprise, surprise – was the drawn face of William Lowe, who, before Kimmi could react and work whatever sorcery he was doing, fired twice.

The first bullet went slightly high and the second clipped the thing's ear. The response was instantaneous. The thing flew up to the corner of the ceiling where it hung upside down with its maniacal grin. The sound of the pistol in the small room was deafening and the smell of cordite quickly permeated the space. Easton's ears were ringing. Then, like some nightmare spider, Kimmi scuttled along the ceiling then leapt diagonally, narrowly missing Lowe's third shot. There was a scrambling along the bookcase – dozens of books went flying in all directions – then the ifrit landed square in the middle of the octagonal table, sending the candelabrum tumbling off to one side. Candles pin-wheeled and tossed sparks and splatters of hot wax. One blob landed on Leffert's cheek and must have seared the skin, but there was nothing he could do. The creature appeared to be enjoying this new diversion. It feinted left, then right, then made a ridiculous pawing motion like a frustrated animal, which tore large divots out of the table surface. Then it went back on its haunches as it prepared to leap.

If Lowe was nothing else, he was either a dependable shot or extremely lucky with a sidearm. Cool as cucumber, he lead slightly, corrected for lift, and fired.

The shot went true and right through the thing's left eye, which erupted in a blinding flash. A withering scream cut through the air and the creature that was Kimmi expanded briefly then imploded inwards as if it had been yanked into another dimension by an insanely powerful vacuum. The body it had inhabited, presumably the late (and sorely misinformed) Maghra the magician, collapsed in a heap of ruined skin and bones to the table. The screaming continued, but it was muted and appeared to be traveling at a high rate of speed on through the house.

At that instant, whatever spell had held the group in its paralytic grip ended. The white tendrils of smoke flitting around near the ceiling had vanished as well.

Chairs toppled over. Someone began screaming in a high pitched wail (it was Delgado). Easton caught himself staggering backwards and almost went over his own tipped chair. Hilderman stood in shock, looking at the mutilated body of Washington next to him, the head nearly completely severed and a small pulsing fountain of blood burbling out of the severed jugular. Wang doubled over and vomited.

In the entrance to the library, Lowe collapsed to one knee, only his hand gripping the door frame keeping him from pitching completely over. Easton ran over to him and realized that he was seriously wounded. His left shoulder had been sliced open, right through to the collar bone. The lobe of his right ear was missing and there was a deep slice along the cheek.

"Jesus, Lowe, what the bloody hell have you been up to!?"

He looked pale but managed a weak smile. "Oh, little this, little that...I came back...Knightbridge...called, I had to get back here ...something terrible has happened at the caretaker's house...Knightbridge is alive – he went to get help. Gave me a gun. Told me shoot for the eyes...something attacked me in the driveway...sorry, not much for an old man..."

Easton was already tearing off his right sleeve to press it into Lowe's wound to staunch the blood, tearing off another piece to bind it in place. "We've got to get you to a doctor. Do you have a phone?"

"Left jacket pocket."

Easton looked but there was no left pocket. It had been sliced away. And Lowe was bleeding from another serious wound there as well. An edged weapon, and, from the looks of it, sharp as a scalpel. He looked up at Easton with glassy eyes. "John...yes, I know who you are...you have to get the hell out of here...all of you, I came to tell you it's off. Van Eyckmann and his request can go to hell. I'll give everyone their money...but there are some strange things...don't know what in the bloody heck they are but they're awfully good with swords...."

Delgado had stopped screaming and was standing there, hands over his mouth, trembling in shock. He looked like he was about to fall to the floor and start babbling like an idiot. Anderson and Hilderman were looking in disbelief at Van Eyckmann and making a concerted effort not to look at Washington's mangled corpse. Wang was on his knees with one hand on the table, wiping vomit from his mouth with the back of his hand. Lefferts stomped over to Van Eyckmann and held up his hands before him, clenched as if he was about to grab the man's neck and start wringing it.

"Jesus H. Fucking Christ on a stick, what in the blue fuck was that, Lars!!??"

Van Eyckmann was looking off in the distance, head slightly tilted, like a man who was listening to a tune only in his head. "A djinn," he said absently, "but had you been paying attention you would have known that."

Lefferts made several wild gestures with his hands like a man looking for something, anything, to smash on the floor as he began to pace back and forth. He finally settled on picking up a book and slamming it down on the floor. "A djinn! You mean a genie? That was a fucking genie? Where were the tits and chiffon robes and batting eyelashes!!!?? The blonde hair? Ruby lips and seductive smiles? That wasn't a genie; that was a fucking refugee from Hell! That was something that ran off the set of a goddamn John Carpenter flick. Jesus Mary and Josephine Baker, Lars, what the fuck is going on here!! You're supposed to be dead! What? Too afraid of your own funeral!!? Now start talking, or I'll...I'm going to-"

"You're going to shut up, Lefferts," Hilderman cut in. His voice was shaky but controlled. "Lars, where did that thing go? Is it dead?"

Lars was still listening. "No. Not dead. Thrown off its game for the moment. Moving around between this plane and the next. But he will be back. You may count on it."

Hilderman thought for a moment. "Right then. Now, let's say for a moment I'm buying in on all this. What is that thing and how do we deal with it?"

"It is an ifrit, you idiot, a malicious entity from another...dimension? Very powerful and evil, but with no real capacity to plan far in advance. It pretty much works on the fly. Regarding how to 'deal' with it, that is a problem I've been working on for quite a long, long time."

"Right out of The Arabian Nights," Anderson said absently.

Yes, right out of The Arabian Nights, thought Easton. Right down to half the story it just told...just like a story one might find in a library. Or a study.

Never one to stay quiet for long, Lefferts jumped in again. "Whoa, you really mean to say you're three – wait, four hundred something years old?"

"I claim no such thing, now if you'll excuse me, Mr. Lefferts...."

A splintering smash came from the front door, momentarily grabbing everyone's attention. Lefferts nearly jumped out of his shoes. "Christ, Lars, what was that? What should we do now?"

"Not my concern any more. But I suggest you run like hell. Out of my way!" And by way of example, Van Eyckmann shoved past Hilderman and bolted past the table and towards the staircase. Easton had time to think "Not bad for an old guy" before something whistled through the air at his head. Letting go of Lowe he instinctively ducked and rolled and that same something bit into the door frame. Right where his head was a moment before.

Easton came to a stop with one knee up. Lowe was slumped down near the entrance, looking like he'd aged ten years in as many minutes. Delgado was still standing before the table with his face in his hands, crying and babbling some nonsense that sounded like "no-no-no-not-realthisisn'treal-okokI'mokokokok..." Hilderman and Lefferts shrank back further in the room, Lefferts tripping over a pile of falling books (toppled by the one he'd just thrown, ironically enough) and landing right on his ass. Anderson, of all the damnedest things, actually drew out his sword.

Standing in the doorway was the weirdest apparition Easton had ever laid eyes on before, excluding the thing that had relieved Geoffrey Washington of his larynx (and life) just a few minutes before. Lowe was too weak to look up but he would have recognized it as quite similar to the thing he had encountered back in the driveway earlier. It was another of the undead Ronin, this one wearing a helmet with two horns that made a 'V' extending out a good foot and a half. Some of its woven armor pads appeared to be missing and the remaining ones were in a serious state of decay. This one had two armored shin guards but no leggings. Its slit and sunken eyes looked around the room for a target and appeared to settle on Delgado.

Yet just as it stomped forward, Anderson leapt in, brandishing his sword like Errol Flynn to the rescue. Easton never would have suspected he had it in him. Delgado continued to babble away, oblivious that death was mere feet from him. Anderson stepped in at a classic swordsman's position, right foot forward, left back and perpendicular, left hand on the left hip and right bent with the sword tip up at eye level. Perhaps he had had fencing lessons in the past. That or he had simply watched too many movies. It was a noble gesture but a moot point, as a split second later the creature swung its Katana with both hands and sliced the top two thirds of Anderson's sword clean off, sending it clanging harmlessly off somewhere to the left. Anderson's eyebrows shot up and the next swing would have decapitated him if Easton hadn't taken the nearest object – it was an old book on taxidermy of all things – and chucked it at the thing's head.

It connected with a heavy "thwack!" and, while doing nothing to prove that the pen was mightier than the sword, it at least got the damn thing's attention. Which left Easton wondering just what in the hell he was supposed to do next.

Lowe lifted his head slightly and limply tossed the pistol at Easton. "The eyes," he was barely able to croak out. Unfortunately, the toss was a weak one and the pistol tumbled only a few feet, although luckily didn't go off. The creature turned its head slowly this way and that, now zeroing in on Easton, whose reflexes once again that day saved him. He ducked and rolled towards the thing and snatched up the Glock, just under the hissing edge of the sweeping blade. The thing turned its head around with the protesting creak of old tendons and bones, only to find the business end of the 9mm an inch away from its glowing left eye.

Easton pulled the trigger.

The head exploded. The thing collapsed like a marionette with all its strings suddenly cut into a heap of bones, moldering armor, and a dusty pall of smoke. The odor of something old, dried, and rotted wafted up. Lowe looked up weakly at Easton.

"Well done...that's two down."

And with that he closed his eyes.

Knightbridge didn't plan to shoot the thing in the eye, despite Wallace's advice, he did simply because the glowing orb was the first target that drew his attention and there was no time to think.

The retort of the pistol in the stairway was enough to make his ears ring.

The sword stroke went wild as the thing's head snapped backwards, then there were loose pieces of armor and old bones and a putrid cloud of dust tumbling around Knightbridge's feet. Hand shaking, he checked the slide on the Glock to make sure it was clear, then cocked his head, listening. He didn't hear anything.

Then he thought he heard a soft thud from downstairs. In the basement.

He crept back down the stairs carefully and froze as he was passing the living room. He could hear Doctor Phil's voice from the big flat screen TV:

"We're back to today's topic, 'Sins of the Father,' with a very, very special guest, Kevin Knightbridge...." Followed by a semi-enthusiastic applause.

"Now, now, Kevin, what you need to understand," the doctor went on in his Texas drawl, "That you are your father's son, not your father," (slightly more enthusiastic applause at this little pearl of wisdom) "despite the fact that your father has done awful things. Immoral and ter-r-rible things, son. And what you also need to understand is that because of his failure as a parent, on every basic level, and your overcompensating need to prove yourself a better man, that directly – and I mean directly – resulted in your getting your gonads blown off by a bunch of trigger-happy towel-heads! In a half-assed backwater goat hole of town in Afghany-stan where they don't even have a pot to piss in!" (Applause and laughter) "I mean your daddy might as well as fired that RPG right at you himself! What a guy!" (More applause)

Mesmerized, Knightbridge found himself easing into the room, his thoughts racing in confusion: impossible, Kevin is dead...what kind of sick joke....? On the big HD screen in glorious full color, the good doctor was seated angled away from the camera across from his son, or what had been his son. He looked like a badly-stitched-together parody of a human being, not the strapping, six-two and buff 21-year-old he last shook hands with at a deployment base in Saudi Arabia. Of course not. The report said the truck he had been riding in took a direct hit from an RPG.

This nightmare version of Kevin looked half conked out, with one eye not quite back in its exploded socket, the other with a glazed, disconnected look. The mouth was a slack-jawed wreck with blood streaming out of it. The intact eye looked right out of the television and directly at Knightbridge and he could see a tear racing down the ruined cheek. He appeared to be trying to respond, but all that came out was a garbled "Dawfgghh..."

Without turning around, the doctor said, "Son, you must think I have 'Stupid' written across my forehead if you think for a second I wasn't aware that your worthless pile of pig feces of a daddy hasn't just waltzed into the room. And you must know that he is going to be deader than a monkey's fart in short order. Wouldn't ya like to see that? Everyone, a big round of applause for Paul Knightbridge!" (Big applause, random laughs). "He'll be getting his nuts diced working for a dead guy who ain't even dead, how 'bout them apples?"

The doctor turned around and despite the bald head, the face was Kimmi's, complete with a mouthful of razor teeth. ""Well, hiya neighbor.

Say, you ain't from Texas, are ya?"

Knightbridge aimed right for the forehead. "No, I ain't." and fired.

There was a spark and a flash and the screen shattered and went black.

Knightbridge was shaking. Every man has his Achilles heel and Kevin was his.

He'd been through plenty of messed-up situations in his career, but this one was clearly taking the cake. Somebody was seriously fucking with him. And the inference that Van Eyckmann was alive?

Another thump from the basement.

He went down the hallway to the kitchen at the back. It was one of the more modern parts of the whole estate, someone had remodeled it in the '90s with cream-colored tiles, rich mahogany cabinets, and high beamed ceilings. It also boasted modern stainless steel appliances and white marble countertops although the broad planked floor had been restored. The basement door was to the right of the main arch, down a short flight of stairs tucked under the main staircase.

He paused at the door, then swung it open while pressing the old fashioned push-button switch. The stairwell that went down was from another era, lined with heavy plank boards and lit by old-fashioned-looking bulbs. At the bottom landing was a door that led into a laundry room, to the left an arch into the workshop and furnace room.

Neither of which was of much interest to Knightbridge. He was focused on the figure at the bottom of the stairs. Standing under the dim glow of a 40-watt bulb, dressed in heavy denim overalls and a soiled work shirt was the missing gardener.

Arms folded, head bowed, empty pools where his eyes were, he radiated insanity and an aura of death. The desiccated jaw tried to work. Dried tendons and muscles struggled to function. Knightbridge could hear the voice as if it was some bizarre ventriloquist's trick.

"Jokes...not funny...now." It sounded like the creak of a rusty hinge. "I've been looking for you, Paul....Kevvy and I have been talking down here....and you've been such a naughty boy...." There was a scuffling sound as the patchwork version of his dead son came around the corner, blood and fluids leaking at the seams. This time Kevin managed a slurpy "D-da...?"

Then he saw the spiders. Not the small bloated house spiders that he typically saw around the basement but-fist sized brown recluse spiders, and not just a few, or dozens, but hundreds. A veritable pulsing brown wave that came around the corner and began expanding along the walls and ceiling and stairs.

A slow-motion explosion coming at him.

Knightbridge felt as though his boots had been nailed to the stair riser.

Icy trickles of panic seeped into his brain.

Spiders.

Then he broke, and ran.

Out the rear door of the kitchen, hitting it hard enough to knock it mostly off its hinges, and off into the woods at a roughly southwesterly direction. This was a new experience for Knightbridge, having held himself together admirably under extreme duress in the past. Flying bullets, mortar barrages, artillery strikes. Anything another man could throw at him, he could face. But the sight of all those spiders coming at him, with their furry thick abdomens and alien-looking pinprick pairs of variable-sized eyes arranged on their heads and the probing, skittering legs and, above all, the knowledge of those alien mouths with their tiny pincer-like fangs dripping clear venom was too much.

His wits short-circuited.

Knightbridge ran, crashing through the trees and brush like a runaway locomotive, legs pumping faster than his tar-and-nicotine-damaged lungs could comprehend. Branches and the occasional vines whipped his face and hands leaving welts. He ran with nothing more than the blind thought of putting the greatest distance between him and the crawling horrors of that basement in as little time as possible. It was a situation John Easton would have certainly sympathized with. There was no concept of how distance was actually covered, only that at some point a sub-functioning part of his body decided to pull the plug on this whole madness and he collapsed to his knees, hands on thighs, breath coming in great whooping gasps.

He was somewhere in the woods. North of the estate, as he had inadvertently swung east, crossed the drive at some point (which didn't even register), cutting through a copse of spruce trees and into a small clearing of early growth maple and chestnut. He sat back on his haunches for a good ten minutes, conscious of nothing but the thundering whump of his heart in his chest and his lungs heaving like a dried out set of leather bellows.

Thoughts began to seep back into his mind. The first was shame, the sense of shame at how quickly he had just snapped and run like a rookie recruit. The second was the awareness that he was not alone.

Overhead, the trees sighed in the wind but this particular spot seemed semi-protected and only a light breeze played across Knightbridge's face. Beneath the sighing of branches was another sound, another sighing sound that inexplicably made him break out in goose bumps.

Bent over, eyes squeezed shut, he wished it would all just go away. Or just end.

But, overstressed as his cardio system was at that moment, it wasn't granting him his wish to go into permanent-shut-down mode. Instead, it struggled to right itself like a carrier that had just taken a few critical (but not fatal) torpedo hits. His next thought was more resigned: I have to look.

Knightbridge opened his eyes.

At first, he wasn't sure what he was seeing. Spectral entities of a sort were floating through the trees, towards him. They looked like insubstantial wisps of light but even as they drew near him, they gained definition, as if drawing clarity from his own life energy. More than a dozen of the...ghosts (might as wall call a spade a spade here) encircled him. They all appeared to be in period dress, and were all men.

The one directly in front of him looked like a late-19th century business man and must have cut a fine figure in life with his waistcoat, tailored jacket and trousers, and pocket watch with chain. His face had a stern cast and a bushy moustache. He stopped just before Knightbridge, lower legs fading into nothingness, and the other ghosts began to crowd in around him. The sweat on Knightbridge's brow felt like ice.

An equally insubstantial voice touched his ear. Aloud? Perhaps he imagined it.

"All of us....he killed all of us....he killed...he killed....." The one in front of him bent slightly forward, looking into Knightbridge's upturned face. The face melted into a hideous skeleton's mask with a few strips of tattered skin. The penny dropped – these were the previous groups of men that had died here at Taron Hall. Who slept their eternal sleep uneasily in their graves by the chapel.

Then the voice said, quite clearly this time, "He'll kill you too!" And the jaws opened and came at him with a roar.

For the first time in his entire life, Knightbridge passed clean out.

Sometime later he came to.

Overhead, the trees creaked and rustled in the breeze. Knightbridge was lying in the clearing among tufts of wild grass, staring up at the night sky and white tufts of cloud speeding overhead. He blinked hard several times to focus himself, then slowly sat up with a groan. He felt stiff and sore and his legs felt like he'd run up to the top of the Empire State Building, twice. He shook his head like a bear just coming out of hibernation. Then with his free hand he pulled out his cell phone and flipped it open, saw there was one, maybe two bars, then hit the speed dial button.

"Come on, come on...." he said under his breath.

After four rings, there was a click and a pause before William Lowe's voice came on the line. He sounded distracted and vaguely annoyed.

"Hello?"

Knightbridge was whispering. "Bill...Knightbridge. We have a serious problem here. Real serious. I have to call the police."

"Hold on." There was a muffled sound as Lowe covered the phone and spoke to someone else who was with him. When he came back on it was with his complete and undivided attention, "What is going on, Paul? What do you mean call the police?"

"My security team has been murdered, along with our driver, Marco. Someone in the house may be next. God, I hope I'm not too late..." He looked at the phone screen. The time was nearly ten o'clock. He swore under his breath, then continued. "Oh, and Van Eyckmann's body has disappeared from the basement. Bill, this is out of my control, and those men up at the Hall may be next. I have to-"

"Hold on, Paul! Let's not do anything rash. Do not, I repeat do not call anybody until I get there."

"Bill, I don't think you're hearing me. There have been multiple homicides. And I-"

Lowe cut him off again. He wasn't sounding at all like the polite, slightly fussy attorney that had been passing out discreet linen envelopes that morning. This sounded more like an old fighter who had just strapped on his gun belts. "Paul, I don't think you're hearing me. I'm still in Wyvern Falls. I'll be there in less than ten minutes. In the meantime, pull it together and do the damn job you're getting paid for. Still getting paid for."

Knightbridge didn't say anything, his lips a compressed line. One thing he didn't tolerate well was anybody questioning his professionalism.

"Right," he said, then thumbed the End Call button.

Lowe made it in nine.

There was a squeal of brakes as his Lexus fishtailed into the drive outside. A minute later, he came stumbling through the front door, looking harried but ready to take charge. Until he saw the driver nailed up on the ceiling of the atrium. For a moment he simply stood, speechless. A career in estate litigation hadn't prepared him for anything like this. Knightbridge was sitting waiting for him on the stairs, gun still in his hand. He had come back to the house to find his car battery dead and his tires slashed. Same as on the other vehicles.

"In God's name....what on earth...?" Lowe stammered, whatever agenda he had earlier folding up and flying out the window. Knightbridge caught the whiff of somebody else's cheap aftershave on him.

"Neither of those terms would apply here, Bill. Still not keen on calling the police in?"

Lowe didn't look clear on anything at all, other than that he looked like he was about to lose his dinner. He pulled out a silk handkerchief from his pocket and covered his mouth as he gagged.

"Bill, you need to get up to the house. I need to check the barn to see if anything is drivable and then I'll meet you up at the Hall. Take my

Glock…."

17. TRICK OR TREAT

The clock on the mantel piece chimed 11:00.

They had crossed the hall over to the parlor where Lefferts and Wang had helped Easton carry Lowe and lay him out on the tiger-skin rug. Easton did his best to field-dress the wounds and got Lowe to take a few slugs of Scotch, which at least got a bit of color back in his cheeks. He would have preferred not to move him at all but it was hard to focus with Washington's devastated corpse in the library as a backdrop. Delgado was still in shock and sitting on the edge of one of the parlor chairs staring off into space, Lefferts was at Easton's side, and Hilderman stood by the fireplace smoking the pipe which he had left there earlier. Anderson was poking around the Samurai statue over in the corner, a snifter of brandy in one hand. Wang was sitting next to Delgado, his head in his hands.

Whatever horror was loose in Taron Hall, it was ratcheting up a notch.

Easton had run into the kitchen looking for a first-aid kit which he found under the sink, but there was no sign of the cook or maids there. Well, not exactly. There were splatters of blood and a dropped tray of dirty plates. The back door was open, banging in the wind. From somewhere upstairs had come a high-pitched scream which trailed off into gurgling cries before stopping abruptly. Who and what has caused that Easton had no idea and no time to find out just yet. Throughout the house, strange sounds could be heard – objects being smashed in some of the rooms, howling shrieks, heavy thuds, a muffled giggling. It was if the place was coming to life as some sort of haunted insane asylum.

The dining room had become a study in carnage. Kimmi, or something, had been a busy beaver.

Easton had run in to grab the bottle of Scotch (This time a 15-year-old Dalwhinnie) and stumbled into a charnel-house room of horrors. Blood and body parts strewn over the table and chairs everywhere. A strip of something bloody hanging from one of the paintings. The corpse of Mr. Theater-Type Waiter had been placed at the head of the table, minus his head, an upright fork in one hand and knife in the other in a parody of an eager diner. In the center of the table was one of the silver serving platters with the decapitated head of the flirty brunette on it. The air was thick with the coppery smell of fresh blood and excrement. Easton forced himself to shut it out and focused on getting the bottle and getting back to the parlor.

As he walked past the dining table, first-aid kit and Scotch tucked under one arm, the Glock in his right hand, the eyes of the woman's head flew wide and glared at him.

"How about a little kiss, sugar?" she said with a wink.

Easton did a quick two-step backwards in shock.

Then: "You're going to die, Johnnie! You're going to die tonight, my friend. I can taste it!!" she growled through blood-streaked teeth, which started chittering in laughter. He almost dropped the bottle of Scotch. Then he reached over and grabbed a platter lid that was upended nearby and slammed it down over the plate. "Keep it to yourself, then" was all he could think to say.

In the parlor, he was trying to formulate a plan while dressing Lowe's wounds. They didn't look good – if they couldn't get him to a hospital quickly, Easton didn't think he'd last more than a few hours tops. It depended on how much blood he had lost and Easton had no idea exactly where and when he had been wounded. It was the one in the side that had him most worried. He needed to get Lowe into an ER and quickly.

Lowe looked at Easton weakly. "Knightbridge called me on his cell…I never went back, I stayed in town to keep a close eye on matters…more at stake than you know…he said something terrible was happening, he was going to have to call in the police. I told him absolutely not…to wait until I came back here to assess myself…I'm sorry, that wasn't terribly bright of me…Oh, God, it hurts…I…"

He was cut off. "Derek, do you really think that's a good idea? What if that thing is one of them?" Lefferts had been assisting Easton best as he could, keeping pressure on the compress on Lowe's shoulder.

Anderson was tapping the masked helmet with his finger. "Joe, this thing is covered in dust. And cobwebs. It's not even the size of a normal man and besides, it doesn't look like this old gal is going anywhere except to an estate sale in the near future." To demonstrate, he held up his finger. It did in fact have a thick smudge of dust on it. He then knocked on the top of the helmet for good measure. "Hello? Anybody in there?" The sound was dry and hollow.

Hilderman took a long draw on his pipe. "So what are you thinking,

Mr. Easton?"

Without looking up Easton replied, "We should be looking for the quickest way to get the hell out of here. And right now the garage is at the top of my list."

"Yes, of course. The garage."

"Derek, what the hell are you doing?" Wang, having finally looked up, sounded annoyed. Anderson was peering into the recesses of the statue's helmet as if there was something of interest lurking there.

Anderson glanced back over his shoulder. "Joe, for God's sakes it's just a -"

The sentence wasn't destined to be finished. A small gloved fist shot up and snatched Anderson by the nape of the neck, the other drawing out the shorter Wakizashi sword with a sliding 'snick' sound. In one swift motion, Anderson was pulled back off-balance by the neck; in the next, the blade licked across his midsection, slicing through doublet, shirt, and abdominal muscles alike. Anderson made a gargling screaming sound as his intestines looped out of the gaping wound and fell over his legs like so many bloody ropes, then the screams were stifled as the blade was thrust upward into the heart and lungs.

Easton jumped up, the pistol in both his hands. He fired one shot which punched through the thing's helmet, then two more that disintegrated the face guard. A splintered, skull-like face leered through the pieces of brittle, shattered metal. Pushing aside Anderson's body, it took a couple of steps forward, joints creaking and popping in protest. Easton stepped up, the butt of the 9mm resting on his left hand to steady it, took careful aim, and pumped the fourth round into the thing's eye.

He would have kept firing but the magazine was empty. He went through a few empty clicks of the trigger before realizing it. The thing toppled over backwards in a heap.

Then he heard another click. He felt something cold and heavy pressed against his temple and knew immediately that it was bad news.

Hilderman was holding an antique looking Webley .38 revolver to his head. It was one of the Mark VI models with a ring at the base of the grip.

He heard Lefferts from behind him. "David, what in the hell are you doing?"

"Exactly what I need to do," came the steely reply. "Mr. Easton, it's time for you and me to take a walk."

Easton had a feeling that was bad news as well. "Hilderman, now is not the time and place to..."

"Now is the time and place. Now toss the gun aside carefully."

Easton complied.

Lefferts stood up. Wang just sat there, not saying a word. Delgado was nowhere to be seen. During the excitement, he had up and bolted out of the room and out the front door.

Panic was creeping into Lefferts' voice. "David, what's going on? I mean…Oh, my God, Anderson, Oh, Jesus...this is all crazy. This is nuts. I mean what...Delgado just split… Jeffrey, say something..."

But Wang wasn't saying a word. For the moment, Brooklyn's premier clothing designer was looking shut down, not open for business. Easton had a sinking feeling the situation was going completely south in a hurry. "Hilderman, let's sit down and talk this out like rational men."

"I'm sorry, Easton, but the situation has changed. Two of the men I was counting on are dead and you're not part of the game plan anymore." He placed his hand firmly on Easton's shoulder and shifted the barrel to the base of his neck. The he looked over at Lefferts. "Actually, Joe, I'm not entirely sure I can count on you either. Why don't you step out ahead? Out into the hallway and towards the basement, if you please."

"David, we just can't leave Lowe, the guy is dying, we need to get him …"

"Never mind him. He'll be dead if he isn't already. Now move."

Lefferts looked like he was ready to break down in tears, but he got moving.

Hilderman forced them down the hallway and through the basement entrance under the main staircase. He made them go down the stairs but stayed at the top. "You two can play around down there for a while. Do stay out of trouble. And don't even think about trying to come back up. I'd hate to shoot a police officer, but I will if need be. Goodnight, gentlemen." And with that, he stepped back and closed the door. Easton heard the sound of a heavy key turning the lock.

Lefferts slid down the cold stone of the basement wall on his haunches, face buried in his hands. The brassy over-confident investment hound had been replaced by a terrified and haggard-looking middle-aged man with trembling fingers. The hallmark bright shirt and tie now looked limp and absurd. "Christ what's going on?" he sobbed. "Did you see what that thing did to Anderson!? Oh, God. I don't deserve this...this isn't happening!"

Easton didn't care much for what he was seeing. All the hallmark signs of a traumatized personality about to collapse. He stepped over and yanked Lefferts to his feet and looked him close in the eye. "Yeah, well, it is happening." He grabbed the end of the crazy-looking tie and flicked it across the blinking face. "From your kids? They're going to want to see their dad come out of this mess. In one piece. Who the hell else in the world are they going to buy these ridiculous things for?" Leffert's hands were still shaking, but at least he was standing up straighter. "Step one is to work on getting the hell out of here, now." First he needed to get to the phone he had seen earlier in the meat locker. The one he could dial "0" on to get an outside line. Then they needed to find Knightbridge.

Upstairs, Hilderman walked into the parlor. Wang was still sitting there, face in hands. Hilderman went up and stood in front of him. "Jeffrey?" No response. Then one eye peeking through the fingers. The force of Hilderman's will was almost a physical thing. In such close proximity, its steeliness was all but overpowering. "Jeffrey, listen to me. We have to move quickly and I need your help. Can I count on you?"

Wang pondered this for a moment. Then he nodded his head.

"Very good. We have to go over to the study – there's something we need to get. Then we're getting the hell out of here. All bets are off. If we don't get out of here soon, we'll be dead. Understand?"

Another nod.

"Good. Now, eyes open, follow me." With that, Hilderman checked the Webley to make sure the chambers were all loaded and walked carefully out of the room, looking in all directions before entering the main hall. Upstairs came another muffled scream and a thud. Somewhere a door creaked and a shutter started slamming.

Halloween at Taron Hall was now in full swing.

Hilderman and Wang stepped into the study, which still had the remnants of a banked fire flickering away in the hearth but which otherwise looked more or less unchanged since the afternoon. With the exception of the Bantu demon sculpture, which neither men noticed had disappeared. Aside from that, the room now had an empty, forlorn air. A trace of cherry tobacco smoke still hung in the air.

Hilderman walked quickly over to the desk and pulled out a duffle bag from underneath where he'd stashed it earlier, pulling out a large mallet and iron chisel.

"Jeffrey, this is for Plan B."

Wang seemed to rally his senses, enough at least to offer a semi-witty response: "What, David, are we going to chisel our way out of this mess?"

Hilderman snorted in reply. "Hardly. Grab one of those chairs and give me a hand. We need to get that coat of arms down off the mantle."

This threw Wang even more. "You've got to be kidding me – you've dragged me in here to steal the Van Eyckmann coat of arms? For Christ sakes, we need to get the hell out of here, now!"

"You need to learn a little patience, Jeffrey. The older one gets, the more it pays dividends." They pulled up the chairs and Hilderman instructed Wang to hold one side of the coat of arms, which was a good two feet across and seemed cast out of iron, while he went to work with the mallet and chisel, hammering from the bottom up to loosen it from its hangers.

"I tried to move it earlier but it wouldn't budge. Damn thing must be rusted in place." He kept hammering this way and that, denting the metal and gouging the plaster on the flute in the process, apparently without regard to the damage he was doing. Wang found this even more unnerving – the impeccable David Hilderman acting like a desperate juvenile delinquent. They had to switch places twice to loosen both sides.

"Jesus, David, what in the hell are we doing?"

Hilderman seemed to grow ever more impatient, the blows with the hammer ever more aggressive and frenzied. Finally with a protesting screech of rusted metal giving way, the whole thing came loose. The two men lifted it off and Hilderman cast it down, letting it drop to the floor with a ringing crash.

"What the...what the hell did you do that for, that's Van Eyckmann's family coat of arms!"

"Piss on Van Eyckmann and his coat of arms, the man is little more than a sadistic lunatic. Now watch and learn. Years of soot had left an outline of the coat of arms over the mantle. Where it had been removed was a seven by ten inch recess. In it was a simply crafted sandalwood box with a tarnished bronze clasp in the shape of a tiny dragon. Blowing dust off the lid, Hilderman carefully carried it over to the desk, clearing a space with a sweep of his arm. He placed it in the center and motioned Wang to sit down before it.

"This, Jeffrey, is Plan B. If my information is correct, I can guarantee you've never seen anything like it."

The box looked like it was old, very old. "What is it?"

"Open it and find out."

Wang put his hands on it gently. From upstairs, came a resounding crash, like that of a large piece of furniture turning over. "But I suggest you hurry."

Wang ran his thumbs over the catch, trying to work the lock mechanism. After a few tries, there was a heavy click and the dragon head snapped down, a nearly invisible blue-tipped barb snapping out briefly and drilling into the pad of Wang's thumb, disappearing just as quickly on its spring-loaded mechanism.

"Shit!" Wang drew his thumb back. A small bead of blood welled up, which he stuck in his mouth.

"Have to be careful with these old locks. Now, behold."

Hilderman reached over and flicked the lid open carefully, from the side. Inside, in a black velvet setting, was the biggest diamond either man had ever seen before. There was a stunned silence. It appeared to gather the flickering light in the room in its depths; a hint of amber, then a streak of deep rich blue.

"The Midnight Star of Molucca, if I'm not mistaken. Second-largest diamond in the world, next to the Hope Diamond."

"My God, I've never heard of such a thing...it's...it's..saying it's beautiful doesn't begin to do it justice. This is...awesome." He shook his hand absently. The thumb was cold and numb.

"This was Van Eyckmann's real treasure. Not even Lowe knows about it. It was his ace in the hole, hidden practically in plain sight."

"How did...you find out? Wang realized his lips were feeling numb and tingly, like he'd just come from a visit to the dentist.

"Kimmi. In one of our many discussions. Information is critical, Jeffrey, if you want to make sure you come out on top."

"Ahh... so this is our...cut?" His heart seemed to be racing, yet his breath was becoming ragged. What was happening?

"Afraid it's become my cut, Jeffrey. If my information is correct, you only have..." He checked his wrist watch quickly, "About three more minutes to live. I'm sorry, Jeffrey, but I'm afraid this is goodbye. Nothing personal, just business." Wang had a look of fear? sorrow? acceptance? Perhaps all of the above. He slumped back into the chair, eyes growing glassy, as Hilderman reached over, carefully tipped the box so the diamond with its filigreed chain rolled onto the desk blotter, then deftly palmed it after setting the box down carefully to the side. He wasn't sure it didn't hold further surprises.

Then, unable to resist, he held it up to the light, its flawlessly-cut facets catching the light. Then he noticed that the center facets formed a double triangle: a Star of David. How odd. He'd never seen a diamond cut that way before. Then he noticed something even stranger. What appeared to be a series of tiny glyphs or characters cut along the outer edges. What the...? He turned it this way and that but they were definitely there. That would reduce the value considerably. He made a mental note to consult with a jeweler he knew on 47th who was known for his discretion. Maybe the diamond should be recut. He pulled out a little velvet pouch from inside his jerkin, dropped the diamond inside and, tying the drawstring, returned it to its hiding place.

Then, as he turned to go he saw someone was standing before the doorway.

It was Lars Van Eyckmann.

"Hello, David," he said, showing his long teeth with a grin that was a half snarl. "I see you've finally run your true colors up the flag pole. 'Piss on Van Eyckmann,' so you say? Scratch an Englishman, smell a swine. Now you're pocketing my treasures with your grubby little hands like a common thief. Sit down, I think you and I have some business to discuss."

"No, I think not," said Hilderman in a level voice, sounding like he was turning down a routine and mildly irritating tennis match. And with that he pulled out the Webley, took aim at Van Eyckmann's chest and shot him.

At about 15 feet, it would have been an easy shot for an amateur. Hilderman was a reasonably accomplished marksman, and the bullet hit Van Eyckmann somewhere in the area of the heart, sending him reeling backwards. Not one to leave much to chance, he then advanced on Van Eyckmann and continued firing. Van Eyckmann stumbled and fell near the doorway.

Four bullets down, one remaining in the cylinder.

He stepped up to the body, cocked the hammer back with his thumb, and prepared to deliver the coup de grace.

Suddenly Van Eyckmann's eyes locked on his.

The Dutchman grinned.

Hilderman's body gave a jolt and he grunted. There was a sound like a spear going through a large watermelon. A rusted point appeared, as if by magic, out of the center of Hilderman's chest. The poleaxe was twisted and thrust again. Blood began to hemorrhage out of his mouth. The Webley fired its last round into the floor as the hand that held it spasmed and then dropped it all together. Then Hilderman dropped to his knees, his expression a study in incomprehension, the look of a dead man who'd never seen it coming. Then he fell over, impaled on the eight foot weapon.

Behind him stood Paul Knightbridge.

Van Eyckmann shoved off Hilderman from where he had fallen over his legs and struggled to gain his feet. "Help me up, damn you!" he said. Knightbridge obliged by bending over and offering his hand.

He brushed off the sleeves of his jacket and straightened his cuffs. There were several bullet holes clearly visible in his shirt and jacket, but not a drop of blood anywhere. "Always were quiet as a cat, Mr. Knightbridge."

His security man nodded. "Aye to that." He gave Van Eyckmann a challenging look. "I've seen men take a bullet or two before, but never quite like that. And for a man I laid out stone dead in the meat locker days ago, you're looking remarkably alive. Care to share how you managed that little trick?"

"It would be quite a long story, Mr. Knightbridge and, unfortunately, time is running short. I need you to find Kimmi quickly and keep him occupied – he's gone mad. He's become a high liability. I need you to take care of it immediately. A year salary for you and your team as a bonus. Where are they?"

"Happy to extend the offer to them, but I'm afraid they're busy being dead."

"Dead?"

"Fatally. Mr. Van Eyckmann, it would be of extreme help if you could tell me what is going on here. I've just dispatched two...best as I can describe it, two very dead-looking things in old Japanese Samurai armor who managed to filet two very capable and well-trained ex-Army seals. As of this minute, you are my employer. Now, to do my job as your security man, I need some clue as to what I'm dealing with so I can keep you safe, yes?" Upstairs, the house creaked and groaned. From somewhere came the patter of running feet. A door slammed.

"Ronin."

"What!?"

"The Ronin. My mercenaries. Not Samurai. At least they were once, but no more. He brings them back every time to torment me. To surgically cut me to pieces and experience the torment I inflicted on her so many years ago....how was I...how would....ah, but wait, you say you destroyed two of them?"

"A bullet through the eyes. Only thing that worked for me."

"How could this be? That has never...occurred." He fell to muttering and distractedly gnawing the knuckles of his right hand. "And yet, this is excellent news!" Clearly excited, he began to pace back and forth. He came up to Knightbridge and grasped his shoulders. "Yes, this is most excellent, Mr. Knightbridge. I applaud you, this is most definitely what I would call a 'game changer'! There may be a way out of this after all!"

Then he stepped over to Hilderman's impaled corpse and began searching. It didn't take long to locate the diamond in its pouch, though it was soaked in blood. Pulling a handkerchief from his side pocket, Van Eyckmann grimaced and, removing the stone, rubbed it down before locating another hanky. He wrapped it carefully and deposited it in his inner breast pocket. Even so, Knightbridge caught a glimpse and his eyes widened. But he said nothing.

"Thank you, Mr. Hilderman. This is the key! Good God, I knew it was here. The devil had hidden it right under my nose all this time. He even hinted at it! But how did you know? He told you didn't he? Didn't he?" He shook his head. "No matter. Mr. Knightbridge, are you properly armed?"

"Of course." He pulled out the Glock he had taken off McGoohan's body and worked the slide. Then a glance over at Hilderman and the poleaxe sticking out of his back. "He had it coming," he offered by way of explanation. "Seemed appropriate, given that ridiculous get up, and besides, he might have heard the gun being cocked."

Van Eyckmann looked disinterested. He folded one arm over the other and began tapping his chin. From somewhere near the back of the house came the tinkle of glass breaking. That seemed to decide for him.

"Come, Mr. Knightbridge. I need your assistance. It is time to complete a trap!"

18. DELGADO'S DESSERTS

Easton stood by the old-fashioned-looking wall phone in the meat locker, his hand on the receiver hook. He tapped the lever again and dialed "0" on the rotary dial. Then 9-1-1. A strange echoing sound like wires being jangled. Then; faint whispers? He was about to hang it up when suddenly a woman's voice came on the line.

"Hello?"

"Hello, this is Detec... this is Jonathan Easton. I'm at Taron Hall off – just north of town. We have an emergency situa¬-"

"How may I direct your call...?"

"You need to send the police immediately, there have been multiple homicides."

"Hello?"

There was an echoing twang, then a loud screech came through the line.

Easton held the receiver away from his head and looked at it in frustration. Then he flicked the receiver lever a few times. "Hello!?" he said.

There came what sounded like a low snickering on the line followed by a burst of static. Then the muffled sound of someone picking up the line on the other end.

"Hello, Detective Easton," said a man in low voice. Then a mockery of Aun-mai's voice: "Do you like me, a little bit!?" A shrill giggle. Then Kimmi's voice loud and clear: "Ah, my friend. I'm afraid you have reached the wrong party. However, not all is lost! I believe we have some accounts to settle! Stay tuned, I shall be around shortly to eat you piece by piece, starting with your feet!" A burst of maniacal laughter followed. Easton held the mouth piece close to his lips and said, "Yeah? Fuck you, Wanker." and hung up without waiting for a response.

Lefferts was looking at him quizzically. "Doesn't sound like we'll be getting any help from the Wyvern Falls Police Department anytime soon."

"No, it doesn't," agreed Easton.

Then the lights went out.

Delgado didn't actually see what happened to Anderson, but he definitely heard it, and, before he could make a conscious decision on a course of action, his legs made the decision for him and had him running at a sprint out of the room and out the front door. He did a few wild circles under the stone arches of the porte-cochere, arms pinwheeling randomly and screaming a high-pitched girly scream, then once again, his legs took over mission control and sent him in a flailing run down the drive towards the barn.

Behind him, a slash of lightening cast the towers and gables of Taron Hall into sharp relief while illuminating a cavernous amphitheater of thunderclouds reaching up into the sky as it lanced off in multiple forks. The thunderclap that followed felt like it might have cracked the bedrock. It was the kind of night and setting a Hammer Films production team would have sacrificed live goats (and maybe a few bare-breasted women) for. A situation lost on Delgado, who had never once seen one of those old classic '60s English horror films.

The doors to the barn were slightly open. Someone had left the lights on inside and a welcoming shaft of light spread out for a few feet along the gravel.

Delgado sidled between the doors and looked around wildly. "Hello? Hello!?" There was no sign of anybody, though he thought he heard a soft rustling thump from somewhere in the piles of junk. Followed by what might have been the patter of light feet on concrete.

A stray cat or maybe a raccoon, he told himself. What if they had rabies?

Wang's dark gray Maserati gleamed under the pool of light cast by the low-hanging green metal farmer-style fixtures. Ignoring the other cars lined up alongside, he glanced in at the lush black leather interior but the ignition slot was empty. Of course. The car had been parked by the valet, had it not? Tommy. Delgado remembered his name because he'd had a brief daydream about him that...was it just this morning? It seemed like weeks ago with all that had happened. This particular fantasy involved Tommy the Valet and an accidental (?) encounter in the shower room at the Sports Club in Brooklyn that Delgado went to three times a week. He felt an urge to relive it but managed to squash the thought. He had to find the car keys and get the hell out of here now. To hell with Hilderman, the creepy house, Van Eyckmann, the money, and everything else in this god-awful place.

The crowded streets and exhaust-clogged air of Brooklyn suddenly seemed as far away as the moon but he couldn't think of any better, safer place to be right at that moment – a world he at least understood.

How whacked out was that?

He remembered what his grandmother used to tell him when he would come in crying after being chased and called names from the neighborhood playground or coming home from school, which was pretty much a daily routine throughout his entire inner-city childhood.

"Mi querido, mi querido...." she would always say, whether it was smoothing his hair, straightening his clothes, or bandaging him up depending on the day and which way his luck was swinging. "You are a good boy, a handsome boy, and you will do many great things...always remember that." The words always soothing, non-judgmental, the one person throughout his formative years who accepted him unequivocally. And somehow, the words did work. He would sit up a little straighter, bear his bruises a little better, and, perhaps more importantly, somewhere in there was planted a germ of confidence that hardened – like a grain of sand into a pearl – and didn't break no matter how many beatings he took, no matter how many nasty names he was called, no matter how many times he ran home scared out of his wits and crying his eyes out. His grandmother, his abuelita, with her jet-black hair always tied up in a tight bun, the always-worried-but-kind look in her eyes, the deft fingers, and the heavy bosom she would cradle him to, while his mother would storm past, shaking her fist or slamming the doorframe: "You turning my son into a sissy! He has to learn how to stand up for himself – look how you spoil him! You want a sissy for a grandson!? Fine – take him!" The words like daggers, even before he understood what names like "sissy" and "faggot" and other, even more descriptive terms meant. And his father? He only recalled meeting him once when he was home on leave and it had been a disaster. He had been six at the time. It was as if his father, who was in the navy, took one look at him and saw right through to his very soul and even then knew. He didn't have to say "sissy" or "faggot." It was written in his eyes. He simply shook his head in disgust and left, never to be heard from again. Years later, he found out that he had settled down in California, though he had sent money to his mother until a few years ago.

But his grandmother, she treated him like a prince. And years later, when he opened his first restaurant, she was there opening night and ushered in like royalty to a special table set up for the occasion, where she took the first bite of the first meal served there and relished it like it was the finest meal served in the history of mankind. Despite the fact that it was Steak Cubano and it was overcooked.

Delgado felt his eyes water as the memory passed. He would have given anything to have his abuelita here right now to make things all better.

But she was dead some fifteen years now, felled by a stroke right in the middle of cooking dinner. The neighbors had come down to complain about the burning smell to find a charred pan on the stove and the cat licking up spilled tomato sauce.

Again the sound of little feet running. Something toppled and crashed beyond where the vehicles were parked. Delgado felt the hairs stand up on the back of his neck. Glancing around, he spotted the small office. The valet's room. Where the keys would be kept. Of course. Then he saw something running low around the cars. It took his brain a minute to register what he was seeing.

It was the Bantu demon doll, sprinting in a loose arc like the world's smallest tight end going full tilt for a long pass. Then it spotted him and altered its path to head straight at him.

Its rows of needle sharp teeth were opening and closing like a sewing machine. Its little eyes looked fierce. And hungry.

Delgado let out a little squeal and ran over to the door, losing precious seconds while he fumbled at the handle. It was an old-style latch, one that one usually opened by depressing the top lever with the thumb, but he kept trying to push it up before his brain finally got a sensible message through to his panicked fingers. The sound of scampering feet was getting closer. Fast.

Suddenly the door clicked.

None too soon, he wrenched it open, jumped through and slammed it shut behind him.

There was a muffled thud.

Then another. And another. And another. The little bastard was nothing if not persistent. And angry. Delgado ran around the room in a panic twice before he spotted the key rack. His hands ran frantically up and down the rows – there was only eight sets in total – before he finally registered the name "Wang" written in sloppy cursive on a tag attached to one of them. He snatched the keys just as the glass window shattered as something came barreling through it.

The thing did a somersaulting bounce, then catapulted onto the desk, a tiny spear held in one hand, and fixed Delgado with its homicidal glare. Then it leaped.

Delgado bounded forward almost simultaneously, the two passing each other by a hair's breadth, the little spear nicking Delgado's ear as it flew past. Delgado did an end run around the desk while the demon creature bounced off the key rack, tumbled onto the floor, then scrambled after him. It was fast, but Delgado was faster. If there was one thing his years of being chased and beaten had hammered into his reflexes, it was the necessity to move and improvise on a dime when the situation insisted.

The situation insisted.

Coming around the desk, he feinted left, then right, then did a double leg-vault over the desk that would have made an Olympic competitor look on in envy. The creature again bounded up onto the desk, jaws snapping, making a bee-line for Delgado. What he got, just as he came within striking distance, was a rolled up high-end sports magazine whacked on his head.

The result was almost comical. If such a thing was possible, the little Bantu demon statue looked startled, almost hurt, before it jumped forward, jaws gnashing. This time, Delgado simply rammed the rolled-up magazine into its mouth. The sewing machine teeth did their work. Shreds of paper flew every which way. By the time the thing spat it out, Delgado had bought enough precious seconds to bolt out the door and make a mad dash for the Maserati.

Within seconds, the creature was hot on his heels.

This time Delgado's fingers were working as required and halfway to the car had figured out that on the key chain was automatic lock release. Switching the keys to his right hand in mid-stride, he held it aloft and pressed the button.

He was answered by a blaring "Awh-awhn!" sound and the welcoming heavy click of a hundred-thousand-dollar sports car's doors unlocking. He made it to the car, wrenched the door open and leaped in, slamming it shut in one fluid motion. The Bantu demon ricocheted off the driver's-side window, then leaped onto the hood and began attacking first the windshield, then, in frustration, began decimating one of the windshield wipers.

Delgado sat back and for a moment took some enjoyment in the luxurious comfort of the hand-made Italian seats. Then he realized someone was in the back seat of the car. In the rear-view mirror was Tommy Robbins.

Only Tommy wasn't looking much suited for a daydream homo-erotic fantasy. Actually he looked like he'd gone a few losing rounds with the thing currently making rubber ribbons out of the Maserati's wipers, which was, in fact, the case. Delgado's mouth opened and closed, but nothing was coming out. Then Tommy reached over from behind and grabbed Delgado's crotch with what was left of his hand and began squeezing and squeezing.

"Want to go for a ride, sailor?" he gurgled into Delgado's ear.

Then Delgado found his voice.

The screams went on for a long time.

In this day and age, it's seldom – in most countries, at least – that one finds oneself in complete and utter darkness, one hundred percent devoid of light, unless one happens to be poking around, say, a mineshaft when the breakers blow. But that was how Easton and Lefferts found themselves.

The first natural urge is to panic. It is the same as being struck completely blind. At the same time, one's other senses do their best to pick up the slack but typically, not being ready for such extra demands, take a while to adjust, to compensate. Even so, one becomes more focused on what one hears, smells. Feels.

The first thing the men became aware of was the cool air, the vague hint of cold meat, the drip of water coming from the tap. From upstairs came some muffled thumps, made even more indistinct by thick tiled walls.

Then they became aware of other sounds. Sounds that were like faint whisperings. And what might have been the faint suggestion of things moving. Then both men heard the same distinct thing from the other side of the room.

The creak of a leather harness. A booted foot taking a step.

Followed by the metallic "Sh-i-i-i-ng!" of a sword being drawn.

"Easton?" Leffert's voice quavered.

Easton didn't say a word. He wasn't sure how well the things could see in the dark – dead or not – and he wasn't keen to give away his location. Instead, he very carefully drew out his sword, muffling the movement with his thumb and forefinger. Then, transferring it to his left hand, he reached into his jerkin with his right and pulled out the Beretta, flicking off the safety first. Hilderman had made him drop the Glock, but thank God he hadn't searched Easton for his own weapon.

Another shuffling footstep. Creak.

"Easton? We have company...I think I'm leaving now..." Lefferts was moving away – the sound of his leather soles on the concrete floor seemed abnormally loud – then a grunt and curse as he banged into something. His arms instinctively flailed out for something to purchase. The sound of metal clanging. Easton winced, mentally willing Lefferts to just shut up and stand still. Then another sound coming through the hallway outside – the stealthy pad of heavy paws.

Big paws. As in a big cat. Then, of all the damndest things, a low growl. The predator's sound of a tiger. In other words, the kind of sound one particularly doesn't want to hear in a completely pitch black room.

"Ah, Easton?? I-I-I.....aggghh!" A swish of air followed by a thud, as whatever it was attacked Lefferts. Followed by a heavy "clang!" and an earsplitting screech.

There came a buzzing sound and the lights suddenly fizzled on, dimly, struggling to reach full illumination. The undead Ronin was standing right in front of him. Easton had heard the term "I felt my blood freeze" but never understood it properly until that moment. He might have gasped. The Katana was already describing its deadly arc through the air. He jumped forward under the swing and, with the sword still in his left hand, he pulled the helmeted head toward him in an awkward embrace, shoved the Beretta in the eye slit, and pulled the trigger.

The lights seemed unable to commit: they flickered on and off. Easton ran over to where the tiger – he could see now that that was what it was – was mauling Lefferts but waffled on a course of action for a second. Lefferts was beating on the thing with what looked like a metal shovel with his free hand and the strobe-light effect made using the pistol an uncertain proposition. Then again, he'd never used a sword in a real situation in his entire life.

He pointed the Beretta and fired. There came the off-sounding bang of a misfire – not enough to blow the barrel but enough to jam the firing mechanism. He debated trying to clear the feed but Leffert's muffled screams forced a decision.

Shoving the pistol back into his jerkin he took up the sword in both hands and, putting all his momentum into an overhead swing, brought it down. Antique or not, the edge was true and he succeeded in severing the torso nearly in half. Steaming gore spilled out both halves over the struggling form of Lefferts. The shovel was dropped with a clang on the concrete floor. Easton used his foot to kick aside the worst of it, then half pulled/half dragged Lefferts out of the mess.

The damage was less than he feared, thanks to the genuine quality of the costume. Lefferts' own leather doublet was badly torn up but had taken the brunt of the tiger's claws. He had a nasty gash on his left arm where he had been bitten but was otherwise alive. His nerves, on the other hand, were a wreck. Easton had hauled him up against the center table to assess the damage. Lefferts was babbling, his breath coming in whooping gasps. "Ohmygod, ohmygod, ohmygod..." until Easton slapped him hard across the cheek, then grabbed his jaw and looked into his eyes.

"Joe, focus! You're okay. Look at me. You. Are. Going. To. Be. Fine."

Lefferts nodded weakly. Easton went over to the first-aid kit, tore the metal top off and yanked out a bunch of compresses, tape, and Betadine, doing a quick field dressing on Lefferts' left forearm. The lights wavered but then came up a little more confidently. Cleaning up the sword with some paper towels over the sink, Easton resheathed it, then checked his pistol to put the safety off. Wouldn't do to have the thing go off by accident.

Shortly after there came the sound of the basement door unlocking, then footsteps coming down the stairwell and after a minute an unwelcome face poked in through the doorway.

David Hilderman.

He took a quick look around at the carnage, alarmed. "You gentlemen having some fun down here?"

Easton just shook his head. He'd just rigged a sling around Lefferts' arm to keep it elevated.

"The situation has changed, seriously. I have to ask you to forgive my earlier actions…I'm not myself tonight. I can explain everything. There's quite a bit going on that you don't know about, but right now Van Eyckmann is up in the tower, he's about to kill Knightbridge and all hell is about to break loose! I need your help, I…" He took a hard swallow and looked at the floor, "…beg of you."

Hilderman led them down the hall but, instead of going back up the stairs, led them over to the old fireplace in the main room. Along the left side was a narrow wooden door that opened into a wood locker where lumber had been stored to dry out, though it was empty, aside from some dusty cobwebs and a few ancient scraps of bark. The locker was tall and narrow and lined with unfinished planks. Hilderman motioned for Easton and Lefferts to follow him in and, stepping to the back about five feet in, pressed a hidden latch. The whole back panel opened up, revealing a narrow staircase spiraling up into darkness.

"This house is honeycombed with secret passages. I heard about this one from Knightbridge," Hilderman said over his shoulder. "This one goes directly up to the attic. Mind your step." Picking up an old fashioned EverReady flashlight on a hook by the door and switching it on, he stepped through the narrow opening and went up.

The staircase was barely a foot and a half wide, so they had to walk almost sideways to navigate it. Made of rough-hewn timber, the steps spiraled steeply up around the chimney with the plaster and lathe of the inside walls on the left and roughly mortared bricks on the right. The trapped air was musty and stale. It felt like they were hiking up a tunnel in a mountain.

After what felt like an eternity of steps, Hilderman finally paused before a black wall, his fingers working at another mechanism until a hidden door opened with a well-oiled click.

He led them into a small garret that was clearly some sort of child's bedroom, or at least a child's room from another era. The wainscoting and plaster walls were painted white and there was a small iron bed with chipped white paint and a lumpy-looking mattress with lumpy-looking blankets on it. They looked threadbare and chewed in some places. He also noticed a small shelf with a rusty pair of handcuffs and what looked like antique sex toys. One appeared to be a cast bronze dildo shaped like an elongated bishop. Easton shuttered. He didn't even want to guess what may have gone on up here, or what Van Eyckmann's involvement was.

On the walls were children's pictures (including an oil painting of a clown whose Chicklet-toothed smile gave Easton the creeps) and a shelf full of old toys and stuffed animals. Everything looked damaged or repaired. Easton noticed that the walls had been gouged and re-plastered, in some places still exhibiting scribbled writing or characters. There was also a small beat-up-looking bookcase with a few tired-looking books including a whole selection of Beatrix Potter.

The garret had four semi-circular windows that would have offered a picturesque view of the Hudson River if it hadn't been marred by the heavy iron bars that covered them. From outside, another fork of lightning snaked through the skies, followed by a thunderclap that rattled the window panes.

"What in the hell is this place?" Lefferts whispered, echoing Easton's own thoughts.

"A shortcut. Also this is where Van Eyckmann kept his bastard child. One of them anyhow. There were rooms for each of them all over the damn house, I've heard. Most didn't live very long. He liked to play with them though. Did you know that? Over a few hundred years, his deviant inclinations took all sorts of interesting forms of expression. Did you know he had Aleister Crowley as a guest here in the 1920s? Crowley bought an island up the river near Esopus. Bit of a sick puppy that one. They spent weeks trying to come up with a way to circumvent the curse – which included plenty of decadent activities. Yes, our Mohican Club leader is a real piece of work. No matter. Follow me."

He led them through a low door – a child-sized door that was made of heavy timber and probably soundproof – and into a low hallway that ran along the eaves of the roof. A series of old dog leashes and collars hung along one wall and there were odd stains on the floor. An old cloth doll lay discarded in one corner. Lefferts looked like he was about to toss his dinner. Easton thought he might join him.

The corridor led to another flush-panel doorway that opened onto a staircase landing. As they stepped out, the door closed by itself with a pneumatic click. It blended in seamlessly with the dark paneling. The staircase went up another dozen steps to a massive oak door. Hilderman put his ear to it and motioned Easton and Lefferts to join him.

Despite the door's thickness, they could hear some sort of chanting from the other side. Easton couldn't figure out the language but the words and phrases sounded arcane and somehow....dark? sinister? oily? He only knew that he didn't like the sound of them. Not one bit.

He looked at Hilderman, eyebrows going up in a what now? look.

In response, Hilderman listened again, pointed to the room on the other side, then held up three fingers. Easton got it: On the count of three.

Hilderman ticked off his digits and when the third came up he twisted the handle, threw the door open and they rushed in.

19. END GAME

In a manner of speaking.

As they ran into the room, Easton saw that they were in fact in a large square turret, perhaps 25 feet across, with tall stained glass windows on three sides. The peaked ceiling vanished up into a gloom of open rafters. The room was lit by large sconces with bulky-looking tapers. It was clearly some sort of martial training room – an assortment of swords, epees, rapiers, staves, and such were set up in racks and displays around the four walls. There was even a modest trophy case with some photos, documents, and an assortment of fencing trophies. In the middle of the broad-planked floor was chalked a large five-pointed pentacle with a lit oil lamp at each point. Around that was drawn, in charcoal, a series of symbols that Easton didn't recognize.

And wouldn't have had time to anyway.

For as they rushed in, Hilderman seized both men by the shoulder and hurled them with enough force to send them tumbling headlong into the middle of the room. More force than a man his size should have managed. Easton had enough time to register that on a small dais on the opposite side stood Van Eyckmann, an ancient-looking book in one hand – it was the tattered copy of S.L. MacGregor Mather's Key of Solomon the King from the study – and what looked like a velvet pouch being held aloft in the other. With his black suit and tie, he might have been a minister about to deliver a rant on hellfire and brimstone. But what really threw him was the figure standing just behind and to the right of him.

It was Paul Knightbridge.

Hardly in any distress, he was standing calmly by what looked like a panel of levers near the wall.

Before Easton could do a double take – he was, after all, tumbling along the floor – there was the sound of screeching metal and screaming pulleys and, with a resounding clang that shook the tower, a large iron cage dropped, imprisoning the two men. Lefferts rolled on the floor with his arm cradled, wincing in pain. Easton had landed on his ass with his hands splayed out. Another two inches and the bottom rail of the cage would have smashed most of his fingers flat.

That didn't even register. He was wholly focused on Hilderman – or a man who looked like Hilderman – standing at the doorway with his arms folded. Even as Easton watched, the air was shimmering around him, features were changing, the whole figure mutating, liquefying as if it was made of wax in a manner he wouldn't have guessed possible outside of a Hollywood special effects house. It hurt his eyes to watch.

Right before his eyes, Hilderman became Kimmi.

Or a nightmare version of him at least.

This version of Kimmi had a much longer, goat-like visage, only a vague approximation of a human face. And he was much taller, easily seven feet. The eyes were fierce slits with reptilian-looking pupils, the nose an exaggerated caricature of its earlier appearance. Two twisted horns bent back from the forehead alongside the crested skull. He now had the shoulders of a linebacker, his arms were thickly corded muscles, and the fingers ended in wicked-looking talons.

The worst, however, was the terrible smile. A mouthful of savage, curved, sharp teeth like those of a Komodo dragon, some bent and blackened, others yellowed, but the better percentage of the rest looking white and deadly and ready for business.

This time when Kimmi spoke, it sounded like three or four voices rolled into one. The effect was just plain weird.

"Ah, my friend, very clever. A trap of purified iron. And a ritual of binding. 390 years of practice so far and this is the best you can come up with?" A gurgling snicker. "I am somewhat disappointed." Then he glided into the room.

Easton went over and grabbed the bars of the cage absently, doing his best to process this unfolding tableau for which he had absolutely no frame of reference in all his 39 years on earth. By virtue of their profession, policemen tend to get considerably jaded as their careers stretch out, the incidents of the bizarre and unnatural becoming fewer and fewer until one pretty much doubts them all. But the past day had taken his increasingly calcified concept of reality, stomped it a few times with its heel, and then torn it up into unrecognizable scraps to be tossed fluttering out the window into the wind. Lefferts was pretty much on the same page, as his arm with its blood-soaked bandages was all but forgotten and he joined Easton, his uninjured hand also grasping one of the iron bars.

Kimmi was expanding. He looked well over eight feet tall now and he looked like a very hungry and homicidal predator about to devour its prey in a slow and very painful manner. The air around him had a shimmering quality as if heat was baking off him in waves. From down the stairs came a muffled stomping.

"The warriors come, my friend, to enact your punishment..."

Van Eyckmann hadn't moved a muscle. But one eyebrow arched up. "Ah, but it seems tonight you are to be short a few hands...?"

Kimmi, who had stopped a dozen feet in front of the Dutchman, look unfazed. "True, but four may easily do the work of ten. And they shalt not tire easily." To make his point, the helmets of the dead mercenaries could be seen as they came trudging up the stairs.

"I am sorry, Kimmi, but there shall be no work for my dead Ronin this evening. It is time for this game to end."

What passed for an amused look crossed the creature's face. But the slitted eyes blinked in puzzlement.

Now Van Eyckmann wore the ghost of a smile. "You foolish, arrogant monster. A cockroach has more brains than you. The trap you have sprung by tossing these two men in first was not the real trap. This entire room is the real trap!" With that, he nodded to Knightbridge who pulled a second lever.

There was a sliding clang as a set of iron bars dropped over the entrance, sealing them in. Easton could see now that there were bars over the windows as well.

Van Eyckmann looked around the chamber. "My entire training room is lined with iron forged from the virgin ore of the Imagi mines, each piece inscribed and blessed by an ancient imam I located outside of Baghdad. It took 60 years to build, a section at a time by different contractors so as not to arouse suspicions. I had to plan a dozen other fake projects to go along simultaneously to mask my plan. Do you have any idea what this cost, you miserable wretch? Go ahead, do what you will, but you still cannot kill me and your magic will not work within these walls, upon my word!"

Kimmi's eyes went wide with alarm and he shot about the chamber, faster than the eye could readily follow, to this wall, that one, over to that corner, his terrible claws slashing at this and that surface. Plaster and lathing flew and crumbled away, revealing a network of iron bars underneath. Kimmi howled and screamed as he flew about, the hideous sound making the men cover their ears in pain. Easton and Lefferts jumped back from the bars lest they lose their fingers as the creature zoomed past, talons flailing. Van Eyckmann was untouchable – possibly his curse could only be inflicted by his contingent of dead Ronin – but Knightbridge wasn't so lucky. After one of the thing's raging passes, he suddenly slumped down to the base of the wall, his chest and face raked by slashing claws, nearly disemboweled.

Then it was off to another wall, toppling the display case and sending Van Eyckmann's trophies and medals flying. This went on for a good five minutes until the creature began to grasp the futility of his actions. He could approach but apparently not touch the iron, nor pass between it. Outside the door, the Ronin gathered, shuffling like the worlds' ghastliest concert-goers muscling for front row seats.

Finally Kimmi came to a stop and approached Van Eyckmann. A sly smile crept across his thick lips as he folded his arms again. "And yet, my friend, you are trapped here with me, no? Shall we spend an eternity in each other's company?" His head tilted and his eyes glittered.

Sometime during all the excitement, Van Eyckmann had removed the contents of the pouch and held the diamond aloft, stopping the creature in its tracks.

"No." said Van Eyckmann. Then he read the name of the symbol carved on the back of the stone. An ifrit's true name.

Kimmi's eyes looked like they were ready to explode in their sockets. There was a moment when the veins stood out around the massive forehead like gnarled roots about to pop and his cavernous mouth yawned wider than seemed possible. Then he imploded and flew into the precious stone with a sonic pop. Easton swore he could still hear the screaming in his ears. It took him and Lefferts a good two minutes to relax their postures and open their eyes. There followed the ringing silence like the one one hears after sitting in the barber's chair for a way-too-long haircut and the clippers are suddenly turned off.

The djinn was gone.

Outside the door, there was a tumble of bones and old armor collapsing as the magic that had animated the long-dead soldiers was snuffed. Van Eyckmann threw up one of the levers next to where Knightbridge lay slumped, then walked over to the iron cage where Easton and Lefferts stood. The bars to the door and windows trundled upward.

"The Midnight Star of Molucca." Turning the diamond over in his hand, he looked highly pleased with himself. "Also known as the Heart of Solomon." Not as valuable as it looks, unfortunately, marred with all these markings. But its value isn't necessarily in dollars and cents. Far from it. It is a very powerful, some say the most powerful, gem of binding one could possess. I had learned of it and spent years searching for it, never knowing that Kimmi, with his twisted sense of humor, damn his eyes, had placed it right here in Taron Hall. Right behind my own coat of arms in my private office!"

Easton stepped up to the bars. "I don't understand."

Van Eyckmann looked at him oddly. "Nor would you, being an imbecilic excuse for a detective. But then there isn't much point in attempting to grasp a djinn's nature, so I will overlook your dim grasp of such matters. They are malicious. Evil. Pranksters. But short-sighted, not much for long-term planning. Every 130 years he has been showing up, inflicting all sorts of mischief, animating things, playing his tricks, harassing, terrifying, bullying. Like having your own private homicidal prankster dropping in for a visit." He peered closer at Easton. "Do I know you? You look a lot like Mr. Matthews. Who, come to think of it, I haven't seen tonight. Where is he? My orders were quite specific! Is he off sticking his noodle in that drossed-up harlot bitch of his? Not that I ever had any intention of giving any of these men a red cent. It was all part of the game. To throw Kimmi off the real plan. Did Matthews ever show up?"

"Actually, he's dead. Hilderman brought me in as a...stand-in of sorts."

"Dead? Well, so is Mr. Hilderman, that backstabbing Shylock, so he's in good company. A shame. I liked Mr. Matthews." He turned to go.

Easton thought a moment, ignoring the Dutchman's barbed comments. "So all this, the snakes, the statues in the garden, the..." he thought about Aun-mai, but held his tongue, "the apparitions and such. All the work of this....djinn?" The word sounded vaguely ridiculous in his mouth. Scratch the vague part. Yet...it certainly wasn't ridiculous to Knightbridge, who was slumped over by the wall like a village drunk, his head slumped over.

Van Eyckmann kept looking at him. "Yes. They can get up to a lot of mischief. But now...now I have him where I finally want him. Where I can control him." He pulled out the velvet pouch and dropped the diamond brooch into it. "And, gentlemen, much as I would like to discourse and discover what simple thoughts are on your feeble minds, time is wasting. I have an appointment to keep. I have a very powerful djinn at my beck and call and I have oh so much work to do...." He turned and headed over to where Knightbridge and the levers that worked the cages were.

"Wait." Easton said in a commanding voice.

Van Eyckmann paused, chin raised, listening.

"The stone. What will you do with it?"

The Dutchman half turned around. "Do with it? You truly are the dim bulb in the box. Do? Why, anything I want. With this I can command reality. Change it. Mold the world in my own image if I so wish. Goodbye."

"Wait! You can't just leave us. We need to get Lefferts to a doctor."

"Mr. Lefferts is an egotistical, loud-mouthed cock with as much value and class as a landfill rat... from Staten Island."

Talk about the pot calling the kettle black, Easton thought.

Lefferts looked stung... and angry.

Van Eyckmann shook his head in disgust and, with that, turned and started walking towards the slumped figure by the wall.

Yet even as he did, Knightbridge's head slowly came up and he caught Easton's eye. Was that a wink? His left hand went up and struck the first lever. There came a clang as the counterweights and pulleys engaged. Then the cage holding Easton and Lefferts began to rise.

Van Eyckmann began to run.

Another inch. Then another. Keeping one eye on Van Eyckmann, Easton waited until the bottom of the cage rose ten or eleven inches, and wormed his way out on his back. Then he jumped to his feet and ran after Van Eyckmann just as the man reached the levers and yanked. The cage dropped with a heavy crash.

Someone began screaming.

Easton glanced back and saw that Lefferts had attempted to follow him by rolling under the rising cage. Hampered by his injured arm, he had almost made it through when the cage came down square on his shin, smashing the bone flat. Easton had no time to consider it further, as Van Eyckmann dashed over to the rack of swords and pulled out a long cup-hilted rapier. Without thinking, Easton reached and pulled out his own sword. Van Eyckmann tore off his jacket, flung it aside and was on him.

In fairness, Easton was a complete amateur, having taken only a few fencing lessons in his misspent youth and a couple of workshops attached to the Karate Dojo he had trained at years back. Van Eyckmann, on the other hand, was not only a seasoned expert in his time, he'd had an additional 390 years to practice. Even so, Easton didn't do half bad. He kept his sword pointed up towards his opponent's neck, weight on the back foot, elbow bent and close in to the body. The most difficult thing was to remain relaxed and focused. Especially when someone was coming at you with a sharp object with the intent of skewering you with it. He struggled to recall his instructor's words: Relax, Balance, Assess…Defense…Defense? Too late. Van Eyckmann was on him. Parry. Thrust. Parry. Feint. Dizzying how fast a sword could move. Nothing at all like the movies. Easton focused on maintaining his calm. Still, it shortly became clear that Van Eyckmann was simply toying with him. Easton was completely on the defensive and had the added disadvantage of not having the correct muscles developed. Within minutes, his arm began to tire as Van Eyckmann forced him back around the room in a large circle. The ring of metal bounced off the walls, mixed with the sound of heavy panting as each man worked at his game.

Van Eyckmann pulled a few quick maneuvers, clack! another parry, feint, a glissade, then a deadly thrust to the abdomen. Clack! The blade was knocked aside but it was a ploy – it came around in a counter-clockwise arc and nicked Easton on the cheek. Van Eyckmann was grinning. Then Easton remembered.

Attack the man. Not the sword.

Van Eyckmann gave a derisive snort, then Easton was at him, this time gripping the hilt with both hands and coming at Van Eyckmann in a redoubled fury, beating him back by sheer brute force. The sword seemed to be alive in his hands, eager to serve its purpose. Time and again, his opponent's counters and parries were knocked aside. He was as surprised as Van Eyckmann, then more so when the older man stumbled slightly under the onslaught and the blade sliced through his shirt and into the meat of Van Eyckmann's right shoulder.

There was a momentary pause as Van Eyckmann realized he had actually been wounded – his face registered shock and alarm – and Easton realized he'd actually just cut a man open with a sword. Blood curtained out of the wound and the shoulder went bright red. Then Van Eyckmann countered with a lunge. Easton managed to keep his blade up enough to deflect the attack, twisting sideways and jumping backward to avoid the point, only to stumble backward over Knightbridge's leg and fall. But instead of pressing home his advantage, Van Eyckmann turned and ran.

Easton found himself looking into Knightbridge's pallid face.

"John, you have to stop him."

Easton gained his feet and leaned over, grasping the other man's shoulder, then looking over to where Lefferts was pinned like a bug, writhing in agony. Knightbridge was clutching his sleeve. "For Chrissakes, Paul, this isn't a game, I don't know shit about sword fighting!"

"You know enough. He's wounded. You have to kill him. You must. And never mind Lefferts...I'll see to him...I can make it. John, go. Now. He can control the djinn....but he needs to invoke it first...GO!"

Easton nodded.

Then sword in hand he began to run.

The trail of blood was quite easy to follow.

The trail led out the back of the house where Easton spotted the lone figure down on the lower terrace overlooking the Hudson River. The rain-slicked flagstones made running questionable but the rain had at least stopped. Across the sky, the wind chased piled-up cumulus clouds across the waning moon. Certainly a witch on her broomstick wouldn't have looked at all out of place up there in the heavens.

As Easton ran down to the lower terrace, sword in hand, he realized Van Eyckmann wasn't performing any hurried incantations or rituals or summoning back Kimmi to remold the world in his megalomaniac vision. No, he wasn't doing anything but standing there waiting for him.

It was almost midnight on Halloween.

And as Easton had observed, there was so often an inevitability to things in life.

Van Eyckmann stood in a relaxed fencer's stance, guard down but foot balanced. The wind plucked and snapped at his clothes. Leaves spun this way and that and the wan moonlight flickered off the surface of the river, snaking through the inky darkness far down below.

As Easton stepped up within the last dozen feet or so, the tip of Van Eyckmann's rapier went up and down a few times. "Yes, I believe we have met. A long, long time ago," he said, his words almost getting carried away in the wind. "What is your name?"

"John Easton."

"John Easton. John Easton." the Dutchman echoed, eyeing him carefully. "I suspect, Mr. Easton, that you and I have some unfinished business to attend to."

Easton wasn't quite sure what he meant, but in a strange way the words did feel about right. Without really thinking, he replied, "It appears so." And both men brought their swords up.

This time the exchange was much more calculated. There was a dead intensity behind each man's moves – there was an unspoken agreement, an almost psychic link that said that this fight was for keeps. Only one of them would be walking away.

Easton, a complete amateur at swordplay, at least had good instincts. Van Eyckmann, who earlier was toying with his opponent and unbelievably skilled, was losing blood fast and was forced to conserve his strength while maintaining the advantage. Back and forth they went across the terrace, swords clanging and whirling. No fancy Hollywood flamboyant antics here, just two men having at each other in deadly earnest while each grew steadily more exhausted. Back and forth. Back and forth. Clack! Clack!

Easton felt his arm going numb. Calling on his experience in karate, he began to conserve his strikes and attacks, letting the fight grow more defensive on his end, hoping to lure Van Eyckmann into a mistake. Van Eyckmann for his part kept working at Easton, trying to wear him down before his own strength gave out. The wound was on his sword arm, seriously hampering his fight, and, for reasons he still couldn't comprehend, the damn Englishman had somehow wounded him.

How? Had imprisoning Kimmi altered the rules of his curse?

There was no time to consider. He kept at it, lunging, feinting. Strike. Riposte. Counter. Keeping Easton as confused and off balance as possible.

And then it happened.

After a particularly quick combination, Easton faltered and slipped in a puddle, feet shooting out and landing square on his back. Quick as a snake, Van Eyckmann was on top of him, foot on Easton's midsection, sword point resting on his heart.

Not in the mood for theatrics at this point, Van Eyckmann simply said, "I am afraid, Mr. Easton, this is goodbye." And plunged the point in.

Easton should have died right then and there.

But he didn't.

Two things – well three things – happened right then simultaneously. One, clear as day, was Aun-mai's voice in his head. He heard the words quite distinctly, erasing all the doubts and fears in an instant: "John. Open your heart. For me." At the same time something did open, something that had been locked shut for so many years. And the white force that plunged through it and through his muscles nearly blinded him. The next was Van Eyckmann's sword point plunging through the leather jerkin into a disk of metal over his chest, one about the size and thickness of a Saint Christopher's medallion, the tip bending with the effort. The third was Easton's own sword coming up, the etched words on its blade appearing to glow in the night.

Verus Cor Justitia

The Heart of Justice.

It cut Van Eyckmann's blade clean in two, sending it flying. Then, gripping the Dutchman's foot and yanking it aside to throw his opponent off balance, Easton bounded up and in one fluid motion sank his sword into Van Eyckmann's chest. All the way up to the hilt.

The two men's faces were nearly touching.

Through a rictus of clenched teeth, Van Eyckmann hissed, "It wasn't supposed to end like this."

"Sorry. It just did." was all Easton could say.

And Van Eyckmann, with what might have been a ghost of a smile, died.

Lars Van Eyckmann's body lay collapsed on the flagstones, blood pooling under his torso propped up by the protruding blade. Easton looked on in shock. Had he really done this? Skewered another man with a sword? Apparently so. It seemed so, well, barbaric.

And yet, he couldn't deny it, it felt kind of, good.

For a split moment the sword had felt...alive...in his hands. As if it had sought out Van Eyckmann's heart on its own. Singing for blood. And that scared the hell out of him.

He fished around on Van Eyckmann's body until he found the pouch with its stone. Even in its covered state, he thought he could feel its promises calling to him. Offering to seduce him. Untold riches. Power. The opportunity to reshape the world to his wildest desires.

The voice of Kimmi.

To hear is to obey, my friend.

Then Easton realized he was hearing the words aloud.

He stood up and looked around. With the wind chill, the temperature had dropped to below freezing and the clouds playing across the moon made the light elusive and the shadows deceptive. Then he looked back at the menacing hulk of Taron Hall. There, standing among the gargoyles hunched along the roofline of the circular tower four stories up at the rear, a lone figure stood, impossibly, on the slate roof tiles, its arms outstretched as if welcoming the night.

Kimmi.

Easton had time to shake his head and mutter, "Fuck."

Then

A blink

The "pop" of an object filling what was empty air a moment before.

Easton wheeled around and found Kimmi standing before him, arms folded. Surrounded by an aura that was like smoldering air, the smell of cordite and sulfur and cooked, rancid meat. His true form was more amorphous, shifting images in the air, sometimes human, sometimes…something else. To gaze too long on it was to invite madness. The eyes were empty pools, black abysses of the deepest reaches of the universe.

What is it you wish, my friend?

Easton sighed. This night just wasn't getting any shorter and his temper was starting to fray. He decided he wasn't much in the mood for rhetorical questions. "For you to go back to whatever poison-aired shit-heel piece of real estate you crawled out of. That'd be fine for starters."

This I cannot do. I am here. I am now. I am Kimmi. I am hungry…

"Well, then I guess its fuck you and the camel you rode in on… My friend."

Kimmi's taloned hands made a palms-out gesture and Easton found himself flying through the air backwards, arms pin wheeling, before he hit, tumbling along the flagstones 20 yards away, banging his shins and elbows and knocking the wind out of him. He came to rest when his back slammed into the large stone fountain, his head snapping back over the rim painfully. He had time to observe upside-down that one of Neptune's mermaids was looking down at him with clinical detachment – no help was forthcoming from that quarter – then, with another disturbing "pop," Kimmi was there, straddling him like the world's ugliest (and extra dimensional) pro wrestler.

What is your wish, Johneaston? I can make it so….?"

"You don't listen too well, Kimmi." Easton coughed, and a sharp pain went up his back. He wondered if one of his ribs might be broken. He heard a line coming out of his mouth like one from a tacky cop movie, but he just couldn't help it. "You should try cleaning the wax out of your ears once in a while. And while I'm at it, you're a sad-ass excuse for a djinn, ifrit, or whatever the hell it is you've been passing yourself off as at this party."

Kimmi cocked his head to one side, as if considering a difficult math equation. Then he laughed his strange and garbled laugh before bending over Easton, putting his hands around the detective's neck and raising his face up to his as if in some obscene lover's kiss. One that, if memory served, was not going to be the start of a productive and mutually nurturing relationship. Easton instinctively reacted by putting his hands in return around Kimmi's neck.

It felt as if he had plunged his hands up to the elbow in molten phosphorous. The pain was excruciating and his teeth clenched like vises. As his hands went numb, he had a moment to consider that he seemed to be making a career out of bad decisions these past few days. Then the gray wool began to gather around his peripheral vision and he knew he was about to black out.

Kimmi bent forward, opening his mouth wide...

As Easton tottered along the edge of his consciousness, it occurred to him that he was about to die, that his options were quickly dwindling to zero, and that he was fighting a force he didn't have a remote shot in hell of overcoming. He felt like he was falling down a lightless shaft, a well from which there would be no return but, perhaps mercifully, there would be the comfort of eternal nothingness. He sensed he was zooming towards the event horizon of his mortality and, helpless, felt an immense calm seep over his consciousness.

At least he had tried.

Time to...

Right then, he heard his Aunt B's voice clear as a bell, as if she was right there and had spoken directly (sexily/forcibly) one simple command in his ear.

"Open the doors, Johnnie. Open them...*now!*"

His mind blinked.

There was a bright, white light approaching like a wave. It was a wave.

There was a suspended moment of anticipation and across his consciousness...

A line from a movie – something wonderful is about to happen – of all the damndest things

Then it swept through him and he was in it. He was in the white.

And the doors opened.

All of them.

It was as if, in his mind, every door to every memory, to every thought, to every event, to everything he had ever seen and done and would ever see and do opened with a perfect, synchronized click like some sort of magic Chinese puzzle box. An epiphany.

Everything made perfect, unquestionable sense.

Then it was as if, as Kurt Vonnegut once phrased it, he became unstuck in time.

There was no time.

He was at a place/thought where there were no questions, no doubts, only absolute certainty, absolute surety of purpose.

A floating sensation. A vague sense of huge objects (celestial spheres?) moving in titanic synchronized motions. Complete disconnect. Images/memories/emotions. Thought. The death of his first dog. The first time he kissed a girl. The sad, resigned look on Pearson's face as he dropped to his knees, his throat pierced by 9mm slugs. The first birthday party he ever remembered, the paper cone hat and the elastic band biting into his chin. His mother kissing his forehead. His first terrified plunge into the ocean. The calloused touch of his grandfather's hand and his old man's smell of whisky, sweat, and cigarettes. The first time he put his hand on the breast of a girl, on the couch of his parents' living room one night – her name had been Carla, she was a cute blond a year ahead of him. He'd been what, 14? 15? The first time he got drunk and vomited over the front seat of his friend's car, and all over himself. Graduation day at the academy…and the angry yet fearful expression of the first man he killed in the line of duty on a hot rainy day. Random memories floating past in the ocean of his life. The velvety warmth of Aun-mai….and the things she whispered in his ear just moments? seconds? hours? before and the conscious landscape began to alter other thoughts and memories and events that weren't his…ones he recognized as his parents'…his birth, his father's haggard grin in the blinding light of the hospital room…their first date…his grandfather's eyes…the terror of German-manufactured bullets whickering past and chopping down the soldiers in the surf at Sword Beach and the numbing *whumpf* of the mortar shell and looking up through Granddad's eyes at the sky and mud and a leg – his leg, by God – falling back down through air with the debris and a pie in his grandmother's kitchen and…

The flow of memories, lifetimes, oceans of existence, and…answers.

His mind picking up the thread of events that led to Taron Hall, the connecting threads woven through everything that was/is/always will be through every event of his entire life, his father's, his grandfather's, his great grandfather's until he could see in hyper-clarity Maghra the magician in his cave and his device, the invocation – going wrong – and the thing that answered his call…not a djinn at all (if there was really ever such a thing) but another, an entity summoned from some other place or dimension entirely, almost in the way that if one called a particularly long international number on the phone and happened to get just one digit wrong in the sequence, an unexpected voice might answer, maybe from another time or place entirely.

And perhaps it is true that, on that time/date sequence that the human race calls Halloween, the membranes and fabrics that separate the dimensions are thinner and more than an unexpected quark particle slips through. In this case, it was an entity from the far reaches of space and time, which answered and arrived at the blink of a thought.

What arrived in the cave on Rhun Island that sweltering evening on October the 31st was at first difficult to articulate. Descriptives like "Demon" were somewhat usable; "Negative Entity" helpful but too abstract. Curiously, the very act of Maghra's senses in interpreting the creature he had invoked in a fashion defined it – and bound it (somewhat) – to the rules he understood and expected. Not unlike the way the act of measuring a quark defines it.

And Maghra, well-traveled and well-read as he was, was an avid reader of the collection of Arabic folklore some of which would eventually be translated and published as The Arabian Nights.

All this Easton grasped in his "unstuck" state.

As well as what Aun-mai told him. The dead apparently talk amongst themselves in whatever dimension or consciousness they move in, because she had told him the creature's true name, not the name Maghra had thought, and thus not the name Van Eyckmann had discovered via Sir Richard Burton's translations and certainly not 'Kimmi' (which was its own fabrication) and even as he thought it, he said

"*Shikk Bazraal.*" Out loud.

The creature recoiled, its mouth mere millimeters from Easton's, its black serpentine tongue rolling back into its gaping jaws like a freakish party favor, its eyes doing a strange double blink with its multiple eyelids like that of an alligator. It was trying to pull itself away, seams and fissures in its skin erupting as it made the effort, but it was as if it was glued to Easton by a force field...

How...? Its jittering thoughts began to run simplistically "johneaston not...not even larsvaneyckmann...but ho..."

Easton's mind blinked again and the creature was screaming, a piercing, keening sound as its body began to shake, shudder, and convulse as if it was in a broken paint mixer. The detective's hand, which still felt like it was full of Novocain, clumsily pulled out the diamond by its chain and managed to hold it up in the air before him.

"Balak shar alazza: Shikk Bazraal," Easton spoke, words which would have sounded like complete and utter nonsense had anyone else been standing within earshot but the creature that was Kimmi understood them quite perfectly. "I bind you." The result was certainly catastrophic for its corporal being. The thing's body disintegrated towards the diamond suspended from Easton's hand as if being pulling into a black hole ("through an extra-dimensional pinhole" might be more accurate). The skin went first, revealing the muscles and veins, then the viscera and the other wormlike inner parts and organs writhed and dissolved, followed by the misanthropic skeleton, like some sort of horror movie toothpaste.

Every molecule of the creature went into the diamond, ending with a somewhat anti-climactic "*pffft!*" sound.

It was gone.

Or, rather, true and officially bound.

Easton staggered to his feet, unable to believe what he had just done. Not entirely convinced he had actually done it. The feeling began to creep back into his arms. He should have been ready to drop dead of exhaustion, but the aftermath of what he'd just been through – cosmic mind-fuck, pseudo-religious epiphany, call it whatever flavor of the week you want – the afterglow of it was still coursing through his veins and he had never felt more awake, more there, more all-cylinders-firing-just-fine-thank-you-very-much, than he did right then. If someone had asked him to walk across the Hudson River in his bare feet right then, he felt that he probably could have done it.

"It didn't work last time," he said to the empty space the creature had occupied moments before, "because Van Eyckmann wasn't much good on slick pick-up lines to win your sweet little heart over." He held the diamond up to the light. He could definitely feel it thrum and pulse in his hand now. A more foolish man might try to control it now, but he also understood it would be like those trainers who work with the Bengal tigers at the circus shows. The control was only an illusion maintained by the ego of the trainer. Sooner or later, one day one when you least expected it, that tiger was probably going to turn around and take your hand off. Or worse.

It was part of their nature.

In that way, it wasn't unlike the djinn everyone had taken it for.

Easton stood for a moment, his eyes half closed, just focusing on the air, breathing in and out of his lungs. Funny the things one takes for granted. In. Out. In. Out. The very function of being alive. The air smelled of dry leaves, the richer textures of river water, the briefest hint of wood smoke from someone's fireplace. He made a promise to appreciate it all more. He'd probably forget about the promise within a week. But at least there was next week to look forward to…

He swore he felt something caress his hand.

Then, in the wind, Easton swore he heard her voice.

"Cinta Kamu."

And then he felt her. Around him. Inside him. The scent of oranges. The trace of fingers along his cheek. Something brushed his lips.

He smiled.

She was gone.

And he had a hunch that she was gone for good.

Upstairs, he found Knightbridge doing what he could for Leffert's leg. It looked pretty bad. The phones were dead but he had scrounged up one of the first-aid kits and had given him a shot of morphine and a handful of other sedatives to knock him out. He'd seen more than his share of major trauma on the battlefield and told Easton he thought that if Lefferts could get through the next 24 hours there was a good chance he was going to survive, though probably minus a leg.

Easton in turn patched up Knightbridge best he could, and while he did, the two men talked.

Easton had grabbed a bottle of Scotch from downstairs and two glasses. Knightbridge swallowed his first glass in one gulp and, wincing, held it out for a refill.

"Thanks, mate. The phones are out and best I can tell the vehicles have all been disabled. When I went for help earlier, the tires had all been slashed, batteries torn out, the works. My guess was either Kimmi or one of his helpers wanted to keep the party cozy and private this evening. I need you to walk down to the main road and either hitch a ride or walk to town – it's only a couple of miles –get to the police station and get an ambulance up here ASAP. That'll give me enough time to tidy up what needs to be tidied up. Not really sure who's left. Wang, Hilderman, Washington, Lowe, and Anderson are dead. Delgado is missing. Some or all of the house staff is dead. Christ, what a fucking mess."

Easton took a pull on his drink. He still couldn't process the whole string of events. "Paul, did all this really happen? Van Eyckmann, the curse, that nightmare called Kimmi, for God's sake?"

"Oh, it happened, John. No one will ever fucking believe it, it may make a half-assed B movie someday, but it most certifiably happened."

"What are you going to tell the police?"

Knightbridge thought a moment, then chuckled to himself. "Maybe about a homicidal house servant who freaked out on drugs during an eccentric dead billionaire's Halloween party. Who then managed to jump off the cliff into the river. Or something like that. The rest they can puzzle out on their own time. You may have to stick around town a few days for questioning, but they'll have nothing to connect you with any of this except that Hilderman hired you to look into a friend's murder. I'll make sure of that. Afraid there won't be any cool millions showing up in your bank account after all."

Easton shrugged. "It would have been bad money anyhow. How did you know about the money?"

Knightbridge took another swig of the Scotch. His cheeks were looking flushed now. "There's a lot I know about, mate. It wasn't a coincidence, you know."

"What?"

"The whole setup. That's what it was. The whole Mohican 'Executive Council' being in dire straits? Van Eyckmann was orchestrating the whole thing all along. Part of his game to keep everyone dancing on hot irons. I did much of the dirty work for him, and that's something I'll have to atone for. Part of it was his sadistic personality. Part of it was a smoke screen to fool Kimmi while he set up the real trap. Part of it was that he was a complete fuckwit who had gone off his rocker. And Hilderman? He was working his own game too. It wasn't a coincidence when he met you on the plane, or what happened to you back on Grand Turk. He wanted Matthews out of the way. Hell, he probably killed him himself."

"Why?"

"Why is a good question, mate, and one we may never get an answer to. I guess we can go downstairs and ask him, but I suspect he won't do much talking. Why indeed? I have my guesses. I think he was working his own plan to get everyone killed off so he could take all the money for himself, or himself and Washington. We'll never know. But story time is over, mate. You need to get a move on so we can save Leffert's bacon. Only one more thing, and you know what that is."

Easton nodded. "Yeah. Have to give that some more thought. But I won't use it. Too much power for one man, too much potential for things to go awry. I think you and I have seen the results of that scenario playing out. A lot of people get dead." He pulled the pouch out from under his leather jerkin.

"What I need to do is find a place, far away from any human's reach."

There was a momentary silence. "I could handle that for you if you like. I'm pretty good at disposing of unpleasant things."

Easton thought about it. He had really grown to like Knightbridge over the course of the past day. But he wasn't sure he liked the look he thought he saw in the man's eyes as he stared at the pouch holding the diamond. "Certainly appreciate the offer. But I think I have to handle this one myself." Putting it back inside his jerkin, he stood up, knees cracking. "Got to run. I'll send help quickly." He gave Knightbridge a tap on the shoulder. "And Paul?"

"Yeah, mate?"

"Thanks."

Easton stood in front of the gates he had just climbed over and headed onto Route 9.

Knightbridge had been right. He'd taken a quick detour into the barn to see if any of the vehicles might work. Wang's Maserati was a charnel house. At least Delgado was accounted for. And Tommy. Easton had no idea what had happened inside the car and decided he didn't want to. Someone had left a creepy-looking wooden statue on the hood, strips of rubber dangling from its serrated jaws. Kimmi's idea of a joke perhaps.

The rest of the cars were unusable. Easton did however find a mountain bike – probably the kid's – which he was able to ride down the driveway to the gates. He would have ridden it all the way to town but the locked entrance and 12 feet of iron bars nixed that plan.

So, just after 1:00 in the morning, he found himself walking down the road toward town. Wyvern Falls. What the hell kind of name was that?

He'd only gone 50 yards or so before a pair of high beams appeared heading south. Easton turned and put his thumb out. As the vehicle neared, it slowed down and he could see that it was a dark green Range Rover. As the car stopped, the window rolled down and Easton could see a youngish-looking man inside with intense green eyes and straight black hair. Easton made him for a landscaper or even a local architect.

"Need a lift?"

"Going into town?"

"That's the plan. Hop in."

The driver gave him a once over as he pulled back onto the asphalt.

"Nice costume. You look like a refugee from a pirate movie. Christ, is that real blood? Sorry for saying so, but you look you've been having a rough night of it."

Easton looked down and realized he had completely forgotten about the clothes he was wearing. "Got that right. Can you drop me off at the police station in town? There's been a bit of trouble."

"Sure thing. Where'd you come from?"

"Taron Hall."

That got a low whistle. "Van Eyckmann's rock pile? No kidding. You run with an exclusive crowd. What the hell kind of Halloween party was he throwing tonight?"

"The kind you'd really want to miss."

The driver nodded. "Ah."

Something about his demeanor struck Easton, but he couldn't quite place it. Like meeting an old friend you hadn't seen in some time. He found himself speaking. "What's your name by the way?"

The driver held out his right hand. "Jim Franks."

Easton shook it. "Jonathan Easton. Detective Jonathan Easton, believe it or not."

Franks nodded. "Nice. British cop?"

"Yep. By way of the Grand Turks and Caicos Islands."

"No kidding? Heard of it. Never been there. But I'm going to guess there's quite a story how you came to be strolling down a road in the middle of the night outside a sleepy Hudson River town. In a bloodstained pirate costume with a sleeve missing. Just a guess."

Easton let out a quiet laugh. "Quite a story indeed. Care to hear some of it?"

"Sure. Just dropped the girl I've been seeing up the road in Peekskill. Halloween Party. Not a bad date. Then again, not a great one either. So I could use a good story."

"Well, you're probably not going to believe this one…"

20. AFTERMATH

The Friday before Thanksgiving at around 10:00 PM, two men sat at Mooney's Bar & Grill, a pub down on lower Main Street. One was nursing a tall pint of Pete's Pumpkin Ale, the other a glass of single-malt Scotch. The pub was essentially unchanged since it first opened its doors in the late 1800s. The actual bar itself was old and banged and dented from generations of drinks and mugs (and certainly a fight or two) along with a few old cigarette burns but the oak had a warm glow and about 50 layers of shellac. Behind the bar was a long mirror in remarkably good shape, with an Art Nouveau framing and etched accents. It never failed to draw a few comments from the more artistic-minded patrons. A few designer bottles of vodka had infiltrated the rows of liquor bottles stepped behind the long counter and the taps favored microbrewery brands these days, but if the great grandfathers had swung by right then they wouldn't have felt too out of place.

The lighting was low and an old fashioned Wurlitzer juke box still lit up the opposite wall, along with some bar tables and stools. Toward the back was a small stage amongst a scattering of dining tables and a row of booths. On weekends one might find a local band, usually a half-decent blues or R&B group, and for a while they had a coffee house on Wednesdays. The juke box had an oddball mix ranging from Roy Orbison, the Who, Tony Bennett, and Patsy Cline to Broadway show tunes, new wave, punk, and even a smattering of obscure local alternative bands like Johnny Society, The Jag, and the dubiously named Rockland Eagles, a hilariously over-the-top arena-rock re-tread. You might hear Tom Waits grumbling about drinking Singapore Slings and playing pool with a midget one minute and the next getting soft and fluffy advice on staying alive from the Bee Gees. At the moment, a forgotten power punk trio known as Bram

Tchaikovsky was harmonizing about the Girl of My Dreams. If anyone was paying attention, they had just gotten to the part where Judy the love doll shows up one morning in the U.S. Mail. No one was. The pub was having a moderately busy night though, the usual mix of college kids and middle-aged adults and, predictably, the regular old-timers supporting the far end of the bar in their well-worn seats. Usually that group consisted of Harry Clanton, Etta Jones, Delores Del Rio, and the owner's nephew, Mike. Sometimes Doris Wilcox joined them but tonight she was home with the flu watching re-runs of Law & Order, SVU with her three cats.

Pat Mooney still worked behind the bar, though he had help these days from a young pretty ex-college student with plenty of tattoos. He had a small kitchen in the back where his sister Irene made some of the best soups in the Hudson Valley and a pretty decent burger to go with it. Oddly enough, the menu even sported a sampling of Cajun dishes, courtesy of an elderly Haitian man named George who had come to Wyvern Falls via New Orleans. He had turned out to be talented enough to earn a coveted slot in Irene's recipe book, which was hidden away like a sacred biblical relic from everyone – including her brother Pat. He stayed long enough to make an impression but vanished after a few weeks as mysteriously as he had arrived.

It had been three weeks since the events at Taron Hall and John Easton was still in Wyvern Falls. The rest of that dreadful evening was still quite vivid in his mind.

Franks had pulled up in front of a reddish brown Depression-era building off Main Street and joined him inside the precinct. The officer working the desk that night was a strapping six and half foot tall Russian with a crew cut and a name tag that said "Krakov," who greeted Franks, then looked at Easton up and down suspiciously. Until Easton explained who he was and gave a highly-edited version of what had happened at Taron Hall which, along with Van Eyckmann's name, got his undivided attention. Then a brief interruption while the police chief was called. Krakov listened patiently as Easton fed him the bare details and took notes in a tiny notebook and tinier pencil stub. Then five minutes later Roy Hendricks, the police chief showed up, a lean, sharp featured man in his early 50s who stood with his hands on his hips, hooded grey eyes drilling Easton as he plied him with questions, getting answers he clearly wasn't happy about. Easton immediately pegged him for a retired state trooper.

Ten minutes later, Easton found himself in the back of a squad car speeding back towards Taron Hall. Four more Village of Wyvern Falls police cars were escorting them, sirens and blue/red blinking lights going full tilt. Four county police cars were already there, waiting along with a couple of ambulances and a forensics team and coroner dragged up from White Plains.

Van Eyckmann was found in the meat cooler, ready for burial. Lefferts was brought down on a stretcher and, as Knightbridge predicted, lost his right leg below the knee. It wouldn't keep him down for long. One surprise was Jeffrey Wang, who was found alive in the study. The poison he had been struck by had lost most of its potency over the past few hundred years and the effect was only temporary paralysis that was beginning to fade by the time the paramedics arrived. He was able to give the detectives the story Knightbridge had already coached him on. The corpses of the other four Executive Council members and their attorney were carried out in body bags, along with the remains of four caterers, the valet, the cooks and two maids (though Juanita would live to serve another day, having left earlier with a slight fever), along with the driver and Knightbridge's two security men.

Kimmi was never found, of course, though an APB with his description was circulated and there were rumored sightings up and down the river. In time he would evolve into a sort of bogeyman of the region who would develop from homicidal killer to nightmare creature with the retelling from campfires and séances to schoolrooms and beauty parlors up and down the Hudson, none suspecting how close to the truth the latter was.

Knightbridge was apparently well acquainted with the police chief, which helped smooth over some of the odd inconsistencies and loose threads with the detectives and county cops that even Knightbridge couldn't cover up in the time he had. Like the stuffed tiger found sliced in half in the meat locker, the story behind the massive iron cage up in the tower, and how Van Eyckmann's driver came to be nailed up in the atrium of the gate keeper's house.

Chief Hendricks wanted clear explanations but was also aware of the level of power and influence Van Eyckmann exerted even in death – Makepeace and Lowe was still involved, despite the loss of their senior partner. In the end, the chief recognized the reality that making it all go away and getting back to whatever the village passed off as "normal" as quickly and quietly as possible was in everyone's best interest.

Easton had crashed on Franks' couch that night, having been allowed to retrieve his clothes and belongings, then took a room in the local bed & breakfast known as Mad Anthony's Arms the next day. Apparently the place was named after a local Revolutionary War hero who'd stayed there on occasion (and at every inn up and down the Hudson) but it certainly had a beautiful old tap room with low, heavy beams and an assortment of period firearms along the walls. Everyone from George Washington to

Aaron Burr was rumored to have slept there.

Easton had called Hutchison the next day to update him on where he was ("No problem, John! See you in eight weeks" was the curt response) and one day began to roll into the next. Then a call to his sister in Kent to let her know where he was. Then a third call somewhat overdue.

The voice on the other end was delighted, but not surprised.

"For shame, it has been a while, Johnnie. Too long a while. But it's so good to hear your voice," said his Aunt Bethany. Her voice sounded raspier (sexier) and still sent a thrill up his spine. "You and I have some catching up to do. But first, do tell, what exactly happened on Halloween? " And Easton told her. This time he didn't leave anything out. Well, pretty much.

Every day he was going to call the airline and book a flight out of JFK back to England and every day the call didn't get made. He rented a car from a dealer down in Tarrytown and took a little time to explore the area and found it quite interesting. Particularly the old cemetery at Sleepy Hollow, the old aerodrome in Rhinebeck with its tattered looking WWI biplanes and, of course, the assorted old mansions and manors up and down the Hudson River. His room at Mad Anthony's had a porch overlooking the river and every morning he would wake up, put on a sweater, and go with coffee in hand to watch what he decided were some of the most beautiful sunrises he had ever seen. He knew he was dragging his heels but couldn't figure out why. Somehow his idle fantasy of France and the Mediterranean began to look a little vacant and brittle, like a painting that really caught your eye the first time you passed the gallery window but the second time you realized it was a slightly bad pastiche.

He'd run into Franks that Thursday having lunch at the local Greek diner and got to talking over bowls of killer Italian wedding soup and cheeseburgers. Franks worked for a web design company in a nearby town called Irvington as an art director and was dating a local Wyvern Falls high school teacher named Karen Evershaw. He had driven up to town that day to talk to a local home renovation company that catered to the high end market – Grainey Restoration on Main Street – about their website. Apparently he had been some sort of hotshot art director in Manhattan but had left a year before after tiring of the urban rat race and decided to try his hand outside the city, stumbling upon the village almost by accident. He also refused to carry a cell phone for reasons he wouldn't elaborate on and he wasn't too keen on the New York City subway system. The slower pace and inspiring views suited him just fine.

When pressed about his plans, Easton said he was about to make his reservations for a flight out that Saturday to head back to England and see his sister. He didn't sound convincing even to himself.

Franks sat back, took a sip of his coffee, and, sounding like he hadn't really heard, said, "Sounds good." Then, "Hey, tell you what, I was planning on taking Karen out for a few drinks tomorrow night, how about you join us a for a few. Send you off on a good note."

Easton thought about it. "Awfully nice of you, but I wouldn't want to be a third wheel." He was thinking about Aun-mai. He'd left out that part in the story he shared with Franks. And with his Auntie B.

Franks shook his head. "Nah, it's no problem. Come on, I'll buy you a few rounds over at Mooney's."

"Fine."

So it was he found himself sitting at the bar with Franks the following night, nursing a glass of 12-year-old Aberlour from Pat Mooney's rather decent selection of single malts behind the bar. Pat had seemed genuinely pleased someone was getting some mileage out of his top-shelf Scotch.

Easton was thinking about a package and two envelopes that had arrived outside his room that very morning. The first package was long and rectangular. Easton had cut it open to find the sword, the very same sword he had left Lars Van Eyckmann impaled upon, carefully wrapped in expensive cloth, cleaned and shining and smelling faintly of oil. The envelope that came with it was postmarked Washington DC. Inside was a short message:

You might want to keep this. Might make a good family heirloom someday.
Have much to atone for, keep an ear out, mate.
Good luck,
-PK

Easton had looked the sword over, turning it in his hands this way and that. He had no idea what in the hell he would do with the damn thing, but somehow he felt glad to have it. It felt...right.

The second note was from Brooklyn. It included a bank statement that included a log-in and pin number. It was in his name. The balance was for $200,000. Easton let out a whistle. Along with it was a note that read:

Sorry it isn't more, it's from a private account of mine and the least I can do. Apologies for poking around but PK helped get your private info to set up the account. All square and above board. Don't even ask. I owe you my life. Call me if you ever need any investment advice.

Included was a business card with Joe Lefferts' name on it, along with his private cell number added in ballpoint ink.

The two men had just been discussing the events at Taron Hall in detail. Franks seemed keenly interested and made passing reference to a disturbing supernatural experience he'd been through back in New York City but wouldn't elaborate.

"You have to admit, John, it's a pretty wild story. Really wild. But since you're a cop, I guess I'm going to have to go along with it."

"Much obliged."

"There are a few points I still don't get though."

"Only a few?"

"Heh. A few dozen. But I'll stick to the big-ticket items. For one thing, what was with the snakes and the Medusa head?"

"Don't know. I think…it's hard to articulate, but it seemed like a lot of secondary strange phenomena were going on, almost like a side effect. This thing that called himself Kimmi may have just attracted other….energy? Entities? Hard to say. So much of this seems ludicrous in retrospect. But he did seem like the classic trickster you read about – just wreaking havoc because he can."

"And what was the whole deal with the Mohican Executive Council and a bunch of middle-aged business men?"

"Don't really know either. Part of some elaborate ruse Van Eyckmann had in mind, but he didn't elaborate and he's not answering questions at this time. At least I hope not."

Franks nodded. "Fair enough. What about Matthews? Are you still going to investigate his death?"

"Well, Hilderman hired me to do it, but he's dead."

"Yeah, but you still have that contract, don't you?"

"Good catch. Yes, I still have the contract…."

Over at the juke box, a gangly-looking dude who might have been Norm McDonald's twin brother was dropping some quarters in the slot. A minute later, the Ramones came on, hitching a ride to Rockaway Beach. When Easton looked again, he realized the kid really looked nothing like McDonald. Christ, was he going to start seeing ghosts everywhere after his metaphysical experience?

Franks piped up again. "Okay, one more."

"Shoot."

"What do you make of this whole pseudo-religious thing you went through, with the doors and all that?"

Easton didn't answer right away but took a draw on his Scotch and considered his response carefully. "Hard to say. It really does sound like a bunch of New Age mystical bullshit when I hear myself talk about it. I guess if I was an unscrupulous type, I could go hawking my tale on one of your daily tabloid shows like Montel Williams, prattling on about how I experienced a 'metaphysical vision that changed my life forever.' Or maybe I could start a mystical wellness cult in California someplace, but I'd probably come off as another self-important opportunistic huckster cashing in on a lot of insecure people with loose wallets, then, wouldn't I? No, I guess it's just one of those things…"

Both men sat in silence for a moment, each in their own thoughts. One thing Easton liked about Franks was that he didn't feel the need to constantly fill up any silences with talk. Meanwhile from the juke box, Chrissie Hynde was managing to make the words "shitting bricks" sound precociously sexy. A few minutes later, Buddy Guy was speculating that the gates of Heaven must be open because he'd just seen an angel walk by. It sounded like a bad pick-up line but Buddy's delivery somehow made it amusing.

Finally, Franks said, "So what is next on your agenda?"

Easton looked up as two women came into the bar. From Franks' description, he presumed the first was Karen Evershaw. She was a sharp-looking brunette with thick waves of shoulder-length hair, strong eyebrows, and a swimsuit figure. It didn't take a second to figure out why Franks was taken with her, everything said Woman about her – it might as well have been stamped on her forehead in bold capital letters. She had on a heavy white cableknit sweater under a down vest and Wellington riding boots. The other woman was slightly taller and Asian, with the kind of looks that stop traffic and get business cards pulled out of wallets in a hurry. She was in a turtleneck and jeans and had on a long black leather jacket with oversized lapels. Her long black hair was pulled up in one of those careless ponytails high up on the head that is apparently a trade secret among certain straight-haired women. She certainly got Easton's undivided attention immediately. For a second, he thought…

No. Of course not. She was much taller for starters, and the features were considerably different. Her most striking features were her eyes, and then an impish smile that flashed as they both shared some private joke.

Easton raised his glass to signal to Pat Mooney polishing glasses down with the regulars. "Next? Looks like next on the agenda is going to be another round of drinks."

Karen's friend, whose name was Vivienne, said in her ear, "Uh, he's like, a little old. Give me a break."

"Oh, shush. It's just for a few drinks. He's an English detective. And, from what James told me, a pretty amazing one."

The two women came up to the bar and introductions were made by Franks.

"John, Karen. And Vivienne. Karen, Vivienne…John, John, Jim, Jim, Karen…cripes, I'm getting old and confused…." He continued on in his deadpan delivery until Karen poked him in the ribs a few times, mussed his hair, and said "Enough!"

Pat Mooney appeared at their end of the bar. He was a hefty Irishman in his late 50s, working on a beer gut but with eyes as young as ever though and a full head of silver hair. More drinks were ordered.

It turned out that Vivienne, whose last name was Lee ("Don't even start with the Scarlett O'Hara jokes," she warned Easton right off the bat, "or you'll be wearing my cranberry and vodka faster than you can say Harold Robbins"), was 29 and a web designer who worked with Franks over at Discreet Media Associates, which had offices in a newly-renovated old warehouse along the waterfront in Irvington. Their conversation was forced at first but warmed up as the evening wore on. Easton went off about the ludicrous antics of some of the more eccentric celebrities who had showed up in his jurisdiction, including a rather humorous story of running into Keith Richards and Bruce Willis at a local seaside bar called Hemingway's and a drink-a-thon that left Easton pitched over a toilet and then passed out on the beach the next day, earning him a second-degree sunburn.

Rounds came and rounds went, conversation flowed this way and that between the four of them. Easton noticed that Franks tended not to talk much about himself but had no shortage of stories about everyone else, usually funny enough to have the three of them laughing to tears. And whatever hadn't been working between himself and Karen back on Halloween appeared to have worked itself out. Easton noticed she touched his hand a lot and her eyes sparkled when she looked at him. She laughed a lot as well, and it was a genuine laugh. He had a hunch she was a few years older than he was, but they looked like a good match.

Initially, he wasn't too keen on Vivienne and wrote her off as another pretty face. Probably used to men jumping all over her; directionless and spoiled. He got the impression she was making the best of a put-up job and, in that sense, he felt some sympathy. But at some point she finally began to thaw a bit and show some of her true colors – in addition to graduating from Parsons the New School for Design, she was a brilliant mimic and had a wicked sense of humor. Alcohol or not, Easton sensed some sort of a connection as the evening wore on, which was confirmed shortly when he looked down and noticed Vivienne's hand lingering on his wrist.

Which was funny as he'd been somewhat reserved all evening and was making a point of not hitting on her. There was a full minute during which she was looking at him curiously. And for split second he could have sworn....

She leaned in and asked, "So what is your game plan, Mr. Detective?" Her eyes looked mischievous and he was pretty sure there was a coded message there.

Without even a second thought, Easton replied, "I don't really know.

But I think I'm going to have to stick around here for a little while and work on it."

January 1, 2011, 5:00 AM

Easton pulled over on the main span of the Tappan Zee Bridge. A large recyclable shopping bag was in his hands. Weeks earlier, he had located a sculptor in Sleepy Hollow who, per his instructions, had taken a small anonymous-looking pouch and sunk it in a concrete form sculpted and finished to look like a natural rock, all while he stood and observed every uninterrupted step of the process. He had told the sculptor it had belonged to his ex-wife who had just passed away and he wanted to bury an important keepsake from the past and start over. Which was at least partly true.

He pulled it out of the bag. He figured he only had a few moments before the police were notified in case he was a jumper, a chronic problem according to the Wyvern Falls Police Chief. He'd chosen a spot just off where he estimated the dredging channel would be and on the south side of the bridge. If they ever got around to replacing the bridge, it would be away from any river construction. That much he had gleaned from a few discreet questions here and there and a visit to the Westchester.gov website.

Over the ensuing weeks, it had become increasingly difficult to face the temptation of that diamond. Potentially the answer to all his – and so many other's – dreams. What if he could find a clever way to control the creature, a way to use it for the greater good? Cure cancer? Stop terrorist attacks? Go back in time and kill Hitler? Save the World Trade Center?

So many possibilities.

Then he remembered his conversation with his Auntie B. Absolutely, unequivocally N period O period. It is a Pandora's Box. You can't destroy it. But you can put it far away, out of reach.

Before he could second-guess himself, Easton cocked his arm and threw it as hard as he could and as far as he could. The "rock" described a long arc, then fell with a splash out in the dark currents of the Hudson. Then he thought about the warm body waiting between the sheets in his bedroom, in an old Victorian house he was renting on Maplecrest Avenue. It was a few blocks from the house Franks lived in on Creighton Avenue. For a moment, he simply savored that moment of anticipation, standing at the guard rail of a bridge in the bone-chilling breeze of an early winter morning, relishing the idea that soon enough he would be home and slipping beneath the covers, cozying up to her...

He jumped back into the car, a Maserati he had purchased as a Christmas gift to himself inspired by Wang. After a moment, he cranked up the heat and headed back to Westchester, passing a police car heading in the opposite direction. He'd picked up the car a few days after the check from Makepeace and Lowe had cleared. After Thanksgiving, he had started investigating Grant Matthew's death, with a little assistance from Police Chief Hendricks, who made a few calls and got him pointed in the right direction. He was still a CID detective after all, and one with a P.D. license in America to boot. The trail was getting cold but he managed to catch a few lucky leads that, with a little help from Knightbridge as well, turned out – surprise, surprise – to point back to Hilderman.

As he pointed out to Franks, Hilderman was dead and his estate was in tatters, which left him with something of a moral and professional dilemma. What decided him was a news bit just before Christmas about his old friend Princeton getting his trial delayed again on a technicality or two (more like dozens, anything his battery of lawyers could throw in the pot), citing severe psychological and emotional distress that culminated in some sort of 11th-hour plea deal.

That was Justice.

It was a conversation he had on the phone with Knightbridge around that time that convinced him. "Make your own little justice where and when you can, mate," he had been told just before hanging up. Hilderman was crooked, manipulative, and probably deserved what turned out to be his final sentence.

But so was Van Eyckmann. And the Dutchman had more, much, much more to answer for.

And the means to pay for it.

So a few days later, the surviving senior partner of Makepeace Lowe received a call, which he followed up with a meeting on a chilly afternoon on a bench near Battery Park. Easton had shown him the contract with Hilderman, then the folder containing a whole stack of documents and photos that, as he explained, linked the illustrious owner of Taron Hall to the deaths of several of the executive members of his own club. These he would be taking to the police and the press unless his original contract with Hilderman was honored. The ensuing legal mess, with wrongful death suits, civil suits, etc., would keep Van Eyckmann's assets tied up in knots for years. Assets that Makepeace and Lowe might seriously need to survive the recession.

"This is blackmail, pure and simple!" an outraged Makepeace had hissed.

"No, this is justice. And this is how it will be carried out…"

In the end, he only kept enough for what he thought he would need to buy a house – he had an eye on a very interesting old craftsman-style place in town he'd seen a For Sale sign in front of – and to get his feet on the ground. He'd worked out an unpaid leave with the Royal Turks and Caicos Islands CID but had some ideas about developing some kind of new position, possibly as liaison between the Metropolitan CID and the U.S.

Army CID, which had a branch office at West Point. And Constable Pearson's family was in for a real surprise this coming year.

As was the Krodos family.

Easton had located the gardener's widow and daughter still living in Wyvern Falls. He was still looking into the events of what had transpired 35 years back, but, after his brief meeting with the widow – he found her living in a run-down third story apartment in near poverty – he decided the executors of the Van Eyckmann estate had another obligation to make good on in the meantime.

The Maserati's window gave an expensive hum as he lowered it at the Tappan Zee Bridge toll booth plaza. He had yet to figure out the whole EZ Pass thing and paid with cash.

Harder to track.

He figured he'd cruise up Route 9 and stop by C-Town to pick up a few things so he could cook breakfast.

For Vivienne.

NOTES FOR THE CURIOUS

First, here's my opportunity to thank you, dear reader, for bearing through this whole mess of a story through to the end. Kudos to you, I say! I sincerely hope you enjoyed this little adventure, enough at least to join me for a few more because, God help me, there are a few more tales to tell about this strange town of Wyvern Falls up on the Hudson.

Being a firm believer, however, in giving credit where credit is due, a few things must rightfully be noted. For starters, more than a bit of this story is steeped in historical fact and,– I'll admit it – historical fiction.

Much of Van Eyckmann's back story is drawn from a real life character, Jan Piertzoon-Coen, who was the real Governor VOC of Banda in the 1600s and did hire Japanese mercenaries to commit horrible atrocities upon the natives of Palau Banda that in fairness make my own fictionalized account look tame. At least some of this was drawn from a factual account of the East Indies Spice Trade called The Scents of Eden: A History of the Spice Trade, by Charles Corn, Kodansha International Press, 1999. There's plenty more available through the internet on Governor Coen and, depending on your viewpoint, he either plays out as a magnificent villain or a national hero. Looking at his actions in the context of the times, probably a little of both.

And for the natives of the Molucca Islands, particularly Palau Banda and Palau Rhun, please forgive me for taking outrageous liberties with both your history and geography. For a place that played such a pivotal role in history, it's surprising how little information is available, so I wound up playing fast and loose with the facts. I hope to God no one ever goes hunting around on volcanoes for a Buddhist temple that was never there.

Aleister Crowley did live at Esopus Island near Kingston for 40 days around August of 1918, where he claimed to have all sorts of visions and spirit travels to add to his ever-expanding portfolio of weirdness, though the true basis of much of his philosophy was made clear when he painted it in big red capital letters on the cliffs of the island: "Do What Thou Wilt Shall Be The Whole Of The Law"

Regarding Aun-mai's gruesome demise, reality is often worse than fiction. There was a particularly sadistic form of torture and execution developed in Imperial China centuries ago known as "death by a thousand cuts," which, according to photographic evidence, was still practiced as recently as the early 20th century. Since it is more of a plot device here, I've spared the reader any of the grisly details of what this really entails.

As to Maynard's journal, he, of course, is a fictional character but much of his dialogue is drawn from the best-known source of the time period, Samuel Pepys' Diary. Mr. Pepys was an English naval administrator who maintained a detailed journal from 1660–1669 that he never intended to have published. It is regarded as one of the best resources of that era and gives us invaluable insights has to how people really spoke and what they really thought at that point in Western history. Granted it's nearly four decades after the events in my own story, but then "beggars can't be choosers," as they say. It has been published online in its entirety and can be accessed readily enough.

For another important piece of the back story, I am of course indebted to the Arabian Nights, as translated by Sir Richard F. Burton, and I freely admit deliberately borrowing whole chunks of it. What a strange and bizarre collection of stories (particularly that of Sinbad's fourth voyage, when he beats people in a grave dump cavern to death with a corpse's leg bone to steal their food, then loots the corpses' bodies for jewels! Nice guy!) As a narrative, however, it falls somewhere between the bizarre and the completely nonsensical in many places and makes some of my own rambling loose ends look positively stone-cold logical by comparison. In fairness, it must be taken for what it is, which is a collection of folk tales told for enjoyment and moral instruction, and not a strict literal and structurally correct narrative.

At the end of the day, that's what it's really all about, isn't it? As one WWII vet I once came across said, "Never let the facts get in the way of a good story." Because we all love a good story, don't we? Heck, I do as much as anyone else. And, as someone who has spent a fair amount of time in his life already working and living in the so-called "real world," I can safely say that reality is highly over-rated.

I'll take a good story over it anytime.

Looking forward to continuing on this little journey,
Robert Stava
April 1, 2011

ABOUT THE AUTHOR

In his former life Robert Stava was a graphic designer and art director who honed his trade in the NYC advertising biz at Young & Rubicam NY and J. Walter Thompson. He went on to head-up the 3D Media Group in the NY offices of Arup, an international design firm based in London, where he and his team developed 3D visualizations and animations for a wide range of major projects in the U.S. and abroad. He's toured around the world as a keynote speaker on the 3D visualization industry, was a lead singer and guitar player in his band The Jag on the alternative NYC music scene for many years, and is an avid history buff.

He currently lives in Ossining, NY with his wife Tomiko, a professional ballet dancer and teacher, and now divides his time between writing, reading, wrestling with his dog, juggling the cat, and painting Hudson River landscapes. Robert serves as a trustee of the Ossining Historical Society Museum, is a member of the Ossining Arts Council, and continues to train in traditional style Japanese Karate at Seido, where he has achieved a nidan (second degree) black belt.

He is also the author and designer of Combat Recon: 5th Air Force Images from the SW Pacific 1943-45 (Schiffer Publishing, 2007), a historical account based on his great uncle's service as a combat photographer during WWII..

Visit his author site:
www.robertstava.com

Or follow him on Twitter:
@robertstava

and the official Wyvern Falls feature site at
www.wyvernfalls.com